Bryony began sorting through the bundle of mail—it was no wonder her mailbox had been filled to overflowing. Among the numerous sympathy cards, bills and junk mail was a small square package. She recognized her father's scrawling, nearly illegible handwriting. He must have posted the package the very same evening he had been murdered!

Was this what the killer had been searching for?

With hands that shook with both nervousness and excitement, Bryony opened the package to find two computer CDs. Hurriedly she booted up her laptop and loaded the first CD.

For over an hour, she tried various words and combinations in an attempt to find the password, when finally, inspiration struck and the file opened.

My dearest daughter,

If you are reading this, then I am probably dead, and I have no doubt endangered your own life, as well, by sending you the two CDs that you now have in your possession.

The CDs represent the culmination of my life's work— a puzzle I have attempted to assemble into a big picture, which, unfortunately, despite all my best efforts, still remains incomplete. But you have the wherewithal to succeed where I have failed, Bryony, for you have always been far braver and more ambitious than I....

However, be warned: You must fear the knowledge the CDs contain. It has brought death to countless men and women through the millennia. I pass the torch now to you, Bryony. You can extinguish it by destroying the CDs, or you can carry it onward, by attempting to decipher the files they hold. The choice is yours—and yours alone—to make.

...Till we meet again, good health and good fortune, my dearest daughter.

Your Dad.

REBECCA BRANDEWYNE

DESTINY'S DAUGHTER

MIRA

ISBN 1-55166-782-7

DESTINY'S DAUGHTER

Copyright © 2001 by Rebecca Brandewyne.

Visit us at www.mirabooks.com

Printed in U.S.A.

For my Welshman,
who knows the many reasons why.
With love.

The Players

IN THE PAST:

On the Island Plain, Date Unknown:

The Fallen One, author of The Book
His sons, Qanah and Hebhel

In Crete, c. 2400 B.C.:

Zeus, the Minos of Crete
Hephaestus, the Master Craftsman,
  brother of Zeus
Pandora, the bride, daughter of Hephaestus
Epimetheus, the groom
Prometheus, twin brother of Epimetheus

In Egypt, c. 1628 B.C.:

Nephrekeptah, a High Priest of Set
Sheshi, the Pharaoh of Egypt
Moshéh, the leader of the Hapiru Exodus

In Babylonia, c. 577 B.C.:

King Nebuchadnezzar II
His favorite wife, Amyitis
Etemenanki, an architect and master builder

In Sogdiana, c. 106 B.C.:

Shahryar, a Petty King of Sogdiana
His brother, Shahzaman
Khirad, the Grand Vizier
Sheherazad, daughter of the Grand Vizier
Dunyazad, daughter of the Grand Vizier

In Judaea, 35 B.C.:

Herod I, called the Great, the
  King of Judaea
His wife, Mariamne
Marcus Antony, a Roman
  general

In Britain, 306, A.D.:

Constantius I, called Chlorus—
  "the Pale"—a Roman emperor
His son, Constantine, later called
  the Great.

In Britain, 500 A.D.:

Arthur, the High King of Britain
Guinevere, the High Queen of Britain
Merlin, the Archdruid
Mordred, a traitor

In Austrasia, 679 A.D.:

St. Dagobert II, the King of
  Austrasia
His wife, Giselle de Razès of
  the Visigoths
Their son, Sigisbert IV, Count of
  Razès
Pepin II, called the Fat, the mayor
  of the Palace

IN THE PAST CONT'D.:

In Septimania, 804 A.D.:

St. Guillem de Gellone, called
Guillem the Lonely and Guillem
of Orange; the Count of Toulouse,
the Duke of Aquitania, and the
Prince of Septimania
His wife, Guibour von Hornbach

In Al-Andalus, 1236 A.D.:

Abraham, a scholar, called the
Wandering Jew

In France, 1360 A.D.:

Nicolas Flamel, a scrivener and
alchemist
His wife, Pernelle
Maestro Canches, a Jew

In Scotland, 1446 A.D.:

Sir William St. Clair, the Knight of the
Cockle and of the Golden Fleece; the
Baron of Rosslyn, the Earl of
Caithness and of Orkney; and the
first hereditary Patron and Protector
of the Scottish Masons

IN THE PRESENT:

In New England:

Simon St. Blaze, a history professor
His daughter, Bryony, an archaeologist
Mrs. Pittering, Bryony's neighbor
Homicide Detectives Rutledge & Atwood
Mrs. Daniels, Simon's secretary

In the United Kingdom:

Hamish Neville, a history professor,
writer and artist

*The Round Table of the
Abbey of the Divine:*

Cauldronbearer
Crownbearer
Hammerbearer
Hornbearer
Lancebearer
Scepterbearer
Scythebearer
Shieldbearer
Staffbearer
Stonebearer
Swordbearer
Torchbearer

CONTENTS

PROLOGUE   19
The Elysian Plain

BOOK ONE   29
The Initiate

BOOK TWO   153
The Adept

BOOK THREE   265
The Master

EPILOGUE   391
The Angel's Face

MAP OF THE EXODUS by Den Robinson

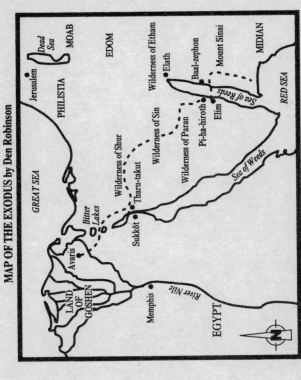

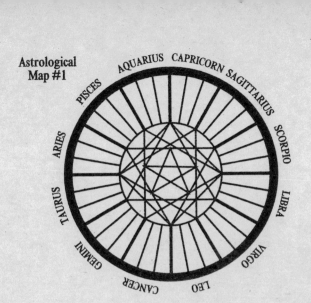

Astrological Map #1

AQUARIUS CAPRICORN SAGITTARIUS
PISCES
SCORPIO
ARIES
LIBRA
TAURUS
VIRGO
GEMINI
CANCER LEO

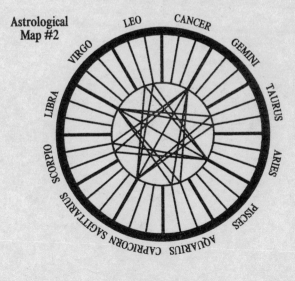

Astrological Map #2

LEO CANCER
VIRGO
GEMINI
LIBRA
TAURUS
SCORPIO
ARIES
SAGITTARIUS CAPRICORN AQUARIUS PISCES

Destiny's Daughter

Destiny's Daughter slept ten thousand years.
Man was a dream unborn, a song unsung,
Silent, the reeds unblown, the harps unstrung.
She slept through the night, not knowing fears.
For ten thousand years, to darkness clung.

Shadows of the Wingèd in fleeting bands divide
The heavens of the world; upon wild winds,
Toward Terra's shores, an Angel bends,
Till he, smitten with his own plagues, doth hide,
And, from his side, all Death's minions sends.
The cloud bears hard on Terra's shores,
Filled with immortal Demons of futurity;
Once, to them, had belonged infinity.
But now, tight-shut be all of Heaven's doors.
Lost, the labyrinthine path to eternity.

Long lay they buried beneath the wasteland ruins so white.
But as the stars rise from the Salt Lake, the Initiates rose in pain,
In troubled mists, o'erclouded by the terrors of struggling gain.
In thoughts perturbed, they rose from the wasteland ruins so bright;
And, silent, followed their fiery King along the Elysian Plain,
Where he sought his ancient Temple of Wisdom, Serpent-born,
That casts its shadowy length along the Island gloomed,
And stretches out endlessly, a necropolis many-roomed,

Heralded by hounds of omen and guarded by beasts of horn.
Once, here, a garden green, a paradise golden, bloomed.

Round the Adepts rolled his clouds of war; silent, the Angel went
Along the unbounded shores of that once green-golden Plain,
Where pride and temptation had proved his sins and bitterest bane.
There had once stood venerable porches; in high-towering ascent,
Their oak- and yew-surrounded pillars had flown and soared, unbent,
Formed of massive stones uncut with tool, baptized with crimson stain,
Standing in their circles, mute sentinels, witnesses to repent....
Stones precious!—mirroring the ever-turning Silver Wheel
Pursued by the savage Hunter in the heavens o'er Terra's keel.
In days gone by, he had known what the words and symbols meant,
And on the Book, in wax, he had pressed his five-pointed seal.

Now arrived the ancient Fallen Master at the southern gate,
Planted thick in yesteryears with trees of darkest leaf,
and in a misty vale,
Obscure enclosed the portentous Stone of Night; oblique in that dale
Long ago hung with purple flowers and red berries sweetly ripe, till fate
Had thrust forth bold its all-powerful hand and torn a gossamer veil
To place both thought and reason into the minds of those called Men.
Now, overgrown with brambles bare, covered with a snowy roof,
Home to naught save wise, old owls and beasts with cloven hoof.
Downward, 'tis sunk, half drowned beneath the sea, a frozen fen,
Lost at the far-flung ends of Terra's earth—hushed, alone, aloof.

Terra's Angel rose upon the Stone of Night, in hand his Book profound,
Which emulous Kings and Priests had copied, had killed for on this earth,
All-unknowing, unenlightened, and without a single truth or worth—
So to be judged from the chariot, the mighty throne become renowned,
The stone seat upon which proud Isis sits, behind her veil...sad mirth.

Since Time's beginning, her secrets no mortal man hath ever found.
Inexorably, blue Terra's sphere travels prescribed rings of Space,

Imprisoned in finite revolutions—and Man now wears the Angel's face,
And hears not the Word, sees not the Way; God, a tyrant crowned,
In whose many names in many tongues, Man dooms the human race.*

---

*Poem adapted from *Europe: A Prophecy,* by William Blake.

Prologue

The Elysian Plain

The immortals will send you to the Elysian Plain at the ends of the earth, where fair-haired Rhadamanthys is. There life is supremely easy for men. No snow is there, nor ever heavy winter storm, nor rain, and Ocean is ever sending gusts of the clear-blowing west wind to bring coolness to men.

The Odyssey
—Homer

Paradise Lost

> To reign is worth ambition though in hell: Better to
> reign in hell than serve in heav'n.
>
> *Paradise Lost*
> —John Milton

A Hollow Hill, the Island Plain, Date Unknown

It was so long ago, now, that he had been cast out that it was sometimes difficult for him to remember the time before. In years past, he had deliberately—determinedly—thrust all those earlier memories from his mind, as though his life had begun here, upon this island plain that had once been a garden green, a paradise golden, but that now had become a wasteland, white and despoiled as far as the eye could see.

In ages past, all manner of verdancy had grown here. The soaring, majestic, purple mountains cutting a jagged-edged silhouette against the distant horizon of the unbounded, deep-blue sky had overlooked hushed forests long with shadows born of tall, aromatic, cone-bearing evergreens and towering, gently rustling deciduous trees dappled with small, hard berries and even harder nuts. Amid the dense woods rich with dank, dark, fertile loam had burgeoned a profusion of lush, exotic flowers bursting with brilliant colors and heady perfumes, a labyrinth of tangled, trailing vines heavily laden with plump, ripe fruit whose mellifluous juices had stained and steeped the fecund soil. Beyond the sweeping hillsides and thick copses, endless vistas of open terrain had stretched, decaying peat bogs and still, stagnant marshes choked with slender reeds and tuberous water lilies merging with wild, stony moors green-gold with thorny hedges and rippling grasses, chessboard fields planted with sprawling vines and swaying grains, and fragrant orchards abundant with sweet, succulent fruit.

But summer came no more to this plain at the ends of the earth. Only winter, dark and endless, reigned here now. For in bringing what had been forbidden to this place, he and his followers had brought Death, as well.

And still, they were called the "Sons of Heaven" by the Daughters of Men.

For a moment, his carnal mouth twisted sardonically at that irony. Well, so they must have seemed to those poor, ignorant creatures, so different from him and his own kind. His was a proud breed—tall, slender, lithe, hard of muscle, fair of skin, and with eyes so blue that they had often been likened to pieces of the sky above this earth. But most of all, it was their long, glossy mane of hair that set them apart from the others, glorious hair the red-gold of the sun that had once blazed in shining splendor above the plain.

His own hair had now, with age, turned as pale and silver as the moon. But it was still the source of his great strength, cascading, unshorn, down his back—a shimmer of silky waves that rippled gently in the night wind, soughing like a last, dying breath across the plain.

With each low, moaning sigh, his solitary candle flickered, throwing a wavering silhouette upon the walls of the hollow hill that was his final refuge. Beyond the gaping mouth of the cave, in the black firmament that stretched away infinitely into nothingness, the distant stars glimmered like eternal echoes of his candlelight. At the sight, a small, peculiar ache he had thought long banished suddenly pierced his heart. It was aeons now, it seemed, since he had viewed the heavens from other than this plain. Stranded, earthbound, bereft of winged flight, immortal no more...that was the price he had paid for his fall from grace.

It had cost him dear, indeed.

Once, he had been a prince of his kind. But pride, vanity, ambition and temptation had driven him to seek more than that—and his reach had exceeded his grasp. As it did the plain and Men, Death now stalked him, too, as punishment for his sins. He who had once been forever young had grown old, his time remaining in this existence short. Yet, unlike Men, he did not fear what hunted him, for it was known and understood by him. It was both end and beginning, a gate, a door, in the perpetual circle of life that, like the great Silver Wheel in the night sky above this earth, was ever turning.

His time would come again.

But perhaps his memories would not. They were buried deep in his subconscious, like swirling mist lying low in the hollows of the land and drifting across the sea, veiling aught in its path, parting only now and then to provide tantalizing glimpses of what was otherwise obscured.

At that thought, he resolutely shook himself from his reverie, directing his attention once more to the task he had set for himself—the book that would be the key to unlock his memories, should they be forgotten. For they would be irretrievably lost if he could not recall them when he came again—lost not only to him, but also to Men; and then the debt he owed to Men for bringing Death among them could never be repaid, and he and they would be doomed to a never-ending cycle in which Death would ever triumph, the heavens always just beyond reach.

For many long moons now, he had labored ceaselessly on his manuscript, writing by hand and candlelight, for of all he had ever once known, only knowledge itself had been left to him. Everything else had been ruthlessly stripped from him when he and his followers had been outcast to the plain. ''Magick,'' Men called his knowledge, for they were as yet newborns in this regard, knowing nothing themselves beyond their own primitive instincts for survival—awed and frightened when he had struck two stones together and thereby shown Men how to make fire.

In return, they had given him many names, among them those meaning ''Light-Bringer'' and ''King of the World.'' These were far different names from that one, meaning ''Adversary,'' which his own kind had bestowed upon him before exiling him from their ranks because he had presumed to take the throne of a king—and a queen promised to another. Like so much else, she whom he had once desired, calling her ''Life,'' was lost to him now, moldering in the earthen grave he and Death had brought to her.

Unwittingly, in an ancient language long unused and thus

rusty on his tongue and to his ears, he murmured her name. A whisper of shame and regret, it reverberated softly in the hollow hill before it was whisked away on the wind, leaving him again in silence broken only by the draft itself and the faint dripping of water from a stalactite into the dark, silvery pool at the center of the cavern. On many a night just such as this had he gazed into the basin's depths, seeing not only what had once been, but also what was to come in the future, and his heart had grieved at the knowledge. Heavy indeed was the burden he carried, for the weight of the world sat upon his shoulders. Still, he must bear it. That was the penance for his crimes.

Picking up his quill, he dipped it into his inkwell and began once more to write, ancient letters and arcane symbols flowing across the parchment pages. Even so, he despaired of the work, for how to condense into a single tome knowledge that could fill dozens? How to cloak the Mysteries so that they might be revealed to the learned and adept, but concealed from the ignorant and inept? How to guard the Secrets so that their power was used only for good by the wise and benevolent, instead of for evil by the foolish and malevolent? And always, somehow, he must remember....

Outside, the moon slowly waned in the black, celestial vault, and the stars dimmed one by one. The wind keened its lament for the dying island plain and crept inside the hollow hill to sing an equally sorrowful song to his single candle and the crackling fire that burned in the simple hearth fashioned from a ring of small stones. With each plaintive note of the draft, the folds of his long, hooded robe, woven from goat's wool and dyed blue from the woad plant, ruffled and whispered about him where he sat upon his huge, imposing throne. This last had been cut from a single piece of solid, gray rock, each strong, massive arm chiseled into the likeness of a ram's head. A thick, shaggy goatskin of purest white and a ram's curling fleece that had been dyed with saffron to a golden hue cushioned the cold seat. From where they perched behind him on the throne's tall back, his two mated ravens, named "Thought" and "Memory," who were his constant companions, watched over his shoulders as he worked. Now and then, he paused, stroking his snowy beard as he reflected on the words and symbols that filled the pages of his book.

At long last, toward dawn, there was nothing left for him to write. The manuscript was finished. Gently, he blew away the remaining vestiges of fine sand he had used to dry the fresh, black ink. Then, taking up the nearby brass candlestick, he tipped it slightly to one side so that the melting beeswax of the taper ran down into a warm splotch on the final page. Firmly, he pressed his gold signet ring with its five-pointed seal into the congealing wax, setting his mark upon it for all time.

There. It was done.

After a seemingly interminable moment, he slowly closed the tome, gazing silently at its cover, which was made of two pieces of goat leather much heavier and coarser than the pages themselves. The front piece had been dyed a deep green from malachite, the back a dark crimson from shellfish. A depiction of a key had been branded into the front and further blackened with coal. Above it were three words in his own ancient language, also inscribed in black. Other than that, the cover was bare of either design or word.

Fleetingly, he wondered if the book would have been better left unwritten, whether he ought even now to consign it to the flames that blazed in the hearth, casting eerie, dancing shadows on the cave walls. In the end, however, the temptation passed. Grown old now, even he had learned that temptation was often best resisted. For good or ill, the manuscript existed, and he would not destroy it.

Carefully, to protect it, he wrapped the tome in two fine linen cloths, one white, the other black. Then he placed it into the puzzle box that he had spent as many long hours preparing for the manuscript as he had writing the book itself.

The box was one cubit in length and half that in width and height. Constructed of strong, intricately interwoven layers of wood from oak and yew trees, it was lined inside and out with sheets of gold, silver and copper, hammered into an elegant thinness. It rested on four feet, each of which was carved in the shape of a different animal's paw or hoof. At the center of the box's lid was set a rare, chatoyant jewel cut into the figure

of a large, wide eye that mysteriously shone green in daylight
and red by candlelight. Above the gemstone, engraved into the
precious metals, were the same three words as were emblazoned on the cover of the tome.

Finally, he shut the lid to the box. Now, it could only be
opened if one possessed the secret to the puzzle of the box
itself.

With the difficulty born of the infirmities of an old age his
body was unprepared for, he rose from his great, stone throne.
The twining serpents tattooed with blue woad on his wrists
seemed to writhe in congress in the wavering, red-orange half–
light of the fire as he reached for the goatskin and ram's fleece
lying on the seat and draped both around his shoulders to guard
himself against the winter's chill outside.

Then, grasping his gnarled, wooden shepherd's crook and
the decorative box, he limped decisively from the hollow hill,
into the raw, bitter darkness beyond, his two ravens fluttering
like familiars behind him.

Their strange, croaking cries echoed mockingly on the icy
night wind...*haw, haw, haw*....

Book One

The Initiate

For the whole earth is the sepulchre of famous men; and their story is not graven only on stone over their native earth, but lives on far away, without visible symbol, woven into the stuff of other men's lives. For you now, it remains to rival what they have done and, knowing the secret of happiness to be freedom and the secret of freedom a brave heart, not idly to stand aside from the enemy's onset.

The History of the Peloponnesian War
—Thucydides

One

Death Comes as the End

The boundaries which divide
Life from Death are at best shadowy
and vague. Who shall say where the
one ends, and where the other begins?

The Premature Burial
—Edgar Allan Poe

Thornfield University, New England, the Present

It was late. Lost in his life's work, Professor Simon St. Blaze
had not realized exactly how late until just this moment, when
the cloud of smoke slowly but surely filling his office had finally alerted him to the fact that he had set his desk on fire—
again.

He never actually *meant* to do it, of course. It simply happened, in the same way that other such accidents plagued him
constantly, all due, according to his secretary, Mrs. Daniels,
directly to his absentmindedness. In this particular case, his
lack of attention concerned his cigars, which he would light up
and then forget were burning in the large, glass ashtray that sat
upon his battered, old desk. Since this piece of furniture—as
well as his entire office, for that matter—resembled a musty

attic, with every single nook and cranny crammed full of books, knickknacks and other, peculiar, unidentifiable odds and ends, there was never any room to be found. So he would inadvertently lay his file folders, notes, research materials and other papers down on his ashtray, and there, they would subsequently catch fire from his smoldering cigars.

Observing that he had unwittingly started yet another blaze, Simon had shouted for Danny, as he fondly called his secretary, for it was she who always dealt with such contretemps. It was only when she had not immediately appeared in the doorway of his office that he had at last recalled that she had bade him good-night sometime ago, and he had glanced at his old-fashioned pocket watch and been astonished to discover the lateness of the hour.

As a result, he was now horrified and at a complete loss as to what to do, for surely, if he did not somehow cope with the situation, and quickly, the smoke detectors in Wiltham Hall would shortly begin to screech, summoning not only campus security, but also the local fire department. At the thought of the inevitable dressing-down, utterly scathing in its excruciating politeness, that he would receive from Leslie Whittaker, the dean of the College of Liberal Arts and Sciences, for causing such a tempest in a teapot, Simon's agitation measurably increased. It never paid to draw the attention of the authorities to oneself, especially in academia, where the egos were as inflated as the politics were cutthroat. Never mind that he frequently broke his own rule to rail rebelliously at the dean, whom he considered a prissy, pretentious, bean-counting snob, with no understanding whatsoever of history and even less appreciation for it.

As Simon glanced wildly around his office, inspiration abruptly struck. Hastily, he grabbed his foam coffee cup and flung its long-cold contents onto the flames, gingerly poking the few still-burning papers that had escaped the sudden deluge back into the sodden, stinking, black puddle he had, with his action, created in the ashtray. Thank heavens, that had done the trick! Now, no one need ever know how close he had come to another disaster. Well, that wasn't exactly true. Danny would know. She invariably did, somehow. But that wouldn't matter, because she always watched his back and covered up for him however she could. Unlike the rest of the world these days, Danny still understood the meaning of loyalty.

That being the case, it would hardly do to repay her by leaving his ashtray swimming with coffee, blackened papers and soaking, half-smoked cigars. With that thought in mind, Simon dumped the entire mess into his metal wastebasket. Then, with some napkins he discovered left over from his lunch, which he had, as usual, eaten in his office earlier today, he wiped out the ashtray and mopped up his desk and the floor.

He hoped the lost papers hadn't been important. Really, it was difficult to know, with the endless stacks of file folders, notes, research materials and other papers he had scattered all around his office. He sighed heavily. He supposed that he truly ought to sort through everything and put it into some kind of order. Danny nagged him about it continually, labeling his office everything from a pack rat's haven to a fire hazard. But every time Simon actually got started on the monumental task of cleaning it up, it entailed his reading all that he had accumulated over the years, in order to determine whether or not he really needed any of it, and then he would get so interested in reacquainting himself with information he had long buried in some dusty corner of his eccentric but brilliant brain that he would entirely forget what it was that he had originally been intent on accomplishing. Besides, it never really paid to throw anything away, either. One never knew when one might require it for some unknown purpose.

Simon comforted himself with the thought that the lost papers were most likely the usual, tiresome memos from the dean, in which case he needn't worry about them. Danny, the soul of efficiency, would already have taken care of everything and left the memos on his desk in a vain attempt at prodding him into paying more attention to what was going on in the world of academia, in general, and at Thornfield University, specifically. But Simon didn't care about any of that. While Danny might believe he deserved to be made chairman of the History Department, Simon himself was perfectly content just as he

was, buried in his small, out-of-the-way office, concentrating
on his life's work, emerging only to teach his popular classes
in ancient history. His ambition in life wasn't to run the History
Department at Thornfield University. It was to unlock the mil-
lennia-old secrets of the Mysteries.

A distant, muted noise from beyond the confines of his office
abruptly startled Simon from his reverie. It had sounded to him
as though a door had opened or closed somewhere down the
long hall. A bit anxiously, he slowly crept to his own doorway
and furtively peered out into the dimly lit corridor that ran the
length of the upper story of Wiltham Hall.

"Hello…?" he called out tentatively, his voice echoing eerily in the sudden silence. "Is—is anyone there?"

Much to Simon's dismay, there was no answer. After a moment, he resolutely forced himself to shrug off the uneasiness
that assailed him. No doubt, whatever he had heard had been
only the building's janitors, cleaning up, or else campus security, making their usual nightly rounds. It might even have
been the normal creaking and settling noises of Wiltham Hall
itself. After all, the edifice was more than one hundred years
old. Or perhaps it had simply been the spring night wind, rising
outside, or even his imagination.

In all truth, he had been even more distracted than usual
lately, and not sleeping well, either. For several weeks now,
Simon had experienced the distinct, disturbing impression that
he was being followed and spied on. There was nothing concrete that he could actually put his finger on, just the weird,
unnerving sensations that caused the fine hairs on his nape to
prickle, as they were now. Unaccounted-for noises, footfalls
behind him that quickly ceased whenever he stopped to look
back over his shoulder, and, once or twice, glimpses of strang-
ers who didn't seem to belong on campus, or even in the small
town of Thornfield itself, would give him pause.

Right or wrong, Simon felt himself to be in grave danger. It
was something to do with his life's work. He just knew it! For
millennia now, clandestine societies composed of powerful
men had zealously guarded what they had learned of the secrets
of the Mysteries. Small-scale murders, large-scale massacres,

countless inquisitions, acts of terrorism, and even wars…the most fanatic members of these covert organizations had stopped at nothing to protect their knowledge from the unwashed masses, who were deemed too ignorant, too stupid and too unenlightened to be made privy to what would only prove far beyond their meager ability to comprehend, anyway.

But even those who had never been initiated into these concealed orders were capable of undertaking their own investigations into arcana and esoterics, and it was precisely this to which Simon had devoted most of his entire life, beginning with a childhood fascination with King Arthur and the Knights of the Round Table. Sometime ago, quite by accident, Simon had become aware of a group of men who believed themselves to be the reincarnates and blood descendants of King Arthur and his legendary warriors and questers for the Holy Grail. They belonged to a society so surreptitious that even Simon, despite all the information he had painstakingly accumulated over his sixty-five years, had never before heard its name: the Abbey of the Divine.

Of course, it was highly doubtful that the modern abbey was actually a true monastic one, although it might well have originated as such in centuries past, particularly if it were, as Simon deeply suspected, some heretofore unknown sect of the famous Knights Templar, which had begun its existence as the Order of the Poor Knights of Christ and the Temple of Solomon. Still, how the Abbey of the Divine had managed to remain hidden for nearly eight hundred years was itself an enigma. Other organizations of its ilk were well known to the world, no matter how often sparsely or distortedly documented.

These days, innumerable Web sites on everyone from the Freemasons to the Rosicrucians, from the Hashshisheen to the Illuminati, filled the Internet, inundating information-highway surfers with pages and pages of gnosticism, hermeticism, mysticism and occultism—much of it not only grossly historically inaccurate, but also as crackpot as many of the amateur Web masters disseminating the material. The Internet had proved to the planet what karaoke had to nightclubs. Weekend Frank Sinatra wanna-bes were everywhere, and now, anyone with a

computer and a modem could hold himself out to the public
as an expert on anything.

It wasn't the Age of Aquarius. It was the Age of Mis- and
Disinformation!

What, indeed, was the world coming to? Simon wondered,
shaking his head bemusedly and more than a trifle sadly, temporarily forgetting his apprehension. But then he heard the
muffled sound again down the hall, and fear returned to haunt
him. It was after ten o'clock at night, long past closing time at
Wiltham Hall. The other instructors and the staff had left hours
ago. As far as he knew, he was all alone in the building. Worse,
what if he weren't? What if the Abbey of the Divine had sent
an assassin to kill him?

His heart pounded frantically in his chest, despite his attempts to reassure himself, telling himself how ridiculous and
paranoid he was being, and that the very same imagination that
enabled him to bring ancient history vividly alive for his students was now running away with him. Well, even if it *were*,
he still needed to be getting on home to his town house.

Rather more rapidly than was his usual wont, Simon began
cramming his file folders, notes, research materials and other
papers into his battered, old, leather satchel, then buckled its
straps firmly. He shrugged on his light, tweed overcoat and
clapped his felt hat on his head. Gathering up his umbrella,
satchel and a package he had prepared earlier to mail to his
daughter, Bryony, he turned off the lamp on his desk and
stepped warily out into the corridor, closing and locking his
office door behind him.

Much to his relief, no one came bounding down the dusky
hall to assault him, and as he headed toward the staircase,
Simon breathed a little easier. He was just a foolish, old fogey,
he told himself, scaring himself like a child envisioning monsters in the closet. Really, Danny was right. He ought to spend
more time socializing with his daughter, friends and colleagues,
and less time buried in his office, with only his books for company, poring over ancient texts and dwelling on the Mysteries,
secret societies and assassins. No wonder he was starting at
shadows in every corner! But since losing his wife many long

years ago to cancer, and Bryony, his only child, having long since grown up and moved out on her own, Simon was left to himself and his own devices. He had turned ever more inward, increasingly shunning a world he had come to view more and more with a mixture of pity and contempt.

If only people would study history and learn the lessons it taught, then they might not be doomed to repeat it over and over! But they wouldn't, and the older he had got, the more Simon had despaired that they ever would. Imbeciles!

Muttering irascibly to himself, he tramped down the three flights of stairs that led to the ground floor of Wiltham Hall. It was so late that he ought to have saved himself the tiring trek and taken the elevator down. But this was the only exercise he got, and his huffing and puffing informed him that he needed it—regardless of what he stoutly insisted to the contrary to his doctor, the damned-fool quack! But when Simon at last reached the bottom of the steps, his heart leaped so suddenly and sickeningly in his chest that for one terrible moment, he was half afraid he actually *was* suffering cardiac arrest.

"Good God, Jessup!" he gasped out, dropping his parcel, one hand clutching his chest as he staggered back against the nearest wall, the other brandishing his umbrella like a weapon. "What a fright you gave me! What do you mean...looming out of the shadows at me like that? Why, it's a wonder you're not having to summon an ambulance for me, my heart is racing so!"

"I'm so sorry, Professor." Jessup, one of the building's janitors, smiled ruefully by way of apology, stooping to retrieve the fallen package, returning it to its owner. "I thought maybe you was one of the students, in here playing some prank, or else a burglar. Security told all of us cleanup crews to keep an eye out, that there's been some vandalism and a couple of break-ins on campus recently. Ain't you got no notice about it?"

"Probably." Now that he thought about it, Simon *did* seem to recall Danny mentioning something along those lines to him a couple of weeks or so ago. Well, thank goodness! That explained everything, then. So much for his wild idea that the

Abbey of the Divine was out to silence him permanently so that he couldn't reveal his knowledge of their existence, much less all he had discovered about the Mysteries. "Please forgive me, Jessup. I didn't mean to snap at you. I'm just a trifle jumpy tonight, I guess."

"That's all right, Professor. Don't you worry none about it. I understand. I'm a little on edge myself this evening…always am when the fog sets in thisaway. It's as thick as pea soup out there tonight, and it's starting to drizzle again, too. You'd best be careful going out to your car. Those old sidewalks get awful slick at times like these."

"Yes, they do." Simon nodded in agreement, images of the cracked, worn, uneven bricks that paved the sidewalks on campus filling his mind. "Thanks for the reminder. I'd hate to slip and fall and break a leg at my age—especially when I know Dean Whittaker's always on the lookout for any excuse he can find to get rid of me!" His eyes twinkled conspiratorially.

The janitor chuckled appreciatively, for although Simon was popular on campus with almost all the faculty, staff and students, his ongoing feuds with the dean of the College of Liberal Arts and Sciences had long been notorious at Thornfield University. "Don't know why Dean Whittaker takes such exception to you. Wiltham Hall just wouldn't be the same without you. Well, I reckon I'd better get on back to work now. 'Night, Professor. Have a good evening."

"The same to you, Jessup. Good night."

Considerably cheered by the chance encounter, Simon continued on his way, whistling as he pushed open one of the heavy main doors of the building, letting himself outside into the darkness. Spindrift-tinged mist rolling in from the Atlantic Ocean swirled ghostly around him as he paused beneath the hazily lit portico to turn up the collar of his overcoat against the spring chill and to put up his umbrella against the fine, light rain that fell from the black night sky. Beneath the gray-white fog, the droplets glistened like tears on the bloodred bricks of the sidewalk dimly illuminated by the clouded, silver moon.

At the end of the gently winding sidewalk flanked by soft-glowing, Victorian-style streetlamps stood a blue, steel U.S.

mailbox for stamped mail, into which Simon shoved the parcel addressed to Bryony. He had missed the last pickup, but that didn't matter. The package would go out sometime tomorrow morning, and she would receive it a day or two later. Simon hoped he were doing the right thing in sending it to her. God forbid that he should unwittingly be endangering the life of his only child. But there was no one else he could trust, and besides, his fears of being stalked were undoubtedly due solely to his imagination, coupled with indistinct recollections about campus pranksters and burglars.

The curving, oblong road in front of Wiltham Hall had always reminded Simon of Rome's Circus Maximus, and tonight was no exception. As always, he envisioned horse-drawn chariots hurtling turbulently around the small park at its center...Charlton Heston as Ben Hur. Now, *there* was a movie— not like the trash filled with sex, booze, drugs and mindless violence that Hollywood churned out these days, undermining whatever morals the nation had left after a shameful, pathetic president like Slick Willie Clinton, and giving young people all the wrong ideas about life. No wonder fully one-quarter of the planet's prison population was incarcerated in the United States! That alone ought to let Americans know there was something drastically wrong with the country. But Simon doubted that most of them were even aware of the statistic. Instead, they were like Nero, fiddling while Rome burned...history repeating itself in an endless cycle....

His older-model Mercedes-Benz sat on the opposite side of the street, in front of the English building, Lennox Hall, where he had only just managed to find a parking space when he had arrived on campus early this morning. To reach the car, Simon would either have to walk clear around the oblong or else cut through the park. For a moment, he was undecided about which path was best. If only it weren't so late and so foggy! Normally, he enjoyed strolling through the trees, shrubbery, flower beds and Victorian benches that composed the park. But tonight, the thought of someone lurking in the bushes was unsettling.

Nevertheless, chiding himself sternly for his trepidation, Simon finally chose the shortcut, reasoning that it would surely be quicker and less dangerous than the wet, slippery, rough-brick sidewalk that meandered its way around the one-way street.

In the end, it wouldn't have mattered which route he had taken.

The instant Simon started across the road toward the park, the dark automobile that had been waiting stealthily, patiently, at the far end of the oblong, its engine purring quietly in the stillness of the spring night, suddenly lurched into motion. Skidding on the damp asphalt, its tires squealed threateningly as it barreled around the curve to accelerate furiously on the straightaway. But the warning sound came too late for Simon. At the last possible moment, the vehicle's headlights flicked on brightly, blinding him where he stood, frozen with surprise, confusion, and then terror as Death raced toward him, a horse-less chariot of dark-tinted glass and bone-crushing metal.

It smote him down with a vengeance, the impact knocking him from his feet, hurling him through the drifting blanket of mist, sending his satchel, umbrella and hat flying. He struck the windshield of the onrushing car, smashing it into an intricate spiderweb. His key ring sailed from one pocket of his overcoat, clattering onto the street as the impact of his collision with the automobile's windshield knocked him sideways with such force that his bloodied body rolled several times, finally coming to rest in a thick cluster of bushy evergreens.

Without slowing, the vehicle circled the oblong, coming around again to the place where it had hit Simon. For only an instant, it paused, a seemingly disembodied hand reaching out to snatch up both the fallen satchel and the key ring. Then the ominous car sped away into the foggy darkness.

Like the wings of a raven, the black, silk folds of Simon's broken umbrella fluttered and flapped in the cool night wind.

Two

Temptation and Knowledge

> He who learns must suffer. And even in our sleep pain
> that cannot forget falls drop by drop upon the heart, and
> in our own despair, against our will, comes wisdom to us
> by the awful grace of God.
>
> *Agamemnon*
> —Aeschylus

A Reed Vessel, the Sea, Date Unknown

The vessel carrying Qanah and the other Children of Death across the ocean to the new land to the east had been constructed of tightly woven reeds dried green-gold from the sun and sealed with resin from pines. The mast was a tall, slender tree trunk rigged with ropes of hemp and bearing a single sturdy sail fashioned of strong cotton dyed a dark crimson from shellfish. As the sea wind lifted, the sail billowed like a flowing tide of blood in the bright, yellow sunlight, causing Qanah to cringe inwardly.

So Hebhel's life's blood had flowed when, in a rage, Qanah had struck him down. That memory would haunt Qanah to his own dying day.

He told himself that he had never intended to murder his brother. But the fierce, hot lust aroused in his loins for Hebhel's sultry, dark-haired, dusky-skinned wife, named Lilitu after her mother, Lil, had proved a greater temptation than, in the end, Qanah had been able to resist. So he had taken his sister-by-marriage, and then, to keep her for his own, he had killed his brother.

Father had known at once, of course, what had transpired with Lilitu. For when Qanah and Hebhel had brought their annual gifts of bounty to him, Father had accepted Hebhel's offering of the sucklings of the flocks, but had rejected Qanah's own of fruit, nuts and grain from the orchards and fields, saying that the fruit, halved, was like unto the soft, hidden folds of a woman, the nuts unto the equally soft but bold pouch of a man, and the grain unto his seed, planted in her secret core. But for a man to till and sow the fertile soil that belonged to another was forbidden.

"Why are you so angry and cast down?" Father had asked, seeing the mutinous expression on Qanah's proud, handsome visage. "If you are well disposed, ought you not to lift up your head? But if you are ill disposed, is not sin at the door, like a crouching beast hungering for you? You must master it, or you will be mastered by it. This, I know to my own regret to be true."

But Qanah had not been appeased by the quietly spoken explanation. Instead, infuriated, he had sought out Hebhel and suggested, "Let us go out." So, together, they had gone to the open countryside, ostensibly to hunt, and there, with the stout cudgel Qanah had carried in one hand, he had beat his brother over the head until Hebhel lay dead, his life's blood staining the grass and seeping into the ground.

"Where is Hebhel, your brother?" Father had queried sharply, when Qanah had returned alone.

"I do not know. Am I my brother's keeper?" Qanah had cried wrathfully, to conceal his guilt and shame.

But as he always did, Father had known the truth. Muttering something under his breath about the sins of the fathers being visited upon the children, he had, with his own two hands, set a mark upon Qanah.

"You are the Child of Death," Father had asserted gravely, "as are all those of your ilk."

After that, as it had been doing for quite some time, the climate had continued to worsen, gradually turning what had once been a green-gold paradise into a white wasteland, driving those who had peopled it from their homes, forcing them into exile.

Qanah and his followers had been among the last to leave. On the cold, dark, wintry night before they had departed, Father had sought him out, bearing a most beautiful but strange and somehow powerful, portentious box, which he had given to Qanah.

Now, as he sat in the vessel skimming across the ocean waves, Qanah felt not a little fear and curiosity as he contemplated the enigmatic box. It contained a book Father had written. That much, he knew. He was tempted to open the box and read the manuscript therein. After all, when questioned in this regard, Father had not forbidden him to do so. But on the other hand, nor had Father, smiling cryptically, revealed to him the key to the puzzle of the box, which meant that if Qanah wanted to open it, he must learn the secret for himself.

"Always remember, Qanah, that what is hard come by is inevitably of far greater value to he who has toiled for it than that which is simply bestowed upon him by another."

As he recalled Father's words of wisdom, Qanah scowled darkly, knowing it might take him many moons to unravel the mystery of the box, and even were he to prove successful, there was no guarantee that at the end of his labors, he would actually be able to read the tome inside. Father could both speak and write an ancient language known to none but his own kind, and it seemed likely that it was this that he had employed in the manuscript.

Qanah had never studied the ancient language. He knew only the common tongue. Now, he regretted that he had never learned the other. Still, he vowed he would eventually somehow open the box and decipher the book.

But not today—for this afternoon, the sun was shining like saffron in the endless, azure sky, as Qanah had not seen it in countless moons, and in the bow of the vessel sat Hebhel's sensual wife, Lilitu, eating fat, rich, sticky dates and slowly licking her fingers one by one, her long, dark, coarsely curling tresses rippling like writhing snakes in the sea wind.

Three

Sad Tidings

> Give sorrow words; the grief that does not speak
> Whispers the o'er-fraught heart and bids it break.

Macbeth
—William Shakespeare

Thornfield, New England, the Present

Bryony St. Blaze was currently in between digs, taking what she herself considered to be some necessary time off following the number of long months she had devoted to her most recent archaeological investigation, an ancient but only relatively newly discovered Iron Age Celtic site in the transalpine region.

She had been home for several weeks now, since winter had finally set in, making any further work on the site impossible until late spring at the earliest; and she was reveling in sleeping until noon or later in her own cozy canopy bed instead of rising at the crack of dawn from an uncomfortable cot, and in cooking in her own small kitchen instead of on a camp stove. Not that Bryony was complaining, of course. She adored archaeology, carefully digging away successive layers of fertile loam or dusty earth to expose the past, the ruins of those who had once peopled what was now history. Everything about the ancient ones fascinated her, how they had been born and had lived and died, what they had reflected on, believed in and revered.

Whenever Bryony walked among the remains of their aeons-old habitats, she often fancied she could hear the faint but unmistakable echoes of their voices and laughter on the wind, of their footfalls in the solitary silence of a breaking dawn or descending twilight.

Still, although she frequently longed for a time machine to transport herself back through the ages, Bryony must, however reluctantly, return to the present at some point—and there were *some* compensations, such as being home in her own snug, little bungalow, not having to live out of a carryall, and lingering beneath her goose-down comforter with a cup of strong, black coffee, if she so chose. Today, she did.

From her thoroughly modern—and undeniably convenient—coffeemaker, prepared last evening and set to begin brewing automatically at ten o'clock this morning, Bryony had retrieved a steaming mug of Colombian Supremo. Juan Valdez would be proud. She had also fetched her copy of the newspaper from her front porch, then settled back into her bed, hauling the duvet close around her.

Now, she sat cross-legged, propped up against her bed lounger and several fluffy, goose-down pillows, sipping from her cup of hot, black coffee, reading the *Thornfield Times* and wondering idly when work on the Iron Age Celtic site in the transalpine region would commence again. Although spring had come, it was still chilly in northern Europe, just as it was here in New England, and despite how much Bryony loved archaeology, she wasn't in any great hurry to freeze her backside off.

Not that she would have to, of course. She didn't need the money—which was a good thing, since most archaeologists didn't make a whole lot to begin with, anyway, relying on grants, endowments, private investors and public contributions to subsidize their undertakings. Bryony was fortunate. She had a sizable trust fund that her father had established for her at her mother's death, purchased with the proceeds of a life-insurance policy. Bryony had been only twelve years old when her mother had died of cancer. Since that time, through shrewd, calculating management of her portfolio by financial advisers, her trust fund had grown to a sum that, if she were equally clever and careful, would support her for the rest of her life.

While she wasn't rich, she wasn't poor, either; and unlike the vast majority of people, she didn't need to work to earn an income. So she was free to devote herself only to those archaeological digs that particularly interested her, and that were willing to include her as a team member.

Although Bryony had traveled all over the world, investigating ancient peoples from the Egyptians to the Incans, it was the Celts who especially intrigued her. At one time, they had been perceived as the fiercest, boldest warriors on earth, unafraid of death, and their holy sect, the Druids, as the keepers of a secret knowledge learned by rote over a period of twenty years or longer. Over her lifetime, Bryony had accumulated a vast amount of information about the Celts, particularly in regard to their preeminent Dark Ages ruler, King Arthur, and his Knights of the Round Table, and she was invariably eager to learn more. So the discovery of the Iron Age Celtic site in the transalpine region represented an exciting opportunity for her.

Nevertheless, for the first time that she could ever remember, Bryony wasn't champing at the bit to get back to work. To the contrary, with the onslaught of winter, she had, in fact, been anxious to leave the dig and return home to Thornfield.

Over the passing months, she had grown increasingly worried about her father, Simon St. Blaze. An ancient-history professor at Thornfield University, he was utterly brilliant, but despite how much Bryony loved him, she wasn't blind to the fact that he was also extremely eccentric. Of late, his e-mails to her had hinted at strange, dark mysteries, secret societies, and that he was apprehensive that his life was in grave danger.

In all truth, Bryony had believed it more than likely that her father's lifelong obsession with arcana and esoterics, coupled with his ongoing feuds with the dean of the College of Liberal Arts and Sciences at Thornfield University, were the real root of his paranoia, that there was actually nothing concrete or sinister behind his suspicions. She had been concerned that her aging father was becoming senile—or even slipping into dementia—in his advancing years.

So she had been glad to come back to Thornfield, to spend some time with him. But despite much insistent, however gentle, inquiry on her own part, her father had refused to elaborate on his trepidations. Instead, he had claimed he ought not to have said anything to her at all, that he had doubtless only been imagining things; he had dismissed all further questions determinedly, however casually, with a nonchalant shrugging of his shoulders and an airy waving of his hands.

"I'm growing old, Bryony," Simon had declared ruefully, only a few evenings ago at his town house. "Not addled or crazy, I assure you. Besides which, as you probably know yourself, it's relatively easy for those who live alone to fancy that the normal settling noises made by their houses at night are instead the sounds of a burglar stealthily prising open a rear window, or of the footsteps of a murderer creeping up the staircase. Only the dullest of persons, totally lacking in either intelligence or imagination, have not, in the wee hours, thought such unnerving things at one time or another, especially in this day and age."

"I could always move back home, Dad," Bryony had immediately offered, in sympathetic understanding. "You know I would be more than happy to do so."

"Yes, I know, poppet." Simon had smiled at his daughter gratefully, giving her a quick, affectionate hug. "But you have a life of your own now, and a wonderful job that you adore. Besides, you are always trekking all over the world for months on end. I wouldn't even begin to dream of taking you away from all that. I'm fine, really. I oughtn't have worried you so with my e-mails. I guess that old cliché is true, and there's no fool like an old fool."

"You're not a fool, Dad," Bryony had admonished sternly, frowning and shaking her head at the very idea.

"Well, perhaps not," her father had conceded. "Nevertheless, I somehow feel quite certain Dean Whittaker would *not* agree with you!" Simon had chuckled at the assertion, his eyes sparkling with mischief. "Now, how about that dinner I promised you?"

Bryony and her father had spent a pleasant evening together, eating the simple meal he had prepared, consisting of a mixed garden salad, thick New England clam chowder and crusty French bread, all washed down with an inexpensive but excellent white wine. For dessert, there had been an assortment of fresh fruit and cheeses.

All during supper, and long afterward, as they had drunk

from mugs of strong, black coffee before the crackling fire in the living room hearth, Simon had happily entertained his daughter exactly as he did the many students in his popular ancient-history classes—with fascinating stories detailing actual historical personages and events, which were interspersed with his own witty observations, outrageous tall tales and amusing jokes. Bryony's father was an excellent raconteur, and he had been at his very best that evening, striving hard to dispel his daughter's anxiety about him. And at last, sitting there in his town house, listening to him as she had so often during her childhood, seeing him looking and behaving just as he always had, she had been able to dismiss her fears.

But now, this morning, a tiny vestige of her earlier concern had returned to haunt her. At sixty-five, Simon was no longer a young man, and although he was in good health for his age and had reassured her about his mental faculties as well, Bryony still knew she needed to think about staying home in Thornfield and spending more time with him. Although her father denied it, insisting that his books were all the company he required, she thought he must still get lonely. Since the death of her mother, Simon had never remarried and, aside from feeding the squirrels who inhabited the small garden he maintained at the rear of his town house, he didn't even have a pet for companionship.

The ringing of her doorbell abruptly jolted Bryony from her reverie. Since she couldn't imagine who else might be calling at this relatively early morning hour, she thought it must be her next-door neighbor, Mrs. Pittering, whom Bryony fondly called "Aunt Pitty-Pat." Mrs. Pittering was an inquisitive but kindly, well-meaning, elderly spinster, with no children of her own. She had taken quite a liking to Bryony and, learning that her mother had been dead for many years, had rather adopted her. Mrs. Pittering often turned up on Bryony's doorstep, bearing such treats as fresh-cut flowers and home-baked pies.

Grabbing her chenille robe from where it lay at the foot of the bed and tying it firmly around her slender figure, Bryony went downstairs to open the front door. Much to her surprise, however, it wasn't Mrs. Pittering who stood outside. Instead, it was two unknown men dressed in dark suits and light, wool overcoats, with black umbrellas raised over their heads against the morning drizzle. Instinctively, Bryony shrank back into the foyer, cursing her own stupidity and drawing her robe more closely around her, gripping its edges tightly at her throat. Living in a small, quiet, neighborly town like Thornfield, she easily forgot the dangers that lurked in today's world. For all she knew, she might have just unlocked her door to a couple of mobsters or homicidal maniacs!

"Ms. Bryony St. Blaze?" the taller of the two men inquired politely. At her affirmative nod, he removed a black, leather wallet from the inside pocket of his suit jacket, flipping it open to reveal an official badge and a laminated photo identification card. "I'm Detective Rutledge. This is Detective Atwood." He indicated his partner. "We're with the Thornfield Police Department—Homicide Division, ma'am. May we come inside?"

A sickening sense of foreboding abruptly seized Bryony in its fist, clutching hideously at her heart.

"*Homicide Division!* Oh, my God! What is it? What's wrong?" she asked fearfully, her voice rising as she numbly moved aside so that the two men could enter the cottage. "My father…has—has something happened to my father? Is he all right?"

"No, ma'am. I'm afraid there's been an accident." Detective Rutledge's own voice was somber as he closed his umbrella, shook out its wet folds over the front porch, then stepped inside. He was joined a moment later by Detective Atwood. "Look, there's no easy way to break this grievous news to you, Ms. St. Blaze. I'm so sorry, but your father is dead."

"D-D-Dead?" Bryony parroted lamely, stunned and disbelieving. "No, that can't be. That just can't be! Why, we had dinner together only a few evenings ago, and he was fine!"

"I'm sure he was, ma'am. As I stated earlier, Detective Atwood and I are with the Homicide Division."

"But—But you just said there'd been an—an accident…." Bryony's now-ashen, tearful face revealed her distress and confusion. "I-I don't understand…."

"According to the Crime Scene Unit, Professor St. Blaze was the victim of a hit-and-run driver, ma'am, sometime last night on campus, probably between ten o'clock and midnight, the coroner has estimated, and this has been confirmed by one of the janitors on campus, who told us that your father left

Wiltham Hall sometime between ten and eleven." Detective Atwood spoke for the first time. "Homicide is routinely called in on such cases, to rule out the possibility of foul play, you understand? I know all this has come as quite a shock to you, Ms. St. Blaze. Is there somewhere we can sit down—can I get you anything...a glass of water or something stronger, perhaps?"

"The living room's just beyond, and there's—there's some coffee in the kitchen...." Bryony's voice trailed away helplessly as she continued to stand frozen in place, dazed and uncomprehending, still attempting to make sense of what the two men had told her.

Obviously, however, Detectives Rutledge and Atwood were well accustomed to dealing with such situations. In minutes, the former had her installed in a comfortable chair in the living room, and the latter was returning from the kitchen, carrying a coffee tray.

Detective Rutledge got out a pen and opened a small, spiral-bound notebook.

"Ms. St. Blaze," he began, "I know this isn't going to be easy for you, but we'd like you to answer a few questions about your father for us. Then we'll need you to come down to the morgue with us to make a positive identification of his body."

His body. Her father was dead. Even now, when Bryony knew it must indeed be so, that the two homicide detectives wouldn't be here at her bungalow otherwise, she still couldn't believe it. She kept on thinking she must be dreaming, and that if she only shook herself hard enough, she could awaken from the nightmare. But she couldn't.

"Positive identification...? Then...you could be wrong, couldn't you?" Her heart leaped with sudden hope. "It might not be my father."

Understanding, Detective Rutledge shook his head sadly.

"No, ma'am, I'm sorry, but I'm afraid the body is definitely that of Professor St. Blaze. His secretary, Mrs. Daniels, and several of his students have already identified him—and his wallet, containing his driver's license, was found in his pocket, as well. So identification by the next of kin is, in this case, merely a formality."

"You said Dad was—was struck down by a hit-and-run

driver last night." Bryony attempted valiantly to collect herself. "Why am I just now being notified about the accident, then? Why didn't anybody get in touch with me yesterday evening? Did anyone see what happened? Do you know who the driver was?"

"Unfortunately, no, not yet, ma'am," Detective Rutledge said, responding to her last question first. "However, we're working on it. So far, we haven't managed to locate any witnesses to the accident. As to why you weren't contacted before now, your father's corpse wasn't discovered until this morning, when he failed to appear for his first class. I understand that Professor St. Blaze was somewhat…absentminded. So some of his students thought he might have lost track of time or even forgotten about his class entirely. They went to look for him, but he wasn't in his office, and when his secretary, Mrs. Daniels, learned that he hadn't shown up for his first class, either, she became quite concerned that something might have happened to him—particularly when his car was found to be parked on the street in front of Wiltham and Lennox Halls. A search ensued, and your father's body was finally discovered lying hidden in some bushes in the park at the center of the oblong. It was apparent that his death had been the result of some violent mishap rather than from natural causes. That's when campus security and the police were both called in."

"I see," Bryony said quietly. "Then…do you think that whoever ran over him deliberately concealed his—his corpse?"

"No." Detective Atwood answered. "It's clear from the crime scene that the impact of the vehicle is what knocked Professor St. Blaze into the shrubbery. That means that whoever did this was, despite the fog last night, traveling at a relatively high rate of speed when the accident occurred. Further, the culprit evidently made no attempt to slow down, as there are no skid marks at the collision site itself, although we did find some recent ones at the west curve of the oblong. Ma'am, what that suggests to us at this point in time is that someone may have been lying in wait for your father and deliberately run him down. Did Professor St. Blaze have any enemies that you know about?"

"No, but—" Bryony broke off abruptly, biting her lower lip. Although her father had later dismissed his worries as the product of his imagination, his earlier e-mails to her *had* hinted that his life was in jeopardy.

"But...what, Ms. St. Blaze?" Detective Rutledge glanced up sharply from his notepad.

"Well, he did seem a trifle on edge lately. I thought—I thought that perhaps he hadn't been feeling well or was under stress. Academic politics can be as cutthroat as corporate ones, and my father was frequently at loggerheads with Leslie Whittaker, the dean of the College of Liberal Arts and Sciences at Thornfield University—not that I think Dean Whittaker would have intentionally run over my father, of course. In fact, I believe the two of them actually rather enjoyed their little skirmishes. They'd been having them for years, after all."

"Anyone else, ma'am?" Detective Atwood asked.

"No, my father was well liked and very popular on campus, and he lived a relatively quiet life, seldom socializing beyond an occasional dinner or an evening out with me or his friends. He was a widower—my mother died when I was twelve—and he never remarried, nor had any special lady in his life or, at least, not that I am aware of. He always claimed to be content with his books for company. His field was ancient history, you know?"

"Yes, we know, Ms. St. Blaze." Detective Rutledge closed his notebook and slipped both it and his pen back into his jacket. "Would you mind accompanying us to the morgue now?"

"No...no, of course not. If you'll—if you'll just give me a few minutes to—to compose myself and get dressed...." Swallowing hard, avoiding the two men's eyes, Bryony rose to make her way slowly upstairs to her bedroom. Her heart was thudding in her breast, and her palms were sweating.

This just couldn't be happening—this couldn't be real. No matter what the two detectives had told her, there must be some mistake, she thought desperately, as she sank down on the edge of her canopy bed. But deep down inside, she knew better. Her father was dead, run over by some as-yet-unknown driver on campus—perhaps even on purpose.

Homicide. *Murder.*

The words rang ominously in her mind. She ought to have told the two detectives about her father's e-mails—all his wild talk of strange, dark mysteries, secret societies, and his fears for his life. But some warning instinct had kept her silent. What if her father actually *had* been right in his suspicions? There was no telling what he might have uncovered or who might be involved. Although Detectives Rutledge and Atwood certainly *seemed* legitimate, perhaps they were part of the plot her father had envisioned.

"Oh, God. That's really crazy, Bryony! Get a grip," she muttered to herself, astounded by her own musings. Nevertheless, she was still cautious, upset and frightened enough to quietly pick up the telephone and call the police station to confirm that the two detectives downstairs in her living room really *were* with the Homicide Division. Her relief that they were was immeasurable.

Her doorbell rang again. This time, Bryony was sure it must be Mrs. Pittering from next door. An unfamiliar vehicle parked in front of Bryony's cottage was bound to arouse not only Mrs. Pittering's curiosity, but also her suspicions and her trepidation about whether or not Bryony was all right. That was one of the nice things about inquisitive neighbors: One wasn't nearly as likely to be burglarized, beaten, raped, killed or otherwise terrorized in one's own home, without somebody noticing and creating a stir about it.

"Bryony…? Bryony, dearie, is everything okay over here?" Mrs. Pittering's slightly shrill voice now echoed up the staircase from the foyer below.

"Aunt Pitty-Pat." Bryony ran down the steps to greet her elderly neighbor. "No, I'm afraid everything isn't okay. These are Detectives Rutledge and Atwood," she said, introducing the two men, who had now appeared in the foyer. "They're with the Homicide Division. Detectives, this is my next-door neighbor, Mrs. Pittering. Aunt Pitty-Pat, Dad is—is dead."

"Oh, no!" Mrs. Pittering's hands flew to either side of her face, and she began to shake her head, stricken. "Oh, no! I'm so sorry, Bryony…just so very sorry. How? What on earth happened?"

"A hit-and-run accident on campus. If you don't mind, I need to go back upstairs and finish getting dressed so I can accompany Detectives Rutledge and Atwood to the morgue, to—to identify the—the body." Bryony blinked away the sudden tears that assailed her. "Would you—would you mind keeping an eye on things while I'm gone?"

"No, of course not, child. I'll be glad to. Whatever I can do to help. You know that. Oh, my. This is terrible news…simply terrible. Poor Professor St. Blaze! Such a nice man! I guess that even the streets of a small town like Thornfield aren't safe anymore. What the world's coming to, I'm sure I don't know. You go on now and get dressed. I'll keep these two gentlemen company until you come back downstairs."

"Thanks, Aunt Pitty-Pat. I really appreciate that."

"No thanks are necessary, dearie, I promise you. It's no trouble at all. That's what good friends and neighbors do— lend a helping hand to one another, especially at times like these," Mrs. Pittering insisted stoutly.

Minutes later, having washed her face, brushed her teeth, given her hair a quick combing and attired herself in a pale pink cashmere sweater and a pair of matching stretch pants, Bryony had rejoined the others in the living room.

Shortly thereafter, she and the two detectives were en route to the morgue.

Four

Losses

> Though nothing can bring back the hour
> Of splendor in the grass, of glory in the flower,
> We will grieve not, rather find
> Strength in what remains behind.

Ode: Intimations of Immortality
from *Recollections of Early Childhood*
—William Wordsworth

Thornfield, New England, the Present

The next several days passed in a blur for Bryony. Years later, whenever she would remember them, it would always be as though she were viewing them through a glass darkly, disconnected vignettes of images soft and misted at the edges, as though the harsh reality would be too difficult for her to bear. She thought that during those days, some kind of grief mechanism, born of her instinct to survive, must have seized control of her, allowing her brain to absorb only as much shock and sorrow as it reasonably could without dragging her down into some dark, inward place from which it would have been very hard for her to escape.

Following Bryony's formal identification of her father's body, an autopsy was conducted by the coroner to determine the exact cause of death, after which the police finally released the corpse to her. Simon St. Blaze's funeral was held three days later, on a dreary afternoon gray with spring drizzle, and cool with mist and wind from the sea.

Despite the fact that the dismal weather was miserable for the large crowd of mourners who had gathered at the graveside, Bryony was glad of the day's gloominess. She had always found sunshine somehow incongruous at a funeral. As her father's bronze casket was slowly lowered into the cemetery's dark, dank earth, she wished fervently that she could go home now, to be alone with her sadness. But there was still the reception, in her father's honor, being held at Thornfield University, which she must attend.

"How're you holding up, Bryony, dearie?" Mrs. Pittering's kindly, wrinkled face was filled with concern as she patted the younger woman's arm.

"I'm all right." Bryony smiled wanly, her pale hands idly twisting a fragrant gladiolus taken as a keepsake from the spray on her father's coffin. In some dim corner of her mind, she knew that from this moment on, the heavy scent of the tall, elegant flower would always remind her of death. She was grateful for Mrs. Pittering's support as they finally left the graveside, walking to the waiting limousine that would drive them to the campus reception. Bryony settled into its plush backseat. "I know it's terrible, but I-I just wish everything were all over."

"I know." Mrs. Pittering nodded in sympathetic understanding. "But like it or not, and as strange and even distasteful as it may seem to you, funerals are social occasions, too...hardest on people your age, I think. We oldsters know we don't have much time left ourselves, so we like to reminisce and make the most of it. As for children, well, I believe that for them, death is something that only happens to elderly folks, and that's as it should be, because the saddest sight in the whole world, I've always thought, is a small casket. But for people your age, Bryony, death—especially the death of a parent—is not only a reminder of one's own mortality, but also a passing of the torch, so to speak. Both your mother and father are gone now, and when that happens, you can never be a child yourself again...childlike, yes, but never really a child, with a mother's comforting bosom or a father's strong shoulder to cry on."

Rummaging in her pocketbook, Mrs. Pittering produced a clean, old-fashioned handkerchief of fine linen embroidered in pale blue with her initials, its edges delicately tatted with lace. She handed it to Bryony. "There, there, child. Get it all out now."

"I'm—I'm so sorry." Bryony wept copiously into the handkerchief for a few minutes before trying to compose herself. "I didn't mean to break down like this."

"Better now than at the reception," Mrs. Pittering observed keenly. "Heaven only knows how long that will last. But you needn't stay until the end. Nobody expects that, although they'll all want to offer you their condolences, of course. Despite his feuds with Dean Whittaker—or maybe even because of them—your father was quite a favorite on campus, and it helps people with their own sorrow to pay their respects and share stories about the deceased. Still, I should think an hour or two at the most will be sufficient for you to receive everyone's sympathies, and then you can go on home, Bryony— although I know the professor wouldn't want you grieving your poor heart out for him."

"No, I'm sure you're right about that, Aunt Pitty-Pat," Bryony acknowledged truthfully as she withdrew her compact from her handbag and set about repairing the damage her tears had done to her makeup. "Dad always said that life was for the living, and that when his own time came, I shouldn't mourn his passing but, rather, think of him as being reunited with my mother, in heaven. That's the only thing that gives me any solace at the moment."

At last, the limousine drew to a halt in front of the house of Thornfield University's president, where the reception for Bryony's father was being held. The two women got out of the vehicle, then slowly climbed the short flight of steps to the portico.

Inside, the house was filled to bursting with campus faculty, staff and students, as well as with Simon St. Blaze's nonacademic friends, all of them talking and laughing, nibbling on hors d'oeuvres and drinking punch. As a result, the reception was more in the nature of an Irish wake than a sober occasion, and Bryony felt certain her father would have loved it. She herself didn't know whether to laugh or cry.

Somehow, she got through the remainder of the afternoon, taking comfort in the fact that Simon had been so well liked and would obviously be missed on campus—Dean Whittaker not withstanding, since even he confessed to her that he felt like a chess player who had suddenly been deprived of his principal opponent.

"A sad, dreadful business all this has been," he remarked gruffly, shaking his head. "Do the police have any leads yet, Bryony?"

"Not that I'm aware of, sir."

"I simply can't imagine why they think someone would have deliberately run Simon over. Who would want to do such a thing, and why?"

"I don't know, Dean Whittaker. It is totally implausible."

Indeed, the more that Bryony had dwelled on the matter, the more convinced she had become that the police must be mistaken in their assessment of the accident. The crowd alone, congregated at the president's house, was proof of her father's popularity on campus—how little anybody would have wished to harm him. That he could have fallen victim to some secret society was a theory so fantastic that Bryony had yet to mention it to anyone, including the police. That she had even considered it credible, she had chalked up to her own shock and upset at her father's death. It was just too wild to be believed, and she didn't want her own and other people's memories of Simon to be tarnished by the thought that he had become senile or even a bit of a kook at the end.

Finally, after making arrangements with Mrs. Daniels, her father's secretary, to retrieve all of Simon's personal files and other effects from his office in Wiltham Hall the next day, Bryony was able to depart from the reception.

As the limousine carrying her and Mrs. Pittering home swept down the winding drive, Bryony happened to notice a man seated in a dark car on the street beyond. Vaguely, she thought she recollected having seen the same vehicle at both the mortuary and the cemetery. On impulse, she tried to catch a glimpse of the face of the man in the automobile. But he was wearing a fedora, its brim pulled down low over his brow, shadowing his visage, and his head was bent to his chest, as though he were grabbing a quick catnap while waiting for a passenger to return. Perhaps he had driven one of her father's older friends to the funeral and reception, Bryony thought.

But still, for some strange, unknown reason, a tiny, icy shiver chased up her spine, and she was abruptly glad of Mrs. Pittering's presence at her side, and of the limousine driver up front, a big, burly man who did not look the sort to be easily intimidated.

Bryony slept very poorly that night, and at last, toward dawn, knowing further attempts at slumber to be useless, she rose to stumble into the small bathroom located between her own upstairs bedroom and the guest room across the hall.

The sight of her listless reflection in the mirrored medicine cabinet over the Victorian-style pedestal sink dismayed her. She had rarely ever looked this bad, even after months of living in a trailer or tent at an archaeological dig. Her waist-length blond hair was a rat's nest from her having tossed and turned all night long, and her sea-green eyes were red-rimmed and swollen from crying, shadowed beneath with dark circles. Her finely chiseled nose was red, too, and her full, generous mouth was chafed where she had gnawed it ceaselessly in her grief. Her skin, pale and fair to begin with, was ashen and pasty. Traces of makeup she hadn't bothered to remove yesterday evening streaked her face.

"Good God, Bryony, you look like hell," she abruptly imagined her father chiding her reprovingly.

"You're absolutely right, Dad. I do. Somehow, I've just got to pull myself together."

A shower would do for a start. Discarding her oversize, cotton nightshirt, Bryony turned on the taps, adjusting them until the water from the faucet was an agreeably steaming temperature. Then she stepped into the claw-footed, Victorian-style bathtub and flipped the lever for the showerhead. She shampooed her hair, scrubbing it vigorously and rinsing it until it was squeaky clean. Then she lathered herself luxuriously with soap. When she had finished washing, she dried off with warm, fluffy towels from the nearby heated towel rack, wrapping one like a turban around her damp head.

After brushing her teeth, she carefully applied fresh makeup to cover the worst of the ravages her sorrow and lack of sleep had wrought. Then, thinking about what cleaning out her father's office on campus was going to entail, Bryony dressed herself in a pair of old, stone-washed blue jeans and an equally old, faded T-shirt emblazoned with the words *Thornfield Titans*. Thirty minutes with a blow dryer turned her long, thick mass of hair into a cascade of gleaming corn silk, which she swept up into an artful French twist, so that it would be out of her way while she worked in Simon's office.

Downstairs, she forced herself to cook and eat a proper breakfast, finding the first joy she had known in days in the simple task. She lingered over her coffee and the morning newspaper before slipping on a pea jacket and going outside to traverse the serpentine, cobblestone path that led from her bungalow to Mrs. Pittering's own next door. As Bryony had hoped, since the rain had now stopped and the sun was shining, her elderly neighbor, an early riser, was already out in her garden, cutting fresh spring flowers and filling the various bird feeders that hung from the trees.

"Aunt Pitty-Pat," Bryony called, waving, "I wanted to remind you that I'm going up to the university today to lend Mrs. Daniels a hand with cleaning out Dad's office."

"Thanks, dearie." Mrs. Pittering nodded and smiled. "Don't work too hard."

"I'll try not to."

Sometime later, having obtained a visitor's parking permit from campus security, Bryony pulled her late-model Jeep to a halt on the oblong street in front of Wiltham Hall. Much to her surprise, both a campus-security vehicle and an unmarked police car were already there ahead of her. Her heart pounded hard with alarm. Slamming her door shut, she hurried across the road and up the sidewalk to the history building, wondering what was amiss.

Inside, she discovered from the student receptionist that someone had burglarized her father's office.

"Or, at least, that's what Mrs. Daniels claims," the young receptionist, Theresa, declared, smacking her chewing gum. "I'm sure I don't know how she can tell. No offense, Ms. St. Blaze, but the professor *was* a bit of a pack rat, if you don't mind my saying so."

"No, not at all. I'll just go on up, then, all right?"

"I'll let Mrs. Daniels know you're on your way." Theresa picked up the switchboard's receiver and punched one of the intercom buttons.

After climbing the flight of steps to the third floor of Wiltham Hall, Bryony found not only Mrs. Daniels and campus security in attendance, but also Detectives Rutledge and Atwood.

"Danny, is it true that somebody's broken into Dad's office?" Bryony inquired.

"Yes, indeed. I'm just positive someone's been here, although neither security nor these detectives have found any sign of a forced entry." Mrs. Daniels sniffed, indignant at the idea that the law-enforcement officers might not believe her story. "However, I'm sure it's entirely possible that whoever ran down the poor professor also stole his key ring. Was it among his personal effects, do you know?"

"No...no, it wasn't," Bryony said slowly, startled by the realization. "And...and now that I think about it, Dad's satchel was missing, too!"

"Really?" Detective Rutledge quirked one eyebrow upward, his pen momentarily poised over his notepad. "Now, that's very interesting, Ms. St. Blaze. It strengthens our suspicion that your father was intentionally struck down—because after all, if it were only an unfortunate hit-and-run accident, then why take Professor St. Blaze's key ring and satchel? No, the culprit must be looking for something. Do either of you two ladies know what that might be?"

"Why, I simply can't imagine," Danny insisted, astonished. "The professor taught ancient history, and when he wasn't doing that, he researched ancient history. That was his entire life. Look around you, Detective." The secretary indicated the clutter in the office. "What could the poor professor have possibly possessed that would have been of any value to anyone but him?"

"I don't know," Detective Rutledge commented. "Do you, Ms. St. Blaze?"

"No." Bryony shook her head, deliberately avoiding his gaze. "I suppose somebody might have wanted his research, to publish it and thereby claim credit for it. Academic theft of that kind is relatively rare, but it does happen. However, it hardly seems a motive for murder, Detective. I mean, it's not as though new theories about ancient history have any real monetary value."

"Mrs. Daniels—" Detective Atwood spoke up "—you say that various things in Professor St. Blaze's office have been moved about. Has anything actually been taken?"

"I'm—I'm not sure…." The secretary glanced around thoughtfully, frowning. "Perhaps some files and papers… I don't know. It's very hard to tell. As you can see, the professor seldom, if ever, threw anything away. Even so, I just know someone's been here!"

"My apologies if it sounded as though I thought otherwise, ma'am. I'm not doubting your word—merely attempting to establish the facts. How about you, Ms. St. Blaze?" Detective Atwood turned to Bryony. "Would you know if something was missing?"

"No, I'm afraid not, Detective. I haven't been in Dad's office since I dropped by to have lunch with him several days before…before the—the accident."

"And following Professor St. Blaze's death, Mrs. Daniels, you never unlocked his office again until this morning?" Detective Rutledge queried.

"No. I had no reason to. I only opened it today because Bryony was coming to help me sort through everything," the secretary explained. "The professor's death has hit everybody very hard, but life has to go on. And since there's obviously a great deal to take care of in the professor's office, I believed it was best to get started on it as soon as possible. There are quite a number of books, files and other personal belongings of the professor's here that I thought Bryony would want to have, and I wouldn't like to be responsible for them, you understand?"

"Yes, I do." Detective Rutledge closed his notepad and put away his pen. "Well, I don't know that there's anything else we can do here, ladies. However, should either of you discover that something's definitely been stolen from the professor's office, I'd appreciate it if you would please notify either me or Detective Atwood immediately. Even if it seems unimportant to you, it still might assist us in developing a motive for Professor St. Blaze's murder.''

"Then...then you definitely believe my father was killed on purpose, Detective?'' Bryony blanched at the notion.

"Let's just say that at the moment, it appears to be the likeliest scenario, ma'am. Hopefully, we'll learn more as we continue our investigation. Good day to you, ladies.''

After the two detectives and campus security had taken their leave, Bryony and Mrs. Daniels determinedly set to work, deciding to tackle the many tomes lining the bookshelves first, since this would make room to stack the piles of file folders and papers that littered Simon's office. Yesterday, Bryony had arranged for a large quantity of boxes to be delivered to Wiltham Hall by a local packing company, and these had already arrived and were now sitting in the hall beyond Simon's office. So all she and Mrs. Daniels had to do was assemble them and reinforce them with packing tape, which they did as needed. As they labored companionably, they conversed quietly, speculating about Simon's death and why someone might have wanted to kill him.

"Danny, did Dad ever talk much to you about his research?'' Bryony questioned as she dusted each of the volumes taken from the bookshelves, checked its pages to be sure there was nothing concealed between them, and then placed it into an open carton.

"No, not really. However, I do know the professor had worked on a number of different things for many years... translating old manuscripts, comparing countless myths, legends, fairy tales, folklore, poetry and historical texts, poring over ancient maps and sea charts...stuff like that. I don't really know what he was trying to find out or prove, however. Even so, I certainly can't believe someone killed him for it. My goodness gracious! It isn't as though anything he worked on wasn't easily obtained from libraries, bookstores and, these days, the Internet, as well. Even the most ancient of manuscripts are being translated and uploaded to the World Wide Web all the time now, and there are online services that conduct extensive searches for out-of-print titles, too.''

"I know, but, well, what if Dad had—had somehow stumbled across something truly important?''

"If he did, I've really no idea at all what it might have been, Bryony," Mrs. Daniels asserted firmly. "I mean, it isn't very likely that the poor professor chanced upon some valuable lost manuscript, is it? History just isn't the same in that way as archaeology, you know. Monuments, tombs and even cities can lie buried for aeons beneath the earth until being discovered by one method or another. We're all aware of that. But with a few notable exceptions, such as the Nag Hammadi Library and the Dead Sea Scrolls, the odds of previously unknown historical texts turning up are actually pretty remote, I should think. And most things, like the Rosetta Stone and the Sumerian Tablets, for instance, are the result of archaeological digs—not of somebody falling into a hole and uncovering a hoard of clay jars filled with ancient manuscripts."

Bryony sighed heavily.

"Yes, you're right, Danny. I know you're right." She paused, thinking hard. Then she continued. "Well, maybe Dad *deduced* something important then, from all his research."

"Maybe," the secretary agreed, as she pulled a long strip of packing tape from the weighty dispenser on Simon's desk. "But even so, I simply can't imagine how anybody else would have known about it—unless, of course, the professor told someone. But if he did, it wasn't me whom he confided in."

"Do you know who it might have been?"

"Well, *you,* I would have thought, Bryony. After all, you were the professor's only child, his only living relative, for that matter. Who else could it have been?"

"I don't know, and that's what's bothering me. Before I came home to Thornfield, I had received several rather disturbing e-mails from Dad, in which he talked about strange, dark mysteries and secret societies, and told me that he believed his life to be in peril."

"Bryony!" Mrs. Daniels cried, stricken. "If that's true, then why didn't you tell the police about it?"

"Because after I got home, Dad dismissed it all as the product of his wild imagination. So I didn't really know what to think after that. But now that he's been killed, I'm worried that there might actually have been something to those e-mails—only it all sounds so...so *fantastic* that I can still hardly credit it, Danny. I'm half afraid that if I go to the police about it, they'll just believe Dad was getting senile in his old age, or else turning into a-a complete crank. And I couldn't blame them for that, because I couldn't help but wonder the same thing myself at the time. You know how eccentric Dad was, even under the best of circumstances.''

"Yes, I know. So I can understand your hesitation. I certainly wouldn't want to do anything, either, that might somehow diminish the professor's good name and reputation. He may indeed have had his own peculiar, little quirks. Don't we all? But he was still the sanest person I ever knew. Still…strange, dark mysteries and secret societies…truly, it all sounds like something out of a James Bond movie,'' Mrs. Daniels commented skeptically. ''Of course, history *is* filled with all kinds of orders like the Rosicrucians and the Illuminati, and it's undeniable that the professor spent a great deal of time studying them because of his interest in arcana and esoterics. But they're hardly secret societies, Bryony—more like societies with secrets, I should say. I don't believe anyone's ever quite determined the true origins of the Freemasons, for example, or solved the various mysteries surrounding the Knights Templar. But even if somebody had, it's scarcely the kind of thing to be murdered over, is it? No, I think it's wholly possible you may simply have misunderstood your father, and that's why he made light of his e-mails to you. However, don't worry. Perhaps we'll find something in all this mess that will help.''

"I sure hope so.''

Nevertheless, Bryony sighed deeply once more. It seemed doubtful to her that anything would turn up, especially since Mrs. Daniels felt so strongly that someone else had already been through Simon's office and, apparently, had had several, uninterrupted days in which to conduct a lengthy search.

Five

Pandora's Box

Sweet spring, full of sweet days and roses,
A box where sweets compacted lie.

The Temple: Virtue
—George Herbert

The City of Knossos, Island Kingdom of Crete, c. 2400 B.C.

"I don't *want* to wed Epimetheus, Father! He's not only old, but a fool, besides!" Pandora cried, stamping one dainty foot upon the brilliant, mosaic-tile floor of their open, spacious house—one of the largest in Knossos, and in all of Crete, for that matter.

Her father, Hephaestus, the Master Craftsman of all of Crete, sighed heavily. He had known that persuading his strikingly beautiful, strong-willed daughter to agree to the proposed marriage would prove difficult. He had just not realized how much so until now.

"I feel for you, Daughter. Do not think I don't. I know Epimetheus is not a man whom you would have chosen for yourself. Nor do *I* favor him for you. Nevertheless, your grandfather has commanded the match. There is nothing we can do."

"I hate Grandfather!" Pandora shook with emotion, and tears brimmed in her wide eyes. Her grandfather, Zeus—

Hephaestus's own father—was the Minos of Crete, its all-powerful king. If Zeus had decreed that she wed his cousin Epimetheus, then her father was right, and there was no escape for her. "I'm sorry, Father," she continued more quietly, equally upset by the anguish on Hephaestus's face. "I don't blame you. I know it's not your fault."

"But it is," he said simply. "If I hadn't been born a cripple—"

"You are *not* to worry about that, Father!"

"I don't, not anymore—at least, not for myself. But the truth is the truth, and it cannot be changed, Daughter. Were I not lame, I would be a prince of Crete, in line for the throne, just like my many brothers. Instead, I am nothing more than a mere metalsmith, the keeper of the flame, the tender of the royal forge."

"That's not true! You're the Master Craftsman of all of Crete, Father—and maybe even of the whole world!" Pandora insisted stoutly. "Do traders not come by the Great Sea from not only the nearby islands, but also from the most distant, foreign lands to seek your work?"

"Yes." Hephaestus nodded. "They do. But still, that does not alter the fact that I'm a cripple rather than a prince of the realm, my royal blood counting for nothing, so I cannot even spare my own daughter from marriage to a man all of Crete knows to be little more than an elderly buffoon!"

"But...why Epimetheus? I, too, am of the royal blood, yet I'm only a pawn on Grandfather's chessboard. The granddaughter of the Minos of Crete is surely of much greater political value as a bride to some prince—or even a king!—than to be parceled off to one such as Epimetheus! Why does Grandfather not seek to obtain a powerful political alliance with some foreign land through my marriage? Why is his old cousin to be my husband instead?"

"That, I cannot answer, Pandora. I know nothing beyond the fact that ever since Epimetheus spied you at your studies with your aunt Athena, he has claimed to be utterly besotted by your incomparable beauty and so asked Zeus for your hand. But had I to venture a guess, I would have to say that Zeus means no good by bestowing you upon his clumsy, scatterbrained cousin but, rather, hopes somehow to punish Epimetheus's twin brother, Prometheus, by it. Zeus is still very angry about Prometheus stealing the live coals from my forge, so the common people could learn to build equally hot fires in their own hearths, and he is also angry about Prometheus stirring up the villagers against him, so they no longer make nearly as many sacrifices to Zeus as they used to. What's more, now, they hide all their biggest, best bulls from him, too, parading only their smallest, scrawniest beasts before him, so the bull-leaping contests aren't nearly as challenging and exciting as they were in the past, and the slaughter of the animals afterward provides only a scanty, stringy feast."

"Maybe so, Father. But I'm afraid that even so, I *still* don't see how wedding me to Epimetheus is going to bring any ill upon Prometheus—or upon the common people, either, for that matter." Pandora's fair brow was knitted in a puzzled frown.

"Nor do I, Daughter. Nor do I. *This,* I do know, however. Even if Zeus *is* the Minos of Crete and my own father, as well, I'm not blind to his many faults. Among other things equally unpleasant, he is a capricious, bullying liar—and *not* to be trusted. Promise me that you'll remember that, Pandora, for it may stand you in good stead someday."

"Yes, Father, I will remember, I promise."

Her heart heavy and sore, Pandora turned away, retiring to her bedroom. From its wide windows, she could see, beyond the city walls, the mighty Great Sea that lapped continuously at the shores of Crete and, to the west, in the distance, the imposing peak that was Mount Ida, which towered over Knossos. Normally, these wondrous sights gladdened her heart, filling her with an immense awe and joy. But today, she felt nothing but depression. The city walls might as well have been the confines of Zeus's subterranean prison, which lay beneath the Great Palace whose construction he had started at the beginning of this year. Sometimes, for cruel sport, he ordered a bull taken below to the dungeons and one of the men incarcerated there turned loose from a cell, to be chased by the beast through the dark, winding passages. If the prisoner could escape, then he would be granted his freedom. But so far, all had fallen victim to the bull, savagely gored to death by its horns and brutally trampled beneath its hooves.

Such was not to become Pandora's own fate, but still, she

felt no less condemned as the weeks passed and her wedding day inexorably approached. All too soon, it seemed, arrayed in elaborate finery, she stood within the walls of the Great Temple at Knossos, being married to her grandfather's old cousin Epimetheus, in a lengthy ceremony at which her own boyish cousin Eros, the High Priest of Crete, officiated.

Afterward, in the Great Hall of the Great Palace, Pandora sat in a place of honor next to her new husband at the high feast table, where they received their wedding gifts. Last to be bestowed upon them was Zeus's own present. As she stared at the strange, somehow ominous, ornate, gold, silver and copper box placed before her, Pandora felt an abrupt, icy tingle chase up her spine, raising the fine hairs on her nape.

"For Pandora, the fairest bride in all Crete...an all-encompassing gift no less beautiful than she herself," Zeus announced, causing the large crowd assembled in the Great Hall to break into a round of appreciative laughter and applause for the witticism—for her name, Pandora, meant "All-Encompassing Gift." After several long minutes, in which he basked in all the attention he felt his due as the Minos of Crete, her grandfather, his eyes sly, continued, "Well, go on, Pandora...open the box—if you can."

Inexplicably, her graceful hands trembled as she laid them on the top of the box, only to snatch them away as she felt a surge of something unknown but undeniably potent rush through her, as though she had somehow been struck by a fiery bolt from the heavens. Slurping drunkenly from his golden wine cup, Zeus guffawed at her.

"It's a box not meant to be opened, you see, Pandora," he declared, waving his chalice about carelessly as he spoke, sloshing red wine onto the colorful, mosaic-tile floor of the Great Hall. "The Cyclopes—the 'Circle-Eyed Ones'—those pastoral giants of Gozo, Malta and Sicilia, presented it to me some years ago as a tribute...a pretty enough trifle, I suppose. They claimed it possesses the secrets of lightning and thunder, and perhaps it does, I don't know. I've never actually opened the box myself—there's a puzzle to it, you'll find—and I don't believe you should open it, either. In fact, since I'm well acquainted with the inevitable curiosity of women, I command you not to."

Gazing steadily at her grandfather, recalling Hephaestus's warning to her, Pandora knew, of a sudden, that Zeus had lied to her—that he *had* opened the box, and that despite his order to the contrary, he wanted her to open it, too. It must contain something dreadful, she thought uneasily, something that would somehow punish not only Prometheus, but perhaps all the villagers on Crete, also, if her father had been correct in his assessment of why Zeus had wished her to wed Epimetheus.

"I am your obedient granddaughter, Minos," Pandora asserted, with an outward calmness she did not feel inside. "Because it is a treasured gift from you, the box shall hold the highest place of honor in our household—but remain unopened, as you have decreed."

And that was how it would have been, she knew, if not for her witless, old husband. From the time they entered their new house together following their wedding feast, Epimetheus became just as obsessed with the box as he had been with gaining her as his bride. That was the way his simple mind worked, she quickly discovered. It focused determinedly on one thing, to the exclusion of all else. Regardless of how many times she reminded him of Zeus's directive, Epimetheus would nevertheless sit for hours, holding the box, turning it this way and that, poking and prodding, utterly fascinated by it.

Often, much to Pandora's horror, his whole body would radiate with a pale, eerie glow afterward, as though he had become a fetch, a shade. Sometimes, clumps of his hair fell out, too.

"Epimetheus, you simply *must* leave the box alone! Do you understand me?" she asked impatiently, for the umpteenth time, upon discovering him with it yet again, quelling the strong desire she felt to box his ears smartly. "If you disobey Zeus, your cousin, the Minos, he might grow so angry that he'll have you cast into the dungeons, to be chased by the bull! Or else chained to the big rock on the coast, for the sea eagles to pluck at, just as he did your twin brother, Prometheus!"

"No, your uncle Heracles would come and free me, just as he saved Prometheus, Pandora," Epimetheus stated, scowling reprovingly at her, as though *she* were the stupid one. "You're my wife, and it's not your place to give me orders! I'll open the box if I please! Only think what I could become if I could learn the secrets of lightning and thunder! I'd be Zeus's equal then—and I'd have a much better gift for all the common people, too, than those old, black lumps of coal Prometheus took from your father's forge and gave them.''

"Prometheus is a thief! He ought not to have done what he did. It's not wise for the villagers to have fires that burn hot enough to fashion weapons. Swords are for soldiers—not merchants and farmers!''

"The common people say my twin brother gave them the fire of life.''

"The fire of *death*, more like,'' Pandora sneered, exasperated. "They would do far better to make plowshares than weapons!''

But like a stubborn, belligerent child resolutely bent on having his own foolish way, Epimetheus would not listen. He was nothing but a silly, old goat, she thought—too stupid, she hoped, to ever manage to figure out the puzzle of the box.

And so the dreary days of their married life passed—until one inauspicious night, when her husband came running into their bedroom, excitedly shouting her name and bearing in his hands the peculiar, decorative box, its lid flung back. Somehow—quite by accident—he had hit upon the secret of the puzzle.

Pandora shivered violently as she stared at the ancient manuscript lying inside the box, for she knew instinctively that it was aeons old—and powerful beyond even Zeus's own grasp.

"Look. It's a massive book, Pandora,'' Epimetheus told her, unnecessarily. "But I can't read it. It's written in some language I've never seen before, and there are strange pictures and symbols, too. But you've studied with your aunt Athena. *You* read it to me, and tell me what it all means. Then I'll know how to make lightning and thunder, and I'll be greater than even Zeus himself!''

In the end, despite all her wisdom and better judgment, the temptation to examine the aged pages of the tome proved more than Pandora could resist. At last, her heart pounding rapidly in her breast, she slowly lifted the manuscript from the folds of its black-and-white linen shroud, then carefully turned back the dark green, goat-leather cover....

Six

Et in Arcadia Egô

> The woods of Arcady are dead,
> And over is their antique joy;
> Of old the world on dreaming fed;
> Gray Truth is now her painted toy.

> *Crossways: The Song of the Happy Shepherd*
> —William Butler Yeats

Thornfield, New England, the Present

When Bryony arrived home at her cottage that evening, she was exhausted from having worked all day long, cleaning up her father's office and sorting through all his books, research materials, and other possessions he had accumulated over the course of his lifetime.

In several respects, clearing away Simon's decades of clutter had been just like scraping away the layers of earth at an archaeological dig, exposing his life in the same way that ancient sites were slowly revealed. Even Bryony had been amazed at the extent of her father's interests and the information he had compiled through the years—and not just with regard to history, either. Simon's scrutiny had covered every discipline from anthropology to zoology, every esoterical subject from acanthus to zodiac.

His tomes had run the gamut: On his bookshelves, Catholic and Protestant Bibles had sat alongside the Gnostic Gospels, the Qu'ran, the Talmud, the Egyptian and Tibetan Books of the Dead, as well as volumes on the Druids, Wicca, mysticism, occultism, voodoo and Satanism. File cabinets had contained hand-labeled folders devoted to such diverse historical person-ages as the eponymous Adam and Eve and the notorious Ma-dame Blavatsky and Aleister Crowley. It had seemed that noth-ing had escaped her father's notice and investigation.

But just what had he been doing with all this? That was the million-dollar question—and Bryony had yet to find any real answer, much less a final one. Like Mrs. Daniels, she simply couldn't imagine that Simon had been deliberately killed for any of it. As his secretary had noted, it was all material that could be obtained by anyone from almost anywhere, especially in this electronic day and age.

Inserting her house key into the lock of the bungalow's front door, Bryony sighed. She was too tired to try any more today to figure out what her father had been up to. It could have been almost anything—from tracing the lost Ark of the Covenant to postulating that the Nazca Lines in Peru were runways for alien spacecraft to hypothesizing that the structure of the solar sys-tem had been much different as recently as only five thousand years or so ago. For all she knew, Simon St. Blaze had been intent on joining the ranks of Graham Hancock, David Talbot, Immanuel Velikovsky and Erich von Däniken, among several others—in which case, whatever her father had been working on would, at the very least, have fallen under the dubious head-ings of "speculative" and "controversial."

Still, that was hardly a motive for murder, she thought. Steal-ing and selling nuclear secrets to the Russians and Chinese was one thing, as was ripping off the Mob or a Colombian drug cartel. Evolving and peddling theories about Atlantis, Bigfoot and Roswell to the public, however, was quite another thing entirely.

Bryony pushed open the door and stepped into the small foyer beyond, switching on the light and then deactivating her alarm system. Shrugging off her pea jacket, she hung it on a brass hook on the ornate hall tree, then slipped off her running shoes, setting them to one side. Advancing down the narrow hallway to the kitchen, she cursed herself silently. Despite how much she usually enjoyed the task, she felt too weary tonight even to cook supper for herself. After hauling the several boxes she and Mrs. Daniels had managed to get packed up at her father's office over to his town house and unloading them, Bryony ought to have stopped on the way home and picked up a cheeseburger or a pizza. But it was too late now for that.

Beyond the swinging door leading into the kitchen, however, she discovered a note from Mrs. Pittering, lying on the counter. It stated that there was a Yankee pot roast on Low in the oven, keeping warm for Bryony's return. As she read the message, tears at her elderly neighbor's kindness and consideration started in Bryony's eyes.

"Oh, bless you, Aunt Pitty-Pat," she murmured with heartfelt gratitude.

She knew there were some who would have thought Mrs. Pittering an annoying, nosy, old busybody. But once Bryony had realized her neighbor's curiosity stemmed not from any malice, but from loneliness, interest and caring, she had been glad to befriend Mrs. Pittering. Bryony's doing so had been rewarded many times over, in ways just like this one. On impulse, she picked up the telephone receiver and dialed her neighbor's number.

"Hello?"

"Aunt Pitty-Pat, this Yankee pot roast you were so sweet and generous to leave me is an awful lot for just one person. If you haven't already eaten, would you like to come share it with me?"

"Why, I'd be delighted to, child. I'll be right over."

Minutes later, Bryony and Mrs. Pittering were bustling companionably around the kitchen, the latter taking the pot roast, potatoes and carrots from the oven, while the former got out her everyday crystal and a bottle of Beaujolais.

"Well, that's odd." Bryony frowned with puzzlement as she glanced down at her utensils drawer, which she had opened to retrieve a corkscrew for the wine.

"What's odd?"

"This drawer…it's all…disarranged somehow, as though someone's been rifling through it, looking for—" Bryony broke off abruptly, a chilling feeling suddenly raising the fine hairs on her slender nape. "Aunt Pitty-Pat, did you let anyone into my cottage today with your key?"

"Why, no." The older woman was visibly surprised. "Nobody but myself, that is, when I brought over the pot roast. You know I wouldn't let anyone in here unless you had given me instructions. Why? What's wrong?"

Bryony was now in the process of opening all her kitchen drawers and cupboards one by one.

"I'm—I'm not sure. This morning when I arrived at the university to help Danny with Dad's office, the police and campus security were there. Danny had telephoned them because she thought somebody had broken into Dad's office. In the end, it didn't appear that anything had been stolen, although it was hard to tell, seeing how disorganized and untidy Dad was. But still, Danny was certain someone had been there—and now, tonight…I don't know, Aunt Pitty-Pat. Maybe I'm just jumpy and imagining things because of all that's happened this past week, but I could swear somebody's been through my kitchen."

"Well, then, perhaps we had better check out the rest of the house, too," Mrs. Pittering suggested, a martial glint in her eye at the very idea that an intruder might have burglarized Bryony's home. "And if there's anything missing, we had best call those two nice detectives right away. Just let me pop the pot roast back into the oven…. There, that's done. Now, we'll soon find out what's what."

Cautiously, the two women made their way through the cottage, Bryony's consternation growing as she noticed more things slightly disordered or otherwise out of place.

"It wasn't nearly as easy for an intruder to search my house without its being obvious as it was for him to go through Dad's office," she observed quietly. "I'm not a pack rat. To the contrary, I'm a neat freak."

"Well, *I'm* really worried, Bryony." Mrs. Pittering's brow

was knitted with anxiety. "I don't like the notion that some stranger has not only been prowling around our neighborhood, but has also actually somehow managed to get into your bungalow—and without my being aware of it! Oh, I should have kept better watch! Shouldn't we contact the police?"

"All they can do is take down the pertinent information and file a report, Aunt Pitty-Pat. Nothing more. They couldn't do anything else this morning at Dad's office, either, because number one, Danny didn't have any proof that someone had really broken in, and number two, it didn't appear that anything had actually been stolen. It's the same case here. Whoever's been here must have used the key to my house that Dad kept on his key ring, and besides, there's nothing missing. Whatever the intruder was after, he didn't find it here, either. Damn it! I should have paid more attention at Dad's town house earlier! Whoever's doing this has probably been through it, too. But I didn't even think about it when I was there. All I wanted to do was unload the cartons Danny and I had packed up at Dad's office, and then get home."

"That's understandable, child. You've been under a terrible strain this past week, and you must be utterly exhausted by now, especially after cleaning the professor's office all day. But, Bryony, how do you suppose whoever broke in here got past your alarm system? And what do you think the intruder wanted?"

"I don't know." The younger woman shook her head, mystified and distressed. "But I'm going back downstairs right now to call a locksmith to change my locks tonight, and then I'm going to enter a new code for my alarm system, too."

The two women returned to the kitchen, where Mrs. Pittering once more retrieved the pot roast from the oven and began preparing their plates, while Bryony telephoned a locksmith, then altered the code for her alarm system. After that, she picked up the corkscrew she had laid on the counter earlier, and opened the bottle of Beaujolais, pouring the dark, red wine into glasses.

"If you're not going to call the police, Bryony, I *do* think you should at least come home with me to spend the night,"

Mrs. Pittering urged, swigging her wine to steady her frazzled nerves. "I don't like to think of you being all alone here, without even a dog to bark a warning, particularly when whoever did this doesn't seem to have been deterred by your alarm system."

"To be honest, I'd really appreciate being able to stay over at your cottage, Aunt Pitty-Pat," Bryony confessed. "So you're not going to get any argument from me on that score."

"Good. Then it's settled. To tell you the truth, all this has got my poor, old heart beating so erratically that I'll be quite glad of your company. Besides which, Tam won't let anybody get into *my* bungalow, I assure you!"

Tam O'Shanter was the older woman's Shetland sheepdog, an extremely intelligent and highly protective animal. So Bryony had no doubt that her neighbor's claims in this regard were to be believed. It *would* be a comfort to know the dog was standing guard, listening for any sound of an intruder. Living alone, Bryony had often wished for just such a pet herself. But she was out of town so much that she would only have wound up having to board a dog in a kennel for months on end, and that wouldn't have been fair to the animal.

By the time the two women had finished their dinner, the locksmith had arrived. While Mrs. Pittering oversaw his changing of all the locks in the cottage's two exterior doors, Bryony ran upstairs to pack an overnight bag, tossing in clean clothes, a nightshirt, makeup, toiletries and her laptop computer. She thought it might help to try to make some notes of her own, to attempt to figure out what her father might have been working on, and why it had apparently been so important to some unknown individual or organization that he had been deliberately killed over it.

Briefly, she reconsidered her decision not to get in touch with Detectives Rutledge and Atwood. But she knew what she had told her neighbor was true, that without proof of a break-in and theft, there was, realistically, little or nothing the police could do. So there didn't really seem any point in telephoning them. She would surely see the detectives again soon, at which

time she could relate to them her suspicions about her bungalow having been searched.

Once the locksmith had finished the job and departed, Bryony and Mrs. Pittering, beaming flashlights in hand, walked the
short distance to the latter's cottage together. Tam met them at
the front door, barking excitedly and wagging his tail enthu-
siastically.

"Down, Tam," the older woman ordered, chuckling. "Bryony doesn't want you jumping all over her like that."

"It's all right, Aunt Pitty-Pat. I don't mind. Really. It's about
the only sane, normal thing that's happened to me this entire
week. Hello, Tam. Hello, boy...such a good doggy. Yes, you
are." Obligingly, Bryony patted Tam's head, stroking and
scratching his ears, in the way she knew he adored. In return,
he licked her hands, then sat and politely offered her one paw.
Laughing, she shook it. "I'm very pleased to see you again,
too, Tam!"

"Oh, my, I just *knew* there was something that slipped my
mind this evening." Mrs. Pittering turned from the brass coat-
rack in the foyer, where she had been hanging up their jackets.
"I declare. With all this upset, I don't know whether I'm coming or going." Picking up a sheaf of mail from the dark, marble
top of the beautifully painted, antique bombé chest that stood
against one wall, she handed it to the younger woman. "Here.
I meant to bring this over to you when I came for dinner earlier.
The mailman retrieved it all from your box today and delivered
it to me. He said your box was getting so full that he couldn't
put anything else into it. He thought that perhaps you'd gone
out of town again, and that I was collecting your mail, like
always, but had either forgotten or else simply hadn't got
around to it yet. I told him, no, that poor Professor St. Blaze
had been killed, run over by some maniac on campus, and that
under the circumstances, I felt sure that your mail was the last
thing on your mind."

"You're absolutely right, Aunt Pitty-Pat. I hadn't given it a
single thought." Bryony shoved the mail into one of the side
pockets of her carryall, then followed her neighbor upstairs to
the guest room.

"Now, you just make yourself right at home, dearie," the older woman insisted as she turned down the four-poster bed and plumped up the pillows. "There're fresh towels and soap in the bathroom cabinets, and if you get hungry, you know you're most welcome to anything I have in the kitchen, too."

"Aunt Pitty-Pat, I don't know how I would have managed without you this past week. I really don't. I can't tell you how deeply I appreciate all you've done for me. You've been like a second mother to me for a long while now. I hope you know that...how much I've come to care for you."

Mrs. Pittering's wrinkled cheeks flushed with emotion, and tears sprang to her clear-blue eyes.

"Why, Bryony, that's the nicest thing anybody's said to me in many a long day. And I couldn't love you more if you were my own daughter, either. Don't stay up too late, now. You need to get some rest, and you can sleep easy here. Tam will protect us."

"I know. Good night, Aunt Pitty-Pat."

"Good night, child."

After her neighbor left the guest room, closing the door gently behind her, Bryony switched on the small television set on top of the chest of drawers to catch the nightly news while she unpacked her overnight bag. She folded her clean clothes neatly on the wing chair that sat to one side, stripped off her dirty garments and tossed them into the carryall, then pulled on her nightshirt. Her makeup and toiletries, she laid out on the dresser, arranging them tidily. Then, sitting cross-legged on the bed, she began sorting through the bundle of mail Mrs. Pittering had given her.

It was no wonder her mailbox had been filled to overflowing, she thought. There were numerous sympathy cards mixed in with all her bills and the usual junk mail. There was also, Bryony observed, her heart starting to thud rapidly in her breast, a small package from her father—a square, bubble-padded manila envelope, the kind used to send computer CDs or disks through the mail. Although there was no return address on the parcel's label, she recognized Simon's scrawling, nearly illegible handwriting. He must have posted the package to her the very same evening as he had been murdered! Unbeknown to her, it had probably been sitting in her mailbox for days!

Was this what the killer had been searching for?

With hands that shook with both nervousness and excitement, Bryony prised open one end of the envelope, carefully plucking the staples free. Inside was a jewel box containing two computer CDs, labeled *Ancient History 101* and *Ancient History 102*. Hurriedly rising from the bed, she grabbed her laptop computer from her overnight bag and set it up on the bed, plugging the cord into a nearby outlet. Once the computer had finished booting up, she loaded the first CD into the appropriate drive and typed in the necessary command to browse the disk's files. A list came up, and from it, she selected the first one, titled *Introduction*.

After a moment, the command "Enter password" appeared on the screen. Canceling the action, Bryony chose another file and then another. All were password protected. What would her father have used? She bit her lower lip, thinking hard. It couldn't be anything difficult or obscure. Instead, it had to be something he would have known Bryony would be able to figure out, something familiar to both of them, but not likely to be easily deduced by anyone else.

For more than an hour, she tried various words and combinations that occurred to her, but none of them worked. Finally, however, she remembered how her father had always ended his classes, and inspiration struck.

At the password prompt, Bryony typed in "historyrepeatsitselfhistoryrepeatsitself," and the file labeled *Introduction* abruptly opened. She eagerly read her father's words to her.

My dearest daughter,

If you are reading this, then I am probably dead, and I have no doubt endangered your own life, as well, by sending you the two CDs that you now have in your possession. For that, I am deeply ashamed and aggrieved. I would have given anything not to have been compelled to burden you with all this. But there was no one else I could trust, as you must now trust no one, either—not even the

"Quester," for although he may indeed be an ally, he might also just as easily be the enemy. I don't know. He has proved as cautious as I, so that I have not even learned his true name. Nor is he aware of mine, knowing me only by my Internet handle of "Torchbearer." But this, I do know: Whether he is friend or foe, you are going to need him, Bryony, should you decide to set your own feet, too, upon the esoterical road he and I have traveled these many long years now. Reach him at: quester@dragon.co.uk. If he is a friend, then I feel quite certain his own life is in grave danger, as well.

The CDs represent the culmination of my life's work—a puzzle I have attempted to assemble into a big picture, which, unfortunately, despite all my best efforts, still remains incomplete. With the exception of this *Introduction*, you will need to decode all the rest of the files contained on the CDs. More than that, however, I cannot tell even you, my dearest daughter, lest the CDs should somehow fall into the wrong hands. So I will say only this: He who rides the tiger dare not dismount—and a swallow cannot know the lofty ambitions of an eagle. When I began my life's work, I did not realize I had mounted a tiger, nor that I was, in truth, only a swallow overshadowed by eagles. But you have the wherewithal to succeed where I have failed, Bryony, for you have always been far braver and more ambitious than I, and your own intelligence and erudition will stand you in good stead, also.

However, be warned: You must fear the knowledge the CDs contain, as I feared it, too. It has brought death to countless men and women through the millennia. I am by no means its first victim, nor will I be its last. But do not mourn for me, my dearest daughter, for death is only a door to another dimension of existence, where the soul lives on, as the ancient ones knew. I am at peace. I died pursuing what I believed in, on the age-old quest for enlightenment, and no man can ask for a finer end to his life than that. It has been a good journey. I pass the torch now to you, Bryony. You can extinguish it by destroying the

CDs, or you can carry it onward, by attempting to decipher the files they hold. The choice is yours—and yours alone—to make. Whatever you decide, always remember that your mother and I both loved you with all our hearts. Till we meet again, good health and good fortune, my dearest daughter.

Your Dad.

After reading her father's letter, Bryony cried for a long time, pressing her face into the pillows to muffle her sobs. Then, at last, she forced herself to gather her composure. Despite the fact that her father had said that the decision about whether to destroy the CDs or decode them was hers alone, she knew he would not have entrusted them to her had he not hoped she would carry on his work...work he had clearly believed so important that he had died for it, probably placing her own life in jeopardy, as well. She would not, *could* not, allow his faith in her to go unanswered.

Glancing at the alarm clock on the nightstand, Bryony observed that the hour had grown late, and she had had a long, grueling day. Tomorrow would be soon enough to get started on trying to decipher the disks. But there was still one thing she could do this evening. Plugging her modem into the telephone jack, she brought up *Netscape Navigator* on her computer and composed an e-mail to the man her father had called the "Quester." Then, before she could change her mind, she logged on and clicked the Send button.

In the blink of an eye, the e-mail she had written vanished, winging its way via the Internet across the Atlantic Ocean to the United Kingdom.

Hamish Neville was, by choice, a recluse. For many long years now since his divorce, he had lived alone in an old sheep-farm cottage on a sweeping hillside of the Grampian Mountains in the Scottish Highlands, overlooking the beautiful city of Aberdeen. He was an historian by trade and kept his professorial hand in by teaching an occasional class on medieval history at King's College, at the University of Aberdeen. But he derived

most of his income from his work as an historical author and
an artist, his latest published book being one he had written
and illustrated on knights, armor and heraldry through the ages.

At the moment, Hamish was on sabbatical and in between
professional projects. He did, however, have plenty to occupy
his time. For far too long now, engrossed in his studies, research, books and drawings, he had neglected his bungalow, to
the point that he was vaguely surprised it hadn't fallen down
around him.

As a result, he had spent half the morning and afternoon
diligently repairing the roof, ripping away worn-out shingles
and replacing them with new. Now, the job finished, toolbox
in hand, he climbed down the ladder and made his way around
back to the old-fashioned lean-to, which currently served as a
mudroom where he hung coats, dropped off muddy Wellies,
and stored his tools and gardening implements. After stowing
his toolbox, he entered the cozy kitchen just beyond, pouring
himself a cup of black coffee from the coffeemaker and grabbing a scone.

Munching on the biscuit, he continued on through the bungalow, trekking up the narrow staircase to the upper floor
tucked snugly away under the eaves. Here, Hamish had turned
one of the two modest bedrooms into a study and library for
himself, where he could work undisturbed, inspired by the
wild, rugged majesty of the Highlands revealed by the small
windows. Sitting down at his desk, he switched on his computer to check his e-mail. It had been several days now since
he had heard from Torchbearer, and Hamish was becoming
concerned. For a number of reasons, he didn't want to lose that
contact.

But once he had logged on, a quick glance at his computer's
desktop showed him that Torchbearer's folder was empty.
There was, however, one e-mail that caught Hamish's attention. Its subject heading was *Introduction to Ancient History
101*, and its unfamiliar sender was identified as "wild-
vine@ringmail.net." The reference to history alone would have
intrigued him, but the fact that the sender was on the same
Internet service provider as Torchbearer was what really made

Hamish sit up and take notice. Quickly, he opened the missive. He read curiously as he consumed the last of his scone, then took a long swallow from his coffee mug.

> To Quester,
> Torchbearer's bright flame has been extinguished. From beyond the grave, he advised seeking out one who quests for enlightenment. Should you be inclined on your long journey to rescue a damsel in distress, you may find that she holds the key that will unlock a treasure chest. Will you heed her plea or ride on by, knight errant?
>   Wildvine.

Hamish stared at the message, thinking hard. Torchbearer was dead—or, at least, so the woman who had identified herself only as "Wildvine" would have him believe. Who was she? He wondered, his mind filling with speculation and countless questions. How had she obtained this particular e-mail address for him? How had she become aware of his correspondence with Torchbearer? What kind of help did she think he, Hamish, could give her? What did she mean that she held the key to unlock a treasure chest? But most important of all, was her note to him a clever ruse, designed to draw him out?

Like Torchbearer, Hamish knew that where history, arcana and esoterics were concerned, there had always been dangerous forces at work—individuals and societies who had, through the millennia, done whatever was necessary to attain, wield, and preserve Power with a capital "P." High priests and priestesses, kings and queens, counselors and warriors, architects and builders, alchemists and necromancers…keepers of the flame, guardians of the Mysteries, questers for the Holy Grail, Crusaders of the Cross, seekers of Truth and Enlightenment. Whatever they had called themselves and whatever they had sought, they had all shared a common goal in the end: to rise like the Phoenix from the ashes; to obtain the *Book of Thoth*, the elusive Grail, the Elixir of Life, the Philosopher's Stone; to unveil Isis….

Reaching for the pack of Marlboro Lights that lay on his

desk, Hamish shook out a cigarette and lit it up, dragging on it deeply as he continued to study the message on his computer screen. He was a skeptic by nature, a stickler for details, insisting on proof, relying on facts. Had he been one of Jesus Christ's Apostles, he would have doubted, just like Thomas. But Hamish was also inherently curious, and whether he liked it or not, this aspect of his character had been piqued by the e-mail he had received from the woman calling herself Wildvine.

At long last, having carefully considered all the pros and cons of his action, he typed a cryptic reply to her and sent it off.

"Let's see what you make of that, milady," he said, raising his coffee cup in a silent toast to his new, unknown correspondent. Then he laughed softly—a low, devilish sound that echoed mockingly in the stillness.

Despite her exhaustion last night, Bryony had nevertheless lain awake until the wee hours, the wheels of her mind churning furiously. Her grief for her father was still fresh in her heart and mind, but she was gradually coming to grips with it. Somehow, his letter to her had helped. Time would do the rest, lessening the pain until her memories of him would be fond and happy, tinged only faintly with sadness at his loss.

Growing, however, was her strong sense of determination to find out who had murdered him—and why. What special knowledge did the two CDs contain that he had been killed for it? And most of all, who was the Quester, and how did he fit into the big picture?

When she had finally fallen asleep in the early hours, Bryony had dreamed about him. Somehow, even though she knew nothing about him, not even his true name or what he looked like, she recognized that the man who haunted her nightmare was the Quester. He had appeared to her like the Roman god Janus—two-faced, one looking toward the past, the other the future. Dressed in the accoutrements of a high priest, he had stood in a strange, ancient temple, before a large, stone sepulchre that had dominated a chessboard floor composed of alternating, black and white squares of marble. Flanking the imposing crypt had been two tall pillars, one black and rising from a white square, the other white and rising from a black square.

With one strong, slender hand, the Quester had beckoned Bryony forward. She had been reluctant to go, but the power emanating from his compelling figure had proved irresistible, and in the end, as though hypnotized by his dark, piercing eyes, she had slowly moved toward him. She had been dressed in a virginal, flowing, white gown that had seemed to float like drifting mist around her when she had walked. An ornate circlet of gold had adorned her brow; matching bracelets had banded her upper arms and wrists. Heavy, gold earrings had dangled from her ears. As she had advanced across the temple floor, the massive lid on the ponderous tomb had begun, of its own accord, to slide inexorably to one side. When she had reached the coffin, the Quester had motioned for her to look inside.

Bryony had expected to see her father lying there. Instead, a huge, red dragon had suddenly uncoiled itself from the bottom of the sepulchre to lunge toward her, mouth agape and breathing fire.

Screaming soundlessly, she had awakened in a cold sweat, her heart thudding horribly in her breast. She had not been able to get back to sleep after that. But it hadn't mattered. By then, dawn had already broken on the horizon, and she had heard Mrs. Pittering moving about in the bathroom that lay between the two bedrooms.

Hearing the older woman finishing her morning ablutions and starting down the staircase, Bryony forced herself to rise and head for the shower. As the steaming water sluiced over her, she thought what a bizarre, unnerving dream she had had! She wondered what, if anything, it had meant. Had it been a psychic warning of some kind about the Quester? Or perhaps just the nightmarish product of her subconscious, born of all she had been through since her father's death? She didn't know. But in the wake of her dream, she half hoped the Quester wouldn't respond to the enigmatic e-mail she had sent to him last night.

Bryony hoped in vain, however. After eating breakfast with Mrs. Pittering, she returned to her own cottage to set up her laptop computer and log on to check her e-mail. She discovered that she did, in fact, have a message waiting for her. The subject heading was *Re: Introduction to Ancient History 101*, and the sender was identified as "quester@dragon.co.uk."

She was almost tempted to delete the e-mail without even reading it. But that would be foolish. Her father had said that she would need the Quester's assistance, whether he was a friend or a foe—and she might as well start trying right now to find out which he actually was. So, at last, she clicked on the note, opening it.

"To Wildvine," she read, her brow slowly knitting in a scowl. *"Et in Arcadia Egô?"*

That was all. He hadn't even signed his e-mail name.

"So, Quester, you want to play games with me, do you?" Bryony muttered, annoyed as she contemplated her computer screen. "Well, Professor Simon St. Blaze didn't raise any esoterical ignoramus—as you are about to learn." She hit the Reply button to respond to the Quester's message, then swiftly typed the proper answer to his question:

"Et in Alphêo Eris."

Seven

The Lady and the Warrior

Every lover is a warrior, and Cupid has his camps.

Amores
—Ovid (Publius Ovidius Naso)

Aberdeen, Scotland, the Present

As the airplane finally touched down at the Aberdeen International Airport, Bryony stretched this way and that in her seat, trying to loosen her muscles, cramped from several hours of exhausting flight. Not only was she suffering from the usual effects of jet lag, but she had also lost a day in the process, the United Kingdom being five hours ahead of New England.

Once the plane had taxied down the runway to the terminal and come to a complete halt, she unfastened her seat belt and stood, slinging the strap of her leather purse over one shoulder, then opening the overhead compartment to fetch her carryall. Inside the terminal, she retrieved the rest of her luggage, then proceeded through Customs, falsely declaring her visit to Scotland to be for purposes of a long-anticipated holiday. Guiltily, Bryony wondered what the penalty was for lying about such things in the United Kingdom, and whether or not she would be imprisoned in the infamous Scottish Tolbooth, if it even still existed. She half expected to be exposed as a fraud and arrested at any moment.

All that happened, however, was that her passport was examined and officially stamped; she and her baggage were cursorily searched; then she was cleared for entry into the United Kingdom. Fleetingly, Bryony wondered if, in her deep grief at her father's violent, untimely death, she had taken total leave of her senses, embarking upon this journey to meet the as-yet-unknown Quester. Still, it was pointless to be having second thoughts now. She had arrived at her destination, and it was too late to turn back to New England.

She would feel much better about her decision after some strong, black coffee and a hot breakfast, she reflected. The terminal boasted various catering areas, and a restaurant called "Brophy's Self-Service Buffet" was open and looked inviting. Before going inside, Bryony purchased a local newspaper at Books Plus, folding it up and stashing it under one arm. She would read it while she ate. Being in no particular hurry, she had time to linger over coffee and the newspaper—not to mention the fact that she wanted to scrutinize her surroundings to determine if anyone seemed especially interested in her. For all she knew, the Quester was watching her at this very moment!

Still, Bryony had to admit that was probably unlikely. He would have had to wait around the terminal all morning, checking out every single American woman coming through Customs. Although he had been apprised of the date of her arrival, she had still been very careful not to give him any flight number, or even an airline. Despite the fact that over the passing days, their e-mail correspondence had progressed from their initial brief messages to lengthier letters, always in the back of her mind had remained the recognition that she might be writing to the enemy. Nor had the Quester himself proved any less cautious. It was she who had eventually suggested that they meet face-to-face, and it had been only reluctantly, she believed, that he had finally agreed, instructing her to fly into Aberdeen. She only hoped she hadn't been sent off on a wild-goose chase!

No one that she could discern appeared to be paying her any

particular heed. So, at last, Bryony turned her attention to her breakfast, famished after her long flight. After dining, perusing the newspaper and indulging in a third cup of coffee, she determined that if anybody actually *were* spying on her, she had wasted enough time demonstrating that she was entirely alone. Collecting her handbag and luggage, she exited the restaurant, making her way to the Travelex bureau de change, which was located near the main entrance to the terminal.

Wincing at the current exchange rate between the United States and the United Kingdom, she cashed a traveler's check for a billfold full of British pounds, having used what few she had got from the bank before leaving New England. Then, from the rank on the terminal forecourt, Bryony engaged a taxi to drive her to the Ardoe House Hotel, where she had booked a room and which was not far from either the airport or the Aberdeen City Centre.

The hotel, an elegant, loftily turreted mansion built in 1878, was fashioned in the Scottish baronial style and reminiscent of Balmoral Castle. Situated on seventeen acres of beautifully landscaped grounds, it provided views of both the River Dee and the Royal Deeside. Once inside, Bryony discovered that the Grand Hall, where the reception desk was located, was in its own way just as breathtaking, a picture of Victorian splendor, luxurious with burgundy-carpeted floors; ornate, wood panels, columns and arches; intricately carved fireplaces; stained-glass windows; and molded cornices and ceilings from which massive, gleaming, brass chandeliers hung. A huge, richly detailed main staircase led upward to an open lounge area overlooking Reception below.

For a moment, after she had stepped into the Grand Hall, Bryony just stood there, drinking everything in, lost in sheer delight at her environment. Thus, the slender but strong hand that, without warning, seized firm possession of her waist nearly startled her out of her wits, causing her to gasp. Instinctively, she began to protest and pull away from the stranger who taken hold of her, but much to her shock and fear, he abruptly pressed a semiautomatic pistol threateningly against her side.

"If you value your life, don't scream, and don't make a scene," he hissed in her ear, in a low, refined voice that bore only a trace of Scottish brogue.

Then, before Bryony could do anything else but nod mutely, he hurried her from Reception and propelled her through a side door leading to the hotel's exterior. After dragging her to a nearby late-model Volvo, he tossed her baggage, which he carried slung over one muscular shoulder, into the trunk. Then, opening the driver's door, he shoved her into the vehicle, pushing her across the five-speed gearshift into the passenger's seat before climbing in beside her, inserting the key into the ignition and starting the engine with a roar. Horrified, Bryony tried to unlock the passenger's door and escape, but the man swiftly grabbed her, giving her a rough, little shake and once more jamming the gun against her waist.

"Try anything like that again and you'll be sorry, I promise you!" he admonished sternly. "Now, be a good girl, and fasten your seat belt."

Her mouth dry with apprehension, her hands shaking as they fumbled with the strap and its buckle, Bryony did as her captor had ordered, unable to believe what was happening to her, that she was actually being kidnapped in broad daylight from an exclusive Scottish hotel, with nobody appearing even to notice, much less lending a finger to help her. She thought of how her father had died, and she wondered if this stranger abducting her was the man who had run him down on campus—if he would kill her, too. Her pulse raced, and it was all she could do to force herself to try to remain calm, knowing that to panic would not help.

Tires screeching on the pavement, the car accelerated away from the hotel, turning on to the main highway, weaving deftly in and out of traffic. Bryony's assailant expertly shifted the gears as the Volvo sped toward the open countryside. She attempted to keep track of where they were going by making a mental note of signs and landmarks. But after they left Aberdeen and its smaller surrounding towns behind, winding through the Grampian Mountains, the countryside, while breathtakingly beautiful, also grew very desolate. So there was little to mark the way. Her heart sank at the realization.

She started to ask the stranger who he was and where he was taking her. But not knowing whether talk and questions would anger him, Bryony decided that it was best to remain silent and watchful instead. Surreptitiously, from beneath the heavy fringe of her long, sooty eyelashes, she studied the man who had kidnapped her from the hotel.

He was tall, perhaps a shade under six feet, she judged, lithe and lean with the grace and hard muscles of a natural athlete— or predator. This last notion caused her to shiver. His rugged, weather-beaten skin was inherently dark, hinting at a Pictish as well as a Celtic ancestry, she thought. He was tanned even browner from long hours spent in the sun. A mass of glossy, black hair feathered with gray framed a handsome, hawkish face with thick, black brows that swooped like raven wings above deep-set, penetrating, molasses-brown eyes. An aquiline nose hooded a sulky, sensuous mouth that hinted at a carnal nature, while the thrust of his square jaw revealed both arrogance and determination. There was a slight, entrancing cleft in his chin.

Although he was casually garbed in a short, denim jacket; a blue, chambray workshirt open at the collar; a tight-fitting pair of Levi's button-fly jeans; and black, leather boots, the stranger looked as though he would be equally at home in a *breacan*— the plaid, blanketlike garment worn by Celtic warriors centuries ago. Bryony supposed that he must be just as barbaric as his ancestors to have abducted her in this fashion. Involuntarily, she shuddered again at the alarming idea.

Her captor drove around for quite some time, keeping an eye on the rearview and side mirrors, as though to make certain the Volvo weren't being followed. Then, at last, he wheeled the vehicle onto a narrow, serpentine, uneven, dirt road that eventually led to an old sheep-farm cottage surrounded by a low, stone fence and tucked away on a sweeping hillside. After pulling the car to a halt around back and switching off the engine, the man retrieved Bryony's luggage from the trunk, once more slinging the two bags over one shoulder. Then he instructed her to get out. With the pistol, he motioned her toward a lean-to at the rear of the bungalow, where he unlocked the door, then stepped back so that she could precede him inside.

"Straight on through to the kitchen," he directed, pointing toward an open doorway. "Sit down at the table, and in just a few minutes, I'll fix you a nice, hot cup of tea and a bite to eat, if you like."

This surprising courtesy was the very last thing Bryony had expected. Still, she was glad of what she viewed as a tentative reprieve from whatever dire fate the stranger had planned for her. Somewhat relieved, thinking that while he was bustling about in the kitchen, she might have a chance—however slim—at escape, she settled into one of the wooden farmhouse chairs drawn up around the kitchen table. Tossing her luggage to one side on the floor, the man joined her there. He started to speak again, but then, much to her distress and utter confusion, he suddenly burst into laughter instead, burying his face in one hand.

"I'm so terribly sorry," he eventually managed to choke out, in between chuckles, as he wiped the streaming tears from his eyes. "But, my God, I can't believe it actually worked!"

Her assailant must be a complete lunatic! Bryony reasoned, horrified. To her dismay, as he observed the stricken expression on her face, the man once more dissolved in mirth.

"Oh, Lord, I truly *am* sorry," he finally apologized again. "This is all really too bad of me—especially when you must be totally terrified and thinking I belong in Bedlam, besides."

"You mean you don't?" she snapped tartly.

"No—or then, again, perhaps I do. In all truth, I can't believe what I've done to you. But I honestly couldn't think of anything else on the spur of the moment. And I'm even more astounded that it actually worked. Thank God, you're an American, and therefore accustomed to a gun culture, because otherwise, I might not have succeeded." From the waistband of his jeans beneath his denim jacket, the stranger drew forth his semiautomatic pistol. "Handguns are highly illegal in the U.K. I'm afraid I bought this particular one at MacTavish's Toy

Shop this morning,'' he explained dryly. Then, aiming the weapon at one kitchen wall, he squeezed the trigger.

Bryony started in her chair at the loud, hissing noise followed by an equally loud pop. But much to her amazement and fury, nothing more than a tiny BB emerged from the barrel, embedding itself in the plaster.

''Why, do you mean to tell me that's only an air gun? Oh, you…you *tricked* me!'' she cried, outraged.

''Yes, dear lady, I most certainly did,'' her captor admitted ruefully. Then, laying the toy pistol on the table, he asked, ''Whom does the Grail serve?''

''It serves those who ask the question,'' Bryony replied, nearly collapsing with profound, unanticipated relief. ''My God, you're the Quester! Why didn't you just say so in the first place, you dreadful, wicked man? Why did you put me through such a horrible, terrifying ordeal?''

''Because I had no guarantee that even if you were informed of my identity, you would trust me enough to leave the hotel with me, no matter what I said or did, and you couldn't stay there. Others are not only aware of your presence here in Aberdeen, but also that you had made a reservation at the Ardoe House. Good Lord, woman! Your father has been murdered, and you yourself have been followed and your house searched, or so you told me in your e-mails. So just what were you thinking of—booking a room at one of Aberdeen's premiere hotels, and in your own name, besides, instead of keeping a low profile and concealing your true identity? Do you believe these people we're dealing with are idiots, that they don't know who you are?''

''No, I-I suppose they must.'' She bit her lower lip hard, appalled at her own stupidity. Of course, she realized now, she ought to have made two reservations, one at the Ardoe House, in her real name, and another at some small, out-of-the-way accommodation, under a fictitious moniker, where she should also have checked in. ''I'm—I'm afraid I'm not used to this sort of thing. I guess I'm not very good at it—yet,'' she added defensively, ''but I'm a fast learner. And that still doesn't explain how *you* knew who I was and where to find me!'' she accused suspiciously. "After all, I never told *you* my real name or where I was planning on staying!"

The Scotsman pointed toward her luggage, its identification tags plainly visible.

"It didn't take a rocket scientist to figure out the connection between 'Wildvine,' 'Torchbearer' and Bryony St. Blaze. In addition, there are only a limited number of airlines that fly from the States to Aberdeen. So, since I *did* know the date of your arrival, it really wasn't all that difficult to cover this morning's incoming flights, and to watch for a solitary American woman coming through Customs, one who would probably be discreetly shadowed by one or more men, given the fact that whoever was spying on you in New England would undoubtedly either have reported your movements to their British counterparts or else tailed you themselves. You were the only disembarking passenger who fit the bill. When you stopped at Books Plus for a newspaper, I managed to get a glimpse of your baggage identification tags. After that, it was only a matter of telephoning hotels to discover where you had booked a room. Fortunately, the Ardoe House was at the top of the alphabetical list. So, after a brief stop off at MacTavish's Toy Shop for the air gun, I immediately drove to the hotel to wait for you."

"And just what would you have done if I hadn't shown up?" Bryony inquired, both miffed and frightened at what an easy target she had unwittingly made of herself.

"Returned home and waited for you to e-mail me with a meeting place, as we had agreed, and hoped you turned up. Realistically, there was nothing else I could have done."

"But...I was quite careful at the airport, and I saw no one watching or following me, including *you*," she insisted, still puzzled and skeptical.

"You weren't meant to see me—or anybody else, either. I'm not a fool—and neither are these people we're dealing with. Two men tailed you at the airport, just as I did. And they also used their mobile phones, just as I did. I feel quite sure there were others waiting for you at the Ardoe House, and since I had no idea what their intentions toward you were, it was imperative that I get you out of there at once, as quickly and quietly as possible.''

"I see." Bryony paused, thoughtful. ''I-I suppose I ought to thank you, then, since it's entirely possible you may have saved my life. Nevertheless, I shall never forgive you for what you put me through!'' She scowled at the Scotsman. ''Why, you've probably taken twenty years off my life, you gave me such a scare!''

"For which I have already apologized profusely, sweet lady—and now do so yet again.'' Flashing her a roguish grin, he pushed the toy pistol across the table toward her. ''I'm incredibly sorry. Will it help if I permit you to shoot me?''

Despite herself, Bryony's breath caught in her throat as he turned the full force of his engaging smile and charm on her. Damn the man! Her job where he was concerned would have been a hell of a lot easier if he hadn't proved both so attractive and clever. He could be the enemy. She mustn't ever allow herself to forget that. For all she knew, his alleged ''rescue'' of her might actually be nothing more than an unbelievably ingenious setup to gain her trust and confidence.

Picking up the toy pistol, she pointed its barrel at him purposefully.

"I'll forego my revenge only on one condition,'' she announced.

"What's that?''

"I still don't know *your* real name.''

"Oh, sorry. In all the excitement, I quite forgot. It's Hamish…Hamish Neville. Would you care to see some identification to confirm that?''

"Yes, as a matter of fact, I would.'' She smiled with feigned sweetness at him.

Inadvertently, Hamish drew in his own breath sharply. It had been quite some time since he had had a woman, and from the instant he had first laid eyes on her at the Aberdeen International Airport, he had thought Bryony St. Blaze was one of the most gorgeous females he had ever seen. At the time, he had been intensely aware of the fact that he wanted her, and now, his groin tightened painfully again with desire. Hooding his eyes to conceal his lust, he slowly reached into the inside pocket of his denim jacket to withdraw his black, leather wallet, flipping it open to reveal his driver's license and holding it out for Bryony's inspection.

"Of course," he observed casually, "you must know how easy it is to forge documents such as this. Technology has got so sophisticated and prolific that these days, one can even purchase fake driving permits, credit cards, passports and so forth on the Internet, I do believe."

"Has anyone ever told you that you're a fiend?" she asked, grimacing at him.

"Yes...all too frequently, I'm afraid."

"So...how do I know that's your real name and driver's license?"

"You don't. You're just going to have to take my word for it."

"All right. I will, then—for now, anyway, seeing as how I really don't have any other choice in the matter. Not to mention the fact that I'm not harboring any illusions whatsoever about this air gun being any kind of an influence where *you* are concerned." Bryony continued to frown at him, sorely tempted to put a BB into the wall behind him, just to give him a scare.

"No, not hardly. Some of us," Hamish declared loftily, grinning impudently at her again, "have sense enough not to be deceived into thinking a toy pistol is actually a real semiautomatic handgun."

"Well, it was surely a natural mistake, under the circumstances," Bryony asserted stiffly, feeling totally ridiculous. "Anyone might have been taken in. I mean, I was frightened out of my wits, and it looks just like the genuine article— besides which, I never really even got a good look at it, until now."

"But that was the whole point, dear lady. After all, how on earth would it have done me any good whatsoever if you'd seen that it was, in reality, only an air gun loaded with BBs instead of bullets?"

"Believe it or not, I probably would have given serious thought to your accidentally putting out one or both of my eyes with it. That's the trouble with air guns. But, yes, you're quite right. It certainly wouldn't have persuaded me to keep my mouth shut and get into the car with you.'' Sighing at how easily she had been duped, Bryony finally laid the toy pistol down on the table. "So, Hamish, where do we go from here?"

"I'm not sure. I do, however, suggest that we first have that cup of tea and bite to eat that I promised you. I'm not a half-bad cook, if I do say so myself—besides which, I've some delicious bannocks if you'd care to have a sample?" He raised one eyebrow inquisitively.

"That sounds wonderful. Is there anything I can do to help?"

"No, no. Please. You just sit there and relax. I know I've given you a dreadful scare this morning, and I imagine you're suffering the inevitable effects of jet lag. So I'll just put the kettle on, then, shall I? Will some Brodie's Famous Edinburgh tea suit you?"

"Yes, it would suit me just fine."

While Bryony sat at the old farmhouse table, watching her intriguing host, Hamish busied himself preparing the light repast. From one cabinet, he took down a tin tea canister decorated with the Brodie hunting tartan, a box of Nairn's Traditional Oatcakes, and a beehive-shaped jar of Denrosa Royal Deeside Heather Honey. As the kettle boiled and both the bannocks and honey heated, he set cups and saucers, small plates, forks, teaspoons and a honey dipper on the table, along with a sugar bowl, a creamer filled with fresh milk, and a little dish of sliced lemon.

When everything was finally ready, he served Bryony and then himself. She took her hot tea with both lemon and sugar, and then, after drizzling the warm, rich, tangy honey over the equally warm oatcakes, she dug in. It seemed like hours since she had last eaten, and traveling always left her inordinately hungry.

"Hamish, this is absolutely scrumptious!" she remarked appreciatively, as she tucked away the tasty bannocks and sipped from her steaming teacup.

"I'm glad you like it." He smiled, obviously pleased. "I

thought you might enjoy a bit of Scotland's traditional fare. Now, Bryony, not to dampen your appetite, I hope, but would you mind filling me in a little more fully about our current situation than you did in your e-mails? Clearly, Torchbearer—your father, that is—was killed because of something he either knew or possessed, and just as clearly, you yourself are now being followed and may also be in grave danger. The police, you told me, are investigating your father's tragic, untimely death, so I'm curious as to why you came to me instead of giving them whatever information you think you may have uncovered in connection with his murder.''

''My father's real name was Simon...Simon St. Blaze,'' Bryony said slowly. ''He was a professor of ancient history at Thornfield University. I came to you instead of the police for two reasons, Hamish. Number one, even though the police believed my father was, in fact, deliberately run over and killed, I didn't know whether they would take my story about esoteric mysteries and secret societies seriously. My father was...rather eccentric and highly imaginative, too, and all this was well known on campus. So it was altogether possible that the police would have thought him a crackpot, even though he actually *had* been murdered. I confess that when he mentioned his suspicions and fears to me, I wondered whether he had grown senile, or even lost his mind. Number two, my father insisted that if I somehow became involved in all of this, I was going to need your help—and that not only my life, but also your own might be in jeopardy. So...here I am.'' Taking up the dipper, she dripped more honey onto what remained of her bannocks. ''What I don't yet know is exactly *what* my father had learned or acquired that proved so fatal to him, how *he* ever got involved in all this himself, and how you and he got hooked up together in the first place.''

Hamish was silent for a moment, reflecting soberly. Then he spoke.

''Whilst I'm not yet aware of the extent of your own knowledge, Bryony, I *do* suspect you're withholding a great deal of information you *are* currently cognizant of—and I can understand that. After all, apart from exchanging a few e-mails, we've only just met, and heaven knows, I've given you no good reason whatsoever for trusting me. You may even think me an utter lunatic, threatening you with a toy pistol and hauling you off from the Ardoe House the way I did—and I wouldn't blame you for that, either. Nevertheless, since you're plainly already at some risk, I guess it won't matter if I enlighten you further.''

Pushing away his plate, Hamish removed a pack of Marlboro Lights and an elegant, gold lighter from his jacket pocket.

"I know it's not politically correct these days, but do you mind if I indulge?'' he queried.

"No, not at all.'' Bryony shook her head. She had had her fill of what every Tom, Dick and Harry deemed politically correct in this day and age, giving every single ill-mannered, immoral moron on the planet a license to ram his doctrines and pet peeves down everybody else's throat.

"Thanks. I appreciate that.'' Taking a cigarette from the pack, Hamish lit up, inhaling deeply, then blowing a stream of smoke from his nostrils before speaking again. "I suppose it's entirely possible that, just like most other people fascinated by arcana and esoterics, Simon might have studied and researched the Mysteries his whole life without attracting any undesirable attention or placing himself in peril. Unfortunately, he had the very bad luck of being the unwitting recipient of an e-mail he should never have got, much less read, or investigated.''

Hamish took another drag of his cigarette, then drank from his teacup.

"If I'm covering ground you've already trodden, then I'm afraid you'll have to forgive me. Suffice to say, therefore, that for nearly eight hundred centuries, there has existed a highly secret order called the 'Abbey of the Divine.' Just like various others of its ilk, it began as a sect of the Knights Templar, with which I assume you're familiar.'' At Bryony's nod, he went on. "Unlike its known counterparts, however, the Abbey's existence has never been publicly exposed, whether because it has always chosen its members extremely carefully or because it is so fearsome an organization that its members dare not cross it. At any rate, it guards its privacy zealously, to the point of murder, I believe. I feel certain it was members of the Abbey who killed your father.''

"But…why?'' Bryony's brow was knitted in a confused frown. ''If this…Abbey of the Divine is as secret as you claim it is, then how could my father have possibly learned of its existence?''

"Through the e-mail I mentioned earlier. Within the upper echelons of the Abbey, there is one whose e-mail address is 'torchbearer at ringmail dot org.' I'm sure it must now be clear to you that a letter intended for that recipient was inadvertently misdirected to your father, whose own Internet service provider was, like your own, 'ringmail dot net.' Employing 'net' instead of the proper 'org' would have been an easy-enough mistake to have made. But I'm afraid the consequences to your father were lethal. Because of that simple error, he received something he was certainly never intended to see. That in itself might not have created a danger to him, as, presumably, the e-mail was encrypted. However, like most of those inclined toward the study of arcana and esoterics, your father adored a mystery. By some means—probably through a student with sophisticated hacking abilities—he managed to decode the message.''

"Do you know what it said?'' Bryony asked, her voice somber.

"Yes.'' Hamish nodded, drawing on his cigarette again. ''It wouldn't have been so bad if all the e-mail had done was reveal the Abbey's existence to your father. He might have paid the letter little or no heed, thinking it was simply some monastic correspondence gone astray. Unfortunately, however, the e-mail detailed the Abbey's origins, its background and its purpose.''

"And are you familiar with all that, as well?''

"Yes. As I said earlier, the Abbey of the Divine began as a sect of the Knights Templar. As you are probably aware, on the thirteenth of October, Thirteen Oh Seven, Philippe Le Bel or Philip the Fair, who was King of France at the time, had the Knights Templar charged with heresy and arrested. In all actuality, the vast majority of Philip's claims were most likely baseless. He coveted the brotherhood's immense wealth, and the only way he could seize its money and other assets was through accusations of heresy, necromancy and so forth. Many of the Knights Templar escaped, however. Several of those in France fled here to Scotland, while those elsewhere, such as in Portugal, simply renamed their order and carried on business as usual. It was presumably at this time that the Abbey broke away completely to follow its own path." Crushing out his cigarette in the ashtray, Hamish stood. "Would you care for some more tea?"

"Please." Bryony handed him her cup and saucer.

As he refilled their teacups, Hamish continued his tale.

"Having originally composed an elite sect within the Knights Templar, the Abbey's members had always considered themselves special—even divine. They were all of Celtic ancestry, and they believed themselves to be descended from King Arthur and his Knights of the Round Table and, as such, the true and rightful heirs to the Holy Grail—whatever that may be. I'm sure you know it's thought to have been everything from the silver platter that bore the disembodied head of John the Baptist to the silver chalice that Jesus Christ drank from at the Last Supper. Some have even argued that the mysterious word for the Grail, *Sangraal,* should be rectified as *Sang Réal*...'Holy Blood,' and hypothesized that this is the name of a bloodline—the Merovingian kings—that descended from Jesus himself."

"Yes, I know," Bryony stated, a trifle dismissively. "Henry Lincoln, et al. I have a deep, abiding interest in the Celts, so I've studied the Grail at some length, and it's my own belief that *Sang Réal* is a grossly inaccurate translation for *Sangraal.*"

"And you may indeed be right," Hamish agreed, shrugging as he rejoined her at the table. "Who knows? There are dozens of theories. Lacking the necessary data to draw any reasonable conclusions in the matter, I myself make no judgments one way or another. I'm merely relaying the information. Whether Jesus Christ did not die on the cross, but instead wed Mary Magdalene, who, along with Joseph of Arimathea and others, subsequently immigrated to Gaul, is a topic for debate. It is, however, what the Merovingian kings of the Frankish Empire later asserted, insisting that they were descended from Jesus and Mary Magdalene's children. The Abbey, however, took all this even a step further, claiming that King Arthur was actually Jesus Christ himself reincarnated and that the original twelve Knights of the Round Table were the Apostles likewise born again.''

"Now, I've heard everything." Bryony shook her head with skepticism and wry amazement.

"Yes, well, it takes all kinds," Hamish observed dryly, lighting up another cigarette. "It also helps, of course, that there is considerable confusion in the Arthurian literature as to just exactly how many warriors made up the original Knights of the Round Table, and who they actually were. Lancelot, Kay and Bedivere spring to mind first, obviously. But which Disciples to equate them with...? Peter, James and John? In all but Scottish tradition, Mordred is a traitor, so he's clearly Judas Iscariot. As for the rest...? Again, who knows? At any rate, this is the foundation on which the Abbey of the Divine was built, the cornerstone on which the beliefs and principles of its members have rested for nearly eight hundred years. The Abbey's supreme goal, of course, is the same as that of fanatics and terrorists the planet over—to impose the so-called New World Order, with the Abbey's inner sanctum of thirteen as the ruling oligarchy. As in all such similar cases, this would be laughable if these people weren't in such deadly earnest, so dangerous and well financed."

"But if there are only thirteen of them—" Bryony began.

"Thirteen who comprise the inner sanctum or, as they call it, the Round Table," Hamish corrected her politely. "Worldwide, there may be countless others, most of whom are probably completely ignorant of the Abbey's existence, but nevertheless employed by it through various individuals and corporations all ultimately controlled by the Abbey."

"And all this is what my father learned from the e-mail he mistakenly received and deciphered?"

"More or less, yes."

"All right. I'll buy that. But that still doesn't explain how *you* came to know so much about everything."

"From your father...some of it, anyway. The rest was imparted to me by the Abbey itself. You see, it was *I* who was the primary subject of the letter your father got."

"You?" Bryony exclaimed, startled.

"Yes." Hamish's mouth curved in a wry, self-deprecating smile. "The Abbey, it seems, has decided that I am Mordred—and thus Judas—reincarnated and that I must therefore take my proper place at the inner sanctum's Round Table. Your father—God rest his soul—was obviously a very decent, caring man. After decoding the Abbey's message, which contained my e-mail address, he got in touch with me—to warn me that certain people I would be in contact with were not at all what they might appear to be. That was approximately three months or so ago, by which time I had come into contact with an enigmatic man known to me only as 'Cauldronbearer,' which I had at first taken to be his Internet handle. Ostensibly, he was interested in my work. I'm a sometime medieval history professor at the University of Aberdeen, and I've also written and illustrated several books on various aspects of the Dark and Middle Ages. But the more we corresponded, the plainer it became to me that he was discreetly sounding me out—not only about history, but also about arcana, esoterics, the Mysteries, secret societies, King Arthur and the Knights of the Round Table, the Holy Grail and so on."

Hamish paused, taking another long swallow from his teacup.

"I'd be lying to you if I said I weren't intrigued. I was. Still, even had I not been warned by your father, my nature, whilst curious, is not by any means blindly trusting. So I would have been suspicious of Cauldronbearer under any circumstances. As it was, thanks to your father, I was privy to a great deal of information that Cauldronbearer didn't know I already possessed. I'm just guessing now, but I think it was days, maybe even weeks, before the error that misdirected the e-mail to your father was discovered. Perhaps whoever made the mistake kept quiet, for fear of reprisal. I don't know. Then, of course, it would have taken the Abbey some time to learn your father's identity and how much, if anything, he actually knew. That he was an ancient-history professor who had studied and researched arcana and esoterics all his life undoubtedly sealed his fate, since both would have made him a threat to the Abbey—especially as, after decoding the letter, your father apparently started digging into relatively obscure areas, to see what else he could uncover. No doubt, the Abbey had been spying on him for quite a while before making its move against him."

Having now smoked his second cigarette down to the filter, Hamish ground it out in the ashtray.

"The problem now is this. Until your father was murdered, the Abbey could only speculate about whether or not he had ever been in communication with me. Certainly, *I* never let on that he had been. Needless to say, it wouldn't have been to my advantage for the Abbey to learn that I was already aware of its existence, background and purpose. But my ongoing association with both your father and Cauldronbearer had gradually begun to convince me that your father was right—these people *were,* in fact, dangerous. Now that your father is dead and his office, and probably his town house, as well as your own bungalow, have been searched, it seems quite likely to me that the Abbey has gained access to his computer and, thereby, access to his correspondence with me."

"Oh, good Lord!" Bryony gasped with dismay, as understanding suddenly dawned. "Believe it or not, until just this moment, it never even occurred to me that Dad's computer might have been broken into. But of course, the Abbey would have wanted to see what was on it...." Her voice trailed away, and she chewed her lower lip nervously, blanching.

"I see you have followed my own line of reasoning. Undoubtedly, the Abbey is also cognizant of the fact that *I* am the reason for your trip to Scotland, and therefore, they must be aware that you, too, have learned of its existence. There is a further complication. Only a few weeks ago, Cauldronbearer at last disclosed to me his true reason for contacting me, telling me about the Abbey and its belief that I am Mordred reincarnated, and inviting me to be initiated into its ranks. I refused to give him an immediate answer, insisting that I wanted at least a fortnight to think about it, which Cauldronbearer granted me. However, I have not heard from him since your father was killed, which undoubtedly bodes ill for me. My guess is that the Abbey is waiting to find out what I will do next, whether I will accept or decline its invitation. If I do not e-mail Cauldronbearer with an affirmative response, I strongly suspect that I shall be placed on the Abbey's hit list—and you along with me. That is surely why your father feared that my life was in jeopardy.''

"But...Hamish, if all this is true, then shouldn't we be doing something about it? Making plans to escape, instead of just hanging around here like a couple of sitting ducks?'' Bryony's pale face revealed her consternation.

''I can't be certain, of course, but I think we have several days' grace, at least,'' he replied thoughtfully. ''If we're lucky, maybe even as much time as two or three weeks, in which to make plans and prepare. I am, by nature, an extremely private and reclusive individual, with a great dislike of intrusion of any sort, which I myself have not invited. I have all my snail mail directed to a postal box in Aberdeen. No one—not even University—has my home address, and my telephone number is ex-directory, as well. Fortunately, the Abbey will have been hindered in finding out where I live by the fact that, unlike the States, the U.K. has what is called the 'Data Protection Act,' which makes the obtaining of personal records very onerous here. Further, that you have not yet checked in to the Ardoe House will create additional havoc for the Abbey. The inner sanctum will no doubt initially assume you took a room elsewhere, under a fictitious name. So they will waste valuable time searching all the other hotels for you, unaware that we are already together. Naturally, in the meanwhile, you'll stay here with me.''

''Naturally,'' Bryony echoed weakly, unnerved by the idea but reluctantly seeing no other rational course of action.

The longer Hamish had talked, the more she had recognized how highly intelligent and shrewd he was. For all she knew, she was the victim of an exceedingly brilliant song-and-dance routine designed to lull her suspicions and gain her immediate trust and confidence. At the moment, she might not have a choice as to the music or her partner, but she could still hold him at arm's length. And would, Bryony vowed to herself determinedly.

That this might prove difficult, due to how handsome and captivating she found him, was a notion she resolutely shoved from her mind. She was not some silly, young schoolgirl, to be infatuated by a dark, hawkish visage blessed with a pair of mesmerizing eyes the color of smoky quartz and a saturnine, sensuous mouth. She had already been through one bad marriage, followed by an even worse divorce, both of which had left her instinctively wary of men, in general, and of highly attractive men in particular, no longer trusting her own judgment where the opposite sex was concerned. So, no matter how attractive and charming he was, it behooved her to remain on her guard against Hamish Neville.

"Have I quite bored you to tears?" Without warning, he interrupted her reverie. "You look as though you're about to fall asleep in that chair."

"The ill effects of jet lag, I'm afraid. I've been fighting it valiantly ever since I arrived at your airport. But honesty compels me to confess that if I don't get to a bed real soon, I *am* liable to crash and burn right where I sit."

"How lucky for you that I've a small, snug trundle bed tucked away under the eaves upstairs." Hamish rose, collecting her luggage. "Admittedly, it's not much. Nevertheless, it's the best I can offer—and I promise that the sheets, at least, are reasonably clean and that the mattress is passably comfortable."

"Don't worry. It can't be any worse than a camp cot." At his cocked eyebrow, Bryony explained, "Sorry. I forgot I hadn't told you what I do for a living. I'm an archaeologist."

"Ah. Having long contemplated becoming one myself, I am now green with envy. This way, sweet lady."

Even as Bryony trailed obediently after Hamish, she thought in some dark corner of her mind that she must be as mad as a hatter. She had met this Scotsman only this morning, when he had hauled her from the hotel by means of a deceptively employed toy pistol, no less! She knew next to nothing about him, other than what he had just shared with her in the kitchen; now, he was escorting her upstairs to a bed, where, for all she knew, he would suddenly fall upon her and ravish her. Even worse was the fact that despite everything, she had to admit this scenario held a certain undeniable appeal.

For pity's sake, she really *must* be losing it! She had, by choice, been celibate now for so long that she was actually ready to hop into the sack with the first and only man she had found physically attractive since her divorce several years ago.

"Here we are." Courteously standing to one side of the doorway so that Bryony could precede him into the bedroom, Hamish indicated the trundle bed where he normally slept. "As I said, it's not much. I don't usually have visitors, so I'm afraid I haven't any guest room. But don't worry." He grinned cheekily at her again. "Despite the indisputable appeal of the idea, I've no intentions of imposing my rather dubious charms upon you. Whilst you're here, I'll sleep on the sofa in my study across the hall."

"No, really," Bryony protested, feeling enormously guilty at the notion of displacing him from his bed. "I wouldn't dream of turning you out of your own room. I'll take the couch."

"Nonsense! You're my guest—and the sofa is terribly lumpy from all the late nights I've fallen asleep on it. So it won't be any real hardship for me to use it, I assure you."

"Well, in that case, then, it's a deal."

After setting her baggage down on the braided rug, Hamish turned down one corner of the bedclothes and plumped up the two pillows.

"The loo's there." Returning to the doorway, he motioned toward the end of the short hall beyond. "I'll just lay out some clean towels and soap, shall I? And if there's anything else you need, please don't hesitate to let me know."

"Thanks. It's very good of you to take me in like this, Hamish, especially when you're not used to company."

"Yes, well, in all honesty, I've the feeling that I actually *could* grow quite used to yours. Why, you're blushing," he observed, with feigned innocence. "Have I said something amiss?"

"I can see, now, that regardless of the situation, you truly *are* just utterly shameless and incorrigible," Bryony told him, flattered and trying hard not to laugh.

"Who, me?" He pretended to be dumbfounded by her accusation.

"Yes, you!"

"No-o-o, I don't believe it! Sleep well, dear lady," he advised. Chuckling, he exited the room, shutting the door softly behind him.

For a moment after he had left her alone, Bryony continued to stare at the closed door, feeling a warm glow of delight suffuse her entire being. So…apparently, she wasn't the only one who was suffering from the effects of that mysterious phenomenon known as "sexual chemistry." On the one hand, the fact that the physical attraction between her and Hamish was mutual excited her tremendously. On the other, it could not help but dismay her, for she knew it would only make keeping a wary distance from him that much more difficult. She sighed heavily.

Then, forcing herself to put her budding relationship with the Scotsman from her mind, Bryony took stock of her surroundings. Although slightly smaller than hers, Hamish's cottage was nevertheless similar to her own in layout. Also like hers, it was scrupulously clean and neat, for which she was extremely grateful, as she couldn't abide slovenliness of any sort. Shortly after their marriage, having previously put his best foot forward, her ex-husband had most irritatingly reverted to his true self as a slob extraordinaire—one of the reasons why she had eventually divorced him.

Hamish's bedroom was simple but pleasing to her eye. The rough, plaster walls had been painted a soft white, which contrasted sharply with the dark-stained, wood beams and floor, and the few well-placed, vibrant seascapes in oak frames. Examining the paintings more closely, Bryony observed from the signature that they were Hamish's own work. He was quite a talented artist, she realized. In addition to the trundle bed, there was an armoire, an old-fashioned gentleman's chest—which was something of a cross between a dresser and a chest of drawers—a night table, and a comfy, overstuffed chair. Further accoutrements included small stacks of books, most of them classics and nonfiction, as well as nautical memorabilia, such as an old, brass ship's bell and an antique sextant. Clearly, Hamish had a love of reading and of ships and the sea, all of which were things that Bryony shared.

In all but Scottish tradition, Mordred is a traitor.... Hamish's words echoed in her mind, sending an icy tingle up her spine.

Deep down inside, she already knew she was going to be devastated if he turned out to be the enemy. Sighing again, she at last began to strip off the now-crumpled clothes she'd worn on her long flight. Then, unlocking and unzipping her luggage, she tugged out a cotton nightshirt and pulled it on over her head, thinking ruefully that it certainly wasn't at all the kind of garment designed to entice a man. For the first time in ages, Bryony longed for something black, sheer and sexy, which would appeal to a potential lover.

Good heavens, what was she thinking? She simply *had* to force all thoughts like that out of her head, focusing her concentration instead—no matter how dangerous—on the Abbey of the Divine, on exposing her father's killers and seeing them brought to justice. That goal must be her one and only priority.

With that idea uppermost in her mind, Bryony slowly tiptoed to the bedroom door. After briefly pressing her head against it to be sure Hamish had now gone back downstairs, she quietly turned the old-fashioned lock—not because she was afraid he would assault her while she slept, but because she feared that he would search her baggage and purse. There was nothing in her luggage that would be of any assistance to him, not even her laptop computer. Her handbag, however, was a different story altogether, for in it were copies of the two CDs her father had sent to her. The originals, she had left at home, securely locked away in a safe-deposit box.

Carefully removing from her purse the jewel box containing the copies she had made, Bryony glanced around the bedroom, looking for a hiding place. Finally, she slipped the jewel box inside the pillowcase on one of the pillows. It would have to do for now, until she managed to think of some better means of concealing the copies. At least this way, if Hamish attempted to take the jewel box from the pillowcase while she slept, she would surely wake up.

Bryony crawled into the trundle bed, momentarily reveling in the clean, masculine, musky scent of Hamish that lingered in the sheets, enveloping her like a sweet caress.

Minutes later, she slept like the dead.

Eight

The High Priest and the Pharaoh

And with the blast of thy nostrils the waters were gathered
together, the floods stood upright as an heap, and the
depths were congealed in the heart of the sea.

The Bible
—Exodus 15:7-8

*The City of Avaris, the Land of Goshen, the Two Kingdoms of
Egypt, c. 1628 B.C.*

Things were not going well for Nephrekeptah, the High Priest
of Set at the ancient city of Avaris. Despite all his prayers and
sacrifices to the gods, it seemed that everything had gone
against him ever since Moshéh had returned to the Two Kingdoms of Egypt, talking like a madman about his One-God,
Yahweh, and his people, the Hapiru—the "Desert-Travelers"
or "Caravan-Travelers"—threatening the uncivilized, foreign
Pharaoh, Sheshi, with various fates worse than death if he did
not let them go. Nephrekeptah thought the many long years
Moshéh had lived beyond the Sea of Reeds, in Midian, in self-
imposed exile after he had killed a man and fled from Egypt,
had unhinged his mind. For if the Hapiru were granted their
freedom, then who would labor to make the bricks and build

the monuments and cities of the Goshen region of the Two Kingdoms?

Between Moshéh's apparent insanity and the Pharaoh's barbarism, as well as his complete ignorance about the Hapiru's great ancestor Yoseph, who had long ago served as an important vizier of Egypt, saving its people from starvation, and who was thus revered by the Hapiru and Egyptians alike, the Nile Delta was in upheaval. Sheshi was one of what the Egyptians called the "Heka-Khaswt," which meant "Rulers of the Foreign Hill-Country"—land that lay beyond Egypt. But ever since Moshéh had come back to Goshen, spouting his fiery rhetoric and brandishing his shepherd's crook threateningly, many of the common people had taken to referring derisively to the Pharaoh as "Hyk-Sos"—"Shepherd-King."

After invading the Nile Delta, conquering and subjugating Memphis, the capital of the Lower Kingdom, and pilfering many of its wondrous treasures, Sheshi had set about rebuilding and fortifying with strong walls the city of Avaris, located just east of the Bubastic Branch of the River Nile and which was the capital of the Sethroite nome or province. Avaris was dedicated to the god Set, whom the Pharaoh had equated with his own god Baal, and for this reason, he had chosen it as his favored seat.

With Moshéh's return, work on the ancient city had virtually ground to a total halt—and still, there had been no convincing Sheshi of Moshéh's lunacy! With every passing day, as plague after plague had beset Avaris, the Pharaoh had grown increasingly irresolute, wavering in the face of Moshéh's zealous bombast and peremptory demands to allow the Hapiru to leave the Two Kingdoms. Moshéh had claimed the plagues were the work of his almighty One-God, Yahweh, a judgment on Sheshi. But the High Priest had spies everywhere, and a few days ago, he had received reports that the learned island of Kalliste had exploded and drowned beneath the waves of the Great Sea, simultaneously spewing fire, thick clouds of ash and a hailstorm of black stones unto the heavens, wreaking havoc for miles in all directions, causing the lands to quake and the oceans to rise and flood far over their shores. The whole world, it seemed, was in chaos, as a result.

It was surely no coincidence, Nephrekeptah thought shrewdly, that all the plagues that had descended upon Egypt had begun at this same time.

First, large patches of reddish brown seaweed had suddenly bloomed on the surface of the River Nile, after which all the fish had sickened and died, their open, putrid sores draining so much blood into the Bubastic branch that its polluted waters had finally run bright red, terrifying the people. With all the fish dead, there had been no natural predators to feed upon the frog eggs hatching their tadpoles in the River Nile, and in consequence, massive hordes of frogs had shortly streamed from the defiled waters, seeking to escape the foulness. Many of these had also died, their amphibian bodies decomposing all along the banks, attracting a multitude of filthy insects. Hosts of midges and stable flies had then risen from the carcasses to settle on the people and livestock, biting them and raising festering boils on them, carrying the pestilence from the dead frogs to humans and animals alike. Men, women, children, camels, horses, mules, asses, cattle, sheep, goats and pigs had died by the hundreds.

If this weren't bad enough, a roaring combination of fire, ash and black stones had rained like hail from the skies, also, decimating the planted crops in the fields and the fruit trees in the orchards, and what little that had survived had subsequently been devastated by a swarm of locusts. Then, for three days, a horrendous sandstorm born on the wings of a violent khamsin had darkened the skies, burying and baking the harvested crops stored in the granaries for times of famine, causing the cached wheat and barley to swelter and rot. Blotches of black mold had appeared on the walls of the granaries and on the cereals themselves. But by then, little else had remained to provide sustenance. After consuming the spoiled grain, all the firstborns, who, as the eldest children, received a double portion of food in accordance with Egyptian tradition, had fallen ill and died, as had countless others, as well. So many had died that there had been no way to carry out the proper funeral rites, the dead having to be hastily interred in shallow, mass graves instead.

Even now, the pharaoh mourned his oldest son and heir, and in his madness and grief, he had commanded Moshéh to take the Hapiru and leave Egypt forever. Moshéh had tarried no longer. Accompanied by several thousand Hapiru men, women and children, together with their animals, carts and meager belongings, he had set out at once from Avaris, slowly wending his way southeastward, toward the Papyrus Marsh and the Seas of Weeds and Reeds.

Upon entering the Great Temple of Set, the High Priest discovered that sometime before departing from the city, Moshéh—once a prince of Egypt and therefore privy to its deepest secrets—had broken into the large, stone sepulchre between the two tall pillars at the heart of the sacred edifice and stolen from it the intricate puzzle box containing the holy *Book of Thoth!* He must be fetched back immediately!

Nephrekeptah's heart pounded with horror at the realization. The *Book of Thoth* was Egypt's most prized possession! It was ancient—older, even, than the pharaohs themselves.

The sacred manuscript was rumored to have come from the distant land of Nod, brought there by the Marked One who had murdered his brother, and then passed on through the ages to those known as the ''Cult of the Dead,'' wanderers who had traveled for aeons far and wide across many lands. Architects and astronomers, the Cult of the Dead had, among other things, constructed massive, labyrinthine temples and a vast hypogeum—a subterranean necropolis—on the islands of Gozo and Malta in the Great Sea, and built a huge, stone henge, a monument to the stars, in the fabled land of Hyperborea, which was said to lie beyond the north wind. Some even claimed that the Cult of the Dead was responsible for erecting the Great Pyramids of Egypt, and although, publicly, Nephrekeptah always denied this, he privately thought it might well be true.

It was claimed that two Minoans, Pandora and Epimetheus, fleeing from the wrath of the Minos who had then ruled the isle of Crete, near Kalliste, in the Great Sea, had borne the *Book of Thoth* with them to Avaris nearly a millennia ago.

Later, it had been taken to Memphis. But upon seizing the throne, Sheshi had removed the tome from the capital of the Lower Kingdom and reinstalled it at Avaris for safekeeping from the provinces of the Upper Kingdom, who, although they grudgingly paid him tribute, still teemed with rebellion against the hated, foreign Pharaoh.

The high priests of Egypt had been studying the *Book of Thoth* for centuries now, trying to decipher its ancient, cryptic language and symbols, laboriously, painstakingly, making copies of its highly elaborate, detailed pages. But there were so many of these last that even after all this time, no complete copy of the mysterious manuscript as yet existed, only bits and pieces that had seemed of primary importance.

The book must be got back!

Determinedly pivoting on his heel, the fine, linen folds of his long, white robe whispering around him, the flapping of his papyrus sandals—the only kind an Egyptian priest was permitted to wear—echoing softly in the silence across the marble of the black and white chessboard floor, Nephrekeptah hurried from the Great Temple of Set toward the Palace. Ignoring the guards, knowing that whatever their orders might be, they would not dare to halt him, the High Priest of Set, who was feared even more than the despised, foreign Pharaoh himself, he pushed open the heavy, golden doors that barred the Great Hall against all intruders, and entered.

Except for the single torches blazing brightly on either side of the gilded throne that stood upon the dais at one end, the vast room was in darkness. But as Nephrekeptah had known, Sheshi was there, ensconced upon his royal seat, his head bowed in sorrow at the loss of his eldest son and heir.

"You interrupt my mourning, Nephrekeptah," the Pharaoh announced after a moment, his voice low and throbbing with torment. "I left instructions that I wished to receive no one this day—especially you, who have failed me in my darkest hour. You are no longer favored. The gods have turned against you, and against me and my kingdoms, as well. The One-God of Moshéh, this...Yahweh...has prevailed, cursing us with one plague after another, and now, my firstborn son is dead. Go,

Nephrekeptah! I would not look upon you, who have proved so useless to me, my son and my kingdoms! Go—as Moshéh and the Hapiru have gone—and leave me alone with my grief!''

"My deepest apologies, Your Majesty, but I cannot," the High Priest declared insistently, shaking his head. "For I have come to you on the gravest of matters, of the utmost urgency. Regardless of the cost, you must set aside your sadness for the time being, gather your mighty army and pursue Moshéh and the Hapiru to the very ends of the earth, if necessary! They have stolen the hallowed *Book of Thoth!*"

"By the Great God Baal, is this true?" Even the savage Sheshi understood the tome's priceless value. One strong hand tightening into a fist, he abruptly sprang to his feet, stricken and outraged. "Sacrilege! Ingrates! I gave them their freedom—and this is how they repaid me! Why do you just stand there, High Priest? Go! Hurry! Sound the alarm! Summon my troops! We must make haste to overtake Moshéh and regain the *Book of Thoth* at once!"

Sometime later, standing haughtily in his heavy war chariot, its horses snorting and prancing with nervous excitement, the Pharaoh departed the city, his powerful military force massed behind him—more than six hundred chariots strong—vehicles that had been little used by the Egyptians until the advent of Sheshi and his soldiers. Accompanied by a multitude of infantry and as though the greatest of evils were hard on their heels, the cavalcade traveled swiftly through Goshen, toward the Papyrus Marsh, the Bitter Lakes, and the Seas of Weeds and Reeds. Day and night, they journeyed, pausing only to rest their horses, following the southern route Moshéh and the Hapiru had taken from Egypt, the northern being far more dangerous, due to the Philistines who peopled that region.

At either end of the east-west, wooden bridge spanning the broad canal that joined the Bitter Lakes with the Sea of Weeds stood the great, twin fortresses of Sukkôt and Tharu-takut, from where Sheshi and his legions struck out across the Wilderness of Sin, which lay between the fork of the two seas, toward the land of Etham. Then, instead of heading for Elath, the oasis at the far-north tip of the Sea of Reeds, the Pharaoh and his war-riors turned south, pushing on toward the fortress of Pi-ha-hiroth, situated on the sea's western shore. His scouts had re-ported that Moshéh and the Hapiru were now encamped upon the vast, white-gold strand there, at Elim, an oasis of bubbling springs, where, in late summer, the wandering tribes gathered dates from the dense groves of palm trees.

Obviously, the Hapiru were bent on reaching Midian, the homeland of Moshéh's wife, Zipporah, and where Moshéh himself had lived since his self-imposed exile from Egypt. It made sense.

Knowing that once his theft of the *Book of Thoth* had been discovered, he would be relentlessly pursued, Moshéh had wisely decided to seek out land with which he was intimately familiar, and where he could hope to elude the Egyptians, guided by his revered One-God, Yahweh, who had first ap-peared to him there, in the form of a burning bush. Once safely in Midian, Moshéh could then turn northward, toward Edom, Moab and Canaan.

But to have first reached Pi-ha-hiroth—the "Mouth of the Gorges"—and Elim, it had been necessary for Moshéh and the Hapiru to traverse an eighteen-mile stretch of serpentine chasms and wadis that were like a labyrinth, only a single one of which opened on to the tremendous beach where the fortress, with its *migdol* or watchtower, stood guard at the northern end. Both Pi-ha-hiroth and Elim were overlooked by mountains to the west, which stretched to the coast, cutting off any further travel southward from the oasis. Directly opposite, on the east-ern bank of the Sea of Reeds, lay the Midianite fortress of Baal-zephon, beyond which, to the southeast, the canyon of Horeb snaked its way to the foot of Mount Sinai, the highest peak in the region.

It was Sheshi's intention to trap Moshéh and the Hapiru on the strand between the mountains and the sea, and to slaughter them for their unspeakable, audacious theft of the sacred *Book of Thoth.*

The Egyptian army was halfway through the maze of twist-ing gulches and wadis when, without warning, a deafeningly thunderous discharge split the heavens, and the earth itself began to rumble ominously.

From his own weighty vehicle, Sheshi frantically shouted commands, attempting to keep his troops from disintegrating into chaos. The loud blasts blown on the rams' horns of his trumpeters rang out strongly, carried to his soldiers by the now-forebodingly rising wind, which presently began to billow with fine clouds of ash and sand, just as it had only days ago. Stinging grit filled the eyes, nostrils, and mouth, no matter how well shielded.

For several long minutes, it seemed as though the cavalcade would break ranks and run. But gradually, through the sheer force of his authority and will, his arrogant visage grim and bent on prevailing, the Pharaoh managed to impose order on his frightened legions, compelling them to press on through the chasms.

From his own light, gilded chariot—designed for priestly ceremonies, not war—at the rear of the troops, Nephrekeptah gazed anxiously at the increasingly menacingly darkening firmament. He thought of the island of Kalliste, which had so recently exploded and sunk, and he feared that something equally disastrous had occurred, from which the labyrinth of winding gorges and wadis had thus far largely protected the procession.

Soon, it was as though night had fallen, so shadowed had the day grown. In the unnatural, blinding murkiness, it was nearly impossible to see. Still, goaded on by the knowledge that recovering the hallowed *Book of Thoth* was paramount, Sheshi resolutely plowed on, directing that torches be lit to illuminate their path, and, seizing hold of his war chariot's long, leather reins himself, instructing his charioteer to disembark and lead the terrified horses forward. In this excruciating way, the host of vehicles and warriors progressed relentlessly, gaining precious ground inch by inch.

All sense of direction was completely lost, but, mercifully, the army was hemmed in by the canyon walls rising on either side, and the roaring sound of the roiling Sea of Reeds served as its own guide, as well. Even so, both Nephrekeptah and

Sheshi worried that despite all their stalwart efforts, they would not succeed, but were doomed to defeat by the maddening elements. Then, finally, when it appeared that their cause was indeed hopeless and must be abandoned, the tall watchtower of Pi-ha-hiroth suddenly loomed ahead, casting a dark, soaring silhouette against the dreadful, fiery dawn breaking on the horizon, turning the Sea of Reeds bloodred.

"By all the gods!" the High Priest exclaimed, utterly daunted and stupefied as he stared with horror at the sea and what lay beyond.

Mount Sinai, the preeminent, lofty pinnacle that dominated Midian, had violently erupted—that was what had caused the thunderous explosion some hours ago—and from its blackened summit, a towering pillar of flame and smoke now gushed forth unabated, raining a hailstorm of fire, thick clouds of ash and black stones from the tenebrous skies. The colossal initial blast had hurled such horrendous shock waves across the earth that the land had quaked savagely for miles in all directions, and the Sea of Reeds had brutally shifted and heaved, splitting in two to expose what had previously been an underwater land bridge joining its banks.

Due to the distance and smoke, Moshéh appeared as only a small, unidentifiable blur on the eastern horizon. Still, somehow in his mind, the High Priest perceived that like a madman, Moshéh, his long, hoary hair and beard flowing wildly in the wind, stood poised upon a desert outcrop on the far side of the aberrantly upsurging waters white with foam. His dark, weather-beaten face was encrusted with brine, and his garments were torn and burned, so he resembled a man possessed as he shouted and feverishly flourished his shepherd's crook, urging the last stragglers among the desperately fleeing Hapiru across the now–revealed land bridge.

"After them!" the Pharaoh bellowed imperiously to his troops. "They must not escape! They have stolen the holy *Book of Thoth* from the Great Temple of Set!"

Lashing his long, snakelike, leather whip so that it writhed cruelly across the backs of his lathered, whinnying horses, he drove the struggling beasts onward, heedless of the hapless charioteer at their heads, who was viciously trampled to death beneath their abruptly churning hooves. Careening recklessly, the vehicle bounced and raced toward the land bridge, the rest of the Egyptian chariots pounding in its wake.

"Hurry, Your Majesty!" Nephrekeptah exhorted fiercely under his breath, clinging tightly to the curved sides of his own golden chariot to keep from being thrown out as, under the guidance of his charioteer, it pelted forward across the marshy tangle of slender reeds, papyrus, grasses and other sea plants bared by the tumultuously swelling and whirling waters on either side. "Hurry!"

The passage of the thousands of Hapiru had crushed not only the verdant vegetation, but also a mass of driftwood, seashells and coral firmly into the muddy seafloor, thereby unwittingly forming a compact veneer that enabled the Egyptian horses and chariots to cross the land bridge without becoming mired. But even as they rushed onward, the seabed started to grumble and quiver again, and suddenly, it seemed to shift and slide precariously beneath them. The turbulent waters began to spill back over the land bridge, swamping the spinning wheels of more than six hundred chariots strung out along its exposed surface. Panicked, the shrilly neighing horses lunged and thrashed crazily, many of them tearing free from their traces to gallop furiously away, stranding the helpless vehicles.

Both the High Priest and the Pharaoh cried out in sheer terror as, in horrifying, torturous slow motion, the now–titanic walls of frothy water crashed down pitilessly upon them, sweeping them and all the rest of the chariots away, drowning the hundreds of occupants, then casting the broken bodies up to strew the ash-blackened shores.

The Egyptian charioteers had perished to the last man—and the *Book of Thoth* was gone.

Nine

False Colors

> Ambition drove many men to become false; to have one
> thought locked in the breast, another ready on the tongue.
>
> *The War with Catiline*
> —Sallust (Gaius Sallustius Crispus)

Aberdeen, Scotland, the Present

"**F**ailure will *not* be tolerated, Shieldbearer." The voice that
spoke into the telephone receiver was cold, low and sibilant,
like a chill, moaning wind. "You *are* aware of that, are you
not?"

"Yes, I am, Nautonnier." Shieldbearer's own voice, at the
opposite end of the line, quavered slightly with fear that he
could not conceal at the icy anger displayed by the current
Grand Master of the Abbey of the Divine.

"And you are also aware, are you not, of the first two rules
of survival?"

"Yes, Nautonnier. Rule number one states that in order to
defeat your enemy, you must first enter his mind, since knowing your enemy allows you to predict his thoughts and actions,
thereby giving you the advantage and lessening the chance that
you will make the mistake of underestimating him. However,

in accordance with rule number two, you must still always expect the unexpected.''

"But so far, you have failed miserably on both those counts, have you not, Shieldbearer?'' the man called Nautonnier— ''Navigator''—inquired frostily.

"Yes—I have,'' Shieldbearer reluctantly conceded, perspiring profusely. Then, resolutely marshaling his courage, he declared, ''But it will not happen again, Nautonnier, I assure you.''

"Let us hope it doesn't, because I warn you that if it does, the consequences to you will be...most unpleasant. Find the woman...this Bryony St. Blaze. Who knows what information her father managed to pass on to her before Hammerbearer struck him down? Obviously, she is cleverer than you and Lancebearer thought, and she has checked in to some hotel other than the Ardoe House, employing a fictitious name. And regardless, locate that damned bastard Neville, as well! He's not only utterly brilliant, but also too cagey by half. I don't trust him. I haven't from the very beginning. He is Mordred, the traitor, and Judas Iscariot, the betrayer. So there's no telling what game of his own devising he may be playing with us. He *must* be brought to heel. He is likely determined to find the lost Knights Templar treasure, and also intent on keeping it all for himself, should he actually find it. And he and the woman have surely made contact, besides. Otherwise, she wouldn't have flown to Aberdeen.''

"No, Nautonnier, I agree.''

"Then do not fail again, Shieldbearer.''

With a soft click, the line abruptly went dead, buzzing as ominously as a pair of hissing serpents in Shieldbearer's ear. As the image of two writhing snakes flooded his mind, he closed his eyes and swallowed hard, shuddering violently. Cleopatra might have chosen an asp—it was actually much more likely to have been a cobra—as the means of her own demise and becoming one with Isis. But no matter what, he, Shieldbearer, wasn't at all eager to follow in her footsteps.

When Bryony awoke, she did not, at first, know where she was. The bedroom in which she lay was in blackness, and the bed itself was unfamiliar—smaller and less comfortable than her own. For a few minutes, she lay still, trying to collect and orient herself. Then she remembered. She was at Hamish Neville's cottage, just outside of Aberdeen, in Scotland.

Reaching out with one hand, she fumbled in the darkness for the lamp and switched it on, wincing slightly as soft, white light flooded the room, momentarily blinding her before her eyes adjusted to the illumination.

It was raining. Bryony could hear the gentle pitter-patter of the drizzle upon the bungalow's roof and against the small windows. It was a familiar, soothing sound, reminiscent of home, as was the damp, spindrift-tinged scent of the air. Still drowsy, she was almost tempted to snuggle deeper beneath the bedclothes and go back to sleep. But a glance at the alarm clock on the night table informed her that she had already slumbered the day away. It was nearly eight o'clock in the evening. Besides, from below wafted the aroma of something that smelled heavenly and whetted her appetite, causing her to realize she had not eaten since this morning.

Rising, Bryony rummaged through her luggage until she found her robe, which she wrapped around her slender figure, tying it securely at her waist. After that, she retrieved the jewel box with the two CDs from where she had hidden it earlier in the pillowcase, and returned it to her purse. Then, carrying that and her small train case, she unlocked the bedroom door and made her way down the short hall to the bathroom, where she showered.

Where could she hide the jewel box? Bryony wondered as she changed into fresh clothes. She couldn't keep lugging her handbag all over the cottage. Hamish couldn't help but grow suspicious of that. He wasn't stupid. She could always just secure the jewel box in her baggage, except that she knew from experience that luggage locks were usually easy to open—she herself had even managed the job with a penknife once in a pinch.

As she gazed around the bedroom, her brow knitted in a frown, it finally occurred to Bryony that the frame on one of

Hamish's paintings was fashioned in such a way that she might be able to conceal the jewel box behind the picture, especially if the canvas were stretched over a wooden support and unbacked, as its mounting in the frame seemed to suggest. Raising one corner of the painting from the wall, she saw to her satisfaction that this was indeed the case. Carefully, she eased the jewel box behind the picture, so that it rested on the top edge of the support's lower piece, against the backside of the canvas. Then she gingerly maneuvered the painting back into place against the wall. Being of oak, the frame was heavy enough that only a significant jarring would shake the jewel box loose from its hiding place. She sighed. It wasn't perfect, but it was the best she could do.

After that, following her nose, Bryony went downstairs to the kitchen, where she found Hamish at the stove.

"Ah, there you are. Awake at last, are you?" he asked cheerfully, by way of greeting her. "Quite a good thing, too, since dinner's almost ready, and I was just about to come upstairs and roust you out of bed."

"Is that coffee I smell?"

"Among other things, yes. A caffeine addict, are you? Would you care for a cup?"

"Yes to both questions," she replied, smiling ruefully as she took a seat at the table, which Hamish had already set for supper. "I'm afraid I'm one of those much-to-be-pitied people who finds it nearly impossible to get moving without a strong jolt of caffeine almost immediately upon rising."

"Then we have something in common. That's a start. Cream? Sugar?"

"No, just black, thanks."

"Colombian Supremo." He set a stoneware mug filled to the brim with steaming, black liquid down before her. "I hope you like it."

"I do. In fact, it's my own preferred brand of poison."

"Better and better. Let's hope you like Mediterranean garlic shrimp equally as well."

"I positively *adore* Mediterranean garlic shrimp!"

"Indeed? Then how soon would you like to get married?"

"Married?" Bryony cried, starting to laugh.

"Well, yes, isn't it obvious? We're perfect for each other. It's fate, destiny—"

"It's a complete crock, is what it is. We've only just met!"

"True," Hamish acknowledged with mock seriousness. "But, then again, that's precisely why it's best to get the wedding out of the way right now—isn't it—*before* we begin to discover each other's faults!"

"Why? Do you have a lot of those?"

"More than my fair share, I fear. Is that a yes to my proposal?"

"No, that's a no."

"What a shame—and here I was, thinking that perhaps I wasn't going to be condemned to my lumpy, old sofa, after all!"

"Now, I feel bad. Really, I don't want to turn you out of your own bed," she protested. *"I'll* sleep on the couch."

"No, no. You're my guest, and I insist on treating you as such. However, should you happen to change your mind about sharing the trundle..." His voice trailed away, and he glanced at her meaningfully, his dark eyes raking her slowly. "Why, you're blushing again. I didn't know women could still do that. It's really quite refreshing and enchanting."

"And *you* are really quite a rogue!"

"Flattery will get you everywhere. I'm easy—not just *like* Sunday morning, as the song goes, but *on* Sunday morning, and on every other morning, too, for that matter!"

"Is that so? Well, speaking strictly for myself, I've always thought that nothing worth having ever comes easily," Bryony observed, trying but failing to suppress a grin.

"Ouch! The rose has thorns! I should have known! In that case, I was only kidding. In fact, contrary to all previous appearances, I have *such* extraordinarily high standards that even the Queen Mum herself couldn't find fault with them."

"That sweet, old lady?"

"Plainly, you don't know the Queen Mum. She is a stickler of the very first order, I do assure you. Now, dear lady, I thought we'd start our dinner with some antipasto, followed by minestrone, the Mediterranean garlic shrimp, stuffed artichokes, a mixed salad with feta and some fresh fruit—all washed down with an excellent white wine. After that, if you're a good girl, we'll have espresso and tiramisu in the living room, before the fire.''

"That all sounds absolutely divine, Hamish! But, truly, you needn't have gone to so much trouble on my account. While I *do* appreciate good food, I'm not a particularly picky eater, and I don't want to put you out any more than I already have.''

"Actually, I've very much enjoyed preparing dinner. It's seldom that I have anyone but myself to cook for, and when I'm alone, I'm afraid I tend to eat out of cans and boxes. Besides which, Italian and Greek fare are my specialities.''

While Hamish put the finishing touches on their meal and opened the promised bottle of white wine, Bryony lit the two candles on the table. She had always believed there was a great deal to be learned about a man by the way he served supper at home. Hamish's table was plainly but elegantly and properly set, indicating to her that he knew and valued such niceties, and that however frankly and wittily outrageous he was about sex, he was nevertheless a romantic at heart. Otherwise, he wouldn't have bothered with the candles. The appetizing meal he had prepared was served in traditional Italian fashion, in the order in which he had enumerated the courses, which meant he appreciated the customs of other cultures, another mark in his favor.

Despite her resolve to maintain a wary distance from Hamish, as their savory dinner progressed, Bryony found herself growing increasingly drawn to him. He was not at all like American men of her acquaintance—and that, too, was no doubt a part of the attraction, she realized. There was an old-fashioned, old-world air about him that strongly appealed to her. As her father had been, Hamish was also a highly knowledgeable and entertaining raconteur, who delighted and entranced her with his historical tales all through their meal, making her laugh with his clever repartée and dry, wicked sense of humor. Bryony couldn't remember when she had had such a good time with a man in ages. Despite the fact that the two of them had met only that morning, it seemed she had known him for years, and that just made it all the harder for her to keep on reminding herself that he might, in truth, be the enemy, setting her up for a very bad fall. After all, regardless of the reasons why, he *had* kidnapped her—and at gunpoint, too, even if it *had* only been a BB pistol!

Whenever she thought about this last, it was all Bryony could do not to giggle with amusement. In retrospect, the notion that Hamish had actually gone to a toy store to purchase an air gun with which to abduct her seemed comical—not threatening—and for all his impertinent, sexy talk, he had, in reality, done nothing in the least untoward or intimidating to her. To the contrary, in fact. He had done everything possible to put her at ease and make her feel welcome in his home.

Which was exactly what the proverbial spider had done all the while it had coaxed the fly into its parlor, she thought suddenly, once more unsettled.

After supper, despite Hamish's protests, Bryony helped him clear the table and do the dishes. Then the two of them carried their espresso and tiramisu into the living room, where Hamish had built a cozy fire.

Outside, rain still drizzled, drumming melodiously on the roof and running in rivulets down the windowpanes. The wind keened in low harmony.

"I'm afraid I don't know any underworld figures," Hamish announced as he settled into the other chair. "However, whilst you slept the day away, jet-lagged from your travels, I was busy online, exploring our options. As I surmised, it is possible to purchase false identification on the Internet, which I fear we may find ourselves in need of, should the Abbey of the Divine manage to locate us here and we be compelled to flee. Before the advent of computers, we could have just disappeared. Nowadays, though, people are easily tracked, especially through credit-card transactions. I didn't find anywhere to buy fake passports, per se. But I *did* discover that for slightly less than five hundred American dollars, one may obtain what is called a 'camouflage' passport."

"What's that?"

"A semilegitimate passport issued under the aegis of a country that no longer exists...New Hebrides, for example, which is now Vanuatu, or Upper Volta, which is now Burkina Faso, and so on. Such passports are, it appears, often used by people wishing to deceive terrorists. For instance, being an American, you're undeniably a target abroad—Osama bin Laden, et al. Thus, were a group of Arab terrorists to skyjack an airplane on which you were traveling and demand to see everyone's passports, if you had a camouflage passport, you could produce it instead of your real passport, so it wouldn't be learned that you were, in reality, an American."

"Actually, that doesn't sound like a bad idea at all to me," Bryony remarked. "But if these camouflage passports are for sale on the Internet, don't you think terrorists know all about them, too?"

"Undoubtedly," Hamish agreed dryly, nodding. "However, just because these various countries no longer exist doesn't mean that their own citizens don't still possess perfectly legitimate passports issued under the countries' old names and which have yet to expire. So it would be difficult for a terrorist to know whether yours was real or not. Further, the camouflage passport can be issued in any name you choose, and an international driving permit also comes as a part of the package, as well as still a third form of identification, such as a press card or travel-club card. Do you see where I'm going with all this?"

"Yes, we could use something like that to prevent ourselves from being traced by the Abbey, while at the same time producing our own legitimate passports and driver's licenses in the event that it proved necessary at a border crossing, for example."

"Precisely! Clever girl! I knew you were."

Bryony grimaced ruefully.

"Not so clever that the Abbey and you both didn't learn that I had booked a room at the Ardoe House, and not so clever that *you* didn't manage to kidnap me."

"Yes, well, I daresay you aren't accustomed to being spied upon or abducted from elite hotels, either. So we won't hold any of that against you. Now that you are aware of the kind of people we're dealing with, you won't be so imprudent or easily fooled again.''

"No, I won't."

"Good. Now, I'm afraid we must discuss the indelicate subject of money. For around one thousand American dollars, we can get debit cards issued in any names we wish, simply by providing notarized copies of photo identification cards bearing those particular names. The debit cards can be used both for purchases and to withdraw cash from ATMs almost anywhere in the world. For approximately twenty-five hundred American dollars, we can also, via the Internet, have set up for us through an offshore bank what is known as a 'bearer share corporation.' This is basically a dummy company that will enable us to obtain anonymous debit cards, issued in the corporation's name. The beauty of this particular scheme is that these cards don't even require a signature. Any or all of these accounts can be managed from any personal computer that has *Client Bank* software installed on it.''

"Truly, I'm astonished," Bryony confessed, shaking her head in disbelief. "I simply had no idea that one could do all this through the Internet. A few thousand bucks, and you, too, can be Double-Oh-Seven...."

"Or a master criminal—not that I'm advocating anything like that, of course." Hamish grinned hugely. "Somehow, I've the indisputable feeling that the Queen Mum would *really* frown on that, and one simply *must* maintain one's high standards, or else where would one be?''

"Easy on Sunday mornings?" Bryony suggested impishly, her eyes wide with pretended innocence.

"Cheeky! Not that I'm complaining, however. I adore a woman with a bit of high spirit. It heightens the challenge and makes her surrender all the sweeter!''

"Indeed? Didn't your mother ever teach you that it's unwise to be so certain of yourself, that you might be doomed to disappointment?''

"Yes, and in all honesty, I've had my fair share of those, to be sure. Still, one can always hope.''

"In vain!''

"We'll see. Now, where were we? Ah, yes, our nefarious arrangements. If you agree with me that these measures would be sensible precautions under the circumstances, then we need to take three passport-size photographs of ourselves this evening, so we can get all the paperwork completed and the various documents in the works as quickly as possible. I thought that for the camouflage passports, we'd use the British West Indies as our homeland. That would account for both our accents—not that *I* have one, naturally—"

"Excuse me?" Bryony raised her eyebrows inquisitively.

"Well, I don't. I make it a point to speak quite correct and accent*less* Queen's English."

"Maybe it's accentless to *your* ears. However, it's not only accented to *me,* but it's also tinged with a slight Scottish brogue."

"No, it isn't."

"Yes, it is," she insisted firmly.

"Dear lady, I dinna know what you're talking aboot," Hamish rejoined, in a pronounced Scottish brogue before he burst into laughter. "Did you like that? Will it help my cause where you're concerned if I speak that way all the time?"

"I'm sure I don't know," Bryony said primly, unable to prevent the tide of crimson heat she felt creeping up to stain her cheeks once more.

"You're blushing again."

"That's because you're behaving badly again! In fact, I feel quite certain the British West Indies won't claim you!"

Still chuckling, Hamish said, "Since this collection of islands was both British and located in the Caribbean, a Scot and an American can both easily have originated there. I'll say my parents were missionaries, and yours can have been ambassadors who took up permanent residence after their tour of duty had ended. Yes, that's good, because then your camouflage passport can be a diplomatic one, and having the two different types will be even better!"

"Are you *sure* you're a history professor—and not wanted for international espionage?"

"*Moi?* Quite sure. I'm a history lecturer, actually."

"Speak French, as well as Scottish brogue, do you?"

"*Mais oui*—and German, Italian, Spanish, and even a little Greek, too, the result of my having bummed around all over Europe every summer in my wild, wayward, misspent youth. Now, if you've finished your tiramisu and wouldn't mind doing the honors by getting us some more espresso, I'll just nip upstairs and fetch my camera, so we can take all the necessary mugshots."

However dismayed she was by the idea of Hamish going upstairs alone, Bryony knew she had no real choice but to agree, since otherwise, he might suspect that she had something to hide. Carrying the serving tray with their cups and plates on it, she made her way to the kitchen while he vanished up the narrow staircase. She wondered if he had hit upon this notion as a means of searching her belongings. If he found the jewel box containing the two CDs, what could she possibly do about it? She was all alone here in the bungalow with Hamish, and he was physically bigger and stronger than she was. She could hardly force him to give the jewel box back, could she? Her heart sinking, she knew she couldn't. If he wanted to take it from her, there was no way—short of somehow disabling him and escaping from the cottage—that she could stop him. And she didn't even have a car to get away *in*. She would have to steal his, and then he might report her to the police!

Returning to the living room, Bryony set the serving tray back down on the tea wagon, biting her lower lip and glancing anxiously at the staircase in the tiny foyer beyond. From upstairs, she could hear the sounds of Hamish busily rummaging around in his bedroom, opening drawers. A few moments later, and much to her relief, he reappeared, camera—but no jewel box—in hand. Still, that didn't mean that he hadn't discovered the disks and concealed them elsewhere.

"Let's see…we'll need some better light," he observed, gazing around the living room, "and a neutral background. We'll do this in the foyer, I think. There's an overhead light out there and a wall that will serve nicely as a backdrop. Come on, then. You first."

In the foyer, Hamish flicked on the overhead light, then had

Bryony stand against one white wall. With a small meter, he measured the amount of light now in the foyer, adjusting his camera for it, so that the flash would be strong enough. Then, just as a professional photographer would have done, he gently brushed a few strands of hair from her face, carefully arranging her tresses to suit him.

"You're absolutely gorgeous, do you know that?" he asked softly, with no hint of laughter now in his voice. "I wish I were photographing you just for me—and not for false-identification purposes."

"I don't think I'm truly beautiful, although I *do* try to make the most of what I have. But thank you for the compliment. Like most women, I do appreciate them." She paused, then continued. "Do you really think the Abbey will try to kill us both, Hamish?"

"I certainly hope not. However, in light of your own father's murder, we would be wholly foolish not to prepare ourselves for the worst."

Bryony sighed heavily.

"I know you're right," she said quietly. "But, still… somehow, it all just seems so…so *unreal*—like something out of a movie or a novel, a…a Robert Ludlum conspiracy!"

Positioning the camera lens fairly close to Bryony's face, Hamish quickly snapped three pictures of her, not even needing to advance the film, since the camera—an obviously expensive belonging—was equipped with an automatic winder. Momentarily, she was blinded by the brilliance of the built-in flash. Then it was her turn to photograph him.

"I'll have the film developed in Aberdeen first thing tomorrow morning," he told her as she returned the camera to him. "Meanwhile, you need to think of a name you'd like to use for your alter ego, so I can fill out all the obligatory forms tonight on my computer. It should be something easy to remember, something that you'd recognize at once if you heard yourself being called by it for some reason, and also something suitable to the British West Indies."

"Hmm…how about Jessamine? That's one of those rather exotic flower names, just like my own, actually, favored by

Americans and the British in years gone by. Jessamine Winthorpe. How does that sound?''

''Like the name of some upper-crust ambassador's daughter!''

''Well, that's what I'm supposed to be, isn't it?''

''Quite. And I'll be Ian MacCallum—a good Scottish name.''

''More Scottish than Neville,'' Bryony commented.

''Neville is Old French. Like those of many Scotsmen, including the Bruces, the Frasers, the Ramsays, and the Sinclairs, my paternal ancestors came here from France,'' Hamish explained. ''As I'm sure you already know, Scotland and France were often allies in the past, particularly against England. Celts from Brittany, Normans from Normandy, Knights Templar fleeing Philip the Fair, and, from this side of the Channel, Jacobites fleeing the English…the traffic back and forth between Scotland and France has been considerable over the ages.''

''Well, it's getting late, and I'm afraid that despite all the coffee and espresso, I'm fading fast, thanks to my long flight today. If you don't mind, I think I'll go on upstairs now, take a hot bath in your loo, as you call it, and then turn in.''

''Not at all. I'll be right across the hall if you need anything. On my lumpy, old sofa,'' Hamish added pointedly with a rueful smile, although, without warning, desire smoldered in his dark eyes before he hooded them against her.

''Which I have offered twice to sleep on instead,'' Bryony declared, a trifle breathlessly, her sooty lashes veiling her own gaze, her heart suddenly beating too fast. ''But since you have also twice behaved the gentleman and refused, I don't intend to offer again. Good night, Hamish.''

''Good night, sweet lady.''

She fled, scared that if she didn't, the powerful temptation to invite him to share his trundle bed with her would prove utterly irresistible.

In all but Scottish tradition, Mordred is a traitor….

Ten

A Deed of Dreadful Note

Ere the bat hath flown
His cloistered flight, ere, to black Hecate's summons
The shard-borne beetle with his drowsy hums
Hath rung night's yawning peal, there shall be done
A deed of dreadful note.

Macbeth
—William Shakespeare

Drumrose Cottage, Scotland, the Present

The following morning, Bryony awoke early. Quietly, not knowing whether or not Hamish still slept, she rose and dressed. Then, unlocking the bedroom door, she stepped out into the hallway beyond. The study door was open, and inside, Hamish lay sprawled on the sofa, snoring gently, a quilt thrown over his lower extremities. As she could see his naked chest and one bare leg, she surmised that he either slept in his underwear or else nude. His chest was dark, muscular and neither too heavily nor too lightly matted with hair. Bryony liked the way he was built—"lean and mean," she had always called it. Unbidden, an image of the length of his body pressed against her own crept into her mind. She felt herself blushing, and she turned away, half ashamed of herself for spying on him while he slumbered.

He must have worked very late last night, she surmised, taking care of all the paperwork for the preparations the two of them were making to try to protect themselves from the Abbey of the Divine. At the thought of the secret order, Bryony shivered. The thirteen men who comprised its inner sanctum, its Round Table, *must* be complete fanatics who would stop at nothing to achieve their goals! How could she and Hamish possibly hope to prevail against them? There was no telling what such unscrupulous men might do. Perhaps it would be better if she and the Scotsman went to the police. But even as the idea crossed her mind, Bryony rejected it, for surely, the authorities would never believe such a wild story, and would probably think she and Hamish were just a couple of conspiracy nuts and the Abbey a total fabrication on their part. She sighed heavily. As much as the notion frightened her, she knew that until she and Hamish could obtain at least *some* kind of proof about the Abbey, especially in connection with her father's death, they were on their own.

After using the bathroom, Bryony went downstairs to the kitchen. She didn't think the Scotsman would mind if she made coffee—or even breakfast, for that matter. After all, he had cooked for her twice already. She definitely owed him a meal in return, and if she were going to continue to stay at his bungalow with him, gratis, she would certainly feel much better if she pulled her own weight. Searching his cabinets, she found a sack of coffee beans on one shelf. Both the coffee grinder and coffeemaker sat on the counter. Moments later, she had the coffee dripping into its glass pot. Then, after checking to be certain the cottage didn't possess an alarm system, Bryony opened the front door, in search of a newspaper.

It was still chilly outside, but the rain of last evening had stopped, and the morning sun glowed softly on the horizon, its rays just beginning to dissipate the gray mist that lay thick and low in the hollows of the sweeping land. Around the bungalow, dewdrops sparkled like thousands of aurora–borealis beads scattered in the grass. The scent of the spring air was crisp and clean, and Bryony inhaled deeply, filled with pleasure as the fragrance of the rich, dark earth permeated her nostrils. As always at such times, she was glad she had never settled for an office job, that her work kept her outdoors, close to nature. Her eyes swept the mountainous Highland terrain. She could see why Hamish had chosen to live up here in this isolated spot. One could easily imagine oneself all alone in the entire world up here, she thought. Besides being far from the madding crowd, it was wild, rugged and breathtakingly beautiful.

She strolled down the serpentine, dirt drive to the gate, where the mailbox hung, but no newspaper was in sight. Bryony surmised that the Scotsman either must not subscribe to one, or else he must not have rural delivery and so had to buy his copies at the nearest village shop.

She returned to the kitchen, where she stood at the stove, frying bacon and scrambling eggs when Hamish appeared, obviously still drowsy with sleep, although he had now donned a T-shirt and a pair of jeans.

"Good morning," she said, smiling at him.

"'Morning," he replied, stifling a yawn. Then, spotting the pot of coffee, he smiled back at her, his eyes lighting up. "You really *are* a woman after my own heart!"

Understanding his need for caffeine, she poured a brimming cup and handed it to him. He sat down at the old farm table, closing his eyes and reverently breathing in the aroma of the steaming coffee before taking a long, grateful sip. He made no other attempt at conversation, so Bryony didn't, either. She wasn't big on chatter first thing in the mornings herself.

By the time she had finished preparing their breakfast, Hamish had downed half a mug of coffee and was obviously feeling much more himself.

"You didn't have to cook," he told her, as she dished up the food and set their plates on the table.

"Yes, I did."

"No, you didn't—but I very much appreciate the fact that you did. And," he continued, after a few bites, "I see you're as good a cook as I am!"

"Thanks. I try."

After breakfast, they cleared the table and did the dishes. Then Hamish asked Bryony if she wanted to ride into town with him.

"I want to get the pictures developed as quickly as possible," he reminded her. "Even with a courier express service, it's going to take several days to get the camouflage passports and other documentation we need."

"I know. I sure hope the Abbey's inner sanctum doesn't find out where you live before then." Her expression revealed her anxiety at the idea.

"Believe me, I've given that some thought, and I've decided that the best thing to do is for me to e-mail Cauldronbearer and tell him that I've made up my mind to join the Abbey's ranks. By doing that, I may gain us some more time, even if it's only a few days."

"But...what if he wants to meet you and asks where you live?"

"I'll stall him, say I'd rather rendezvous in Aberdeen, that I'm a recluse and value my privacy highly. That is, after all, the truth—and undoubtedly one of the things that drew the Abbey to me in the first place."

"And if he persists?"

"Trust me. I'm far from a pushover. I shall be polite but equally insistent that some quiet pub, restaurant, or wine bar in Aberdeen would suit me much better as a meeting place, and that, too, is the truth. I don't know Cauldronbearer or any of the rest of those who make up the Abbey's Round Table, and since I've demonstrated a certain amount of skepticism from the start, asking a great many hard questions and offering relatively little information in return, I doubt that Cauldronbearer will question my continued reticence."

"That makes sense to me. Let's just hope Cauldronbearer buys it, too."

"I think he will. At any rate, we'll see."

The drive into Aberdeen was a much pleasanter experience than the last time Bryony had traveled the road. Unlike yesterday, the time passed in companionable conversation, with the Scotsman pointing out all the local sights and expanding on their history. Royal Deeside, which lay just beyond Aberdeen, was home to several castles, among them Balmoral.

"This whole area is truly beautiful," Bryony observed with enthusiastic appreciation as she gazed out the car's windows.

"It's considered some of the finest landscape in all of Scotland. I'd really adore showing you around the entire countryside and the Aberdeen City Centre, too. However, I'm afraid sightseeing excursions wouldn't be wise at this juncture. The Abbey is no doubt searching all of Aberdeen for you, so we won't even be going into the city proper, but only to one of the outlying villages instead, just to be on the safe side."

After they had dropped off the film for processing, they returned to the bungalow, Hamish taking great care to ensure they weren't being followed. Upon reaching the cottage, he steered the Volvo around to the rear, and pulled it right up to the back door of the lean-to.

"I think we need to be prepared to leave here at a moment's notice," he asserted, scanning the open terrain for signs of movement as they got out of the automobile. "In fact, we probably ought to get everything we might require and pack it into the car as soon as possible."

"I agree that's a wise precaution."

"Good. Then that's what we'll do."

So they spent the next few days making lists and collecting supplies, which included nonperishable foods, bottled water and camping gear that the Scotsman had stowed in his attic, as well as a tent, a camp stove and sleeping bags.

"Do you *really* think we're going to need all this, Hamish?" Bryony queried, as they shifted things around in the trunk of the Volvo for the umpteenth time to make room for all they continued to assemble.

"I don't know. I hope not. But I'd rather be safe than sorry, and even with the false identification, we might find that we're better off avoiding hotels and motels if we *are* compelled to make some kind of a getaway from here. I'm almost tempted to go to the police and inform them about all our suspicions. The trouble is that I doubt we'd be believed, but, instead, written off as a couple of loonies. After all, we don't have even a single shred of concrete proof that the Abbey actually exists, much less that the inner sanctum murdered your father. Even my e-mails from Cauldronbearer could be viewed as total fabrications.''

"Yes, I know. I've realized that myself."

"Right. So that's that, then. We'll just have to make out as best we can on our own, and I truly don't know any way other than this, Bryony. Do you?''

"No," she confessed. "I guess it's just that it all continues to seem, well, *unreal* to me."

"Like a bad dream."

"Exactly!"

"Don't worry. I know what you mean. I feel the same." Then Hamish smiled at her encouragingly. "Nevertheless, do *try* to keep your spirits up. We *do* have *some* advantages on our side, you know, including the fact that the Abbey apparently hasn't—at least for the moment—managed to locate us. Nor are they aware of the steps we've taken to protect ourselves, and to prepare to escape from them, if necessary. In the end, it may not even come to the worst. Actually, Cauldronbearer seemed quite pleased to receive my e-mail, and to learn that I'd decided to join the Abbey's ranks. Of course, I'll be in a much better position to judge our situation after I've seen him tomorrow in Aberdeen."

"Perhaps, but even so, I'm worried about your meeting with him, Hamish." Bryony gnawed at her lower lip nervously. "It may be that the Abbey's suspicions really *haven't* been allayed by your decision—that the Round Table's only pretending to believe you, and that this rendezvous is therefore just a trick to draw you out into the open."

"That's quite possible. However, I *will* be in a public place, with lots of other people around, and I simply don't see any other choice but to keep the appointment. If I *don't* show up, the Abbey will surely suspect that something is wrong, and that I've just been stringing them along—given their own paranoid outlook."

"Yes, I agree."

"It's settled, then. I'll go into Aberdeen tomorrow, meet

with Cauldronbearer, then pick up the identification package from my postal box. All the documentation we ordered ought to have arrived by then.'' He slammed shut the trunk of the automobile. ''Meanwhile, I'm going to remove all the critical files from my computer's hard drive, optimize it, then do a government wipe of the free space. That way, there won't be anything vital on it if the Abbey should somehow gain access to it.''

''It's definite then—Neville is going to meet with you to-morrow afternoon, Cauldronbearer?'' The hushed, serpentlike voice that spoke into the telephone receiver held a triumphant note of satisfaction.

''Yes, Nautonnier.'' Cauldronbearer could tell that his su-perior was most pleased, and he breathed a deeply felt sigh of relief. It did not pay to anger the Abbey's Grand Master, and Cauldronbearer was aware that for the past few weeks, he had been walking a tightrope. He knew that the Nautonnier had been almost as annoyed with him as with Shieldbearer and Lancebearer, thanks to Neville's seeming hesitation and inde-cision about joining the order's Round Table. ''All the arrange-ments have now been agreed upon. We're to have lunch to-gether at the Wild Stag pub, at noon.''

''Good. You know what to do? You have the necessary elec-tronic equipment in hand?''

''Yes...delivered to me by special courier this evening from Hornbearer. It is a micro-tracking device that I shall discreetly attach to Neville's vehicle—after which, we won't have any difficulties at all in discovering his home address and keeping abreast of his location at all times.''

''Excellent... It has been...most annoying...this reclus-iveness and secrecy of his, this mania for privacy that he has. Coupled with the U.K.'s Data Protection Act, Neville has pre-sented quite a challenge, has he not, Cauldronbearer?''

''Indeed. However, tomorrow, he'll be lured from his lair— and then we'll have him!''

''Yes—and he will either take his proper place at the Round Table, or else we will be compelled to find a replacement, which I shall find *most* upsetting, Cauldronbearer. Neville *is* Mordred. I feel it in my bones, and I am never wrong.''

''No, Nautonnier.''

''Still, we must be careful. Neville has already demonstrated that he's fully capable of duplicity when it suits him. He never once informed you that he was in touch with the late—but hardly lamented—prying Professor Simon St. Blaze. And we must not forget that Neville may, even as we speak, be in contact with the professor's apparently equally nosy daughter, Bryony. Neither Shieldbearer nor Lancebearer has yet to uncover her whereabouts in Aberdeen.'' The Grand Master's ire at and disapproval of this last were plain.

''Dear me. Most unfortunate, Nautonnier.'' Cauldronbearer made appropriate sympathetic noises, although, privately, he was delighted that he had finally managed to succeed with his own assignment, while his colleagues had botched theirs. Failure was never tolerated. At the very least, it resulted in a demotion in rank at the Round Table. The worst–case scenario was better not dwelled upon.

''Keep me apprised of all developments, Cauldronbearer.''

''Of course, Nautonnier.''

Having done with the conversation, the Grand Master then abruptly disconnected the line, leaving the dial tone buzzing loudly in the other's ear. Cauldronbearer didn't mind. Meager though the praise had been, it had nevertheless been high indeed, coming from the Abbey's taciturn, exacting Nautonnier.

After he had driven into Aberdeen to keep his scheduled luncheon appointment with Cauldronbearer, as well as to retrieve the false-identification documents that had finally arrived at his postal box, and to run a couple of other errands, Hamish returned to the cottage to report to Bryony that to the very best of his knowledge and judgment, everything had appeared to go quite well during the meeting.

''Did Cauldronbearer reveal his own identity to you?'' she queried as, following supper, they worked together in the Scotsman's study, he finishing with the cleanup of his computer's hard drive, and she getting all their paperwork in order, preparing simple but credible cover stories for them both.

"He said his name was Roland Kilgour. However, given his own caution and reticence, I shouldn't be at all surprised to learn that was an assumed name."

"Did he ask about your correspondence with my father?"

"No." Hamish shook his head. "I'm afraid Cauldronbearer, or Roland, whichever, was much too clever for that—because even had the Abbey wanted him to question me in that regard, they simply couldn't afford to do so. It would have revealed to me that it *was* their order who murdered Simon, thereby gaining access to his computer files. Nor, for the exact same reasons, could Cauldronbearer inquire about you, either."

"Good. Let's hope the Abbey's still looking all over Aberdeen for me, then. Well, actually, they *must* be, mustn't they? Because if they knew where I was, they'd surely come here for me, wouldn't they? And probably for you, too." Rising from the overstuffed sofa, Bryony attempted to stretch the knots from her back muscles.

"Would you like some help with that?" the Scotsman offered kindly, also getting to his feet. "Believe it or not, I'm quite good with that sort of thing. Here. Cross your arms over your chest and place your hands on your shoulders."

"No, really, that's okay—"

"Don't be alarmed," he reassured her, smiling. "It'll only take a moment, and it won't hurt a bit, either, I promise you." Moving to stand behind Bryony then, he wrapped his own strong arms around her, sending a sudden electric shock tingling through her whole body, curling her toes. "Hmm...nice," he murmured in her ear, his voice abruptly low and husky, his breath soft and warm against her skin.

"I *thought* you meant to try to fix my aching back," she pointed out, her own voice now unsteady, her heart thudding in her breast.

"Yes...right. Down to business, then, shall we? Ready?" At her nod, he lifted Bryony from the floor, bending her back against him, so that the entire length of her spine was gently compelled back into alignment. Then he returned her to her feet, continuing, however, to hold her close. "Better?"

"Much! Thanks! How'd you learn to do that?" she asked in a rush, all too aware of his enticing proximity, of the smoky, masculine scent of him that intoxicatingly pervaded her nostrils, of the thrilling hardness of his body pressed against her own soft one.

"Books, sweet lady. I've got all kinds of knowledge and trivia stored in my head from reading, I fear." At last, reluctantly, Hamish released her.

"You must have quite an excellent memory, then." She slowly turned to face him, her full, rosebud lips parting and her breath catching in her throat as she observed the desire for her that smoldered like twin flames in his dark, brown eyes.

"It's nearly photographic, actually."

The expertly muffled shot came without warning, blasting through one of the cottage's small windows, sending shards of glass spewing like water from a fountain in all directions.

Before Bryony even realized what was happening, Hamish had tackled her violently, knocking her flat upon the dark, hardwood floor of the study, his lithe, muscular weight pinning her down, causing her to gasp. Initially not understanding the smashing sound or his intentions, either, she began to struggle desperately against him, attempting to free herself.

"Bryony, stop fighting me, damn it!" Hamish hissed sharply in her ear, his voice grim, his hands roughly and unceremoniously securing her wrists above her head. "That was a bullet! Someone has just attempted to kill you! Look at the window...the floor...."

"Oh, my God," she whispered, stricken, as she saw all the broken glass. "I thought—"

"Shh." He held one finger to her lips, silencing her, his gaze filled with anxiety. "Stay down. Crawl over to my desk, and hide inside the kneehole. It'll offer you the best protection. Can you do that?"

"Yes...yes..." she whispered, before her voice caught on a soft sob of fear.

Then the lights went out, and the study was abruptly plunged into blackness.

Eleven

The Tower of Bab-Ili

> Therefore is the name of it called Babel; because the Lord did there confound the language of all the world.
>
> The Bible
> —Genesis 11:9

The City of Babylon, the Kingdom of Babylonia, 577 B.C.

The land here in Babylonia was so very different from that of her homeland of Medes, Amyitis thought, sighing gently and smiling a little to herself. Medes, which lay to the east, beyond the River Tigris, was a mountainous, cooler region, while Babylonia was flat and sunbaked. When she had first come here from her father's Median kingdom to marry Nebuchadnezzar, the second king of Babylonia to bear that illustrious name, she had often felt quite sick at heart, longing deeply for the soaring, snowcapped peaks of her homeland and its green foothills and riverbanks.

Despite her constant pining for Medes, Amyitis had nevertheless managed to win not only Nebuchadnezzar's favor, but also his heart. Of all his many wives and concubines, he loved and cherished her the best. There was not a single doubt of that. Proof of it was in his every thought, word and deed—for all the world to see.

Over the years of their marriage, the King of Babylonia had bestowed upon her many fine and beautiful gifts, but the greatest and most wondrous of these were the gorgeous Hanging Gardens that he had caused to be constructed for her in the Southern Citadel of the great, walled city of Babylon, the kingdom's capital.

To build this majestic, artificial mountain for Amyitis, so that she would no longer be so homesick for Medes, Nebuchadnezzar had first dug a basement foundation consisting of fourteen large rooms, each with immense, stone-arch ceilings to support the one-hundred-by-one-hundred-and-fifty-foot, terraced structure he had planned. One room had three huge holes in the floor, for the chain pumps that would be used to bring water from the River Euphrates to the Hanging Gardens, as it scarcely ever rained in Babylonia. Above the foundation, resting upon hollow, cube-shaped pillars, were the vaulted terraces that composed the artificial mountain itself.

Each rectangular platform consisted of massive, stone slabs covered with layers of reeds, bitumen—the strange, slimy asphalt employed as a mortar by the Babylonians—and tiles, over which were laid sheets of lead, to prevent the water from rotting the underpinnings. This had had to be done because almost all of the many edifices in Babylon were fashioned of bricks made solely of clay mixed with chopped straw and baked in the hot, blazing sun, so they swiftly dissolved when soaked with water. This was not usually a problem, since rain was so rare in Babylonia. But the Hanging Gardens were to be exposed to constant irrigation.

Every column had then been filled to the top with rich earth, for the planting of even the tallest and biggest of trees. Over the lead sheets of the platforms, more fertile soil had been laid, sufficient in depth for the growing of other trees, as well as a profusion of shrubs, flowers and vines, which tumbled and cascaded in such thick, lush greenness and brilliant color over the terraces that the gardens appeared to "hang."

One ascended to the peak of the artificial mountain by a series of steps, at the side of which ran the mechanism of the water engines, formed by two giant wheels connected with a chain, on which hung a number of buckets. Just above the three enormous holes in the basement, into which water from the River Euphrates was channeled, the lower wheels of the chain pumps turned, their pails dipping into the pools, then carrying the life-giving water to the pinnacle of the artificial mountain, where it was dumped into a pond, the empty buckets then returning to the basement to be refilled. By means of gates and man-made streams with sources located at the top of the artificial mountain, the Hanging Gardens were thus irrigated, a bevy of slaves continually turning the handles of the shafts attached to the pump wheels in the basement, to operate and power the ingenious contraption.

Truly, Nebuchadnezzar was one of the cleverest and most innovative kings who had ever lived, Amyitis reflected appreciatively, strolling leisurely through the lovely, peaceful Hanging Gardens as she did every day at this late-afternoon hour. It was quite rare, now, that she ever felt the least bit homesick for Medes.

Far beneath her, Babylon sprawled along the shores of the River Euphrates, an astonishing array of daunting walls, vast palaces and temples, colossal statues of solid gold, and a network of roads—including the great, wide processional way that wound through the very heart of the city. All this, Nebuchadnezzar had built.

"Amyitis...Amyitis!" As though she had somehow wished her beloved husband, the King, there beside her, he suddenly appeared on the terrace, hurrying toward her from the ascending steps, his visage beaming with excitement. "Amyitis!" Without warning, he caught her up in his strong, muscular arms and delightedly swung her around as though she were a mere child. "There's been a marvelous discovery! Today, after more than two decades, we have *finally* managed to decipher several important passages in the Book!"

His wife, the Queen, did not need to ask to which book Nebuchadnezzar referred. For the past twenty years, in his mind, there had been only one. He had come into possession of it when his mighty armies had overrun and conquered the Israelites, first sacking their famous Great Temple at Jerusalem and then, ten years later, destroying it completely. The ancient manuscript had been found inside a decorative, gold, silver and copper puzzle box, which itself had apparently at one time been placed into a sacred chest or ark bearing two enigmatic, golden, winged figures on its lid. Someone—a priest, no doubt—had taken the puzzle box from the sacred chest, hiding it beneath the Great Temple, hoping to conceal it from the Babylonian soldiers. Meanwhile, a modest contingent of Israelites had smuggled the ark itself from the city, either to deceive the Babylonians into believing the temple treasure had already been carried away, or else simply wholly unaware that the contents of the ark had earlier been removed and secreted for safekeeping.

The small cadre of fleeing Israelites were rumored to have made their way to Yabu, an island off the coast of the Two Kingdoms of Egypt and famed for its trade in the ivory tusks of elephants. But that hadn't mattered. Nebuchadnezzar had got the Book, and he had had little interest in the two stone tablets the sacred chest was alleged to have also contained.

"So…what have you learned from this priceless, unparalleled book of truth and wisdom, my beloved husband?" Amyitis smiled at him, laying one graceful hand upon his arm, taking pleasure in his enthusiasm.

"It speaks of a gate, my most favored wife—and not just any gate, mind you, but a sacred Gate of the Gods!" Nebuchadnezzar's face revealed his own astonishment and awe. "Amyitis, I have found the way to reach the heavens above us! I am going to build this exalted gate! From the rubble of my ancestor the renowned Nimrod's ziggurat shall this gate—this incomparable, soaring tower—rise, until it gains the very heavens and the great God Marduk-Bel Himself! I shall call it 'Bab-Ili'—'Gate of the Gods'! What do you think of that, my dearest wife?"

"I think it shall be even more wondrous than my Hanging Gardens, Nebuchadnezzar, which all the world speaks about and which the historians make records of for all posterity. Now, they shall talk—and write—of your splendorous tower, as well. Have you chosen an architect yet?"

"Yes." The King nodded. "For such a peerless project, such a monumental undertaking, I will require thousands of slaves—

from even the most far-flung reaches of my empire, and perhaps even beyond. For that reason, I have bestowed upon Etemenanki the honor of designing the tower. Besides a talent for architecture, he has an uncanny gift for languages and speaks not only all those known in my kingdom, but also the foreign tongues of many other lands. With Etemenanki in charge, there will be no confusion among the laborers as to what needs to be done, and the work shall progress quickly and smoothly.''

''And when do you plan to begin building this amazing tower, my beloved husband?''

''Tomorrow—for this day, I mean to spend with you, Amyitis. Come.'' Nebuchadnezzar held out one hand to her, which she took shyly but eagerly, blushing, causing him to smile at her knowingly as he led her from the Hanging Gardens.

Early the following morning, as promised, construction on the King's proposed Tower of Babel commenced. Never in the world had there been such an architectural ambition—to build a ziggurat to the heavens, a Gate to the Gods. North and south, east and west, the King's legions scoured his empire and foreign lands far and wide, marching vast hordes of slaves into Babylon to dig the damp clay and chop the bundles of straw from which the thousands of bricks necessary to raise the stupendous tower were to be made, and to labor on the building itself.

Once the wet clay and pieces of straw were thoroughly mixed, they were poured into molds, then set to bake in the fierce, burning sun that shone over Babylonia. After becoming hard, they were unmolded, enameled a brilliant blue in color, and joined together with bitumen brought from the high plateau to the east of Babylonia. The foundation of the ziggurat was to be not only enormous, but also perfectly square, and aligned with the heavens, just as were the great pyramids of the Two Kingdoms of Egypt.

Night after night, the most highly learned of all the astronomers in Babylonia studied the stars, making their lengthy, detailed calculations for the exact positioning of the tower's massive quadrangular base. Then, under Etemenanki's direction, the bricks were carefully put into place, in accordance with all the astronomers' various measurements, which they themselves had taken under the guidance of the invaluable Book.

As the weeks passed, the groundwork was completed, and the ziggurat itself began to rise, stepped like the terraces of the Hanging Gardens and with a circular staircase that spiraled around the whole exterior. Gold, silver and precious jewels from faraway mountains and seas were set into a number of the bright, blue bricks, and halfway up the eight levels, there were to be seats for those who climbed to rest upon on their long journey to the Gate to the Gods.

The interior would include an elaborate system of pipes, which would drain water away from the structure and its foundation, to keep them from crumbling away. For this purpose, a group of slaves would be assigned to continuously clean and maintain the pipes.

Daily, ringing strongly throughout the city streets of Babylon, could be heard the loud, authoritative voice of Etemenanki, the architect, rising above the constant, confused babble of the slaves as he shouted orders in dozens of languages. Moving from the clay pits and straw fields to the brick–production facilities to the tower itself, such was Etemenanki's vital presence that the city dwellers even took to referring to the ziggurat by his own name. Higher and higher, it loomed as successive layer after layer of bricks was meticulously fixed upon the bitumen slathered on each previous stratum, and narrow step after narrow step was set into position—until, one day, the unthinkable happened.

It was late afternoon, the time when Amyitis always liked to stroll in her Hanging Gardens, where, from the ornately balustraded terraces, she could watch the steady progress of Nebuchadnezzar's huge, imposing tower, which was truly a marvel without equal. But this day, as she wandered languidly through the trees, shrubs and flowers to her favorite observation spot, instead of swelling with pride at her husband's accomplishment, she felt strangely unsettled. All morning and afternoon, the sun had played hide-and-seek with thick, darkening clouds massing in the skies, and the usually hot, dry air had turned peculiarly heavy and humid, as though presaging a coming storm.

Still, that was surely most unlikely, the Queen thought, perplexed and frowning. It hardly ever even rained in Babylonia, only once in a blue moon—much less stormed. Yet, in the vast firmament above her, there came an ominous, unmistakable rumbling sound that she knew could only be thunder.

As she glanced across the labyrinth of city streets to the place where the ziggurat soared, Amyitis spied Etemenanki ascending the serpentine staircase that wound around the exterior of the tower, which was now so very tall and spiring that from the ground far below, it did indeed seem to reach the very heavens. The architect had just reached the summit when, to the Queen's everlasting horror, a jagged-edged bolt of bright, blinding lightning hurled without warning from the tenebrous skies, struck the top of the ziggurat and burned Etemenanki to a charred crisp.

Then, in the blink of an eye, the whole crown of the tower exploded, violently heaving the enameled, blue bricks in every direction. Screaming in sheer terror and in a confusion of foreign tongues, the panicked workers fled desperately, trampling one another in their haste to escape what they inevitably saw as the Gods' abrupt, fiery judgment upon them, for daring to attempt to attain the heavens.

On the verdant terrace from where she watched the terrible unfolding scene, Amyitis stood petrified with stark fear, her whitened knuckles gripping the balustrade tightly, holding her upright as her knees suddenly buckled beneath her. In some obscure corner of her numbed brain, she wondered if Nebuchadnezzar had somehow misunderstood the Book's cryptic passages, and had incorrectly translated its unknown language, which even Etemenanki had never before seen, or if the ancient manuscript contained, in truth, some monstrous, ghastly evil, penned by an utterly diabolical fiend....

Book Two

The Adept

I would win my way to the coast,
apple-bearing Hesperian coast
of which the minstrels sing,
where the Lord of the Ocean
denies the voyager further sailing,
and fixes the solemn limit of Heaven
which giant Atlas upholds.
There, the streams flow with ambrosia
by Zeus's bed of love,
and holy Earth, the giver of life,
yields to the gods rich blessedness.

Hippolytus
—Euripides

Twelve

Into Darkness Peering

Deep into that darkness peering, long I stood
there wondering, fearing,
Doubting, dreaming dreams no mortal ever
dared to dream before.

The Raven
—Edgar Allan Poe

Drumrose Cottage, Scotland, the Present

A second muted shot, followed by a third, and then several others, drilled through the windows of the study, shattering more panes into splinters that, on the dark, hardwood floor, sparkled like deadly diamonds in the silvery moonlight that streamed inside the room. The tiny shards bit into Bryony's palms and knees as she crawled desperately toward Hamish's desk, but such was her terror as the bullets struck the furniture and walls around her that she scarcely felt the pain. Her heart pounded in her ears and throat, deafening her and making her feel as though she were going to choke or pass out. With difficulty, she fought back the sobs and screams that would otherwise have erupted from her throat.

Dimly, she registered the fact that Hamish, too, was moving in the study, snaking his way on his belly across the floor. He seized a double-barreled shotgun that stood in one corner. Then, from a bookshelf, he yanked down a box of ammunition, which broke open as he grabbed it, sending its contents scattering, so that the shells bounced and rolled upon the floor. Swearing, he snatched up two of the fallen cartridges and jammed them into the weapon, snapping the breech shut with a decisive click.

"Bryony!" he called sharply to her

"Y-Y-Yes?" she managed to reply, from where she now crouched in the kneehole of his desk.

"There's a phone on top of my desk. Get it, and dial nine-nine-nine. When the Emergency Services operator answers, ask her to connect you with the police. Tell them to send help to Drumrose Cottage, on Old Kirkton Road, immediately. Do you understand me?"

"Yes…yes."

Her hands shaking, Bryony reached out from beneath the kneehole to fumble for the phone on the desktop above her, then quickly punched in the Emergency Services number.

"Hamish, the phone is dead!"

"Damn the Abbey! Whoever they've sent here must have cut the bloody lines!"

"Now, what?"

From where he crouched on the floor, the Scotsman suddenly stood, flattening himself against the wall before shoving the barrel of the shotgun out one of the broken windows and firing off both rounds. Then, grabbing more shells, he rapidly reloaded.

"There. At least, now, they know we're not unarmed and helpless," he announced grimly. "That ought to give them *some* pause, I hope. In the top left-hand drawer of my desk, there's a mobile phone. See if you can dial out on *it*."

Her hands still trembling, Bryony did as he instructed.

"Yes…*yes*, it's ringing!" she told him, vastly relieved. When the Emergency Services operator answered, Bryony requested the police, giving them a brief explanation of the situation and asking for immediate assistance. "Help is on the way," she said after hanging up.

"Good. It can't get here too soon for me," Hamish replied. Then he shouted out the smashed window, "Whoever you bloody, damned hooligans are, we're armed, and we've used a mobile phone to call the police! They're en route as we speak. Do you hear me?"

There was no answer save for the soughing of the night wind. A chill tingled up Bryony's spine. She wondered what the assailants were doing now. Her imagination ran rampant. She envisioned them dousing the Scotsman's bungalow with gasoline and setting it afire, burning her and Hamish alive, or else breaking into the house to take them prisoner, after which they would be tortured to death.

"Do you think they've gone?" she queried quietly.

"I don't know. Maybe. But I don't believe we should take any chances. So you'd better sit tight until we find out—or at least until the police arrive."

Surreptitiously dropping to the floor once more, Hamish began systematically gathering up all the spilled cartridges, putting them back into their box.

"What're you doing? What if you need those?"

"I've reloaded the shotgun, and the shells aren't going to do me much good on the floor. In addition to which, one is usually arrested here for firing a weapon at intruders, even in self-defense."

"You have *got* to be kidding!" Bryony was astonished by this piece of news. "What in the hell were we supposed to do? Just stand here and let them kill us?"

"No. However, if it's all the same to you, I'd just as soon *not* be taken into custody, either! At the very least, we'll be compelled to spend several long hours at the police station, being interrogated about the circumstances of my having deliberately discharged my shotgun—and such a matter is serious enough that it would probably be left to the Crown Prosecution Service to determine whether or not charges ought to be brought against *me*, and quite possibly you, as well, during which time, we'd both be barred from leaving the country. Is that what you want?"

"No...no, of course not."

"Well, then, when the police get here, it would be best if you didn't mention that I even own a weapon, much less that I actually fired it at anyone," Hamish remarked dryly. "Besides which, I sincerely doubt that at this range, I even hit anything."

"Why? How far away do you think the shooters are?"

He shook his head. "I don't know. It's difficult to tell at night. However, it's my guess that whoever's out there fired those rounds from thirty-aught-sixes...a couple of hundred yards or so from the cottage, maybe."

"But...the electricity's gone off, too," Bryony pointed out, confused.

"No—only the study lights, and *I* turned those off." He chuckled lowly, without humor. "If I hadn't, we would've been sitting ducks, and one or both of us would undoubtedly be dead by now."

"Oh, God...yes...you're right, of course. I'm afraid I wasn't thinking very clearly."

"Jesus, I wonder why...?" The Scotsman's tone was wry. "Hang in there, Bryony. The police are on their way, and in the meanwhile, I believe it's highly unlikely that the Abbey's agents are going to stick around, waiting for them to show up. This is *not* the States. The U.K. is *not* a gun culture. We have very serious laws and penalties here for this sort of thing, I do assure you. The shooters, if sensible, will not wish to run the risk of being caught. They would not get off with a light sentence by plea bargaining their way down to a much lesser crime here, I promise you."

"I'm sure that's true ordinarily," Bryony conceded. "But we're not dealing with sensible people. The Abbey's members are fanatics who will go to whatever lengths necessary to protect their order. They've already killed my father, haven't they?" Her voice ended on a ragged sob.

"Yes. However, these are still *not* the kind of religious maniacs who lack intelligence and reason, however distorted it may seem to us. Neither is imprisonment nor suicide their goal. Nor is generating headlines, either. They could not have concealed the existence of their order for centuries, otherwise."

As she gazed from beneath the desk at the Scotsman, Bryony realized suddenly that even though he was speaking softly and comfortingly to her, his head was cocked a trifle, listening intently to the house and the night, and that he still held the shotgun at the ready, prepared for action in case the Abbey's henchmen should resume shooting, or commence an assault on the bungalow. So, no matter what Hamish had told her, he was not absolutely sure, after all, that whoever was outside had, having failed in their mission, actually departed. His talking to her was simply his way of trying to calm and reassure her. And it *was* true that she was not nearly as terrified now as she had been only moments ago, when the barrage of flying bullets had smashed the study windows and riddled the room's interior. Still, the silence did not necessarily bode well for the two of them, either, as the Scotsman had recognized.

But then, much to Bryony's immense relief, she heard in the distance the unmistakable wail of police sirens. Help had arrived.

"No, stay put," Hamish directed, when she started to crawl from her hiding place. "Let's be sure of things before we leave the relative protection of my study. I haven't detected any signs of anyone having moved in close to the house, nor heard any sounds of a break-in downstairs. However, better safe than sorry, I always say." When finally he saw the police cars driving up to the cottage, blue lights flashing, he continued, "I'll go down first. I'm going to put the shotgun and shells under the bed across the hall, just in case you should need them."

"But...why would I?" Bryony queried, puzzled.

"Well, we won't know it's *really* the police until we do some checking, will we?" he pointed out, abruptly bringing all her fears to the fore again.

Then, reaching for his cell phone, Hamish disappeared from the study. From below, Bryony could hear peremptory knocking on the bungalow door, accompanied by the sound of voices announcing themselves as the police. The Scotsman asked to see their identification. Then he prudently telephoned the police station to confirm the identities of the officers standing beyond the closed front door. At last, satisfied with what he had learned, he admitted them into the house, calling up the stairs, "It's all right, Bryony, you can come down now."

When she joined him downstairs, he was in the process of explaining to the police what had occurred. Pausing, he introduced her to the two officers in charge.

"Bryony, this is Inspector Ferguson and Sergeant MacDuff. Gentlemen, this is my friend Ms. Bryony St. Blaze, from the States, who is my houseguest just at the moment."

"How do you do, madam?" the Inspector said. "I understand you've had quite a harrowing experience this evening."

"Yes, we have indeed."

"I'm very sorry to hear it. However, I do assure you, madam, that something like this is truly *most* out of the ordinary here." Inspector Ferguson directed his attention back to Hamish. "Now, Mr. Neville, you say that you've no idea whatsoever as to who these assailants were, or why they might have wanted to take potshots at your cottage?"

"No, I don't." Hamish shook his head. "None at all. Really, I can only presume that it was drunken hooligans intent on playing some sort of nasty prank. Should you wish to check, I'm sure you'll discover that I value my privacy highly and live very quietly here. I suppose that with my bungalow being so isolated, it seemed an ideal target for whatever mischief the miscreants intended...burglary, perhaps."

"And you've no enemies that you know of, sir?"

"Beyond the usual academic rivals?" The Scotsman smiled. "No, none of which I'm aware."

"Very well, then. We'll just have a look upstairs, shall we?" the inspector asked.

"By all means, please do." Hamish indicated the narrow staircase that led to the second story of the cottage.

Upstairs in the study, the police spent some time digging the spent slugs from the walls and taking photographs and measurements of the crime scene. The officers interrogated Bryony and the Scotsman about what the two of them had done when the shooting had started.

"Well, at first, we thought it was rocks, not bullets, smashing the panes," Hamish falsely reported. "Then, when we realized we were being fired upon, I knocked Ms. St. Blaze to the floor and instructed her to crawl under the kneehole of my desk for protection, whilst I switched off the study lights and carefully made my way to the window, to see if I could determine who was outside and just what was going on. I told Ms. St. Blaze to call Emergency Services and ask to be connected with the police. However, the phone was dead—apparently, the line was down—so she tried again on my mobile phone. It was around this time that the shots abruptly ceased, and we simply waited here in the study until you arrived. That's basically all we know, Inspector."

"Would you concur with that description of the events as they transpired, madam?" Sergeant MacDuff inquired.

"Yes." Bryony nodded. "It all happened so quickly…I'm still shaking, I'm afraid."

"Quite understandable, madam. And neither of you saw anyone at all?" the sergeant continued.

"No. It was dark…I was huddled up under the kneehole practically the whole time, and Mr. Neville, when he glanced out the window, said that he thought the shooters must be a couple of hundred yards away from the cottage, at least."

"Right, then." Inspector Ferguson started toward the study door. "We'll check around outside and see what, if anything, we can turn up. In the meantime, you folks might want to think about spending the night somewhere else, just in case whoever it was should take a notion to return."

"Yes, thank you, Inspector. Under the circumstances that would probably be the wisest course of action," Hamish declared. "I'm sure I don't know what the world's coming to, when people aren't even safe in their own homes."

"I know what you mean, sir. If we learn anything further, we'll be in touch with you. And of course, should you have any more trouble this evening, do ring us immediately."

"I appreciate that, Inspector. Good night."

"Good night, sir, madam."

After the police had finally departed, the Scotsman suggested to Bryony that the two of them finish packing the Volvo and leave the bungalow as soon as possible.

"I don't want to take the chance that the Abbey will indeed try to make a second attempt on our lives tonight," he said soberly. "Damn them! I was *so* careful driving home after my meeting with Cauldronbearer, *so* sure that I wasn't followed!"

"Maybe you weren't," Bryony responded comfortingly. "Really, you shouldn't blame yourself, Hamish. It's entirely possible that the Abbey tracked your address down by some other means...the university, the Internet, a private-detective agency...there are dozens of ways these days to find out where someone lives, and you couldn't realistically have expected the U.K.'s Data Protection Act to shield you forever. For all you know, the Abbey has been aware of your location from the very beginning."

"Yes, that's true," he reluctantly conceded. "Nevertheless, you have to admit that it's still one hell of a coincidence that their assassins showed up on my doorstep shortly after I met Cauldronbearer for lunch. No, somehow, I was followed. I feel certain of it. I just don't know how..."

"A tracking device?" she speculated thoughtfully. "I mean, such things *do* exist, don't they? They're not simply the product of the overactive imagination of some scriptwriter for James Bond movies...."

"Bloody hell! No...no, of course they're not!" After abruptly going into the lean-to and rummaging through his toolbox, Hamish reappeared with a high-beamed flashlight in one hand. "It's dark outside," he said, "and we need to go over my car thoroughly before we hit the road. Because otherwise, if you're right, the Abbey will know every single move we're making."

"Hamish, I think...I think that maybe we should check for a...for a bomb, too, while we're at it. Maybe the Abbey has wired the Volvo to blow up. Maybe that's why they suddenly stopped shooting at us and didn't try to break into the house—and not because you told them that we were armed and had called the police."

"Oh, Jesus! This is a goddamned, bloody nightmare, isn't it?"

"Yes."

And then, quite suddenly, Bryony began to cry.

"Shh. Hush, sweet lady, hush." Somehow, the Scotsman's strong arms were around her, holding her close, one hand stroking her hair soothingly and pressing her head gently against his broad shoulder. "We're going to get through this. I promise you. One way or another, we are going to get through this all right."

"Oh, Hamish, how can you be so sure? I'm frightened."

"Yes, I know you are. I can feel you trembling against me." *And it is not at all an unpleasant experience,* he wanted to add but didn't, feeling that his timing, if not his advances, would be considered horribly inappropriate—and rightly so, he reflected ruefully. Nothing like being shot at with high-powered rifles, and then having to fend off a man who was a relative stranger. "You really must *try* to keep your spirits up and look on the bright side of things. We've still got quite a bit going for us, you know."

"Yes, I know," she agreed, smiling up at him tremulously through her tears. "I'm sorry. I'm not usually given to tears— oh, and now I've got mascara on your shirt—"

"Don't worry about it. I don't mind. If I've given you any solace at all, then it was worth it." He smiled back at her. "Shall we go investigate my Volvo, then?"

Slowly, she nodded, loath to leave the warm comfort of his embrace but knowing that the longer the two of them tarried at the cottage, the greater the risk they ran if the Abbey's agents were to return to attempt to finish them off. Hamish, too, was reluctant to release her, but he recognized that time was of the essence, as well.

Outside, while Bryony maneuvered the flashlight for him, the Scotsman carefully went over every single inch of his automobile.

"Well, the good news is that there's no bomb that I can see. The bad news is that you were right about the tracking device." Sliding his hand from beneath the right rear wheel well, he showed her the small object that had been used to pinpoint the location of his bungalow. "Damn! I cannot believe I was so bloody, damned stupid!"

"It's not your fault, Hamish."

"Yes, it is! I should have thought about something like this—and I didn't. I've grown rusty and complacent, I guess, living so quietly all alone here with my books."

"You're a history lecturer—not a spy."

"Yes, well, nevertheless, I'd better start thinking like one, hadn't I? Otherwise, who knows what might happen next?"

"Hadn't you better destroy that thing?"

"No. Now that we've found it, we can put it to work for us to mislead the Abbey."

"How?" Bryony inquired, puzzled.

"We'll drive into Aberdeen—and stick it on somebody else's vehicle!"

"Hamish! How could you even *consider* doing something like that? I don't want us to be the cause of endangering anyone else—"

"But that's the beauty of it, dear lady. We won't be. The Abbey's hirelings won't want to make a mistake, which would create additional problems for them. They'll want to be sure it's actually *us* before they try anything further, and by the time they've realized we found their tracking device and transferred it to somebody else's car, we'll be long gone, and they won't have a clue as to where, either. It'll give us an advantage that, at the moment, I'd say we desperately need, Bryony."

"Yes, okay, I suppose you're right."

"I know I am. Now, let's finish packing up the Volvo—and then get the hell out of here!"

"What went wrong, Shieldbearer?" The Nautonnier's icy tone expressed his supreme displeasure. "I'm certain I don't need to remind you how long and hard Cauldronbearer worked to entice Neville into meeting with him. Further, I am assured by Cauldronbearer that the tracking device was placed without detection on Neville's Volvo, and was operating properly, and that by this means, the location of Neville's cottage *was*, in fact, pinpointed."

"Yes, Nautonnier, it was." Shieldbearer's forehead was perspiring so profusely that sweat ran down into his eyes.

"Then I ask again...what went wrong, Shieldbearer?"

"Our initial shots missed the woman...Bryony St. Blaze...and Neville reacted very quickly to the assault, knocking her to the floor and killing the lights, so we no longer had a clear target. We fired several more rounds, but these were unsuccessful, as well, and Neville proved to be unexpectedly armed with a shotgun, which he discharged out an upstairs window in our direction. Further, despite the fact that Lance-bearer had cut the phone line, Neville had a mobile phone at hand, and he used it to call the police, shouting this information out the window at us. After some discussion, Lancebearer and I decided that the most prudent course of action was to retreat rather than to run the risk of being arrested, which might have led to all sorts of unpleasant complications, Nautonnier. Of course, we did not want to jeopardize the Abbey."

"Why were the possibilities of Neville's being armed with a shotgun and equipped with a mobile phone not taken into account?"

"They were, Nautonnier. However, given the laws of the U.K., we did not believe that Neville, if armed, would actually fire upon us. As to his mobile phone, in order to have immo-bilized it, it would have been necessary for us to have disrupted one or more relay towers, which would have rendered every single other mobile phone in the entire vicinity inoperable, too, thereby drawing unwanted attention and investigation in the event that our attempt upon the woman's life had succeeded. At the very least, the police would have found it highly sus-picious that not only Neville's phone line, but also his mobile phone had proved conveniently out of commission. As it is, the incident may be thought, by both Neville and the authori-ties, to have been no more than the work of local thugs, intent on robbing his bungalow."

"Well, let us hope that does, indeed, prove to be the case, Shieldbearer." The Grand Master's sibilant voice sent a chill snaking down the other's spine. "Otherwise, we will be com-pelled to deal not only with Neville and the woman, but also with the police. I'm sure I don't need to tell you that would present difficulties."

"Yes, I am aware of that, Nautonnier. What are your instructions? Are we still to take Neville alive? Had it not been for that directive, then Lancebearer and I *could* have succeeded in our mission, moving in to dispose of both him and Bryony St. Blaze. As it was..." Shieldbearer allowed his own voice to trail away, leaving, hanging in the air, the unspoken suggestion that his and Lancebearer's failure had been due not to any fault of their own, but to the Grand Master's orders.

"I am cognizant of the problem, Shieldbearer!" the Nautonnier snapped, annoyed. "However, it will not behoove us to act hastily in this matter. Perhaps it is part of the Grand Design that you and Lancebearer failed in your mission this evening. We do not, I remind you, yet know Neville's true intentions toward the Abbey. Although he has proved to be in touch with the woman *and* saved her life, he may have had good reasons— of which we are ignorant—for both. Her father, Professor St. Blaze, made a lifelong study of arcana and esoterics. He may somehow have uncovered information that we ourselves lack about the missing Knights Templar treasure, and he may have made his daughter privy to this—in which case, Neville may only be using her for his own purposes."

"Possibly. However, if so, he ought to have informed us of all that, Nautonnier." Shieldbearer's tone was disapproving.

"Quite. But he has not yet been initiated into our ranks and ways. Perhaps he hopes by these methods to prove himself worthy of our trust. We do not yet know. On the other hand, however, he may be playing both sides to his own advantage, hoping to find—and keep—the treasure for himself. He *is* Mordred, the betrayer." The Grand Master paused, reflecting. Then he continued. "The tracking device is still in place?"

"Yes."

"Good. Then, for the moment, I believe the wisest course of action is now to wait and see what Neville and Bryony St. Blaze do next. If they leave the cottage, follow them. However, do nothing else against them until such time as we can discover precisely what they know and what they are up to. Meanwhile, Cauldronbearer will keep in touch with Neville—to allay any suspicions he might have that the Abbey was behind the attack upon his bungalow tonight.''

''Very well, Nautonnier,'' Shieldbearer said—but he spoke only to a buzzing dial tone. The Abbey's Grand Master had, as usual, abruptly severed the connection.

Thirteen

One Thousand and One Nights

'Tis all a Checkerboard of Nights and Days
Where Destiny with Men for pieces Plays:
Hither and thither moves, and mates, and slays,
And one by one back in the Closet lays.

> *The Rubáiyát of Omar Khayyám*
> —Edward FitzGerald

The City of Maracanda, the Kingdom of Sogdiana, 106 B.C.

Sheherazad, the eldest of the two daughters of Khirad, the Grand Vizier of Maracanda, in the kingdom of Sogdiana, was more frightened than she had ever been before in her entire life. This day, she was to wed Shahryar, the self-proclaimed King of all of Sogdiana.

This last wasn't in the least true, but since he held the capital, Maracanda, and its surrounding region, including, on the outskirts of the city, Afrâsiâb, the hill where the mighty Citadel that housed the Great Palace stood, he was the highest-ranking and most powerful of all the Sogdian nobles. Further, he had installed his younger brother, Shahzaman, at the nearby city of Bukhârâ. As a result, between them, they now ruled the two most important cities in all the kingdom.

Under normal circumstances, Sheherazad, like any other

young woman, would have been thrilled to have been chosen as Shahryar's queen. Unfortunately the Sogdian King of Maracanda was insane. He had become so when he had discovered that his first wife and his concubines were being unfaithful to him with several of the slaves in the Citadel. In a passionate rage, Shahryar had commanded that all the women be executed. Since that time he had decided, irrationally, that all females were as treacherous, disloyal and untrustworthy as his first wife and concubines had proved—bound to bring shame and disgrace upon their husbands and lords.

But the King lacked an heir, without which the nobles of Maracanda could not rest easy. Sogdiana was located at the very heart of both the Silk and Fur Roads. From the far east came caravans laden with bolts of silk, and from the far north, traders arrived bearing piles of furs, all to be bartered or sold to the lands west and south of the kingdom. Sogdiana was the crossroads of all four corners of the known world. For this reason, through the ages, it had been invaded by any number of barbaric, foreign peoples, all desirous of gaining control of the kingdom and plundering its riches. When the faraway Seleucid rulers had lost their power over Sogdiana, the kingdom had fallen victim to corruption and chaos. To restore order, it must have a dynasty of its own. So Shahryar's advisers had counseled him to choose a second bride, with whom he could beget an heir.

What they did not know—and what Sheherazad's father, Khirad, the Grand Vizier himself, had learned quite by accident only last night, having eavesdropped on a clandestine conversation between the King and the Citadel's executioner—was that although Shahryar had finally acceded to his nobles' demands, he had also secretly instructed the executioner to stand ready to behead the new Queen the morning following her wedding night, so that she would have no opportunity to betray him, once he had taken her maidenhead.

By this time tomorrow, Sheherazad would be dead.

Her heart thudded with terror, and her palms were damp with sweat. With difficulty, she fought down her rising panic as the handmaidens attending her finally completed the task of arraying her in the elaborate, colorful, silk finery in which she was to be married. Graciously inclining her head, Sheherazad dismissed them, and as they exited her chamber in the Great Palace of the Citadel, her father entered.

Much to her surprise, he carried the intricate, gold, silver and copper puzzle box that was his most prized treasure. It had been brought by Alexander the Great from Babylonia to Sogdiana over two centuries ago.

In the mountains of the kingdom rose an imposing fortress known as "the Rock," where Prince Oxyartes of Sogdiana had made his final stand against the conqueror's onslaught. The fortress had been believed to be impregnable. But somehow, several of Alexander's soldiers had managed to scale the high cliffs where the Rock perched like an eagle in its aerie. So amazed had Prince Oxyartes and his own troops been by this incredible, daring feat that they had immediately surrendered the fortress, and eventually, the prince and the conqueror had become good friends.

One of those seized captive at the Rock had been Prince Oxyartes's beautiful, young daughter, Roshanak. Legend claimed that Alexander—who had called her "Roxanne"—had fallen in love with her, and perhaps it was true. Certainly, he had taken her for his wife, although he need not have done so and was not romantically inclined toward women, either. As a mark of his favor and appreciation, he had also bestowed upon her father, Prince Oxyartes, the ornate box that Sheherazad's own father now bore.

"Daughter," Khirad said gravely, in greeting, "I have brought you a wedding present."

"Yes, so I see, Father. I am truly honored that you would entrust to me such a valuable object. Nevertheless...do you think it wise to give it to me? You yourself know better than anyone that His Majesty has lost his reason. If he were to learn what the Book inside that box contains—"

"It might save your life, Sheherazad!" her father insisted, his voice low so that he would not be overheard by anyone who might be spying upon them. "For he will need *you* to tell him what the Book says."

Since she was a child, Sheherazad had read all the annals, histories, legends and texts of all the Sogdian kings, nobles and heroes. In addition, she had collected a thousand or more tomes on the ancient peoples of all the known foreign lands and their own deceased rulers. She had studied the arts, philosophy and the sciences, and she knew the works of countless poets by heart. Considered one of the most learned women in the whole of the kingdom, she had finally managed to translate many of the parchment pages of the ancient, cryptic Book passed down through the Sogdian ages, from Prince Oxyartes to her father.

For the first time since discovering that she was to wed the King, Sheherazad felt her heart leap with sudden hope. Perhaps Khirad was right. Perhaps even a lunatic like Shahryar would perceive the Book's priceless wisdom and wish to learn of its contents.

"But, Father, what if His Majesty, in his madness, thinks it only a trick? What if he does not believe I can read the Book— or at least some of it, anyway?"

"You are not only highly educated, but also very clever, Daughter…perhaps the cleverest woman in all of Sogdiana," her father declared, not without pride. "I have faith that you will think of some means to convince him."

"By tomorrow morning?" She raised one black, raven-wing eyebrow skeptically.

"Ahura Mazda will show you the way." This was the God of those who followed the teachings of the ancient priest Zar- athushti, whom the Greeks called "Zoroaster." "Good thoughts, Sheherazad," Khirad said, reminding her of one of the first principles of their religion. "Now, come. It is time, and you must be away to your wedding."

The ceremony was to take place in the Great Temple of the Citadel. Despite her father's gift of the puzzle box and the hope it offered her, Sheherazad still could not quell her sense of doom as she slowly trailed in his wake from the Great Palace.

Outside, in the bright, golden sunlight that beat down from the brilliant, azure sky, she saw that slaves stood at the foot of the shallow steps of the Great Palace, waiting for her, holding the halter of the elephant she would ride to the Great Temple.

Behind this were arrayed her principal handmaidens, mounted on pure–white mares, followed by three male servants astride camels, then Khirad, alone, on a dun-colored stallion. The remainder of the splendid caravan consisted of the presents she would give to Shahryar, among them a herd of magnificent horses and flocks of peacocks and swans. Like their ancestors and many other of the peoples of the region, the Sogdians were superior horsemen, and the animals were highly prized, a symbol of power and prosperity, while the birds were revered for their beauty and grace.

As the elephant knelt, the slaves assisted Sheherazad into the richly draped palanquin on its broad back. Then the procession began to wind its way through the Citadel, preceded by little girls bearing baskets of red lilies and other flowers, from which they strewed petals upon the beaten clay-brick roads dusty with yellow loess. The inhabitants of the Citadel crowded the narrow streets, cheering as their future queen passed. Choking down her fear, Sheherazad forced herself to smile and wave at all the well-wishers. After all, they did not know what the King had planned for her tomorrow morning. To them, she represented a new beginning—and hope that Shahryar's lunacy would somehow pass.

Inside the Great Temple, the King awaited her. At the sight of him, Sheherazad felt her breath catch in her throat. It was difficult to believe he was not in his right mind, for he was a man tall, handsome and virile—dark of hair, beard and eyes, and in his prime, his lithe figure regal and imposing. He looked every inch the way a king ought to, she thought. Nor was there another man in the entire kingdom as skilled with a scimitar as he was. With this had he won his throne—and kept it, in spite of his insanity. She trembled as his penetrating glance raked her from head to toe as though using his infamous, curved blade, revealing nothing of what might be in his crazed mind. Resolutely emptying her own sane one, she walked toward him.

The wedding ceremony was long, followed by an equally lengthy banquet. Then, at last, Sheherazad was escorted back to the Great Palace. There eunuchs had already prepared the large, mosaic-tiled *hammam*, or bath in the mural-walled bed-chamber, scenting it with musk, rosewater and willow-flower water, and fumigating it with ambergris and eagle wood. Hand-maidens undressed and bathed her, then oiled and perfumed her body before garbing her in a brilliant, silk gown purfled with red-gold, elaborately embroidered with depictions of beasts and birds, and bedecked with priceless jewels. After that, they presented her to Shahryar.

He lounged among huge, tasseled satin pillows set before a low table of wood and brass, laden with fruit and wine. Gold candelabra bearing flickering beeswax tapers illuminated the room. Behind a screen at one end, musicians played quietly, the dulcet sounds of ouds, dumbeks, daffs and zils mingling and echoing on the gentle night breeze that soughed in through the wide, arched windows.

"You have eyes like a gazelle," the King observed, his voice low.

"I hope you find them pleasing, Your Majesty," Sheherazad replied softly.

"*I* hope they are not *all* I find pleasing." His dark gaze swept her intently, making his meaning even more unmistakable.

She shivered, frightened. She expected him to be rough with her, and eventually, when he finally claimed her as his, he was. Still, despite her apprehension, Sheherazad made no protest against him, crying out only once, when he first thrust deeply into her, piercing her maidenhead. Afterward, she lay quietly beside him, biting her lower lip to keep from weeping. Tears would not help her cause and would perhaps even anger or amuse him. She was exceedingly beautiful. He would not have wanted her, otherwise. And she somehow knew instinctively that he had enjoyed possessing her far more than he would have liked. She had been a virgin bride, but not an ignorant one. She had spent her whole life being trained in the arts of making a man such as Shahryar happy.

"I have pleased you, Your Majesty?"

"Yes," the King admitted grudgingly.

"Then perhaps you would grant me a small favor?" She-herazad ventured hesitantly.

"Perhaps. What is it?"

"My father, the Grand Vizier, has given me a wedding present…an ancient manuscript. I had hoped to share some of its stories with my younger sister, Dunyazad, but there was no time today. If it would not trouble you, may I send for her now, to share my father's gift with her? The night is yet young, and I know she would be grateful for your kindness in this matter, as would I, Your Majesty. And perhaps you, too, would like to hear some of the tales the Book contains? Something to amuse you, while you have some food and drink. And then, later—"

"Later, you will please me again, Sheherazad." It was a command, not a question.

"I am your wife—and thus yours for the taking, Your Majesty."

"Yes, you are," Shahryar insisted, in his tone a subtle note of warning and menace, so that Sheherazad knew he was re-membering his first wife and concubines, and their infidelity. For a moment, she was afraid she had lost her opportunity. But then, much to her relief, the King at last decided to be mag-nanimous. "Send for your sister, then. It is a small enough favor you ask, and one easily granted."

"Thank you, Your Majesty."

Rising from the gossamer-draped bed, Sheherazad first pre-pared a dish of sticky dates and a goblet of red wine for Shah-ryar. Then she returned to the *hammam* where, with hands that shook slightly, she washed the virgin's blood from her thighs. After that, covering her nakedness with a loose robe, she sent one of her handmaidens to fetch her younger sister. Presently, Dunyazad appeared in the bedchamber, her lovely countenance filled with concern for Sheherazad.

"His Majesty, my husband, has said that I might show you Father's wedding gift to me, Dunyazad, and read you some of the stories the Book holds," the older sister announced, her own expression silently warning the younger to ask no ques-tions and to say nothing untoward.

"His Majesty is most kind and generous," Dunyazad asserted, paying courteous obeisance to the King before following Sheherazad to a lattice-screened alcove of the bedchamber, where they could be private, although still overheard by Shahryar.

There, the two sisters sat upon large, striped, satin pillows before a low table on which the elder placed the intricate puzzle box that Khirad had given her. Slowly but surely, in the proper order, she maneuvered the complex sliding pieces that would unlock the box and allow the lid to be opened. Then, from within, she drew forth the ancient manuscript, unwrapping it from the folds of its black and white linen cloths. She turned back the front cover.

"As you know, dear Sister, it is said that this Book is as old as time itself and has written upon its pages all the wisdom of the world," she explained, for the listening King's benefit. "There are words and symbols the like of which are unknown beyond this manuscript, and tales beyond our wildest imaginings, too. For this reason, they have been thought by some to be only fables. But I believe they are much more than that...."

On that night—and a thousand others that followed—Sheherazad read, her voice rising and falling as sweetly as the strains played by the musicians behind the screen. And each evening, just like all good storytellers, she ceased her tale at some critical point, so that in order to hear the end of it, Shahryar must keep her alive yet one more day, until, finally, he no longer had any wish to behead her but had come to love and cherish her deeply instead, his madness cured. In that time, she bore him three fine sons, who listened as raptly as their father and Dunyazad, who had wed the King's brother, Shahzaman, and was now as equally beloved as her sister, to the stories their mother recounted from the Book.

"Tonight, I will tell you all the last tale I have been able to translate thus far in this ancient manuscript," Sheherazad announced now, to her small but precious audience. "It is called

Ali Baba and the Forty Thieves—and while you may think it is only a story about a clever, young man and a mysterious cave full of treasure, it is my own belief that it is, in reality, about the means to open some great cosmic gate...."

Fourteen

Flight into Darkness

Ah, love, let us be true
To one another! for the world, which seems
To lie before us like a land of dreams,
So various, so beautiful, so new,
Hath really neither joy, nor love, nor light,
Nor certitude, nor peace, nor help for pain;
And we are here as on a darkling plain
Swept with confused alarms of struggle and flight,
Where ignorant armies clash by night.

Dover Beach
—Matthew Arnold

En Route from Aberdeen to Edinburgh, Scotland, the Present

After taking the time to board up the broken windows in the cottage and get the last of their packing finished, Bryony and Hamish finally drove into Aberdeen sometime after midnight, where they placed the Abbey's tracking device on another vehicle to throw their pursuers off the trail. Then, following the A90 trunk road, they headed south, taking turns at the wheel so that they could travel all night, putting as much distance between themselves and the Abbey's hirelings as possible.

When they reached Dundee, they crossed the Firth of Tay, taking the highway south to Kirkcaldy, and, from there, headed to Edinburgh, as Hamish thought it would be more difficult for them to be followed in the capital city.

After passing through the city center, they came to the dismal Leith docks, then took the old coast road toward Berwick. At last, toward a gray, rainy dawn, just east of Musselburgh, Bryony and Hamish pulled down a short county lane into an isolated wooded area, where they parked the Volvo so that it couldn't be seen.

"I think we'll be safe here," the Scotsman remarked as he shut off the engine. "I haven't seen anybody tailing us, have you?"

"No." Bryony shook her head tiredly. "I'm pretty sure we made a clean getaway. So…are we going to make camp here, then?"

"Yes, I believe that's best, don't you? We've had a long night, and we both need to get some rest. Otherwise, we're liable to wind up falling asleep at the wheel and having an accident."

"I agree."

They unpacked the automobile and erected the Scotsman's dome tent, which was easily set up, then unrolled their individual sleeping bags inside. After that, weary to the bone, and not bothering to do more than strip off their socks and shoes, they crawled into their sleeping bags just as the rain began to come down in earnest.

Bryony thought she would slip into slumber immediately, but much to her surprise, she lay awake, going over in her mind the night's terrifying events. She couldn't imagine what she and Hamish could do to extricate themselves from their current situation. Even though they had managed to escape this evening, they could not run away from the Abbey forever. Perhaps they had made a mistake in not informing the police about the order's existence and the deliberate attempt on their lives.

"What's wrong?" Hamish's voice was soft and low in her ear. "Can't you sleep?"

"No, I guess not. I thought I could. Heaven knows, I'm

utterly exhausted. But now, I don't seem to be able to drift off. Hamish, what are we going to do? Maybe we were wrong not to tell the police everything. I mean, we *had* been shot at. They would have to believe *that*, at least.''

''True,'' he conceded. ''But even if they *had* taken us seriously, what do you suppose they could have done to help us, Bryony? Placed a round-the-clock watch on us? In such a case, the Abbey would most likely have just waited them out—and in the end, we would only have wound up looking foolish, as would the police themselves, when nothing further happened. And then, the odds of getting the authorities to believe us again would have proved pretty slim.''

''But how can we possibly save ourselves—get any concrete proof of the Abbey's existence?''

''Hmm...well, I've been giving that some thought, and it seems to me that one way might be to expose the Abbey in a manner in which we wouldn't actually *need* any real hard evidence.''

''What do you mean?''

''I mean that we could simply put up everything we know about them on the Internet. We could build a Web site devoted to the Abbey and send information about them to any number of other esoterical Web sites already in existence, as well. If we did all that, then the whole world would know about the order, and they wouldn't have any reason to kill us, would they?''

''I don't know. I suppose they wouldn't—except...''

''Except what?''

''Except...well...there's something I haven't yet told you, Hamish,'' Bryony slowly confessed, torn by doubts and conflicting emotions. Surely, she could trust the Scotsman now. Had he not saved her life—twice now—instructed her to telephone Emergency Services and to request the police when the Abbey's henchmen had been shooting at his bungalow? Surely, he wouldn't have done all that unless he really *were* on her side, she reassured herself. ''It's...it's about Dad.''

''I'm listening. What about him?''

''He...sent something to me...right before he was killed.''

The Scotsman abruptly sat straight up in his sleeping bag.

"What?" he exclaimed, staring down at her accusingly, where she lay beside him. "I beg your pardon, but I thought we were in this together!"

"We are…only…well, I'm sorry, Hamish, but I wasn't certain I could trust you! In all honesty, I'm not sure if I should trust you even now! You could be one of them…the Abbey, I mean."

"I see," he said after a moment, obviously offended. "Well, in that case, I'm very surprised that you came away with me, Bryony. Why didn't you just tell the police everything you know—and also inform them that you suspect me of being a part of the entire scheme? Never mind that I've saved your life twice now—and placed my own in considerable jeopardy by doing so!"

"I know that, and believe me, I'm extremely grateful to you. I don't know what else I can do but apologize." She bit her lower lip uncertainly, wondering if she had now made the Scotsman so angry that he would perhaps desert her out here, in the middle of nowhere, loading his camping gear back into his Volvo and driving away without her.

"Well, for one thing, you can try actually *using* the very fine brain that I am aware God gave you!" he declared sternly, frowning at her. "For instance, *if* I were indeed already a member of the Abbey and in on its dastardly plot, then why should I bother to defend you at my cottage—and to have you call the police, besides? In fact, there would hardly have been any need at all for the Abbey's hirelings to fire upon us, would there? I could simply have let them into my bungalow, and given how ruthless they are, we could all have behaved *most* unpleasantly to you until you surrendered whatever it is that your father gave you. I presume the Abbey knows you have it…whatever *it* is?"

"No, they don't. However, I'm sure they must suspect that Dad was on to something." Bryony's expression was contrite and ashamed in the face of the Scotsman's irrefutable logic. "I think that's why they ransacked his office and town house, and why they searched my cottage, too. And the only reason they *didn't* find what Dad gave me was because he had mailed the package to me right before he was killed, and my next-door neighbor, Mrs. Pittering, had collected my mail while I was trying to deal with his murder, the investigation and the funeral arrangements. So she had the disks all the time.''

"The disks?" Hamish went still and alert at the word, so that Bryony was forced to wonder yet again if she were doing the right thing in trusting him.

But she had already told him about the CDs now, so it seemed pointless not to continue. He was bigger and stronger than she was, and they were totally alone here in the woods; besides, it was unlikely that anyone would hear her even if she did scream. Surely, in this weather, not even a lone hiker would be around. Hamish could easily overpower her, tie her up and search her belongings until he found the disks, and there would be nothing she could do about it.

"A pair of CDs containing a number of files," she elucidated.

"What kind of files?"

She shook her head.

"I don't know. They're all password protected, and so far I've only been able to open the first one, which was titled *Introduction*. It was a letter to me from Dad."

"What did it say?" Hamish inquired.

"It said that what the disks contained represented the culmination of his life's work…a-a *puzzle* he had attempted to assemble into a big picture, but which was still incomplete. He talked about riding a tiger, and a swallow being unable to know the ambitions of an eagle. He insisted that the knowledge the CDs held was dangerous, and that countless people over the millennia had died because of it. He told me that if I were reading his letter, then he was undoubtedly dead himself, so he was now passing the torch on to me, and that it was up to me to decide whether or not I wanted to extinguish it, but that if I chose to carry it forward, I would need your help. He called you the 'Quester,' and gave me your e-mail address, so I could get in touch with you. That's about it.''

"And where are these disks now?"

"In my…in my handbag."

"Well, you'd best leave them there, then, since that's probably the safest place for them right at the moment—provided, of course, you aren't one of those annoyingly scatterbrained women who leaves her purse everywhere she goes—and until we can figure out how to open the rest of the files and find out what they contain."

"No, I don't leave my handbag everywhere I go. As to what's on the CDs, I've racked my brain ceaselessly, but I just can't imagine what it might be. A big picture," she mused aloud. "What could Dad possibly have meant? And why would whatever it is be so very important to the Abbey?"

"I have an idea," Hamish answered slowly, "that it might have something to do with the missing Knights Templar treasure."

"The treasure!"

"Yes. As I'm sure you're aware, when the Knights Templar were persecuted and disbanded under Philip the Fair, their great treasure was alleged simply to have disappeared. Speculation has run rife over the centuries ever since as to just exactly what this treasure actually consisted of. The Order was extremely rich, of course, so one idea is that innumerable coffers of gold, silver and jewels were smuggled out of France, and, eventually, by 'Prince' Henry Sinclair, taken to the New World and buried on Oak Island, just off the coast of Nova Scotia, in what has come to be known as the 'Money Pit.' This is a deep shaft that has been excavated on several occasions and at considerable expense—all to no avail. Every time a certain depth is reached, the pit floods with seawater, apparently engineered to do so. Prior to Prince Henry's voyage, however, the pit was thought to contain a pirate's hoard, rather than the Templar treasure. Others claim the treasure is hidden in a concealed chamber at Rosslyn Chapel, but the Sinclairs, who own the chapel, have refused to permit the necessary excavations to determine whether or not this is indeed the case. Still others believe the treasure lies somewhere within the confines of Rennes-le-Château—or, at least, that the mysterious, coded parchments discovered there are the key to the location of the treasure. Some think the treasure and the Holy Grail of King Arthur and his Knights of the Round Table are one and the same, and if that's so, then the Abbey's interest in this regard could be two-fold.''

"But…in all the stories of it, the Grail is never a treasure in the monetary sense," Bryony pointed out, perplexed at the notion. "It's a cup or a platter or a stone, usually."

"True…but, then, there's no evidence that the *real* Knights Templar treasure was ever monetary, either," Hamish observed. "It's simply been assumed that it must have been, because the Order was so immensely wealthy. However, in my opinion, it's highly unlikely that countless chests full of gold, silver and jewels could have been successfully smuggled out of France, with no one the wiser. Philip the Fair had laid his plans carefully, and he had spies everywhere, watching the Templars for weeks, no doubt even months, before he moved openly against them. So any maneuvers made by the Templars on such a large scale would have been noticed, and action taken to halt them, since the primary impetus driving Philip was his greed for the Templar's riches and property. No, my guess is that no matter what the real Templar treasure actually was, it was small—something that could be carried by one man who, in all the confusion, could have got away disguised as a beggarman, perhaps, someone to whom no one would have paid any heed under normal circumstances, much less in the midst of Philip's dismantling the Order and seizing its leaders and property."

"So…you think the treasure *was* a cup or a platter or a stone, then?" she asked.

"No, not necessarily—because if it *were* one of those things, it would obviously have to possess some kind of extraordinary power or history to be utterly priceless…that is to say, something worth killing for."

"Well, yes, but the cup is said to be the chalice from which Jesus Christ drank at the Last Supper, the platter to be that which bore the disembodied head of John the Baptist, and the stone to be the fabled Philosopher's Stone."

"True. The problem is…just exactly how would anyone go about proving any of that? A cup or a platter could, by means

of modern radio-carbon dating, of course, be reasonably pinpointed as having been in existence during the time of Jesus
Christ and John the Baptist. However, that's all that could definitely be said about either object. And in the case of a stone,
it would have to be subjected to all kinds of alchemistic experiments to determine whether or not it truly were the Philosopher's Stone—in which event, an extensive knowledge of alchemy and the properties of the stone itself would be needed,
and according to legend, if one already had all that knowledge,
then one could make one's own stone and wouldn't require any
other."

"Then what do you think the treasure or Grail is?"

"I don't know. There are any number of possibilities that
come to mind. Maybe we'll get some clues from your father's
CDs. In the meanwhile, I suggest that we both get some much
required sleep. Otherwise, we're not going to be much good
for anything, and at all costs, we need to keep our wits about
us," the Scotsman insisted.

"Yes, we do. Good night, Hamish—or, rather, good morning."

"Good morning to you, too."

"I'm sorry I didn't trust you before." Yawning, Bryony
apologized again as she snuggled deeper into her sleeping bag,
soothed now by the falling rain. "I hope you're not still mad
at me."

"No, I'm not. I know you had good reasons for your suspicions. But I *do* hope we can be friends and allies hence-
forth."

"Yes, we will be."

"Is that a promise?"

"Yes, I promise."

"Good." Hamish laughed softly. "Because I don't think I
can sleep with one eye open, in case you should try to cosh
me over the head and leave me behind here for the Abbey to
discover!"

"I wouldn't do that."

"I'm *very* glad to hear it!"

A smile of amusement curved Bryony's mouth at his teasing. She slept.

It was late morning, dark and gray with still steadily drumming rain, when the two of them awoke. Disoriented for a moment, Bryony didn't know where she was. She took stock of her surroundings, and the fact that she had slept in her clothes suggested she was at an archaeological dig. Then, slowly, she became aware of Hamish lying beside her, his right arm wrapped around her waist, his head so close to hers that his mouth—sulky, provocative and carnal—almost touched hers, and she could feel his warm, rhythmic breath against her skin. For fear of waking him, she lay quite still, hardly daring to breathe. Despite everything, there was a joy for her in being held by a man again for the first time in a very long while.

And not just any man, but Hamish. However unwise, she could not deny how powerfully attracted to him she was, and that this feeling was only increasing, the more time she spent in his company.

"Hmm…you feel good," the Scotsman murmured drowsily.

"Oh! I thought you were still asleep." Bryony's soft tone, while accusing, was also filled with smothered laughter at his playing opossum.

"I am." Hamish smiled wickedly, deliberately tightening his grip about her.

"Talk in your sleep, do you?" she asked archly.

"All the time," he answered. "Hmm…you smell good, too. What's that perfume you're wearing? It's delicious."

"It's not perfume. It's a combination of vanilla body cream and vanilla body spray."

"Really? Well, it makes you smell absolutely divine…good enough to eat." Lightly, playfully, he nibbled her earlobe, as though starving and intending to devour her.

Bryony's physical reaction was immediate—and so strong that the pleasure was almost painful. A thrilling electric current coursed down her spine, and her nipples tautened, circles of shocking tingles radiating from their centers.

"Hmm…you even *taste* good," the Scotsman continued,

chuckling huskily as she shivered with enjoyment in his embrace. "And I'm famished. How about if I have *you* for breakfast?"

"Breakfast? It's more like brunch time now."

"Then it's no wonder I'm ravenous."

Without warning, Hamish's mouth traveled warmly—incitingly—across Bryony's soft, rose-tinted cheek to seize her full, generous lips, abruptly parted with surprise and then incredible delight. Her breath caught raggedly in her throat as he tasted her tenderly at first, taking his time discovering and exploring her, pressing sweet, enticing kisses at the corners of her mouth before claiming it completely, lingeringly. His teeth nipped her lower lip gently, sucking, savoring. Tantalizingly, his tongue traced and teased the rosebud shape of her mouth before finally insinuating itself inside the dark, moist cavern, plunging deep, causing her to moan low in her throat, with pleasure. Like smoothest velvet, his tongue twisted and twined with her own, the pressure of his lips upon hers inexorably increasing, growing harder, more demanding, as he felt her enraptured response to his amorous onslaught. Her hands crept up around his neck, fingers tunneling through his glossy, silvery-black hair, drawing him even nearer. Her slender body trembled with longing and excitement in his arms as he went on kissing her urgently, swallowing her breath and the tiny whimpers of entreaty and exultation that he elicited from her pliant, eagerly yielding mouth. Almost savagely, his fingers grasped handfuls of her long, silky, blond hair, holding her upturned face still so that even had she wished to avoid his feverish encroachment, she would not have been able to. But Bryony had no such desire. Quite the opposite, in fact. She wanted Hamish to go on kissing her forever.

Ardently, his mouth moved from hers to rain a stream of kisses along her pearly, swanlike throat, finding its hollow, his tongue licking and dipping tauntingly there, causing her nipples once more to strain and stiffen with delight. As though sensing their high arousal, he trailed one hand down to caress her ripe, round breasts, swollen and aching with passion. Hampered by the sleeping bags separating him and her, he muttered a hoarse curse, yanking at the zipper of hers until he was able to turn back the thick, down-stuffed edge, giving him better access to her burgeoning breasts. His palm closed over one soft, full mound, squeezing and stroking, making her mewl again with yearning and pleasure, before he abruptly pulled up the T-shirt she had slept in, his fingers sliding sensuously over her now-bared belly and rib cage.

Then, his breath coming in harsh, heated rasps, Hamish determinedly pushed up Bryony's lacy, satin bra to expose her pale, naked breasts to his avid eyes and lips and hands.

"You're so very beautiful," he whispered thickly, his breath hot and alluring against her nipples.

He captured one firm, flushed peak possessively between his thumb and forefinger, tugging and rolling it gently, making it pucker and become even more rigid, like a sweet, succulent cherry on the verge of bursting, before he lowered his lips to taste it. His tongue darted forth, flicking and swirling, sending waves of delight rippling in all directions from the tiny bud. His teeth nibbled it delicately; his lips sucked it greedily, while she arched and writhed beneath him, her hands burrowing through his hair and gliding over his shoulders and back, reveling in the feel of his sinewy muscles.

In some dim corner of her brain, Bryony thought she must be mad. She scarcely even knew this Scotsman, still wasn't sure, despite everything, whether or not she ought to trust him, and yet she had never before in her life met anyone else like him. She had felt such a strong, instant attraction and empathy to this man, as though she had fallen in love with him at first sight, knowing she had been destined for him since time's beginning, as though they were...*soul mates.* The word sprang unbidden into her mind. It was a deeply romantic and esoterical—some would say even foolish—notion. What if she slept with him, and he turned out to be the enemy, after all?

"Hamish..." To her despair, what Bryony had intended as a soft but resolute protest came out instead as a prolonged sigh.

Still, the Scotsman was uncannily attuned to her tumultuous emotions and inner conflict.

"I know...I know...." Reluctantly—sighing himself—he at

last drew away from her, abruptly covering her up with the
sleeping bag once more, so that she would no longer prove
such a strong temptation to him. "I'm sorry. I really didn't
mean for this to happen—or at least, not right now," he
amended honestly, flashing her a rueful but winsome smile.
"This is neither the time nor the place. So, as much as it pains
me—literally—" he glanced significantly at his nether region,
so that she could not mistake the fact that he was highly stim-
ulated and hurting from the lack of release "—to behave myself, I shall nevertheless endeavor to play the part of a gentleman."

"It's...ah...not wholly *your* fault," Bryony admitted, blushing with guilt. "I mean, I wasn't exactly discouraging you."

"Well, no, you weren't." He grinned at her now with impudent satisfaction. "Does that mean there's hope for me yet?"

The crimson that stained her cheeks grew even darker and
more pronounced.

"You're a very bad man, Hamish Neville," she declared
primly.

"Yes, I am," he growled teasingly, his voice choked with
laughter. "Come on, then. Let's break camp, go get something
to eat, and then head for Roslin."

"Roslin?" she inquired, puzzled.

"Yes, it's the village where Rosslyn Chapel is located."

"Why do you think it's important that we go there?"

He shrugged.

"We have to start somewhere—and it's close, tied up with
the Sinclairs and the Knights Templar, and therefore as good
a place as any to begin."

Fifteen

The Green Man

Dear friend, all theory is gray,
And green the golden tree of life.

> *Faust: The First Part. Mephistopheles and the Student*
> —Johann Wolfgang von Goethe

Must I not serve a long apprenticehood
To foreign passages, and in the end,
Having my freedom, boast of nothing else
But that I was a journeyman to grief?

> *King Richard II*
> —William Shakespeare

Roslin, Scotland, the Present

Roslin lay nine miles south of Edinburgh, and as Hamish turned left off the Penicuik road on to a narrow byway, the hamlet of Roslin, along with Rosslyn Chapel and the ruins of Rosslyn Castle, came into view.

Bryony's breath caught in her throat at the sight of the chapel itself, for it was truly unique, a masterpiece of Gothic architecture, complete with soaring spires, flying buttresses and beautiful arches. It was not large, but it *was* exquisite, and it possessed a strange, haunting, almost ethereal quality that was only emphasized by the gray drizzle that continued to fall from the cloudy sky. After she and Hamish had got out of the Volvo and paid a small fee to go inside the chapel, Bryony felt as though they had somehow mysteriously stepped back in time, and had been transported to some otherworldly place.

"My God," she breathed as she gazed, awestruck, around the magnificent interior. "I've seen photographs of the chapel, but they hardly do justice to the reality, do they?"

"No." Hamish shook his head as the two of them walked along reverently, drinking in their surroundings. "I think it's safe to say that Rosslyn Chapel is genuinely one of a kind, its closest rival probably being El Pilar, in Zaragoza, Spain."

From the vaulted, stone ceilings to the fourteen pillars that supported them, there was scarcely an inch of space that was not covered in intricate carvings and hieroglyphics. Twelve of the columns were identical; only the two at the eastern end of the chapel were different. The left–hand of these was known as the "Mason's Pillar," while the right–hand one was called the "Apprentice Pillar."

"Symbolically, they are representative of the twin pillars, Joachim and Boaz, of Solomon's Temple," Hamish explained, as he and Bryony studied the two columns quietly. "According to legend, the Master Mason was given, by Sir William St. Clair, who designed and built Rosslyn Chapel, a plan for a pillar of incomparable workmanship. Thus, feeling himself un-equal to the task of creating it until he had viewed the original, the Master Mason journeyed to the Continent, to Rome. In his absence, however, his apprentice took it upon himself to carve the right–hand column as it now stands. Upon his return to Roslin, the Master Mason, seeing what his underling had man-aged to accomplish, was totally consumed with jealousy and anger at the apprentice's presumption and talent. In a blind rage, the Master Mason snatched up a mallet, struck his un-derling in the head with it, and killed him. That carved head over there in the east corner at the top of the roof is said to be the Master Mason, while the one in the west corner, with the scar on its right temple, is claimed to be that of the hapless, murdered apprentice. Just east of the apprentice, under that niche, is the head of the woman thought to be his mother. The apprentice is referred to as the 'Son of the Widow.'''

"Really?" Bryony started visibly at this piece of information. "That's very interesting, because the Grail Quester Perceival—before Galahad eventually displaced him in the Arthurian literature—was also known as the 'Son of the Widow.' Perhaps there's some significance in that, Hamish!"

"I shouldn't be at all surprised. Historically, there are a quite number of men who have been called the 'Son of the Widow,' among them the Egyptian god Horus; Hiram Abiff, who is said to have been the architect and builder of Solomon's Temple; Jesus Christ; and Mani, the founder of Manicheanism. Freemasons also traditionally refer to themselves as the 'Sons of the Widow.' What seems to be of importance in all this is the idea of a master architect or builder as a savior."

Reflecting upon this information, Bryony contemplated the Apprentice Pillar carefully. At its base, eight dragons intertwined with foliage that sprang from their mouths. The vines themselves wound in four double spirals up the column, each different from the others and bound by carved ropes to the post. No fruit grew amid the foliage.

"In addition to the Boaz pillar, it might also be representative of Yggdrasil, the Great Ash Tree, or 'Odin's Steed,' of Scandinavian mythology," she observed slowly, "its Niflheim root being gnawed at by the huge dragon or serpent Nidhögg, in the Well of *Hvergelmir*—the 'Roaring Cauldron'—from which many rivers flowed. Odin is said to have sacrificed himself upon the tree and to have given up an eye to learn the secrets of creation and wisdom from the severed head of Mimir, the nature god, the Norse equivalent of the Celtic vegetaion god, the Green Man."

"Indeed. It will interest you to know that there are over two hundred depictions of the Green Man here at Rosslyn Chapel," the Scotsman declared. "And in fact, Osiris, the husband of the Widow Isis and the father of Horus, is often shown with a green face. Further, Isis herself is frequently referred as the 'Black Madonna,' and many authorities believe there used to be a figure of the Black Madonna in the crypt here at the chapel. The Apprentice Pillar could also be symbolic of the Christian Tree of Life, with its Serpent, Lucifer, and of the Qabbalah's Pillar of Tree, too.''

"And what about the pictures the alchemist Nicolas Flamel claimed to have copied from the *Book of Abraham the Jew*? One of those is entitled *Planetary Dragons on a Hill*, and it depicts several dragons surrounding a hill, upon whose crest a single, large tree grows. Do you know what those vines spiraling up the Apprentice Pillar actually remind me of, Hamish?''

"No, what?"

"Strands of DNA...the double helix of life....''

"You know, now that I think about it, you're absolutely right,'' he mused aloud thoughtfully.

At the east end of the southern aisle, near the Apprentice Pillar, a lintel bore the familiar Latin inscription:

"Wine is strong,
a King is stronger,
women are even stronger,
but TRUTH conquers all.''

Although alleged to have been built to the greater glory of God, Rosslyn Chapel actually boasted comparatively few Christian symbols. Instead, it was an almost overwhelming monument to arcana and esoterics, to the Knights Templar and Freemasonry, despite the curious fact that the latter's so-called origins dated to the sixteenth century, nearly a hundred years after the chapel itself had been constructed, while many people averred that Freemasonry had actually officially begun even later, in 1717, in London.

The whole of the chapel was designed around sacred geometry, with the principal pillars in the east end forming a triple tau, the badge of the Royal Arch Freemasonry and which triple tau was said to mean many different things, among them "a key to a treasure" and "a place where a precious thing is concealed." The arrangement of the columns was thought to be symbolic of the Temple of Jerusalem, and in the Royal Arch

Degree, the Seal of Solomon or Star of David—a double triangle within a circle of gold—meant "Nothing is wanting but
the Key," and "If thou canst comprehend these things, thou
knowest enough," the latter of which was itself inscribed on
the Royal Arch jewel worn by the companions of the order.

In the southeast of the chapel, well-worn steps led to the
crypt below. Halfway down stood a sculpture of a man carrying
a "Hiram" key, the handle of which was a perfect square, a
Masonic symbol. This was the entrance to the scroll vaults,
which had once housed the vast library of the chapel, and
which some people believed still to contain Nasorean scrolls
taken from Herod's Temple at Jerusalem. But the crypt had
long been sealed off, so that Bryony and Hamish were unable
to explore it.

"What does it all mean, Hamish?" Bryony asked, mystified
"Do you really think the Knights Templar treasure is hidden
here?"

"I don't know. However, if I had to guess, I'd say no."

"Why?"

"Because, for one thing, I don't believe the treasure to be
coffers full of gold, silver, and jewels. If it is, then there's no
legitimate reason for the Sinclairs *not* to produce it, *not* to allow
the crypt to be excavated—other than the taxes the Inland Rev-
enue would no doubt demand as its share, of course. Further,
if the treasure is instead a cup, a platter or a stone, then why
continue to conceal that, either? It doesn't make any sense. As
you saw from the protective canopy currently erected outside
over the chapel to enable ongoing restoration and repairs, such
work is badly needed if the building is not to fall into rack and
ruin, and donations are being widely sought for funding. If the
Knights Templar treasure were to be found here, imagine the
publicity value of that, the kind of money that would be generated from books, documentaries, souvenirs, tourists and so
forth. As it now stands, the chapel is really more or less off
the beaten path, so to speak, not considered by most people—
aside from the esoterically inclined, of course—to be much of
an attraction."

"What if...it's the chapel *itself* that is the treasure?" Bryony speculated.

"What do you mean?" the Scotsman queried interestedly.

"I mean that all the ancient philosophies and religions that have given rise over the millennia to secret sects and orders like the Essenes, the Priory of Sion, the Knights Templar, the Freemasons, the Rosicrucians, the Golden Fleece, the Golden Dawn and so on...well, they *aren't* ultimately about money, or even about power, Hamish—or at least, they didn't used to be. They're about the quest for knowledge and enlightenment."

"Agreed."

"So...well...what if Sir William St. Clair intended the structure itself was to be a kind of treasure, to *preserve* knowledge, as it were, by engraving it in stone, in the same way that the Egyptians, for instance, recorded the histories of their pharaohs and kingdoms by carving hieroglyphics into the walls of pyramids and upon obelisks? Would it be so very strange for Sir William to have copied that idea?"

"No. But even so, the chapel *cannot* be the Knights Templar treasure, for the simple reason that it didn't even exist at the time of the Order's persecution and dismantling by Philip the Fair."

"True. However, the Sinclairs were affiliated with the Knights Templar from the very beginning of the Order, so Sir William might have had access somehow to the Templar treasure and employed it in some fashion as the foundation for Rosslyn Chapel. Maybe the *real* Templar treasure was an ancient manuscript of some sort, like the *Book of Abraham the Jew* or the *Voynich Manuscript,* and Sir William had all its symbols carved into the chapel for all posterity. In the Arthurian literature, the Holy Grail is sometimes described as a book, too."

"It's certainly a possibility. However, even if that *is* the case, we're still left with the question of what all the symbology stands for...just precisely how is it to be interpreted? Symbols, of course, are actually a form of shorthand, to be read and understood by those who have been initiated into the Mysteries, while remaining an obscure secret to the ignorant and unen-lightened.''

"Yes, so I suggest that we begin by making a list of every-thing that seems to be of importance here, like the Green Man, the Mason's Pillar and the Apprentice Pillar.''

"To what end?''

"I don't know. But it's as you said, Hamish. We have to start somewhere—and it was *your* idea for us to come here to Rosslyn Chapel in the first place!''

"Yes, it was, wasn't it?'' The Scotsman abruptly grinned at her hugely. "And quite a good one it was, too!''

Sixteen

Herod the Great

Pale Death with impartial tread beats at the poor man's
cottage door and at the palaces of kings.

Odes
—Horace

The City of Jerusalem, the Kingdom of Judaea, 35 B.C.

Herod I—called "the Great"—the King of Judaea, stood
thoughtfully in the splendid Great Hall of his magnificent Great
Palace, surveying the decorative, gold, silver and copper puzzle
box that sat at the center of a high, beautifully sculpted, marble
table that rose at one end of the vast chamber.

"A gift from the Roman General Marcus Antony," the her-
alds had announced when they had carried the box into his
presence.

For his loyalty to Rome, Herod had been made the King of
Judaea, yet some smaller, personal reward from his good friend
and companion had not been unexpected. After all, Herod now
reflected, he had lent considerable financial and military support to Marc Antony in Rome's battles against Parthia. Still,
the puzzle box was clearly such a prize that Herod was somewhat surprised Antony had not sent it instead to Cleopatra, the

Queen of Egypt, under whose seductive spell he was alleged to be falling.

"She will prove the death of you someday," Herod had warned his friend, but to no avail. Antony was bent on his own course of action and would listen to no one.

Ah, well, it was certainly none of his business or concern, Herod reminded himself sharply, deliberately focusing his attention once more on the box. Apparently, the Parthians had stolen it from Sogdiana, and Antony had then seized it from the Parthians, subsequently shipping and entrusting it to Herod for "safekeeping," or so the scroll that had accompanied the puzzle box had declared, Antony being "unable to think of another more deserving of such a trophy."

Was that truly indeed all there was to it? Herod wondered now. Or had Antony, too, suspected that the box had once belonged to the Hebrews—a treasure lost when the Babylonians had twice sacked Jerusalem more than half a millennium ago? At the thought, Herod's inquisitiveness mounted, and a sudden, avid quiver of excitement ran through his body.

Even today in Jerusalem, there were rumors and legends told about just such a puzzle box. It was claimed it had contained an ancient manuscript that King Solomon had used to build his Great Temple. Some said the box and the book had been placed into the Ark of the Covenant, which had later mysteriously disappeared.

Was it actually possible, Herod pondered curiously, that after all this time, the puzzle box had somehow made its way back to Judaea? The idea seemed incredible.

One arm folded across his chest, the other resting on it, hand cupping his chin, he slowly walked around the marble table, studying the box from this angle and that. It certainly *looked* like the box described in the tales he had heard. The precious metals alone were utterly priceless. However, it was really the craftsmanship of the puzzle box that was beyond compare, he reflected. The intricate interleaving of the gold, silver and copper was simply exquisite, unquestionably the work of a supreme master.

"That is the gift from Marc Antony?" his wife, Mariamne, asked as she quietly entered the Great Hall.

"Yes." Herod nodded absently, paying her little heed.

"It's beautiful."

"Yes, it is. I have been admiring it for quite some time now."

"Why have you not opened it?" she inquired.

"For two reasons. One, it appears to possess some kind of a strange energy force, which may be felt when you touch the box, and which grows increasingly stronger and more painful the longer you are in contact with it. And two, in order to open the box, you must first learn the necessary puzzle sequence, the way in which the metal strips have to be pushed into position to release the locking mechanism inside."

Abruptly ceasing his pacing about the marble table and stretching out his hands, Herod demonstrated the procedure for his wife, showing her how the elaborate pieces that formed the box's exterior could be slid out of place, either to the right or the left, on all four sides.

"But…why didn't it open?" Mariamne's face filled with confusion when the box remained closed, despite Herod's tinkering with it.

"Because I have not yet even begun to figure out the proper succession in which the strips must be moved *to* open it," he explained, frowning contemplatively. "You see, there are dozens, perhaps even hundreds, of possible combinations, and even a single mistake will result in the box staying locked. Truly, whoever designed it was utterly brilliant—and perhaps a fiend, as well, I think…."

Seventeen

The Knight's Tour

O, what can ail thee, knight-at-arms,
Alone and palely loitering?
The sedge has withered from the lake,
And no birds sing!

La Belle Dame Sans Merci
—John Keats

En Route from Edinburgh to Mold, Wales, the Present

"So...we now have quite a list of symbols from Rosslyn Chapel," Bryony commented, as she and Hamish climbed back into the Volvo and got back on the road.

"Yes—although I say they can be interpreted in any number of different ways, so I still don't know what you have in mind for us to do with them," Hamish replied. "Esotericists have been studying the chapel for centuries and have yet to come up with any real answers."

"Well, maybe that's because they've all been going about it the wrong way...thinking the symbols were a map of some kind to lead them to a buried Knights Templar treasure of gold, silver and jewels. I just don't believe that's what the symbols are all about. At any rate, we have them in case we need them. So...what do you think we ought to do next?"

"Head for the town of Mold, in Wales."

"Why?" Bryony was clearly bemused. "What's in Mold?"

"A library with one of the world's largest collections devoted to King Arthur. I thought it might be a good idea for us to do some further research on both the Round Table and the Holy Grail, among other things," the Scotsman explained as he drove.

The gray rain continued to fall lightly but steadily, slicking the two-lane highway with a fine coat of moisture that gleamed luminously in the glare of the headlights the Scotsman had switched on. The wipers of the car swished rhythmically across the windshield. The radio played softly, the melodious strains of Heart's "These Dreams," with its lyrics about woods and mist, appropriately filling the vehicle. Beneath her breath, Bryony sang along with the music. Listening to her, Hamish smiled gently to himself. Despite everything, the atmosphere in the Volvo was cozy and congenial. It was hard to believe the two of them were fleeing for their very lives. They might have been out on a Sunday drive.

Three miles north of Carlisle, the Scotsman took the M6 motorway south toward Preston, where he and Bryony stopped for dinner.

"What would you like to do?" he asked, as he pulled slowly into the parking lot of the Blue Boar pub. "Do you want to get a couple of hotel rooms here, set up camp somewhere outside the city or keep on driving?"

"How much longer will it take us to reach Mold?"

"A little under three hours."

"Then I think we should keep on driving. It'll be harder for the Abbey to track us, won't it, if we stay on the move?"

"Yes—as long as we're not leaving behind a paper trail with our names attached to it."

"I guess it's a good thing that we've got plenty of cash, then, isn't it?"

"Yes, but we want to use it as carefully and sparingly as possible. We don't know how long we'll need to make it last."

"Not long, though, I hope."

"No, I hope not, either—but at least long enough for us to

design and upload some sort of a Web site about the Abbey to the Internet and then get information about it to other Web sites, as well. That's one of the things we need to start on right away, if we *are* to have any hope of saving ourselves. Of equal importance, of course, is finding out what those disks your father sent you contain.''

"I agree."

Supper consisted of a savory pot roast served with potatoes, carrots and thick, crusty bread, all of it washed down with a good ale that left Bryony feeling so drowsy that, seeing her yawn tiredly, Hamish insisted on remaining at the wheel.

"Look, even this morning, when you were all bright-eyed and bushy-tailed, it made me nervous for you to drive," he confessed, flashing her an impudent grin. "Number one, *I'm* not used to being chauffeured around by a woman to begin with—or anyone else, for that matter. And number two, *you're* not accustomed to a 'right hooker'—a car with right-hand drive—and you Yanks don't drive on the right side of the road, besides."

"Oh, yes, we do!"

"Okay, I'll grant you that it's the right *lane* in which you drive. Nevertheless, it's still the *wrong* side of the road!"

"Not for the vast majority of the world. Really, it's only you *Brits* who perversely insist on driving in the left lane!"

"And *that,* sweet lady, is one of the reasons why we once ruled an empire upon which the sun never set!"

"'Once' is the operative word in that sentence, Hamish," Bryony asserted, with feigned loftiness, trying to suppress the smile that tugged at the corners of her lips.

"Oh, getting cheeky with me now, are you?"

"If you say so."

"What I say is for you to get in the car, woman—*passenger* side!"

"Oh, getting *bossy* with *me* now, are you?" she inquired archly as the Scotsman opened the door of the Volvo for her, waiting until she had settled herself inside before he leaned in to fasten her seat belt firmly for her.

"If you say so," he rejoined, kissing her swiftly but deeply on the mouth to silence any retort she might have made, before he slammed the door shut, then walked around the automobile to slide into the driver's seat beside her, a smug smile of satisfaction curving his lips.

Next to him, Bryony sat speechless, her mouth tingling and her heart beating fast in her breast.

Darkness had long since fallen on the town of Mold, and along the two-lane High Street, the reproduction, old-fashioned, double-lantern streetlamps lining either side glowed softly, illuminating a mélange of buildings that encompassed architectural styles from Tudor to modern. At one end of the street, the Late Perpendicular tower of St. Mary's church rose, as though keeping a protective watch over the small town. At this late-evening hour, the shops were all closed, and traffic was light.

"The library's not open now, obviously," the Scotsman pointed out. "So we won't be able to visit it until tomorrow morning. Meanwhile, I believe we ought to check into the closest hotel and apply ourselves to the Web site idea and your father's CDs, all of which—for lack of electricity—will be rather more difficult to do if we set up camp instead."

"Right. However, would you mind stopping at a convenience store first, Hamish? Since we're clearly going to be working late, I'd like to get some sandwiches, potato chips and colas, just in case we get hungry and thirsty later on. I doubt that any hotel here will have twenty-four-hour room service."

"No, hardly. Good idea."

They had a cooler with their camping gear, so they were able to fill it with ice, sandwiches, potato chips, and Cokes and Pepsis bought at the Tesco hypermarket. After that, paying cash and employing the fictitious names on their camouflage passports, they checked in to the Bryn Awel Hotel, deciding—in the interest of holding down expenses and because they planned to labor until the wee hours—to rent only one room, with two double beds.

"I trust you intend to behave yourself," Bryony said, as she and Hamish unloaded what they needed from the Volvo and made their way to the hotel room.

"I always do." The Scotsman grinned at her insolently, in the fashion she had come to expect.

"No, you don't! You're incorrigible!"

"Guilty as charged. Do you want the loo first?" he queried after unlocking the door and switching on the lights. He set their bags down in the middle of the floor.

"No, I'm bound to take longer than you. So, please, you go ahead."

"Thanks. I'll just grab a quick shower, then."

While Hamish was in the bathroom, Bryony unpacked her laptop computer, setting it up on the desk, plugging it in, then booting it up. After logging online, she ran a quick check of her e-mail, finding nothing of any importance. Deleting all the obvious junk e-mail without even bothering to open it, she logged off and withdrew from her purse the disks her father had sent, inserting the first one into the CD-ROM drive and calling up the list of files it contained. Skipping the *Introduction*, she clicked on the second file, titled *Chapter One*. As usual, she was then asked to enter the password.

"Damn." Scowling, she bit her lower lip, vexed and stymied.

"What's wrong?" Without warning, the Scotsman stepped from the bathroom.

Bryony had been so engrossed in working at her laptop that she had not heard the faucet shut off, signaling his exit. With a thick towel, Hamish tousled his dark, dripping-wet hair. Except for another such towel, wrapped around his hips, he was completely naked. Bryony's breath caught in her throat at the sight of him. He was simply gorgeous, she thought. He had the lean, hard-muscled body of a distance runner...broad shoulders tapering to a firm, flat waist, narrow hips and long legs. Only a faint smattering of fine hair feathered his bare chest, although his powerful thighs and calves were more heavily matted. The white towel slung low at his hips was in stark contrast to his swarthy skin.

"Bryony, I'm very much afraid that if you keep on staring

at me like that, the towel concealing my…er…private attributes is going to be of little use whatsoever in providing me with even a modicum of modesty."

"Oh…*oh!* I'm—I'm so sorry!" she stammered, blushing crimson and, with difficulty, averting her gaze as she realized he was becoming aroused by her perusal of his body.

"No more than I am, I assure you," Hamish growled, abruptly ceasing to dry his hair and hauling the second towel around his hips, as well. "The loo's all yours."

Bryony stood up so swiftly from the desk that she knocked the chair backward on to the floor. Still flushed, she rapidly righted it, cursing under her breath at having been so clumsy— her mood decidedly unimproved as the sound of the Scotsman's low laughter reached her ears.

"You deserve to have your cheeks smacked for your impertinence!" she told him.

"Are you asking me to turn around and bend over?" he inquired, still chuckling with amusement.

"Oh! For shame, Hamish Neville! That's *not* what I meant— and you know it!"

"Well, I'm very glad to hear it. For a minute there, I was afraid I ought to be worried about whether or not *you* were going to behave *yourself!* I'm a perfectly respectable, normal, healthy Scots male, I'll have you know—not into anything kinky!"

Rendered mute by mortification, Bryony impulsively snatched up a pillow from one of the beds and flung it at him. Deftly, he ducked.

"What a termagant! I suspected it from the very beginning, but now, I'm *sure* of it!" he declared insolently. "With a temper like that, you've just *got* to have some Celtic blood in you somewhere!"

"I do. However, I don't intend to stand around here detailing my ancestry to a man who is practically…*naked!*" Opening her luggage, she removed her nightshirt and fresh underwear. "I'm going to take my bath now. While I do, I suggest that *you* see if you can figure out the password my father used to seal the file named *Chapter One* on the two CDs he sent me—because for the life of me, I can't imagine what it might be.''

''What was the password for the *Introduction*?'' Hamish asked, curious.

'''History repeats itself,' all run together twice. But that hasn't worked for *Chapter One*. So the password for each file must be different from all the others.''

''A sensible precaution. However, with the aid of a password cracker, we should be in business shortly.''

''A password cracker? What's that?''

''Exactly what it sounds like...a program that cracks passwords—usually employing a brute-force method. Brutus and Crackerjack are two of the more popular ones, I believe. Whilst you're in the loo, I'll download one from the Internet and start it running. Then we'll be into your father's files before you know it.''

''So much for all of Dad's safeguards, then!''

''No, he was absolutely right to try to protect his files. It's simply that in this day and age, anyone with the proper knowledge and the necessary time and opportunity can usually manage to circumvent almost all security measures.''

When Bryony emerged from the bathroom, it was to discover that in her absence, Hamish had donned a burgundy, silk robe and a matching pair of pyjama bottoms. He looked very handsome and casually elegant in them, she thought, like some yesteryear lord of the manor, seated at the desk, smoking a cigarette and drinking a Pepsi, his concentration focused on the laptop computer's screen, where combinations of letters and numbers were running in rapid sequence. Even as she watched, utterly fascinated, the password-cracker program discerned the correct combination and locked it in.

''Open Sesame,'' the Scotsman murmured, hitting the Enter key, and the *Chapter One* file itself abruptly appeared on the screen.

''But...it's gibberish!'' Bryony exclaimed, in utter disappointment.

''No, sweet lady, it's in code. You look delightful.'' His dark, hawkish eyes smoldered like twin embers, roaming appreciatively over her slender figure and long, bare legs, revealed by the nightshirt she was now wearing.

Beneath it, she wore only a pair of French-cut panties, so that her full, round breasts were free under the cotton material. At his scrutiny, her nipples involuntarily tautened and peaked against the fabric. Feeling suddenly naked, she crossed her arms over her breasts.

"They're lovely. Why do you hide them from me—especially when I both saw and tasted them only this morning?" he inquired softly.

"I don't know. I just..." She paused, swallowing hard, then continued. "Look, Hamish, it's...been a long time for me, that's all."

"For me, too—believe it or not."

"Well, then, you must know how difficult it is when you...haven't been with anyone for a while. It's always a little nerve-racking, anyway, with somebody new, and when you're out of practice...well, it's almost like the very first time all over again, isn't it?"

"Yes, it is. Don't worry. I understand. You need time. Perhaps we both do. But the attraction's there, Bryony, and for whatever reason...chemistry, pheremones, good vibrations...it's incredibly strong. You know that. I've felt it from the very start, and so have you. Sooner or later, we *will* do something about it."

"Yes, I know. But not tonight, please."

"No, you're right, not tonight. Because tonight, we need to determine exactly how your father encrypted these files. Did he play chess, by any chance?"

"Yes...why? How did you know?"

"Most people who are inclined toward arcana and esoterics usually do. As to the why, are you familiar with something called the 'Knight's Tour'?"

"Of course. It's a kind of...logics puzzle," she said slowly, frowning, "having something to do with mathematics, as I recall, wherein one moves the knight on a chessboard to every single square, without ever landing on the same one twice. What makes it so very difficult is the fact that one has to use the knight's regular pattern of movement to do it—two vertical squares up or down, followed by one horizontal square right or left, or vice versa. So solving the puzzle requires a specific formula, of which there are many, depending upon the size of the chessboard used and the square on which the knight begins the tour. A Closed Tour is even harder, because the knight has to end up on the same square upon which it started.''

''All absolutely correct. I'm guessing that your father employed the Knight's Tour to encode his files. The coded parchments of Rennes-le-Château, you will remember, were also encrypted using the same device.''

''That's right, they were. But, Hamish, if that's the case with Dad's own files, then it could take weeks, months, or even years to decode them!''

''If we didn't have computers and the Internet, yes, it could. Fortunately for us, there are Web sites where Knight's Tour formulas can be run in seconds, so, thankfully, we won't have to do any of the highly complex mathematical computations by hand. All we'll have to do is figure out what size chessboard your father actually used—whether it was a standard eight-by-eight-squares board, or a sixteen-by-sixteen-squares board, whatever, and on what square he began the tour.''

''Then I think we should try the eight-by-eight-squares board first,'' Bryony suggested. ''After all, eight is an esoterically significant number, associated with Isis, Infinity and the quadrivium of Pythagoras, among other things.''

''Agreed.''

It took them until one o'clock in the morning to decrypt *Chapter One*. But in the end, they had something that was no longer incoherent. It read, in part:

Chapter One: The Fount

According to legends, Galahad is the only Arthurian knight who ever succeeded in finding the Holy Grail, and Nicolas Flamel is the only alchemist who ever succeeded in finding the Philosopher's Stone. What did these two men have in common? Galahad was pure in body, heart, mind and spirit; he did not seek to profit from the Grail, but died of overwhelming joy after he had found it. Nicolas Flamel may also be said to have been pure in body, heart, mind and spirit; he did not seek to profit from the Philosopher's Stone, but instead employed his newfound riches for the benefit of others much less fortunate than he.

There is a lesson to the wise in this, Daughter, and it is this: The great, secret treasure that men have sought for millennia cannot be attained by the ignorant, the unworthy and the evil. Therefore, it cannot be a treasure in the monetary sense, consisting of gold, silver, jewels and so forth, as so many have hoped and believed, and have murdered and died for. It is my own belief that this treasure is, instead, a book—an ancient manuscript that is the common well or source of all knowledge and enlightenment here on earth, and from which, over the millennia, bits and pieces have been copied to make their way into the world as a whole.

If one studies the cosmologies, myths, legends, fables and fairy tales of all the ancient peoples, one can clearly see that, as scholars like Immanuel Velikovsky, Robert Graves and others have proposed in part in their own works, these stories, in one fashion or another, recount the very same narratives over and over, indicating that all we know of such things originally sprang from a single fount of wisdom and learning.

For lack of any more certain name, I call this common well Alphêus, in honor of the renowned underground stream of Arcadia. No doubt, this source has had many different names over the millennia. One could just as easily call it Atlantis, Avalon, the Elysian Plain, the Fortunate Isles, the Isle of Apples, or any other such name known to us. There are literally hundreds. Further, I believe this fount was—once—a very real place, and not simply an imaginary "Otherworld" or an equivalent of the Christian Heaven.

In addition, I think that at this place, something catastrophic happened, leaving it a "Land of the Dead," about which there are also many accounts worldwide. On our planet, which we are now able to chart from outer space and so know the entirety of, there is only one continent that may legitimately be referred to as being "dead"— Antarctica. Our scientists would have us believe it has been a frozen wasteland now for millions of years. Yet, it is in Antarctica that we find an actual "underground stream"—Lake Vostok—which lies mysteriously unfrozen and fluid beneath the continent's icy, snowbound surface. Some have suggested that this is due to heat from volcanic fissures, although this is a theory that has yet to be proved.

What else lies beneath Antarctica's surface, we do not yet know. However, it is worth considering the fact that the continent has been unthawed much more recently than our scientists would have us believe—especially in light of maps such as those of Piri Reis, which appear to show the actual coastline of Antarctica beneath its layers of ice and snow, and which we ourselves were unable to chart accurately until the twentieth century.

We must remember that science, like our so-called underground stream, is fluid and thus ever-changing and evolving. Intelligent, educated men of science once believed the earth to be flat, and those like Copernicus and Galileo, who insisted it was a sphere, revolving around the sun, were mocked and reviled. The focus of modern scientists may be said to be equally narrow, uncompromising and ignorant, for even men who are ultimately misguided in their beliefs and hypotheses may still ask wholly legitimate questions, which demand reasonable answers. For scientists to blindly and resolutely discount stories told time and again worldwide is as foolish an approach to the Mysteries as is that of esotericists who, with equal blindness and determination, discount proven science.

Ultimately, however, whether Antarctica or some other place was our original fount is irrelevant. What is important is the recognition and acknowledgment of the common well or source itself by all men, for it is only in the spirit of both curiosity and cooperation that true wisdom and understanding are achieved.

"So...what do you think?" Bryony asked, after she and Hamish had finished reading the chapter. "Do you believe my father had gone completely around the bend?"

"No, because much of what he's said ties in with what we've already theorized ourselves. I *am* skeptical about his conclusions with regard to Antarctica, since there are many legitimate reasons as to why it has probably not been unthawed much more recently than scientists currently hypothesize. However, I will grant you that it's entirely possible that, tomorrow, some new scientific discovery will turn that thinking totally in another direction. Lake Vostok *is* an anomaly, for which there are no as-yet-proved theories. It *shouldn't* exist. Yet, somehow, it *does*. With regard to there having been a common well or source or fount—whatever one wants to call it—for all ancient, worldly knowledge, on that point, I would agree with your father, since it is true that the cosmologies, myths, legends, fables and fairy tales of the ancient peoples do all have clearly recognizable common themes. The dragon, for instance, is depicted worldwide, despite the fact that no such creature is known ever to have existed—its closest approximation being certain dinosaurs, all of which were, however, long extinct before the advent of humankind. The Green Man, of which there are so many carvings at Rosslyn Chapel, is another example of a universal figure."

"And what do you think the Green Man symbolizes?"

"Well, in Egyptian culture, Osiris is usually painted either green or black, and the green Osiris is symbolic of fertility. In one form or another, green has always been the color of fertility, rebirth, hope and renewal, representing, in ancient civilizations, the difference between the desert and the oasis, and therefore between death and life. Similarly, throughout Europe, evergreens such as the mistletoe, myrtle, and fir, pine and yew trees became symbols of survival when the rest of nature withered during the long, dark winter months. Our own tradition of erecting a Christmas tree, for instance, derives not from Martin Luther, as is popularly believed, but directly from the pagan practice of bringing evergreens into houses for good luck during the winter season.''

"Yes, that was a custom of the ancient Celts and Scandinavians, whose Green Man may also be associated with the Celtic 'Cult of the Head.' The Celts were headhunters, severing and preserving heads because they believed them to contain the immortal soul. In the Celtic myth of Brân the Blessed, his disembodied head was thought not only to hold his soul, but also to ensure fertility and ward off plague and Britain's enemies.''

"All of which is also consistent with the Knights Templar and their own 'Cult of the Head'—the so-called Baphomet, which is most likely a corruption of the Arabic *Abufihamet*, which means 'Father of Understanding.' However, the Dead Sea Scroll scholar Hugh Schonfield also applied the Atbash cipher, an esoteric code employed by the Essenes to disguise the true meanings of their scriptures, to the name 'Baphomet' and came up with the word 'Sophia,' which was one of the names of the ancient goddess of wisdom, and who is generally associated with Isis or the Black Madonna. At any rate, the Baphomet head was alleged to have been able to cause seeds to germinate and trees to blossom.''

"Father *was* right, Hamish! Because even with only this small amount of information, we can already start to see all the commonalities! The question now is, once again…what does it all mean?''

"That, dear lady, I suggest that we leave until tomorrow. It's late, and we need to get some sleep, so we can make an early start in the morning. The Arthurian collection at the Mold library is extensive, so it will take us quite some time to sort through it all.''

"And just what is it that you hope to find there?''

The Scotsman shook his head.

"I don't know…maybe nothing, maybe everything. We'll just have to wait and see.''

Eighteen

The Library

Thou art the book,
The library whereon I look.

An Exequy
—Henry King

Mold, Wales, the Present

The following morning when Bryony opened the curtains in their hotel room at the Bryn Awel, she could see the Shire Hall-Crown Court-Library complex shining in the morning light on the slope of the hill directly opposite, a mile away on the other side of the Alyn Valley.

Later that morning, after a breakfast of scrambled eggs, rashers of bacon and slices of toast spread with orange marmalade, it was necessary for Bryony and Hamish, walking hand in hand, to climb a flight of steps to reach the library, before they entered through a set of double, glass doors, and then descended some stairs to the reception desk. Often, this was not manned, Hamish informed her, having himself visited the library previously on more than one occasion. However, today, a librarian was present.

"We'd like to see the Arthurian collection," the Scotsman told the woman.

"Yes, of course," she replied. "Won't you please follow me?"

After taking a key from the reception desk, she escorted them down a T-shaped corridor, turning left into the hallway that led to the business–reference library. There, immediately on their left, was a blank, wooden door, which bore a plate engraved with the words *Arthurian Collection*. Inserting the key into the lock, the librarian opened the door, then stepped aside so that they could enter the room.

"If you need anything else, just let me know," she said politely. "Also, after you have finished consulting the collection, please notify me of that fact, because I'll need to lock up behind you."

"Yes, we will," Hamish answered.

Once the librarian had disappeared back down the corridor, he and Bryony surveyed their surroundings. The walls were lined all around with books and divided into sections that dealt with known history, myth, romance, historical manuscripts and so on. In the center of the room sat a modern library table with four chairs. The only natural light came from long, shallow, frosted windows set high under the ceiling, in one of the walls. The floor was carpeted. All was still and hushed.

"So...what do we do first?" Bryony inquired quietly, awed by the vast amount of material present. Surely, the Mold library's Arthurian collection must rival any other in the world, she thought. "What are we looking for?"

"Any information we can find on the Knights of the Round Table and the Holy Grail." With one hand, he indicated the book-lined shelves. "Name your poison."

"All right, I'll take myth and romance."

The Scotsman smiled broadly.

"Somehow, I just knew you were going to say that! Okay, I'll tackle history and the historical manuscripts. Academically speaking, those are my forte, anyway."

Because of her deep, abiding interest in King Arthur, Bryony was already familiar with a great many of the tomes on the shelves and, in fact, owned copies of several of them herself. Carefully selecting half a dozen books to start, she carried them to the table where Hamish was unpacking her laptop computer, setting it up and plugging it in, so that they could use it to make notes of whatever details they thought might be important.

They labored in companionable silence for several long hours, electing to skip lunch and work straight through the afternoon, until, finally, the waning light filtering in through the high, glazed windows of the room warned them that the day was growing late.

"Do you think we ought to return tomorrow?" Bryony queried, utterly loath to leave the room, even though she knew it must be nearing closing time for the library. "It seems we've hardly made even a dent in all this material. We could spend days here…weeks…months…." Her voice trailed away as she observed Hamish's amusement. "All right, maybe *you* couldn't. But *I* certainly could. Ever since I was a child, I've been completely fascinated by King Arthur."

"Never mind about him!" the Scotsman rejoined, shaking his head and grinning at her. "What conclusions have you reached about the Round Table and the Holy Grail?"

"Well, let's see. The Round Table *may* actually have been some kind of a tangible object, since it is alleged to have belonged to Arthur's father, Uther Pendragon, before having passed to Arthur himself, which is a fact that many Arthurian scholars frequently overlook. It's claimed to have been everything from a real table to an astronomical observatory of some sort. There appear originally to have been anywhere from twelve to twenty-four Knights of the Round Table, excluding Arthur, which number, however, gradually increased over the centuries to a grand total of one hundred and fifty. However, this is apparently due directly to the existence of several Welsh lists naming the various knights, and which lists are patently muddled and corrupt. So it's entirely possible that there may be some basis for the Abbey believing there *were* only twelve knights in the beginning, just as there were twelve Apostles."

"Yes, that coincides with my own findings, as well. It's interesting that the Abbey has cast Arthur into the role of a reincarnated Jesus Christ, however, because Arthur doesn't seem to have been viewed by those of his own time period as a messiah figure. It is only after his death that he appears to have been perceived in that particular light—especially, believe it or not, by modern Arthurian scholars, who have attributed to him the part of a hero who held back the so-called Darkness of the legendary Celtic Twilight.''

"True—by allegedly saving Britain as long as possible from the barbarian Saxon hordes, so that by the time they finally *did* overrun the country, they were more educated and inclined toward Christianity. As for the Holy Grail, it's difficult to say when it first began to be fused with Christian themes. However, it's clear that it was *not* originally associated with either Jesus Christ or John the Baptist. In fact, although, as we've noted, the Grail is usually depicted as a cup or a platter or a stone, it is in some texts described as a *book,* Hamish, just as I told you!''

"In light of your father's disks, that's really a fascinating idea, isn't it?''

"Yes, it is.'' Bryony paused, then continued. "I've been giving a great deal of thought to all this wisdom and death business, Hamish. In the Christian context, of course, death is something that was brought to Man by the Serpent, Lucifer, in the Garden of Eden. But in reality, death is a concept that can only be understood by beings of higher intelligence. Animals, for instance, undoubtedly recognize when another creature is dead. But it's probably safe, even so, to say that they still don't fully comprehend all the nuances of death itself. In fact, it is, to date, *only* with the advent of the Neanderthals that we begin to see actual archaeological evidence of ritual burials, as though the Neanderthals had evolved to a level of higher intelligence than Man's previous ancestors, or else that through whatever unknown means, a level of higher intelligence had somehow been *introduced* into the Neanderthals. We know they had large brains, just as we ourselves do. They may even have been capable of rudimentary speech. So the idea that we ourselves—meaning Mankind—may have been a host for something alien cannot, I don't think, be dismissively discounted.''

"Echoes of David Wood, et al.''

"David Wood? Who's he?"

"The author of a book titled *Starmaster Paladin,* and who has proposed that extraterrestrial beings landed on our planet and, by whatever means, whether through artificial insemination or actual physical copulation, introduced alien genetic material into our prehistoric ancestors. Even the Bible clearly states that the 'Sons of Heaven' came down to earth and mated with the 'Daughters of Men,' although in this regard, I believe the so-called Sons are viewed in the guise of angels rather than space travelers, obviously. They are also known as the 'Lords of Light.'"

"Indeed. However, it's just as Dad said about the common well, source or fount. *What* one calls such beings really doesn't matter, does it? Ultimately, it's the notion itself that's important—and you have to admit that the possibility that something not of *this* world *was* somehow introduced into our prehistoric ancestors does at least exist."

"I don't deny that it does. Personally, I find it an engrossing concept, in fact. However, like much else, it remains mere speculation at this point...a theory for which there is—Erich Von Däniken and his fraudulent clay pots not withstanding—absolutely no hard evidence whatsoever. Oh, yes, we *can* point to such archaeological mysteries as the Egyptian and Chinese pyramids, Stonehenge, Chaco Canyon and so forth, and question *how* the ancients could have built such great monuments and cities, all apparently *without* any kind of sophisticated technology to assist them. But the truth is that we don't actually *know* the answers. Hell. We couldn't even begin today to construct the Great Pyramid at Giza ourselves, even with all our modern technology! Still, the fact remains. No one on earth has ever discovered even one single item that can be incontrovertibly proved to have been brought here by extraterrestrial beings—or angels, either, for that matter. Don't you think that if aliens *had* visited our planet, they would invariably have left *something* behind, no matter how small?"

"No, not necessarily—especially if they had some kind of rule like the Prime Directive."

"The Prime Directive? What's that?"

"Well, now, we know you're not a *Star Trek* fan!" Bryony laughed. "It's a regulation on the TV show *Star Trek*, which prevents the Federation from making contact or otherwise interfering with planetary cultures that have not yet developed warp-drive capabilities. What if our hypothetical extraterrestrial beings or angels or whatever one wants to call them had the same sort of rule? And what if a host of them violated that directive and, by some means, *did* introduce alien genetic material into our prehistoric ancestors, which resulted in their evolving to a level of higher intelligence, so they became sentient and thus eventually grasped, among other such ideas, the concept and significance of death? How might those same extraterrestrial beings or angels have punished their cohorts guilty of such a misdeed? One thought that quickly springs to mind is that they might have marooned them here, *without* any of their actual sophisticated technology, but still retaining their advanced knowledge, so they might have been able to design and oversee the erecting of such monuments as the Pyramids and Stonehenge, for example. They would, in fact, have been our earth's original *architects*, Hamish! The *builders!*"

"I adore it when you get excited like this," the Scotsman drawled, grinning back at her. "Still, this is all only *one* theory—and it may not even be the correct one. So you mustn't let yourself get carried away by all this speculation, sweet lady. Even such lowly creatures as beavers, birds and bees *build* dams, nests and hives!"

"Spoilsport!" Bryony's giggles filled the otherwise quiet library room.

"No, realist. Come on. Let's finish putting the rest of these books away and pack up your laptop. Whilst we now have plenty of food for thought, we have *not* had plenty of food to *eat*, and I'm starving."

"You're *always* hungry!"

"Yes—however, not *always* for *food!*" His dark, gleaming eyes slowly raked her curvaceous body appreciatively, causing her to blush.

"That observation, Hamish, is going to cost you a prime-rib

dinner,'' she asserted, ''complete with a tossed salad and a baked potato smothered with butter.''

''Yes, well, fortunately, I know just the place here to get all that. All that remains for us to decide now is what we're going to have for dessert.''

''Each other. No, don't deny it! I *know* that's what you were thinking!''

''What? You mean *you* weren't?''

Stubbornly, Bryony refused to answer. But she was unable to conceal the fact that her shoulders shook with silent mirth—which only made Hamish's gaze sparkle even more speculatively and sensuously with the heat of desire.

Nineteen

Young Constantine

This is the forest primeval. The murmuring pines and the hemlocks...
Stand like Druids of old.

Evangeline
—Henry Wadsworth Longfellow

The Countryside, Britain, 306 A.D.

From the ranks of the Roman army, Constantius I, called Chlorus—"the Pale"—had become Emperor of the West. He had begun his career as a protector, a tribunus, and a praeses Dalmatiarum. By 288, he had become the Praetorian Prefect of the western Emperor Maximianus Herculius, and five years after that, he had been Maximianus's Caesar. Then, last year, something extraordinary had happened: The eastern Emperor Diocletian had become the first Roman emperor ever to abdicate, due to his having contracted a nearly fatal illness the year before, and he had forced Maximianus to abdicate, as well. The result was that Diocletian's Caesar, Galerius, had been named Emperor in the East, while Constantius had achieved the same rank in the West.

However, to prevent discord and as a sign of good faith,

Constantius had been compelled to leave his oldest son, Constantine, as a hostage with Galerius.

But now, all that was changed, thanks to the fierce, marauding Picti—the "Painted People"—who continued to defy Rome and to attack Britain. Down from the wild, northern highlands, the Picts came, in savage, screaming hordes, their small but strong, dark bodies fearsomely tattooed with blue woad and often naked, as well, their deadly, iron spears glinting in the sunlight. They spoke a strange language none save a few of their Celtic kinsmen understood, and they stubbornly refused to submit to Roman rule, violently attacking without warning, then retreating into the rough hills and deep woods of Britain and Caledonia instead.

Just short of a decade ago, Constantius had commanded an army that had sailed to Britain to put down the revolt of the murderous usurper Allectus. Now, Constantius had voyaged again to Britain—and this time, his son Constantine was at his side.

"Britain is not at all as I expected," Constantine commented now, as he rode at his father's side, toward the northern city of Eboracum.

"No, Son, as we have everywhere else, Rome has managed to successfully establish a civilized culture here in Britain. It is only the Picts in the far north of the island, along with their barbaric Celtic kinsmen across the sea in Hibernia, who continue to resist Roman rule here and to attack Britain. But even over these, we shall eventually triumph, I have no doubt."

"They hold many interesting beliefs, these Britons."

"Yes, indeed they do." Constantius nodded, taking pride and pleasure in his eldest son's company and conversation. "That's one of the reasons why I brought the puzzle box and the ancient manuscript it contains to Britain with us. The last time I was here, I was unable to come ashore myself. However my Praetorian Prefect landed and returned with many fascinating stories about the Britons and, in particular, their spiritual leaders, the Druids. I don't think Rome has ever truly succeeded in destroying these last, as is popularly believed. I think many of them have simply gone underground or become Christian monks. I hope to meet some of them while we are here. It is said that they spend fully twenty years studying, learning vast amounts of information by committing it to memory, for they are forbidden to write it down, and their knowledge is said to be so great that even such esteemed men as the Greek mathematician Pythagoras held them in the deepest of respect and admiration.''

"Have the box and the book always belonged to Rome, Father?''

"No. Following a riot at Caesarea, Gessius Florus, then Procurator of Judaea, as punishment for the uprising, confiscated the Temple treasury at Jerusalem, at which time the box and its manuscript were seized and brought to Rome, where they have remained until now. I do not trust Galerius. So that is why I thought it best to bring them here to Britain with us. Besides which, it may be that these Britons' Druids can indeed shed some light on the book's contents. Despite more than two centuries of study, the few Roman scholars who have been entrusted with the tome have still come up with far more questions than answers about its text and diagrams.''

"What do *you* believe the manuscript says, Father?''

"I'm not sure,'' the elder man replied soberly. "It seems to elucidate upon the means to open some vast cosmic gate. Yet legend claims that when King Nebuchadnezzar the Second of Babylonia attempted to build just such a great gate to the Gods, they grew exceedingly angry with him and struck it down, so terrifying all those present that they began to babble hysterically in a confusion of tongues.''

"Perhaps Nebuchadnezzar didn't have the box and the book to help him,'' Constantine suggested.

"Perhaps not. But then, again, perhaps he did. Who can say for certain one way or the other?'' Constantius shrugged carelessly. "The tome is incredibly ancient, and the language in which it is written unknown, and like no other, besides. So who can know who authored the manuscript, through whose hands it may have passed over the millennia, or what it has wrought upon this earth—and whether for good or ill…?''

Twenty

The Silver Wheel

It was a wine jar when the molding began:
as the wheel runs round, why does it turn out
a water pitcher?

Epistles
—Horace

The ever-whirling wheel
Of Change; the which all mortal things doth sway.

The Faerie Queene
—Edmund Spenser

A Route of Evanescence
With a revolving Wheel—

No. 1463
—Emily Dickinson

Mold, Wales, the Present

"**W**hat do you mean...*you lost them*, Shieldbearer?"

The Nautonnier's voice was the iciest that Shieldbearer had
ever heard it, so icy, in fact, that it seemed to freeze him right
through, so that his entire body shuddered violently, as though

he had been exposed to the full, merciless blast of a raw, Arctic wind.

"I-I mean just that, Nautonnier," Shieldbearer stammered nervously. "The woman and Neville evidently discovered the tracking device that Cauldronbearer had concealed on Neville's Volvo, and they removed it, placing it on a lorry to mislead us."

"Are you telling me that for the past few days, you and Lancebearer have been trailing a goddamned *truck?*" The Grand Master's tone was not only angry, but also incredulous.

"Y-Y-Yes, Nautonnier, I'm afraid so."

The silence that followed this unfortunate admission was so long and deafening that Shieldbearer thought his superior had abruptly severed the connection, as usual, except for the fact that no dial tone buzzed in his ear.

"N-N-Nautonnier...?"

"You and Lancebearer have failed, Shieldbearer." The cold, sibilant accusation rang like a death knell across the telephone line. "There must be retribution for that. In the meantime, I am sending Swordbearer to assist the two of you. You will continue your search—which you will now broaden in scope to include the whole of Europe. I do not expect your task will be easy. By this time, Bryony St. Blaze and Neville could be almost anywhere, unquestionably traveling under assumed names and, if they are smart—and I do not doubt that they are—taking care that there will be no paper trail left behind them for us to follow. Therefore, I am also dispatching Torchbearer to help you. You and Lancebearer are to make full use of both his and Swordbearer's talents. Do you understand me? There are to be no more slipups! Is that clear, Shieldbearer?"

"Crystal. Do we continue merely to maintain surveillance on them, or have your orders in this regard changed, Nautonnier?"

"No, for the moment, I only want the two of them located and carefully watched. Obviously, Neville must have been planning this escape of theirs ever since he met the woman—which can only mean one of two things. Either the bloody, damned bastard's letting his hormones do his thinking for him, or else her father did indeed give her something of great value…something to do with the Knights Templar treasure, I suspect…perhaps even the very site of its hiding place! If that is so, then we must risk allowing the two of them to live a little while longer. If, after all these centuries, the treasure can be found, then the power of the Abbey will be elevated to unconquerable heights!'' The Grand Master's voice swelled with triumph.

"Yes, Nautonnier."

"However, if we should discover that Neville is only desirous of bedding Ms. St. Blaze, or of locating and keeping the treasure for himself, then we will have time enough to be rid of them both. Obviously, since there has been no trouble with the police, Neville either does not know the Abbey was behind the assault upon his cottage—which, given his and the woman's flight, seems highly unlikely—or else he has, for whatever reasons of his own, decided to keep his mouth shut about the Abbey's existence—at least for the time being. That is the one thing that gives me hope, Shieldbearer, that his chosen course of action may be an attempt to prove his worthiness to us.''

"If you say so. However, I remind you, Nautonnier, that as you yourself have noted on more than one occasion in the past, he *is* Mordred, the traitor.''

"Quite so—and we must never forget that. Still, it is never wise to burn a bridge unless and until one is very certain one will not ever need to cross it again.''

Shieldbearer was unsurprised—and vastly relieved—that with those parting words, he was treated to the sudden buzzing of the dial tone in his ear.

Following supper, Bryony and Hamish returned to their hotel room at the Bryn Awel, strolling hand in hand along the sidewalks illuminated by the glowing streetlamps. The spring night was clear and cool. Overhead, the nearly full moon shone as lustrous as a pearl in the black-velvet firmament, and the stars twinkled like a scattering of tiny diamonds. Through the mountains and hills, the valleys and glens, the wind whispered as softly as a sigh, and the greening leaves of the trees rustled.

Once, centuries ago, on nights just as this one, Celtic and Pictish warriors had roamed this wild, rugged land, Bryony thought, and the Druids had enacted their sacred rituals. The ruins of ancient hill forts were still to be found here atop knolls like Moel y Gaer, and later, medieval fortresses rose at places like Conwy, Denbigh and Flint. At the heart of Mold itself, a park commemorated the site of the old motte-and-bailey castle that had once stood on Bailey Hill.

"Although I know it's not so, the land on this side of the Atlantic always seems far older to me than that on my own side," she told Hamish quietly as they walked on toward the hotel. "I suppose it's because, with a few exceptions, history just doesn't seem to live and breathe in the Americas the way it does here in Europe, and in Africa and Asia, too. Unfortunately, we don't have any hill forts or castles."

"No, but even so, your Native Americans are not so very different, in some respects, to the Celtic and Pictish warriors of Britain, as well as other ancient peoples of Europe. Your Comanches, for instance, were horsemen to compare with the Celts and Scythians of old, and the white buffalo sacred to the Sioux and other Indian tribes is simply another version of the white bull revered by the Celts and Minoans, among others."

"More universal symbols?"

"Yes, if you like."

"It's actually quite fascinating how the bull seems to have become such a cult figure during the Age of Taurus, while the same may be said of the ram and the Age of Aries, and the fish and the Age of Pisces. And now, as the song goes, it is the dawning of the Age of Aquarius. If the pattern holds true, then we should expect to see depictions of the water bearer prevail throughout the next two thousand years."

"How so? In truth, astrology is something about which I know very little, compared to other arcana and esoterics," Hamish confessed.

"Really? That surprises me, because the art of astrology is quite ancient—as old as Babylonia, at least. The word *zodiac* is Greek, meaning 'circle of animals,' and it refers, of course, to the twelve astrological constellations that gird the Earth, the *Arianrhod* or 'Silver Wheel,' the Celts called it. As far as individual birth signs go, the zodiac proceeds through the twelve constellations from Aries to Pisces, with each change from one to the next occurring approximately every thirty days. However, for various astronomical reasons, the Earth itself progresses through the signs in exactly the reverse order, from Pisces to Aries, with each change from one to the next occurring approximately every two thousand years. So the Age of Pisces was really the advent of a new astrological cycle. I've always thought it was about all this that Jesus Christ spoke when He said that the first would be last and the last first...Aries being the first sign for individuals and the last for the Earth, in the same way that Pisces is the last sign for individuals and the first for the Earth. All of which means that if Jesus were born in late winter, as many scholars believe, rather than the December twenty-fifth date He is traditionally assigned, He would have been a Piscean, born during the Age of Pisces, making Him both a first and a last, an Alpha and Omega, just as He claimed. And of course, His symbol, the fish, is also the symbol of Pisces."

"I wonder what the Age of Aquarius will bring?"

"I don't know. Like all symbology, it depends on the interpretation of the water bearer."

"And what do you suppose that to be?" the Scotsman inquired.

"Well, traditionally, Aquarius is depicted as a figure pouring water from a jar—as Pandora released all the troubles of the world from a jar or a box. However, a water bearer could actually be a pregnant woman, for example, her belly filled with amniotic fluid, which is virtually indistinguishable from seawater, and the woman herself representative of the Madonna—which might tie in with Isis or the Black Madonna and Sophia, the goddess of wisdom. Alternatively, it could be argued that the Aquarian figure is, in reality, a bearer *over* water, a psychopomp, as it were...Charon ferrying the souls of the dead across the River Styx or Barinthus piloting the souls of the dead across the sea to Avalon.''

"But...that's wonderful!" Hamish exclaimed.

"Why?"

"Because it begins to weave together some of our esoterical threads into a tapestry!"

"How?"

"Well, as you pointed out earlier today, in order to fully understand the concept and significance of death, one must have achieved a level of higher intelligence—or Sophia's wisdom, let us say. Otherwise, death is meaningless, incomprehensible beyond the most primitive of instincts. And rivers like the Styx were underground streams...that is, *sources* of knowledge and enlightenment. So, in other words, to know *death* is to attain enlightenment!"

"Isn't that basically what the Bible and other such holy books preach and promise?"

"Yes. But one doesn't actually have to die, does one, in order to grasp death? You and I are not dead. But we still *know* what death is—and conversely, because of that, we also understand what *life* is. We are sentient beings. We have consciousness. We *know* we exist. The question is...would we be aware of that if we did *not* comprehend death?"

"No," Bryony answered slowly, reflecting soberly on the question. "I don't believe we would. We'd be...well...just like animals, really."

"Exactly! In the Christian context, then, perhaps what the Serpent, Lucifer, brought to Mankind was *not* death itself, but the *knowledge* of death. Perhaps we were never really immortal beings but simply, until that time, did not grasp the concept and significance of death. And it's important that we *do* grasp it, because without that kind of understanding, we can never comprehend the act we have committed in killing another human being, and if we cannot understand that, then we have no reason to avoid war and strive for peace here on Earth."

"No, we don't. That's one of the keys to the Mysteries, Hamish! It *must* be!"

"Yes, I think so, too. However, it's a rather disturbing key, isn't it?"

"In what way?"

"Well, it means that there may not be a heaven, after all, doesn't it? That death really may be nothing more than the end of life, period."

Twenty-One

Love at First Sight

> Who ever loved that loved not at first sight?
>
> *Hero and Leander*
> —Christopher Marlowe

Mold, Wales, the Present

"I just don't believe death is the end, Hamish," Bryony declared as they entered their hotel room at the Bryn Awel and switched on the lights.

"Why not?"

"Well, because for one thing, if it is, then life's really all just a big cheat—like coming to the end of Umberto Eco's book *Foucault's Pendulum* and discovering that the big secret is that there never was any big secret to begin with!"

"Whoever told you that life is fair?"

"I know…I know. It *isn't*. But that's the whole point! If there's no justice or reward to be had anywhere, not even after death, then why bother? If death *is* the end, period, then that would mean that our entire lives are pointless… meaningless, without purpose, that the universe and everything in it are the result of some mere accident or capricious chance—and I simply can't accept that that's so."

"Why not?" Hamish queried again.

"Because there's a pattern and order to it all that isn't consistent with such randomness. The very universe itself is regulated by the laws of physics. Planets have prescribed orbits around the sun. Moons have equally prescribed orbits around the planets. Even comets travel well-defined paths in space—"

"None of which, however, prevents all sorts of objects in the universe from colliding with one another all the time. Meteors, asteroids and even comets smash into planets and so forth. That's one of the causes of craters...why the Earth has such a pockmarked moon."

"Yes, but still, in the grand scheme of things, such events are anomalies, the exception rather than the rule—and even then, such incidents have to be set into motion in accordance with the laws of physics. Suns, planets, moons, comets and so on aren't just blindly wandering all over the place, gleefully bashing one another like a bunch of kids riding the bumper cars at an amusement park!"

"Okay, I'll grant you that. But isn't it entirely possible that that was the case billions of years ago, before the universe finally did settle into some kind of uniformity?"

"I suppose so. However, I tend to believe that if that were true, then every single planet and moon in our whole solar system would be as cratered as the Earth's moon, and that just isn't so—which argues for the fact that there was some kind of regularity in the universe almost from the very start of the Big Bang. So there must have been some master architect or builder of the universe at work...God, the Creator, the Source, whatever one wants to call such an entity. Further, the soul is undoubtedly pure energy, and pure energy doesn't die. It merely transforms its state of being. Thus, at death, the soul must go somewhere, perhaps to heaven or hell, or perhaps elsewhere. Given all that, it seems quite unlikely that death is the end. If it were, I don't know where we would have got ideas about immortality, heaven, hell and reincarnation in the first place."

"All right. I'll buy all that. Truce. We need to return to work on your father's CDs and start assembling a Web site about the Abbey, as well."

"I can do that—if you wouldn't mind driving down to that Tesco hypermarket and getting us some more ice for the cooler, and some more sandwiches, potato chips and colas, too."

"Sounds like a plan to me. I'll be back before you know it." Jingling his keys in one hand, the Scotsman exited the hotel room.

After he had gone, Bryony unpacked her laptop computer, set it up on the desk and plugged it in. As usual, once it had booted up, she checked her e-mail, deleting all the obvious junk. Then she started the password cracker to work on the file titled *Chapter Two* on her father's disks. She decided that while the program was running, she would go ahead and take her turn in the bathroom, leaving it free for Hamish when he came back from the store.

Her head was still in a whirl from all the events of the past several days, and last night, there had not been time for her to do more than quickly shower. Tonight, however, she intended to indulge in a leisurely soak in a hot bath. That always soothed her senses, and Bryony was forced to admit to herself that between having been shot at by members of the Abbey's Round Table, being currently on the lam, and her ever-growing physical, mental, emotional and spiritual attraction to the Scotsman, her nerves were frazzled. To help calm herself, she switched on the radio, finding a station that played a blend of contemporary and oldies mellow pop.

In the bathroom, she turned on the taps, so that steaming water filled the bathtub, and she poured in a generous measure of vanilla bubble bath. The aroma of the sweet fragrance permeated her nostrils as she stripped off her clothes, then wound her long, blond hair up into a French twist, so that it wouldn't get wet in the bathtub. After that, she slid gratefully into the warm, bubbly, perfumed water, wishing that she had some candles to complete the mood. At home, she would have lit at least half a dozen of them. But here, there was only the inevitable, unforgiving glare of a hotel bathroom's light. Shutting her eyes against it, she leaned back in the bathtub, soaking and then wringing out a washcloth, which she laid over her face.

She managed half an hour like this before she heard the sounds of Hamish's return.

"Bryony?" After a moment, he knocked gently on the bathroom door.

"Yes, I'm in here," she called.

"Want some company?" Ill-suppressed glee choked his voice, so that she knew he was grinning to himself at the thought of her naked and blushing in the bathtub at his query.

"You're a wicked man, Hamish Neville!"

A deep, throaty chuckle was his only reply. Hearing it, Bryony giggled quietly to herself. In some obscure corner of her mind, she realized that one of the reasons why she was so very strongly attracted to the Scotsman and enjoyed his company so much was the fact that he was fun and made her laugh. Since her divorce some years ago, she hadn't had a great deal of either fun or laughter in her life. Instead, she had thrown herself into her work, allowing it to consume her. Now and then, of course, she had compelled herself to accept an invitation for a date. But while none of the men she had gone out with had proved disasters, she wouldn't exactly label them successes, either. She hadn't had much of anything in common with any of them, and their friendly but mundane chatter had bored her to tears, although she had known that wasn't their fault.

In fact, up until now, Bryony had felt all her life like a misfit, as though ever since childhood, she had spoken a bizarre foreign language that no one else except her father had ever understood. Because of that, his death had hit her especially hard. Losing a beloved parent was always difficult. But losing someone who grasped the inner workings of your mind and soul, and who knew exactly how to communicate with you, was undeniably traumatic. Hamish had, she recognized, filled a void in her life that would otherwise have proved very dark, lonely and empty indeed. From the very first moment she had ever met him, he had spoken her language. Now, belatedly, she wondered if that were one of the reasons why her father had sent her to the Scotsman. She thought it was probably so. Simon St. Blaze, however eccentric and often irascible, had nevertheless been possessed of an extremely kind heart and thoughtful nature. He had suspected that he might be murdered, and he would have wanted to protect his daughter as much as possible from grief at his death. More than anything else, her father had wished for her to be happy.

And strangely enough, despite everything, she was.

Stepping at last from the bathtub, Bryony gently toweled herself almost dry. Then she generously slathered her entire moist body with the vanilla body cream she used to keep her skin soft and silky. After that, she sprayed herself lightly with the matching vanilla body spray. Carefully, at the mirror over the sink, she reapplied a touch of makeup, then unpinned her heavy mass of tresses and brushed them until they shone. When she had been a child, her paternal grandmother used to tell her that her hair was the color of corn silk. Some of Bryony's most cherished memories were of sitting on her grandmother's front porch, listening to wild, wonderful tales about their Celtic and Pictish ancestors. Whenever she thought about it, she supposed that it must have been there, on that old, cracked, concrete veranda with its wrought-iron-lace railing, that her fascination with King Arthur and the Knights of the Round Table had really been born.

For a moment, sudden tears brimmed in Bryony's eyes at the childhood memories. She had been only eighteen when her beloved grandmother had died, and even now, so many long years later, she still missed her. When she had watched the movie *Peggy Sue Got Married* and Peggy Sue had gone back in time and seen her grandmother alive again, Bryony had without warning begun weeping so profusely that she hadn't been able to stop for hours afterward. As a result, she had never sat through that film again. Now, determinedly, she dashed her tears away, slipping into a pair of white, lacy, French-cut panties and shrugging on one of the cotton nightshirts that she habitually slept in. This one was pink and had fleecy, white sheep on it.

At the sight of herself in it, Bryony was abruptly mortified and didn't know whether to laugh or cry. She had bought the nightshirts because they were practical and comfortable, and nobody was going to see her in them, anyway. But now, she longed for something black, silky, slinky and sexy. She should have bought some new lingerie before leaving the States, she reflected crossly. But, then, she had never dreamed that the Quester was going to turn out to be a tall, dark, handsome Scotsman in his prime, a man she had previously assumed would be her father's age, at least.

"Bryony, have you drowned in there?" Hamish knocked again, this time more peremptorily, startling her from her reverie.

"No, I'm—I'm just now finished and coming out." She slowly unlocked the door and opened it.

"Good thing, too," he declared firmly. "I was really beginning to get worried about you...to wonder if you were all right—"

At that, much to Bryony's embarrassment, the tears she had resolutely brushed away only minutes before suddenly filled her eyes once more, spilling over to trickle down her cheeks.

"Here...here...what's all this, then? I was right. There *is* something wrong!" Crooning to her, the Scotsman gathered her into his arms and, after leading her over to one of the two double beds in the hotel room, sat down upon it and pulled her into his lap, cradling her head against his broad shoulder and stroking her hair. "What's the matter, sweetheart? Can you tell me what's happened to cause all this...to upset you so? Is it...is it something *I've* done? I won't tease you anymore, if that's what's brought all this on, I promise you."

"N-N-No, it isn't that. It isn't that at all," she managed to get out between sobs. "I-I *like* your teasing, Hamish. Really, I do. It's just that...death *isn't* the end. It *can't* be! Because if it is, then I'd—I'd never see my grandmother or my mother or my father again.... And I-I simply won't believe that's true—"

"No, of course it isn't. Bryony, darling, I'm so sorry. I should have been more sensitive to how your father's death has affected you. Naturally, you're still grieving for him."

Sniffling, she nodded.

"I've—I've tried not to dwell on it. Really, I have. But, then, tonight...I don't know...all this talk about—about death—"

"Shh...hush. I know." Reaching over to the nightstand between the two beds, Hamish plucked a tissue from the box that sat there. "Here. Dry your eyes now." Tenderly, he wiped the tears from her cheeks and smoothed back strands of hair from her face.

"I'm sorry," she apologized. "I-I suppose I look all red and ugly now...a complete mess!"

"No, you don't." Hamish smiled at her encouragingly.

"Yes, I know I do." Bryony smiled back at him wanly through her tears. "I'm—I'm not one of those gorgeous women who looks all heart-wrenchingly lovely and tragic when she cries. My mascara and eyeliner run, so I wind up with raccoon eyes. And I've—I've got on this frumpy, old nightshirt, covered with sheep, besides, and I wish I didn't—"

"Oh?" One of the Scotsman's thick, black eyebrows lifted inquisitively, and his smile widened into a grin. "Would you like me to take it off you, then?"

"You're terrible!" She tried but failed to repress an answering grin.

"*You're* wonderful! I adore you, and I want you very badly—raccoon eyes, frumpy, old nightshirt and all. Besides, you know what they say about Scotmen and sheep... I'm head over heels about you. You know that, don't you?"

"No, I don't. You're probably just saying that to be kind."

"Sweetheart, I assure you that kindness is something I retain for those nearest and dearest to my heart—as you have become to me. Otherwise, I suppose—and most people would no doubt agree—I am reclusive and reserved to the point of rudeness, or, at the very least, of brusqueness. Life is far too short for me to be inclined to suffer fools gladly, I fear. You, however, are a treasure...a priceless jewel beyond compare. I need no other. Before you came into my life, I thought I would never find your like in a million years. I had, in fact, quite resigned myself to the idea of growing old alone, of turning into a crazy, cantankerous coot, shut up like a solitary anchorite in my bungalow, with nothing but my books and music for company."

"You could at least get a dog," Bryony pointed out, her mouth so softly vulnerable and tremulous that Hamish couldn't resist kissing it sweetly and lingeringly.

"I'd much rather have *you* instead," he murmured huskily, afterward. "And I warn you that before this is all over, I fully intend to. What do you say, darling? Do you think you could be happy living in Scotland, at Drumrose Cottage, with me?"

"Yes," she whispered breathlessly, feeling suddenly shy. "I do."

"Good—because I'd like that more than anything else in the world, and I mean that with all my heart. So that's all settled, then, isn't it?"

With that, Hamish kissed her again, and Bryony melted in his embrace, clinging to him tightly, reveling in the warmth of his lean, hard body against her own slender, curvaceous one, the ripple of his sinewy muscles beneath her palms. She was grateful for the solace he had offered her, the romantic—as well as the teasing—words he had spoken to her, the tenderness and understanding he had shown to her. But it was not just all that alone that caused her to respond to him now. She wanted him as much as he did her…hungered for him…ached for him. In the face of death, they would make life quicken between them. It was an instinct as age-old as time itself. Without even asking, she knew, somehow, that Hamish felt it, too.

Again and again, his lips tasted hers, as though he had all the time in the world to go on kissing her endlessly, to discover each and every nuance of her mouth, and to explore its sweetness. Delicately, his tongue followed the outline of her lips before parting them to slip inside and drink deeply of the nectar within. With a sigh, her mouth opened and yielded itself to him, like a flower unfurling its petals to life-giving moisture— and that was exactly how Bryony felt, as though she had been parched and dry and dormant for a very long time now, and Hamish were a spring rain, bringing her to life anew.

Perhaps he was her enemy. Deep down inside, she knew that. But still, when she looked at him, she saw in his dark, smoldering eyes only longing and love for her, although the second was something about which he had yet to speak. But his gaze held neither slyness nor guardedness that would have warned her that he was bent on seducing her only to satisfy his lust, and that he withheld his true self from her out of malice and deceit. His eyes were honest with the plethora of emotions that welled inside him as he kissed and caressed her with increasing ardor.

He did not rush her, for he was no callow youth, but a man in his prime, knowledgeable and skilled in the ways of women and their arousal. From her own experience with men, Bryony knew that. Although it might have been a while since Hamish had taken a female to his bed, she marveled at his restraint. He did not simply fling her down upon the mattress and have his will of her. She would not have blamed him if he had. Still, she was glad that he clearly had no intention of hurrying her, meant not only to allay her natural anxiety and feelings of awkwardness, but also to give her every opportunity to change her mind and say no, if she felt so inclined.

One of his slender but strong, sure hands threaded its way through the silky strands of her long, blond hair, tilting her pale countenance up to his own dark visage as his encroaching lips and taunting tongue continued their insistent onslaught upon her mouth and senses. His other hand slid inexorably up her body, from her bare thighs to her covered breasts, his palms gliding in sensuous circles across her tight, hard nipples, which strained against the thin fabric of her nightshirt, causing the slow-burning heat that had, at his first kiss, been ignited within her now to burst into flame, spreading like a raging fever through her entire being. As though delirious, she shivered with mingled nervousness and excitement against him, and a ragged moan that was a sound of both protest and pleasure escaped from her throat.

"Do you want me to stop, sweetheart?" Hamish asked, his voice low and throbbing with emotion, his warm breath a rasp against her lips.

"No...no...I don't...."

"Are you sure?"

"Yes..."

"Then I want very much to see you, darling...all of you...please...."

He pushed the nightshirt up her body, then pulled it off over her head, leaving her clad only in the white, lacy, French-cut panties that she wore underneath. Bryony's initial instinct was to cover herself against him, but this, he would not permit.

"No...no...don't hide yourself from me," he demanded thickly. "You're gorgeous—and I want to see and touch and taste every single, beautiful square inch of you...."

"Aren't you going to undress, too?" she queried softly.

"Yes, in a minute."

He still held her in his lap, and now, once more, he kissed her deeply, his tongue delving between her lips to garland and wreathe her own tongue incitingly. One hand fondled her exposed breasts, cupping and kneading them, thumb and forefinger stimulating their rosy crests, making them tauten and peak even more firmly than before. From their flushed centers, pools of delight radiated throughout her whole body. Her arms tightened around his neck, her fingers tunneling through his thick, glossy, silvery-black hair, before one hand slipped down to his chest, and she began to unfasten his blue, chambray workshirt, yearning to feel him naked against her.

"Witch!" Hamish said, with a low, rueful laugh. "Did no one ever teach you the value of patience?"

"Hmm...no, I guess not." Bryony blushed and buried her head against his shoulder.

But still, emboldened despite herself, she hauled the ends of his workshirt loose from his jeans and drew it from his swarthy torso, running her palm lightly across his bare chest.

"Well...?" he inquired, quirking one eyebrow.

"Well, what?" Feigning innocence, she peeked up at him, her sea-green eyes dancing.

"What about my jeans?"

"What about them?"

"Now, who's the tease?"

"I'm sure I don't know what you mean," she insisted, turning her face into his shoulder again, so that he would not see the mirth that threatened to bubble from her.

"Oh, you don't, do you?" His mouth and hands began to roam leisurely, sensuously, over her body once more, beguiling and titillating her unbearably. "In that case, I suppose I'll just have to show you what happens to my lady love when she wants to play games.''

"What's that?"

"This!"

Without warning, he scooped her up in his powerful embrace and tossed her into the middle of the bed, leaving her gasping for breath and choking with laugher as the weight of his muscular body came down over her, pinning her to the mattress. With one hand, he caught her wrists and pinioned them above her head, his other hand capturing her chin and tipping her face up to his. His legs spread her own, so that she could feel the hard heat of his arousal pressed against the soft, moist heart of her. Suddenly, a hollow, fiery ache seized her there, so that she instinctively longed to be filled by him.

"Now, you're going to be sorry, witch!" Hamish growled, his voice provocative with triumph and smug with glee.

"Oh, I am, am I? Why's that?"

"Because, now, *I* am going to tease *you* until you beg and plead for mercy!" he told her, before his eyes, the color of smoky quartz, abruptly darkened with passion, and his lips seized hers again, hard and hungry now, his tongue shooting deep.

After a moment, he freed her arms, and she wrapped them around his back, fiercely clutching him to her, her palms splayed and playing intensely over his bare flesh, spurring him on. His mouth slashed across her cheek to her temple, the strands of her hair. Bryony could feel his breath, coming harshly against her ear as his own desire and excitement heightened sharply. His teeth nibbled her earlobe lightly, and he muttered words of sex and love there, words that filled her with anticipation and joy, and caused her heart to pound, her blood to sing. One of his hands tangled roughly in her tresses; the other toyed with her full, generous breasts, squeezing them and pressing them high. His lips blazed a trail of kisses down the slender, white column of her throat to the ripe, swollen mounds and closed over one pebbled, pink nipple, sucking covetously, his tongue stabbing her with its heat.

His body rocked slowly, in sweet, savage torment, giving

her no ease, but only increasing her burning need to have him inside her. Whimpers of pleasure and entreaty issued from her throat, but Hamish paid them no heed, moving his mouth instead to her other burgeoning breast, to torture its tightly furled bud as expertly and fervidly as he had its twin. Her fingers entwined in his hair, Bryony strained and writhed beneath him, feeling as though all her bones were somehow dissolving inside her, leaving her entire body a molten, quicksilver mass of painfully exquisite sensation. Everywhere he touched her, she sizzled and melted, like fire and ice, her form melding eagerly to his.

Inflamed and shivering with desire and excitement, breathless in his wake, she kissed and caressed him everywhere she could reach, discovering and exploring the hard planes and angles of his body just as avidly he did her own soft, voluptuous curves. He smelled of cologne and smoke and musk, masculine scents that aroused and dizzied her as she breathed them in deeply. His dark skin tasted of salt when she pressed her lips and tongue to it, bit him gently on one shoulder, eliciting a low, impassioned groan from his throat. The fine, dark hair that lightly matted his broad chest was like silk beneath her palms and against the highly sensitive tips of her breasts, his back as smooth as velvet, its muscles bunching and quivering as he kissed and embraced her, so that she was made acutely aware of his strength in comparison to her own fragility. His corded legs entwined with her supple ones, his erection pressing firmly through his jeans against her, a potent portent. Reaching down, she stroked him, causing him to inhale sharply, his breath catching on a serrated edge. His hand closed over hers, rubbing it even harder against him. Ardently, his mouth sought her own once more, his tongue thrusting deep.

Like the great Silver Wheel of the Celts, time turned, and kept on turning. How much passed, whether minutes or hours, Bryony did not know as she lay in Hamish's arms and let him do as he willed with her. She knew nothing but the irrepressible, exhilarating feelings he evoked in her, that engulfed her like a tide sweeping her away as he touched and tasted her, mouth and tongue and hands unstill. Tantalizing her, he inexorably kissed and licked his way down her rib cage and belly, his tongue swirling and dipping into her navel, before traveling lower still.

His hands grasped her hips, caught hold of her panties, tugged them lingeringly down her long, graceful, bare legs, then tossed the scrap of lacy silk onto the floor. Lowering his head, he pressed fleeting, hot kisses upon her thighs…and then between them, upon the blond down that feathered her lightly there. Then, in a prelude of what was to come, his tongue darted forth to trace the wet, concealed furrow of her, a quick, teasing lap that was agony to Bryony in the face of her craving for assuagement, and that caused her breath to catch raggedly in her throat and then to be released in another low moan of rapture and beseeching.

While she watched, Hamish finally unfastened his button-fly jeans, discarding both them and his briefs, sending them to join her own panties on the floor. Naked then, he knelt before her on the bed, his sex hard and heavy with desire, his hands spreading her thighs wide, so that she lay wholly revealed and vulnerable to him. Her pale, smooth skin gleamed in the soft-glowing lamplight, like the sweet, vanilla fragrance that permeated it, the scent wafting to his nostrils, intoxicating him as surely as though he had drunk long and deep of smoky Scotch. His breath quickened. His groin tightened. She was beautiful, and he wanted her.

He bent his head to Bryony once more, his mouth finding the dark, secret heart of the tender, mellifluous, engorged petals of her that trembled and opened to him of their own exigent accord. His tongue pierced her, dove down into the cinnabar well of her, making her shudder with ecstasy and unendurable yearning. Sensing her suddenly frantic need, Hamish slowly pushed one finger, and then two, deep inside her, only to withdraw them just as torturously, so that her breath caught again on a ragged sob. In response, he slid his fingers into her once more, beginning an age-old rhythm designed to bring her to culmination. All the while, his tongue flicked and circled the tiny, throbbing nub that was the key to her pleasure.

Her fingers burrowed convulsively in Hamish's hair, drawing him even nearer to her. The room misted and spun away as Bryony closed her eyes, no longer even aware of how she arched against his taunting tongue and skillful fingers, but focused solely on her own urgently spiraling need, the tension relentlessly building inside her at the very core of her being. And then her release came, bursting like an explosion within her, overwhelming her, sending such powerful tremors of deep delight throughout her whole body that Hamish felt them, too.

Raising his head and withdrawing his fingers, he poised himself above her. There was between them an interminable instant as highly charged as the air presaging a spring storm, fraught with portent and promise, as though, somehow, all their lives, he and she had been destined for each other, for this joining. Then, at last, he took her, his hard, questing maleness piercing swift and deep and true into her, so that Bryony gasped, then cried out softly at the shock of it. Savagely, his lips smothered her own, swallowing the sound and her breath, his tongue filling and possessing her mouth, just as he himself filled and possessed her. For a moment, he lay still atop her, pushing to the utmost within her, accustoming her to the inexorable, irresistible feel of him inside her, stretching and molding her to accept him, for it had indeed been a while for her.

"You feel divine, my love," Hamish muttered hoarsely against her lips, the hollow of her throat. "I have died and gone to heaven...."

With that, burying his dark visage in the long, tangled mass of her hair, he began to move within her, slowly and steadily at first, his hands beneath her hips, lifting her to receive him as he deliberately ground himself against her, quickly stimulating her to an unbearable pitch. It was as though her body no longer belonged to her at all, but had merged with his to become a part of him. Blind and lost to everything save him, Bryony could do nothing but hold on to him tightly, enfolding him in her embrace, enwrapping him with her long legs, enveloping and immuring him with the slick, heated core of her very being.

Her head thrashed...reeled giddily, as though she were drunk or drugged, as though she had, like Alice, stumbled and fallen down a rabbit hole, although not into Wonderland, but, rather, some dark, tumultuous, atavistic place far removed from the dimly lit hotel room and the bed where she and Hamish made love, the air sharp and sweet with the scent of their now— feverish mating. When her climax came, it was primal, shat- tering, ripping through her like a wild, unbridled wind, as though every single ounce of long suppressed yearning and deep, passionate emotion in her entire body had suddenly been released. Whimpering with unbelievable pleasure, she stiffened beneath him, her back arched, her head flung back, her finger- nails digging into his shoulders, goading him on.

Knowing she had attained her peak, feeling her muscles tighten convulsively around him, the forceful, seemingly end- less waves of ecstasy that rushed through her, overpowering her and sweeping her away, Hamish thrust blindly now into her, his maddened body quickening urgently, frenziedly, against hers. Increasingly harder and faster, he drove into her again and again, until his own throbbing orgasm seized him just as violently and completely, causing the whole length of his body to shudder long and fiercely against her. As he spilled himself inside her, he crushed her to him savagely, crying out, a sound low and dark and harsh with intense emotion and pro- found fulfillment, which mingled rapturously with her own soft keening.

In that moment, they were as one, breast to breast, thigh to thigh, hearts beating in unison, bodies and souls entwined, no space between...no room for another—nor would there ever be.

Twenty-Two

The Last Battle

> I am Merlin
> Who follow the Gleam.

> *Merlin and the Gleam*
> —Alfred, Lord Tennyson

> Follow, follow, follow the gleam,
> Banners unfurled o'er all the world.
> Follow, follow, follow the gleam
> Of the chalice that is the Grail.

> *Follow the Gleam*
> —Sallie Hume Douglas

Glastonia, Britain, 500 A.D.

After three long days, the battle had ended—the last battle—for Arthur, the High King, was dead, as was his much beloved High Queen, Guinevere.

And he, Merlin, Arthur's Archdruid, had gone quite mad with grief at the shock of it all.

The world as he had once known it was gone forever now. All the bright hopes and dreams that the High King and he had quested and fought so long and hard for had been irrevocably destroyed. The ignorant barbarians had brutally murdered bold, glorious Arthur upon the crimson-stained battlefield. In the end, even *they* had been ashamed of their cowardly, ignominious deed, giving Merlin and the High King's six surviving warriors leave to wash and care for his bloodied body—and to build a coffin.

As their ancestors of old had once done for the revered dead, Merlin and the others had felled a huge tree—not an oak or an ash, which were accursed and despised, nor a yew, which was sacred and thus never to be cut down—but a hawthorn tree, as white as sea foam, covered with delicate flowers. Hollowing out its thick trunk, they had fashioned the High King's coffin and carefully placed him inside, folding his arms peacefully across his chest. Just so, they also constructed a coffin for the High Queen, and her ladies had arranged her inside. Then the warriors and the damsels had loaded the corpses onto a gilded barge and brought them here, to Glastonia—the great, powerful tor that pierced the clinging mists, towering eerily over the surrounding marshland, where, some miles to the southeast, the mighty hill fort of Camelot rose.

Merlin and the others had dug the graves deep—sixteen feet—and laid the coffins inside, heads to the east, as tradition dictated. Nine feet up from that, they had placed a lead cross in the ground, then covered the whole with a huge, stone slab, and filled in the remainder of the excavation with the damp dirt. Then they had each gone their separate ways, and the Archdruid had known he would never see any of them again.

Now, he sat beside the rich, dark, freshly turned earth, his head buried in his hands. And he was glad that he had gone clean out of his right mind, for otherwise, he did not think he could have borne the horrific pain and grief. There were some things too deep for tears. All was lost—including Britain's greatest treasures: an ornate, gold, silver and copper puzzle box and the ancient manuscript it contained.

From time's beginning, the box and the book had belonged always to Arthur. Merlin had known that the very first moment the High King had ever laid his strong hands upon the box, his fingers moving surely, sliding first one strip and then another into place in unerring sequence, until the lock had sprung free and the lid had opened to reveal the tome inside. Slowly, Arthur had lifted the manuscript from its resting place. Yet, oddly enough, he had not turned back its cover.

"Do you not intend to open the book, Arthur?" Merlin had inquired curiously.

"No, there is no need."

"May I ask why?"

"Because it is only the three words on the cover that are of importance. They are the same as those engraved on the box, you see."

"Yes, I do. And what do they say?"

"'Remember the word.'" The High King had translated the language as unhesitatingly as he had opened the puzzle box itself.

"And what is the word, Arthur?"

"There are many, Merlin, but only one that matters."

"Yes, but...what *is* the word?" the Archdruid had pressed again.

"When you know that, Merlin, then you will know all," Arthur had responded quietly.

"But, then...what is the purpose of the book?"

At that, the High King had smiled faintly.

"It is for those who do not know the word," he had said.

Now, suddenly, beside the new graves upon the massive tor, the Archdruid leaped to his feet, his solitary figure silhouetted against the westering, fiery-orange sun, his arms outstretched in supplication to the flaming sky, his gnarled, wooden staff held high, his snow-white robe fluttering in the soughing wind, like the wings of an anomalously white raven in flight.

"What is the word?" he cried, his voice rasping and ringing out strangely in the stillness of the marshland. "Tell me! *What is the word?*"

And somehow, as before, Arthur's own melodious voice echoed softly in his ears.

"When you know that, Merlin, then you will know all...."

Twenty-Three

In the Afterglow

O Love, O fire! once he drew
With one long kiss my whole soul thro'
My lips, as sunlight drinketh dew.

Fatima
—Alfred, Lord Tennyson

Mold, Wales, the Present

In the sweet afterglow of their lovemaking, Bryony and Hamish lay quietly together in the double bed of their room at the Bryn Awel hotel, he on his back, one arm wrapped possessively around her, and she on her side, cradled against his chest, her head pillowed upon his shoulder, one thigh covering his. It was an intimately pleasurable embrace, flesh pressed against flesh, their bodies still warm and damp from their lovemaking. In the silence, Hamish smoked a cigarette, its end glowing red-orange in the semidarkness.

"Are you all right, Bryony?" he asked, finally.

"Yes...yes. I'm sorry I broke down earlier. I didn't mean to. I suppose that in some ways, I'm just not as strong as I like to think I am."

"You've nothing to apologize for, darling," he insisted, his voice low, as he stroked her arm soothingly and reassuringly.

You've lost your father, whom you loved—and in a very untimely and horribly brutal fashion. Since then, you've really had little or no time to grieve for him, and you've been thrust into a completely unexpected and dangerous situation that has placed your own life in jeopardy. As well, you've been thrown together with me, a man you hardly know and whom you probably, if you're honest with yourself and with me, still have some slight doubts about, no matter what.''

"I really don't understand how you can say that, Hamish.'' Bryony spoke softly. "I've placed myself totally in your hands, entrusted you with the knowledge of my father's disks, slept with you, and agreed to move in to Drumrose Cottage with you, if that's what you want. Isn't that enough?''

"For the time being, yes. But I'm a realist, sweetheart, and I want you to be sure. I know there's a powerful physical, mental and emotional attraction between us. I've felt it from the very first moment I ever laid eyes on you, and I believe you've felt it, too. And now that you're mine, I don't want to lose you. But I don't want to push you, either.... I guess what I'm trying to say is that I don't want either of us to think that perhaps I've taken advantage of you while you're in a fragile and vulnerable state. That's truly *not* what I intended.''

"No, I don't believe it was. Yes, these past several weeks have been a strain for me. I miss my father deeply, and I'm angry—very *angry*—about the fact that he was so cruelly murdered. He was struck down at a time in his life when he ought to have been taking things easy...socializing with his friends, puttering in his small garden, finding pleasure in his books and, especially, his studies, which always gave him such delight. Deep down inside, his loss has been made more difficult for me, knowing that something to which he had devoted almost his entire life should, in the end, have proved the cause of his death. That is a bitter irony to have to live with, Hamish.''

"Yes, I know, my love. If I were in charge of the world, it would be a much better place, let me tell you! But I'm not, and it isn't. So all I've got to offer you is myself and whatever poor solace I can manage to provide.''

"You *are* a comfort to me!'' Bryony declared, lifting her

head to gaze up at him earnestly. "So please don't think you're not! Because the truth is that I shudder to imagine how terribly alone and frightened I'd feel right now if you hadn't ever come into my life. Earlier, I thought that perhaps that's why Dad had sent me to you. I still think it is—and I'm glad that he did. I *do* have doubts, but not about you, Hamish...not anymore. I worry about what's going to become of us, and whether or not we are going to be able to get out of this alive. Right now, the odds seem overwhelming to me. It's you and me against not only the Abbey, but also the whole world—because we don't know who the Round Table may have in its employ, or what other kinds of resources they may have at their disposal, either. Hell. We don't even know who *they* themselves are...just a bunch of nameless, faceless enemies! I think that's the worst thing of all—not even knowing who it is that we're fighting, and who it was that killed Dad."

"Except for Cauldronbearer, the so-called Roland Kilgour, I wouldn't know any of the others if I saw them on the street. I have to admit I find that a little nerve-racking myself. Nevertheless, we've still got *some* advantages on our side. We made a clean getaway from Scotland, so, at the moment, chances are that the Abbey has little or no idea where we are. That will work in our favor and buy us some time at least, and tomorrow morning, we'll get back on the road again...drive to London. I think it's better if we try to keep on moving and don't stay in any one place too long, don't you?"

"Yes, I do. But...why London?"

"Well, the British Library has a number of historical manuscripts that are relevant to King Arthur, and although the library's in the process of uploading some of them to the Internet, several of the texts simply aren't on the World Wide Web yet. We ought to have a look at them. The Harleian collection, for example, may be of some to use to us, I don't know. I've never before sat down like your father and tried to make one big picture out of all the puzzle pieces. Where does one begin?" After the rhetorical question, Hamish paused briefly. Then he continued.

"Because we know the history of the Abbey of the Divine

and have access to Simon's disks, we've at least managed to home in on some kind of a starting point—the fact that all world cosmologies, myths, legends, fables, fairy tales and so on have a common origin, which your father called Alphêus. While it may *seem* revelatory, however, that's actually not a new idea, but, rather, a very old one. Among countless others, Robert Graves used it in connection with his examination of what he termed the 'White Goddess,' and Immanuel Velikovsky employed it in his own works, such as *Worlds in Collision,* also. The difficulty arises in trying to narrow the focus of one's research. We have managed to do that already, via the Knights Templar, their lost treasure, and the Abbey of the Divine's connection to them, as well as to King Arthur and his Knights of the Round Table. Even so, we've still got an enormous amount of ground to cover and material to work with.''

"Are you saying that our situation is hopeless, then?" Bryony inquired, discouraged.

"No." The Scotsman shook his head, momentarily leaning over to crush out his cigarette in the ashtray. "Simply difficult because we don't yet know what all may be involved, that's all—although we can probably make some educated guesses."

"So, tomorrow, we'll go on to London, then," Bryony said, "and see this Harleian collection for ourselves. What's in it?"

"Among other things, a history collated by a Welsh monk named Nennius, the *Welsh Annals,* and several Welsh genealogies. Whether any of it will be of any help to us or not, who knows? But since it's the Abbey of the Divine we're dealing with, I think we need to understand both the myths and the history that are the framework for their mind set."

"'Know thy enemy,'" she quoted quietly.

"Yes, exactly."

As he looked down at Bryony nestled snugly against his chest, the thought of their adversaries getting their hands on her crossed Hamish's mind. His arm tightened around her, and his eyes darkened once more with a smoldering passion that made her breath catch in her throat. Abruptly tangling his fingers in Bryony's long, blond hair, Hamish deliberately tilted her countenance up to his, claiming her tremulous mouth with a roughness born of strong and primitive emotion. They made love again, urgently, then slept in covetous, close embrace.

Twenty-Four

Retribution

> But when the blast of war blows in our ears,
> Then imitate the action of the tiger;
> Stiffen the sinews, summon up the blood,
> Disguise fair nature with hard-favored rage;
> Then lend the eye a terrible aspect.
>
> *King Henry V*
> —William Shakespeare

London, England, the Present

The next morning, Bryony and Hamish got an early start, the drive to London passing uneventfully but pleasantly and companionably.

This was not Bryony's first visit to the capital city, but it had been some years since she had last seen it. She surveyed the sights eagerly, taking renewed delight in the old-fashioned-looking, black taxis and the bright, red, double-deck buses, in the delightful architecture of Paddington Station, and in the beautiful Regent's Park, which had originally been part of King Henry VIII's great hunting forest.

Fortunate enough to locate a space for the Volvo in the Euro Car Park lot at the St. Pancras train station, Bryony and Hamish paid to park for the day, not knowing how long they would be in the library. Then they stopped off at one of the train station's refreshment outlets, where they bought some sandwiches, "crisps," as the Scotsman called potato chips, and colas for lunch, which they carried away with them as they crossed the street to the library.

First finding an empty bench in the piazza, Hamish and Bryony sat down to enjoy their lunch in the spring sunshine, making something of a picnic of it and, as they ate, tossing crumbs to the cooing pigeons that flocked to the square. Bryony wondered if, seeing the two of them together, passersby knew they were lovers. She thought it was probably so. She and the Scotsman could not seem to keep their eyes and hands from each other, their gazes inevitably meeting and locking, drinking each other in, their fingers constantly touching and interweaving, filling her with a love and joy that she saw reflected on Hamish's dark, hawkish face. They might have been teenagers, she thought, except that there was already a richness and depth to their relationship that was only to be found with age and experience.

Romantic ideals were formed in childhood, Bryony had always believed. But it was only in one's mature, adult years that one fully understood and recognized what it was that one had been searching for all of one's life. Somehow, she knew instinctively that at long last, she had discovered that in Hamish. It was difficult to think she had known him only a short while. It seemed as though they had been friends and lovers since time's beginning. She could not imagine why she had ever thought he might be her enemy. She realized, now, that from the very start of their relationship, he had been intent only on helping and protecting her to the best of his ability.

"Thank you, Hamish," she said quietly, as she fed the last bit of crust from her sandwich to the pigeons.

"For what?" He cocked one eyebrow curiously.

"For everything. With Father's death, the Abbey, and all the rest of it, I…well…I don't honestly know what I would have done without you."

"You're a strong, intelligent, resourceful woman, sweetheart. You would have managed somehow."

"Perhaps. But still, I'm very glad I found you."

"That makes two of us, then. That morning when I first saw you at the airport, it was as though you had stepped out of every dream I'd ever had as a young man. For a moment, I was half afraid you were only a figment of my imagination. Then, when I realized you weren't, I couldn't believe my good luck!" He smiled at her tenderly. "I knew right then that, somehow, some way, I was going to make you mine, no matter what. And as you have no doubt guessed by now, when I put my mind to something, I'm quite determined on succeeding at it—and as quickly as possible!"

"Yes, you are. I can see now that I never really stood a chance against you. I've never lost my head and allowed myself to be swept off my feet before. It's truly most unlike me."

"Are you sorry it happened, darling?"

"No." Bryony shook her head. "I'm not."

"And you never will be, either, I promise you." Leaning over, Hamish kissed her swiftly but passionately on the mouth. "Come on, my lady love. As much as I wish it were otherwise, we just can't afford to sit here all afternoon, idling our time away in this glorious, spring sun."

Once inside the hushed interior of the library complex, the two of them made their way to a reading room and took seats at one of the one hundred and fifty computer terminals available to readers, where they ordered the materials they wanted to peruse. Then, somewhere in the library's inner recesses, a member of the staff searched the vast shelves for the requested information, delivering it to them thirty minutes later.

While waiting for the books, Bryony thought of Hamish, and she felt a warm glow inside at the idea of living with him, of their becoming a couple, husband and wife. She had been alone for far too long, and so had he. Together, the two of them would make a fresh start. Then, at the thought, she shook herself mentally. Before they could do anything, they must find a way to escape from the Abbey of the Divine, and Hamish's plan to upload information about the order to the Internet still seemed their best chance...their *only* real chance, Bryony amended, in her mind. She didn't want to think about what might happen if the Abbey continued to pursue them after that. Perhaps the order would be so angry at being exposed that its Round Table would be bent on revenge. She shivered at the notion.

"Cold?" Hamish inquired solicitously.

"No." Bryony shook her head. "Just...frightened, I suppose. What if we reveal the Abbey's existence to the world—and it doesn't stop the Round Table from trying to kill us?"

"Then we'll have to get some kind of proof about the order, somehow—or else find the Knights Templar treasure."

"Yes, but how will that help us...protect us from the Abbey?"

"Well, I'm certain they wouldn't want details about the treasure and its location uploaded to the Internet!" The Scotsman smiled slowly, wickedly. "In fact, now that I think about it, that threat might be our means of salvation!"

"Possibly. But first, we have to find the treasure!"

"Right. Back to work, then."

They remained at the library, researching, until closing time, when they were finally compelled to leave. By then, dusk had fallen, and the shadows were long and deep between the towering buildings on either side of Euston Road. Bryony, accustomed to being on guard in such situations, was glad that Hamish walked beside her as they crossed the street to the train station and hotel.

As they entered the Euro Car Park lot, she spied the man. Beyond absently noting the stranger's swiftly striding figure coming at them from the opposite direction, wearing a fedora hat and coat, she paid him little heed, assuming that he was, as she and the Scotsman were, merely returning to his automobile. But then, as she and Hamish passed him by, Bryony saw something flicker for the briefest of moments in the man's cold, penetrating gaze as he assessed them, and unwittingly, she stumbled to a halt, surprised and puzzled.

"What is it, sweetheart? Is something wrong?" Hamish asked, when she simply stood there.

"I...I don't know. I'm—I'm not sure. There was... something about that stranger we saw just now. For a minute there, it was as though he was somehow startled to see us. I thought...it was as though he *recognized* us, Hamish! And there was something familiar about him to me—as though I ought to know him...." Her voice trailed away, and she glanced back over her shoulder to where the man now sat in his dark car, talking into a cell phone.

The brim of his fedora was pulled down low over his brow, shadowing his visage. His head was bent to his chest as he held the cell phone to his ear, as though he were either speaking intensely or listening with equal fervor. At the sight of his hunched form in the vehicle, a vague memory stirred deep in Bryony's brain, and then a tiny, icy shiver chased up her spine.

"Oh, my God!" she cried, suddenly gripping Hamish's arm so tightly that he winced. "It's *him!*"

"Who, darling?"

"The man who murdered Dad!"

At that, the Scotsman looked over sharply at the stranger in the vehicle, then back at her.

"How do you know that, Bryony? How can you be sure? Your father was killed in a hit-and-run accident, and there were no witnesses. Even your police have been unable to track down his murderer. Sweetheart, you've been under an enormous strain—"

"Hamish, listen to me, please! It's him—Dad's killer! I know it! He was *at Dad's funeral!* I saw him there, and then again...parked outside on the street at the reception afterward. He was *wearing that same hat and coat!* It's *him,* I tell you...."

Bryony was so certain of this that without even thinking, much less considering the consequences, she began to run toward the stranger's automobile, ignoring the Scotman's urgent, upset shouts of warning behind her as he gave chase. Reaching the car, she wrenched open the driver's door.

"I know who you are, you murdering bastard! You killed my father!"

In the instant that followed her near hysterical accusation, Bryony knew she was right to have made it, for the man's chilling, piercing eyes narrowed, and she could almost see the wheels of his brain churning furiously as he ran rapidly through his options. Without warning, he jerked her into the vehicle, half flinging her into the seat beside him, striking her head painfully against the window of the passenger door. Quickly, not bothering to close the driver's door, he started the engine with a roar and backed the automobile from its space, tires screeching. Then he threw the manual, five-speed gearshift into First and stamped down hard on the accelerator.

By this time Hamish was on the scene, and without hesitation, he attacked the stranger in the driver's seat, trying to haul him out. The car skidded crazily in the lot, bashing into the rear end of another automobile, propelling Bryony and her would-be abductor against the dashboard and pitching the Scotsman onto the pavement. The stranger recovered first, slamming the gearshift into Reverse, backing up, tires squealing as before. But on his feet now, Hamish caught hold of the still-open driver's door, hanging on to it so that he wouldn't be run over as the vehicle fishtailed backward. Simultaneously, using the swaying door as leverage, he kicked out at Bryony's kidnapper. The stranger grunted with pain as his face and chest were impacted by the Scotsman's legs.

The abductor attempted to push the gearshift into First. Now terrified for Hamish, Bryony seized the man's hand and yanked on it with all her might, causing the gearshift to grind horribly. Then, somehow gathering her wits, she leaned over and shut off the engine, snatching the key from the ignition and tossing it out the driver's door on to the pavement. The automobile jolted to a sudden halt, and the next thing Bryony knew, Hamish and her would-be kidnapper were locked in mortal battle, their fists swinging and slugging mercilessly.

Although the two men were fairly evenly matched, the stranger was still slightly taller and much heavier than the Scotsman, and obviously professionally trained in hand-to-hand combat, besides, so that it seemed to Bryony that Hamish stood little chance against him. Scrambling from the vehicle, she glanced around wildly for some kind of a weapon with which to help her lover. Spying her fallen handbag, which she had dropped on the pavement, she grabbed it up and desperately began to beat the man on the back of his head. The blows not only distracted him, but also knocked him off balance.

At the same time, Hamish's fist collided with an audible crack against the side of the stranger's ruthless, scarred visage, sending him sprawling. For an instant, he lay stunned. Then he shook his head to clear it, and his eyes narrowed. Gingerly, he touched his hand to one corner of his mouth, his fingers coming away streaked with blood. His lips twisted cruelly at the sight. As he started to rise, Bryony swung her handbag as hard as she could, smashing him square in the face, sending him reeling again.

Grunting in pain, he reached out and caught hold of her ankle, hauling her feet from beneath her, so that she fell painfully upon the pavement, landing on one hip. Snarling murderous imprecations, Hamish threw himself brutally upon the kidnapper, pummeling him savagely. With difficulty, Bryony somehow wobbled upright as the two men rolled and grappled their way across the car park, the ugly sound of the blows ringing sickeningly in the twilight, so that Bryony was afraid she was going to either faint or be ill. Yet she did neither, for she knew her own life and Hamish's depended on her retaining her senses. She bashed the stranger again and again with her handbag, doing little real damage, but nevertheless proving an annoyance, so that he was unable to devote his full attention to the Scotsman.

Then, from nowhere, the abductor pulled a knife, its blade glittering wickedly in the dim light. He slashed out at Hamish, but much to Bryony's shock and horror, instead of moving out of the weapon's path, her lover stepped right into it, his hands clamping down hard upon the stranger's wrist. For what seemed a hideous eternity, as she watched, frozen where she stood, unable to tear her eyes away from the vicious, morbid scene, the two men struggled frantically for control of the knife, until finally its blade was shoved deep into flesh and, with a grunt of supreme satisfaction, twisted.

"Hamish! Oh, my God! *Hamish!*" Screaming and sobbing,

impelled by sheer terror, Bryony staggered to his side as, grim faced, his breath coming in hard rasps, blood staining his hands and shirt crimson, he stumbled back from her would-be kidnapper. "*Hamish...!*"

Twenty-Five

The Deposed Boy-King

> And nothing can we call our own but death,
> And that small model of the barren earth
> Which serves as paste and cover to our bones.
> For God's sake, let us sit upon the ground
> And tell sad stories of the death of kings:
> How some have been deposed, some slain in war,
> Some haunted by the ghosts they have deposed,
> Some poisoned by their wives, some sleeping killed;
> All murdered: for within the hollow crown
> That founds the mortal temples of a king
> Keeps Death his court.
>
> > *King Richard II*
> > —William Shakespeare

En route from Austrasia to the Pyrenees Mountains, 679 A.D.

It was New Year's Eve. But that didn't matter to the small, three-year-old boy named Sigisbert—the fourth Merovingian king of that illustrious name—who crouched miserably in the back of the humble, wooden cart that slowly and furtively wound its way southward, deep into the foothills of the Pyrenees Mountains.

It was rough, wild, rocky country through which the boy,

his older sister and the rest of those who accompanied them traveled. The land was desolate and forlorn, and grim and icy now, too, with the onslaught of winter. Here and there, beneath the thick, feathery branches of the coniferous trees, snow lay in thin patches upon the ground, and an equally thin layer of frost limned the boulders and outcrops that thrust up from the half-frozen earth. Just ahead, cutting a jagged-edged oblique against the lowering twilight sky, the mountains themselves loomed large and eerily—strangely slanted and looking as though some giant hand had pushed them at odd angles. In the valleys between, clouds of mist drifted and swirled on the chill, sibilant wind.

In one corner of the lumbering vehicle, huddled beneath a wool blanket, the brutally deposed, little Sigisbert shivered—although not just from the cold of the season.

Two days before Christmas, in the fringes of the forests of Wœvres, near the city of Stenay, his father, Dagobert II, King of Austrasia, had been assassinated, by order of the Mayor of the Palace, Pepin II, called "the Fat," who had ambitiously usurped power in the Merovingian kingdom and installed a puppet-ruler on the throne. In Sigisbert's mind, Stenay—also known as "Satanicum"—would forever be an unholy, evil place. It was said that frogs frequently fell from the firmament there. At that thought, without warning, he shuddered violently once more.

Austrasia was currently in such turmoil that no one was sure how his father had been killed. Some people reported that Dagobert had been pierced with a lance through one eye, while others claimed that a lethal poison had been poured into one of his ears. Sigisbert knew only that with his father's murder, his whole world as he had known it had abruptly collapsed.

His mother, Giselle de Razès, of the Visigoths, had died three years before, giving birth to him, so he had never known her. Nevertheless, he had much cause to be grateful to her now, for it was to Rhédae, the Visigoth stronghold, that he fled, in fear for his own life. Although only a three-year-old boy, he was now the true and rightful heir to the Austrasian throne, upon which the Merovingians had sat for centuries—and thus a threat to Pepin the Fat.

The Merovingians were a very old and exceedingly royal family, founded by Merovech, who was said to have been born of two fathers. His mother, already pregnant by King Chlodio, had, while swimming in the ocean, been seduced by the five-horned Quinotaur. In her womb, the blood of the Frankish king and the mysterious sea god had mingled to fashion Merovech, or so legend recounted.

From the Visigoths, who had long intermarried with the Merovingians, descended the sacred blood of Jesus the Nazirite, the martyred Christ, whose wife, Mary Magdalene, had, following his Crucifixion, fled with their two children to Gaul. The family had eventually settled among and intermarried with the Visigoths. As a result, like the Nazirites of centuries past, the Merovingian kings never cut their long, flowing manes of hair, and over their shoulder blades, they each bore a distinctive, red birthmark in the shape of a cross.

Highly learned, occult adepts, they wore robes fringed with tassels averred to possess magical, curative powers, and in their royal tombs were to be found such things as golden bull heads, miniature, gold bees and crystal balls. Often, after their deaths, their skulls were ritually incised or trepanned, as well.

But at this moment, all of this meant little to Sigisbert. The decorative, gold, silver and copper puzzle box and the ancient manuscript that it contained were all that mattered now—and they were safe, nestled close beside him in the crude, wooden cart.

"I have many enemies—the Mayor of the Palace, the Roman Church, and several of the nobility, among them. Should anything happen to me, guard both the box and the book with your lives, my children," Dagobert had urgently charged Sigisbert and his older sister.

"We shall, Father, we promise." And despite being only three and twelve years old, respectively, Sigisbert and his sister had kept their word.

Now and then, as the vehicle continued its long, clandestine journey southward, Sigisbert reverently touched the box to reassure himself that it was still there, that it had not somehow been snatched away and fallen into the grasping, murderous hands of the fearsome Pepin the Fat. It was too holy and precious for that. As young as he was, Sigisbert understood this profoundly.

At the death of his grandfather, Sigisbert III, his father, Dagobert, then a child, had been kidnapped and exiled to the British Isles by Grimoald, who had been the Mayor of the Palace at the time, and the Austrasian throne had been seized by Grimoald's son, Childebert the Adopted. When Grimoald and Childebert had finally met their downfall, Dagobert's cousin Chlotar III, King of Neustria, had secured the kingdom for Childeric II. It had been only upon the assassination of Childeric five years ago that Dagobert had, with the assistance of Wilfrid, Bishop of York, been traced and restored to his proper place upon the throne.

Returning to Austrasia from Rhédae, where he had married Giselle de Razès and found a secure haven among her people, the Visigoths, Dagobert had carried with him the puzzle box and ancient manuscript, which he had obtained from the Irish monastery at Slane, near Dublin, wherein he had sought sanctuary as a boy before moving to Northumbria and thence to Rhédae.

Now, just as his father before him had done, Sigisbert, too, must seek refuge among his mother's people, the Visigoths, at Rhédae.

Rhédae—which, in later years, would be known to the entire world as "Rennes-le-Château."

Book Three

The Master

Dreams surely are difficult, confusing, and not everything in them is brought to pass for mankind. For fleeting dreams have two gates: one is fashioned of horn and one of ivory. Those which pass through the one of sawn ivory are deceptive, bringing tidings which come to nought, but those which issue from the one of polished horn bring true results when a mortal sees them.

The Odyssey
—Homer

Book Three

The Master

Twenty-Six

The Underground Stream

For Nature beats in perfect tune,
And rounds with rhyme her every rune,
Whether she work in land or sea,
Or hide underground her alchemy.
Thou canst not wave thy staff in air,
Or dip thy paddle in the lake,
But it carves the bow of beauty there,
And the ripples in rhymes the oar forsake.

Poems (1847). Woodnotes II
—Ralph Waldo Emerson

En Route from England to France, the Present

"*H*amish! Oh, my God!" Still screaming and sobbing hysterically, Bryony clung to him desperately, running her shaking hands over his chest, trying to unbutton his shirt so that she could see where he was wounded. "Are you hurt? Oh, Jesus—"

"Shh. Hush, Bryony, hush!" the Scotsman demanded gently, catching hold of her wrists, then enfolding her hands tightly in his. "I'm not injured. It's not my blood. Do you understand me? *It's not my blood!*"

Gradually, attempting to gather both her wits and composure, she became aware of her brutal assailant lying on the parking-garage pavement, crumpled into a motionless heap in a pool of blood.

"Oh, my God…" she said again, her voice now a tremulous murmur. "Is he—is he dead?"

"I don't know." Hamish's own voice was low and grim. "But we're about to find out."

With one foot, he tentatively prodded the still body, but the fallen man did not respond. Carefully, the Scotsman knelt on the pavement, laying two fingers on the side of the stranger's neck, searching for a pulse, but finding none.

"Yes, he's dead, Bryony."

"Oh, Jesus… Oh, Hamish…what if—what if this *isn't* the man who murdered my father? What if—what if I've made some horrible mistake…?"

"No…no, you haven't."

"How do you know? How can you be so sure?"

Slowly, the Scotsman turned over the attacker's left wrist, so that she could see the strange symbol tattooed on its inner side. At first, Bryony thought the mark was a caduceus inside a circle. Then, upon closer inspection, she observed that the pair of winged serpents were actually entwined around a hammer. The circle was, in reality, a wheel whose rim bore the Latin words *Sigillum Militum Xpisti*—the "Seal of the Army of Christ"—which had also been the inscription on the Knights Templar seal. Rather than snakes, however, the latter had actually depicted two knights—one a soldier, the other a pilgrim—mounted double on a horse.

"Cauldronbearer has a tattoo similar to this one on the inside of his own left wrist," Hamish asserted as he dropped the dead man's hand, "except that instead of a hammer, Cauldronbearer's mark has a cauldron. What do you want to bet that our corpse, whoever he may have been, was known to the Abbey's Round Table as 'Hammerbearer'?"

"Undoubtedly, then…but who *was* he?"

Rifling the deceased man's pockets, the Scotsman produced a black, leather wallet, which he opened to reveal half a dozen driver's licenses in various names, all with photos of the stranger upon them.

"We'll probably never know." Hamish paused for a moment. Then he continued. "Come on, Bryony. We can't afford to stay here. We've got to make a clean getaway before anyone shows up."

"What? And just—just leave him here?" She indicated the corpse. "Shouldn't we call the police or something? I mean, the man *did* attack us! And you *did* kill him in self-defense, Hamish!"

"Yes, I did. But think, Bryony! Before you ran over to his car to confront him, Hammerbearer was speaking to someone on his mobile phone...probably another member of the Round Table, maybe even the Grand Master himself. From what you told me earlier, Hammerbearer recognized you, and so knew who we were. He *must* have been reporting our whereabouts and requesting instructions. That means other members of the Round Table are doubtless en route to St. Pancras even as we speak! If we contact the police, then it means hanging around here, waiting for them to show up...then going down to the police station to answer dozens of questions—with no guarantee whatsoever that our story will even be believed. And even if it is, by the time we're through with the interrogation and allowed to leave the police station, the Abbey will know exactly where we are, and after that, our chances of escaping from them will be pretty damned slim indeed!"

"But...maybe the police *will* believe us about the Abbey now!" Bryony insisted.

"Why? Because Hammerbearer has a peculiar tattoo on his left wrist and half a dozen IDs in his pocket? I doubt it. We've nothing beyond your own testimony as proof that he murdered your father, and all you can *really* say in that regard is that you saw someone who resembled him at both your father's funeral and the reception afterward. That is hardly irrefutable confirmation of Hammerbearer's guilt, Bryony! *I* believe you, yes, of course, because I know who we're dealing with. But the police will take a great deal more convincing and want a whole lot more evidence than that!"

"I-I guess you're right."

"I know I am." Picking up the knife Hammerbearer had pulled on him, Hamish glanced carefully around the parking garage to be certain he hadn't missed anything else that might incriminate him. "Let's go, Bryony. You drive," he ordered as they headed toward the Volvo. "I don't want to get blood on the car—and open the boot first, please."

After she had popped the trunk, the Scotsman removed a rag from the toolbox he kept in case of a mechanical breakdown. After wiping off his bloody hands and the blade, he wrapped the weapon up in the rag. Then he and Bryony slid into the vehicle, and she started the engine, accidentally stripping the gears, she was still so distraught.

"Take it easy, sweetheart," Hamish murmured soothingly. "About the last thing we want to do right now is attract attention to ourselves."

"Yes…I know…all right."

Slowly, she backed the automobile from their parking space, taking care not to accidentally run over Hammerbearer's corpse in the process. As she steered the Volvo through the parking garage, Hamish tucked the bloody rag and knife into an empty, discarded fast-food sack he retrieved from the back floor of the car. Then he tugged his open jacket discreetly around him to conceal the bloodstains on his shirt. After Bryony had exited from the parking garage, he directed her to the A2 dual-carriageway, heading southeast from London, toward Dover.

"Why Dover?" she inquired as she maneuvered the vehicle onto the A2.

"Not Dover, but Folkestone, actually—because I think we need to get out of the U.K. altogether for the moment, and that's where we can catch Le Shuttle across to France. It would have been easier to take the M-Twenty motorway, but I don't think there are any service stations along that route, and I know there's one on the A-Two, just outside of Rochester—besides which, we can hook up with the M-Twenty at Junction Three. What's your visa status for the Continent?"

"Current for all of Europe. I'm an archaeologist, remember? I never know when I might be asked on short notice to join an expedition. So I keep my visa status up-to-date in several countries.''

"Well, thank God for that! That means we can cross over into France tonight, putting as much distance between ourselves and the Abbey's Round Table as possible.''

Presently, Bryony and Hamish left London behind, driving in silence for a time. Then, just past the town of Rochester, he instructed her to pull off the dual-carriageway into the service station.

"We ought to get petrol before we run low, and I need to get cleaned up before anyone sees this blood all over me,'' he declared. "You'll have to get a fresh shirt for me from my bag in the boot, please, darling.''

"Yes...okay.''

Once she had fetched him a clean shirt, the Scotsman made his way to the service-station rest room. Winding his way through the open corridor that led to the interior, he glanced around to be certain he was alone. Ascertaining that the rest room was empty, he vigorously scrubbed his hands at one of the sinks, washing away every last trace of blood. Then he pushed the button on the air dryer, which came on with a dull roar. When his hands were dry, Hamish stepped into one of the toilet stalls, where he quickly stripped off his jacket and soiled shirt. Careful inspection showed that the former, fortunately, was unsullied. The latter, he rolled up and stuffed into the fast-food bag, which he had carried into the Gents with him. Then he donned the fresh shirt and hauled his jacket back on. Exiting from the rest room, he discovered that Bryony had finished refueling the car, paying cash for the bill.

Minutes later, with Hamish now at the wheel, they were back on the A2 again.

"Hamish,'' Bryony said quietly, after a time, "I can't seem to get the dreadful image of Hammerbearer's body out of my mind. Have you—have you ever...killed a man before?''

"Yes,'' he rejoined tersely.

"My God! When? Why?''

"Years ago, during the Falklands War, when I was under the command of Colonel H. Jones, who was killed there. In my wild, wayward youth before I became a peaceful history lecturer, I served a stint in Two-Para—that's the army's Second Battalion, the Parachute Regiment. It's a crack combat unit, trained to be dropped into areas of heavy conflict. That's why, when Hammerbearer drew his knife on me, I knew that the correct counteraction was to step into his swing, rather than away from it. He wasn't expecting that. Most assailants never are. That's how I was able to deflect the blade and drive it into him."

Bryony didn't know how to respond to that. It abruptly occurred to her that although she had fallen in love with the Scotsman and slept with him, there was still a great deal she didn't yet know about him. It would take time to learn all about his past, she realized now. But still, his unexpected revelation explained a lot…how he had successfully managed to conceal his home address for so long from the Abbey, known how to search the Internet in order to obtain the camouflage passports and other false identification the two of them now employed, how to check for the tracking device, how to elude their pursuers and avoid leaving a paper trail, set up an efficient campsite, and all the other things he had done since she had first met him. Even kidnapping her at the point of a BB pistol had been the act of someone trained to think on his feet and keep a cool head in a crisis.

"I'm afraid that, nowadays, I'm really quite out of practice at this sort of thing," Hamish continued. "Nevertheless, I *do* have some small experience in these matters, which I hope will stand us in good stead."

"It already has."

It had grown dark now, the headlights illuminating the highway before them. When Bryony and Hamish reached the town of Ashford, they stopped for supper, but they did not linger, dining and then getting back again as soon as possible on the M20. Some miles past the village of Smeeth, Hamish left the highway once more, guiding the vehicle into a secluded area near the East Stour River.

"Are we going to camp here?" Bryony asked.

The Scotsman shook his head.

"No, I only want to ditch Hammerbearer's knife and my bloodstained shirt before we get to Folkestone. Otherwise, there won't be any real opportunity to do it once we reach the Channel Tunnel, and we can't take the risk that Customs won't search our car."

Leaving the engine running, Hamish got out of the automobile. Using a small trowel from the toolbox, he dug a hole in the soft, damp earth and buried Hammerbearer's blade. Then, siphoning a small amount of gasoline from the car's fuel tank, he doused the fast-food sack, his soiled shirt and the rag he had used earlier, igniting the whole with his lighter and dropping the bundle on a flat rock to burn, so it didn't set fire to the ground. When it was a charred pile, he scattered the ashes, then got back into the car.

Returning to the M20, he and Bryony followed it all the way into Folkestone, and to the Channel Tunnel terminal. There, at the toll booth's gate, they paid the fare for passage on Le Shuttle.

After the Volvo had simultaneously passed through both British and French immigration services, Hamish drove the vehicle into one of Le Shuttle's bright transport cars. Then, climbing into the backseat of their automobile, he and Bryony settled down together for the thirty-five-minute journey. She nestled against the Scotsman, her head resting upon his broad and comforting shoulder. Presently, despite how wound up she was from the day's harrowing events, exhaustion overcame her, and the rhythmic clatter of the train's wheels upon the steel rails lulled her into an uneasy sleep.

It was late when Le Shuttle finally arrived in Calais. After getting back into the Volvo's front seats, he and Bryony exited the transport car, the Scotsman remembering to steer the automobile on to the right side of the road.

It was a three-and-a-half-hour drive to Paris. Having telephoned earlier from a pay telephone in Ashford, Hamish had managed to acquire lodgings for them at the Hotel Baltimore, a small, quiet, elegant hotel on Avenue Kleber, not far from the Arc de Triomphe, the Place de l'Étoile, and the Avenue des Champs Elysées.

"I've registered us at the hotel under the names of Ian MacCallum and Jessamine Winthorpe, by the way," he explained as he guided the Volvo on to Autoroute 16, heading south toward Paris. "Despite everything, I think it's still highly unlikely the Abbey is aware that those are the aliases we're employing. I think Hammerbearer's presence at the Euro Car Park at St. Pancras was nothing more than a piece of very bad luck for us. He wasn't actually waiting there for us, so I'm quite sure the Abbey hadn't expected us to be at the British Library. Otherwise, they would've sent more than one man for the job."

"Unless they only wanted him to tail us," Bryony pointed out.

"Yes, well, there is that, of course. But in that case, you can be certain Hammerbearer would've avoided being seen by us. He must have known there was a slight, however remote, chance that you would recognize him from your father's funeral and reception. No, I think it was just mere coincidence that Hammerbearer happened to be at St. Pancras at the same time as we were."

"I sure hope so!" Bryony responded fervently.

From the A16, they took Autoroute 26 to the A1, which they followed the remainder of the way to Paris. Sometime later, they pulled up in front of the Hotel Baltimore, an old, stone building with dark, green awnings over the doors and windows, and with wrought-iron-lace railings across the lower portions of the windows of the rooms above the ground floor. Small topiary trees pruned into decorative, ornamental balls stood in square planters out front. Just down the street, at the heart of the *Place de l'Étoile*—the "Place of the Star"—a circular plaza from which several of Paris's main streets, including the Avenue des Champs Elysées, emanated, the magnificent, ornate *Arc de Triomphe*—the "Arch of Triumph"—glowed golden in the soft light that illuminated it in the darkness. A short distance to the south, the Eiffel Tower rose, a spire equally gilded by luminescent light in the night.

After checking in to the en suite room they had booked at the hotel, Bryony and Hamish divested themselves of their clothes, then fell into bed, too tired even to make love. They were so exhausted that they slept until late the following afternoon, finally awakening to the rays of the warm, yellow spring sun streaming in through the windows, pouring over their naked bodies entwined on the fresh, clean sheets of the bed. Stirring ever so gently, whispering sweet nothings to each other and laughing throatily, they did make love then, slowly and lazily, each reveling in the other, mapping anew what they had only explored before in the heat of urgent passion.

They spent the next several days not only sating their lust for each other time and again, but also resting and sightseeing, in between collating and ordering all the notes they had gathered thus far, as well as decrypting more of the files on the two disks that Bryony's father had sent to her before his death. The interlude was, she thought afterward, like some glorious moment out of step with the rest of the universe, as though they two were all alone in the world, even upon the crowded, noisy streets of Paris.

But eventually, she and Hamish knew they had to move on. It was dangerous for them to linger too long in any one place, thereby making it easier for the Abbey to track them down. And one of Simon St. Blaze's encrypted chapters, when finally decoded, had spoken extensively about the centuries-old, secret order known as the *Prieure de Notre Dame de Sion*—the "Priory of Our Lady of Sion"—and a small village located in the south of France, called "Rennes-le-Château...."

Twenty-Seven

The Monastery of St. Guillem the Lonely

> The quality of mercy is not strained,
> It droppeth as the gentle rain from heaven
> Upon the place beneath: it is twice blessed;
> It blesseth him that gives and him that takes:
> 'Tis mightiest in the mightiest; it becomes
> the thronèd monarch better than his crown;
> His scepter shows the force of temporal power,
> The attribute to awe and majesty
> Wherein doth sit the dread and fear of kings,
> But mercy is above this sceptered sway,
> It is enthronèd in the hearts of kings....

> *The Merchant of Venice*
> —William Shakespeare

The Valley of Gellone, the Principality of Septimania, 804 A.D.

Over the aeons, the ruggedly beautiful, sun-drenched land upon which Guillem—Count of Auvergne, Barcelonne, Rhédae and Toulouse, Duke of Narbonne and Razès, and Prince of Septimania—now stood had been home to many peoples. Pagans, Jews, Muslims, Christians...all had called this crescent sliver on the great Mediterranean Sea home. Now, it was the principality of Septimania, bestowed upon the Jews in 768 by the Austrasian Mayor of the Palace, Pepin III, called "the Short," for their aiding the Franks in driving the ever-encroaching Moors back south beyond the Pyrenees Mountains. Pepin the Short had installed Guillem's father, Theodoric, as Septimania's prince and ruler.

As he gazed out over the terrain, a faint, wry smile curved Guillem's lips. More than a hundred years ago, Pepin the Short's grandfather, Pepin the Fat, had ordered the assassination of the Merovingian King Dagobert II, and usurped the Austrasian throne from Dagobert's son, Sigisbert IV, bestowing it upon a puppet-ruler. That Pepin the Short should have placed Theodoric, descended from the Merovingian kings, over Septimania was thus the greatest of ironies.

Since his father's death, Guillem had reigned over the principality. But he had grown old now—and tired; his wife, Guibour von Hornbach, was dead. The chivalrous exploits of his youth, including his defeat of the Saracens at Orange, which had earned him the sobriquet of "Guillem of Orange" and made him famous—the subject of bard song—were long behind him. Soon, he would hang up his bold knight's sword and relinquish his place at Charlemagne's court to devote himself to other matters.

Here in the valley of Gellone, near the town of Lodeve, the academy that Guillem had commanded be constructed was gradually taking shape. It was to be a center for Jewish studies—although after his death, it would become a Catholic monastery, subject to St. Benedict of Aniane, and Guillem himself would be pronounced both a monk and saint, although he had been neither.

Guillem did not know how much time he had left in his life. But he wanted to spend the remainder of it studying the ancient manuscript inside the ornate, gold, silver and copper puzzle box that had been handed down to those of the Merovingian line since the days of Dagobert II. The book was written in a strange, cryptic language like none Guillem had ever before seen. His predecessors had kept notes on their own progress with the tome, which would be of great assistance to him— just as his own research would be to those who followed in his wake. It would, he reflected, take several long lifetimes not only to decipher the manuscript, but also to fully comprehend its contents. It was not a task for one mere man alone, even should he wish to attempt to undertake it.

The book was a puzzle, was as the box itself—deliberately obscure, not easily understood, and thus intended only for the erudite and the enlightened.

Who had written it—and why? Guillem wondered as he strolled through the peaceful, secluded valley. The silence was broken only by the ongoing work on the rising academy, with its two round towers and its single, looming, square one. If he could determine who had authored the tome, then perhaps he would possess the key to unlock its many mysteries, and those, he felt sure, would reveal the secrets of the very universe itself....

Watch and pray, that ye enter not into temptation: the spirit indeed is willing, but the flesh is weak....

As the biblical passage suddenly sprang unbidden into his mind, Guillem shivered momentarily beneath the summer sun that beat down from the endless, blue sky. Then, shaking his head as though to clear it, he walked on through the valley, in the shadow of the towering mountains.

Overhead, a raven winged its way against the white clouds, its raucous cry echoing on the gentle wind that whispered inland from the bounded sea.

Twenty-Eight

The Four-Wheeled Chariot

> There appeared a chariot of fire, and horses of fire, and
> parted them both asunder; and Elijah went up by a whirl-
> wind into heaven.

> The Bible
> —2 Kings 2:11

> He gave him the plans for the chariot, for the golden cher-
> ubs with wings outspread covering the ark of the covenant
> of Yahweh....

> The Bible
> —1 Chronicles 28:18

> For see how Yahweh comes in fire, his chariots like the
> tempest....

> The Bible
> —Isaiah 66:15

These were the living creatures I had seen beneath the
God of Israel by the river Chebar, whom I now recognized
to be cherubim. Each had four faces and four wings;
something like human hands were under their wings. Their
faces looked just like those I had seen by the river Chebar;
each one went straight forward. Each had four faces: the

first face was that of an ox, the second that of a man, the third that of a lion, and the fourth that of an eagle. Such were the living creatures I had seen by the river Chebar. I also saw four wheels beside them, one wheel beside each cherub; the wheels appeared to have the luster of chysolite stone. All four of them seemed to be made the same, as though there were a wheel within a wheel. When they moved, they went in any one of their four directions without veering as they moved; for in whichever direction they were faced, they went straight toward it without veering as they moved. The rims of the four wheels were full of eyes all around. I heard the wheels given the name "whirling wheels." When the cherubim moved, the wheels went beside them; when the cherubim lifted their wings to rise from the earth, even then the wheels did not leave their sides. When they stood still, the wheels stood still; when they rose, the wheels rose with them; for the living creatures' spirit was in them. I looked and saw in the firmament above the cherubim what appeared to be sapphire stone; something like a throne could be seen upon it. He [Yahweh] spake to the man dressed in linen: "Go under the chariot, beneath the cherubim; fill both your hands with coals of fire...."

The Bible
—Ezekiel 10:1-16

Rennes-le-Château, France, the Present

The next morning Bryony and Hamish left Paris, following Autoroute 10 to the A71, then took the A20 through Limoges, all the way to Carcassonne. From there, they wound their way south to Couiza and Montazels, the twin villages set below Rennes-le-Château. After passing through the town center of Quillan, they spied a modern road sign on their left, indicating that Rennes-le-Château lay two-and-a-half miles beyond. It was, in fact, located on a fifteen-hundred-foot-high knoll in the foothills of the Pyrenees Mountains, concealed from the valley below, but commanding breathtaking views from its summit, which would once have made it ideal from a defensive military standpoint. The road that led to it consisted of only two narrow lanes, and the village itself had changed very little in the past few centuries, as though time had somehow passed it by. Yet here, for more than two thousand years, had come Celts and Romans, Visigoths and Merovingians, Cathars and Knights Templar to these rugged hills. Centuries ago, then then called *Rhédae*—"Four-Wheeled Chariot"—Rennes-le-Château had been the center of the Visigoth kingdom of Razès, into which the Merovingian King Dagobert II had married.

Skilled builders, the Visigoths had made Rhédae a stronghold consisting of a town flanked by two fortresses and encompassed by a double set of ramparts. Over the centuries, because of its strategic location, Rennes-le-Château had been overrun time and again, falling prey to King Alphonse II of Aragon and his army; to the Abbot of Cîteaux and Simon de Montfort and his Crusaders, who had been sent by Pope Innocent III to subdue the powerful Languedoc-Roussillon region; to *Les Routiers* from Catalonia, brigands and bandits who had pillaged the countryside, burning houses, destroying harvests and slaughtering villagers. Now, all that remained of the place were the church of St. Mary Magdalene and a few houses tucked around the château that had been built by the Voisins family, upon whom Rhédae had been bestowed by Simon de Montfort before his death.

Tradition stated that the church had been dedicated to Mary Magdalene in 1059. However, it was said that an ancient parchment discovered in a Jerusalem Bible had recorded that in the time of Nein, there had been built in Rhédae a temple dedicated to the goddess Isis, which had, in the year 70 A.D., during the reign of the Roman Emperor Titus, taken the name of Magdala. *Nein* derived from the Hebrew *nain* or "green pastures," and it was the name of a town near the gate of which Jesus Christ had, according to the Gospel of Luke, raised to life the dead son of a widow.

Set in wild, rocky, green land, Rennes-le-Château seemed an unlikely village to have generated the controversy it had over the last century. In 1885, a young priest named Francois-Berenger Saunière had been appointed to Rennes-le-Château, and finding that its ancient church was in dire need of expensive restoration, he had, in 1891, managed to arrange for a small loan, to begin repairs.

It was widely rumored that when the altar had been dismantled, Saunière had found, hidden in a hollow altar pillar, several genealogical charts and Latin texts written on parchments, in a code so complex that it would never have been decrypted had the key to the cipher not fortuitously been discovered engraved on the tombstone of Marie, Lady d'Hautpoul de Blanchefort, in the church's cemetery. It was now known that the altar pillar was not hollow, so it could not have concealed anything—although a small, glass phial that might have held something *had* been found in a wooden rail inside the church. The museum at Rennes-le-Château now had the phial on display.

Others, however, claimed to have seen the priest removing a wooden tube with wax seals on it from the church's *capsa*, a crypt designed to hold the relics of the saint venerated in the church. Later, it was said that this tube had contained a manuscript and two parchments.

In reality, the parchments had apparently been written by Saunière's predecessor, Abbé Antoine Bigou, confessor to Lady d'Hautpoul de Blanchefort, in 1781, in a code that could only be deciphered employing the Knight's Tour, although others had argued convincingly for a solution based on Pythagorean geometry. On the surface, the parchments appeared to contain nothing more than Latin transcriptions of passages from the Gospels of Matthew, Mark and Luke. However, secreted within them had been two very strange messages:

"TO DAGOBERT II KING AND TO SION BELONGS THIS TREASURE AND HE [or IT] IS THERE DEAD."

"SHEPHERDESS NO TEMPTATION THAT POUSSIN TENIERS GUARD THE KEY PEACE 681 BY THE CROSS AND THIS HORSE OF GOD I COMPLETE [or DESTROY] THIS DAEMON GUARDIAN AT NOON BLUE APPLES."

It was said that following his discovery of the coded parchments, Saunière had gone immediately to Carcassonne, whence he had been sent to Paris, to consult with the specialists at St. Sulpice about them, although this was unproved, and that when he had returned to Rennes-le-Château, he had brought with him reproductions of three paintings: *Les Bergers d'Arcadie (The Shepherds of Arcadia)*, by Nicholas Poussin, *The Temptation of St. Anthony*, by David Teniers the Younger, and a portrait of Pope Celestine V, by an unknown artist.

Les Bergers d'Arcadie was a painting of three shepherds, a young woman and a sarcophagus, which greatly resembled a tomb that had once stood in a valley near Rennes-le-Château, but which sepulchre had unfortunately been demolished. On the crypt in the picture were engraved the words *Et in Arcadia Egô*, which translated from Latin to English as *And in Arcadia I*, with the words "death" and "am" often considered to be understood as a missing part of the phrase, as well: *And in Arcadia I, Death, am....* But another, anagrammatical translation was *Behold, I conceal the secrets of God.* Poussin had, in fact, been acquainted with the family at the nearby Château d'Arques, so that it was possible he had indeed visited the Rennes-le-Château region, and the flora in his picture was the same as that still to be found at the site of the destroyed mausoleum.

Further, strangely enough, in the gardens at Shugborough Hall, in Staffordshire, England, stood what was known as the Shepherd Monument, which was a mirror image, in stone, of Poussin's painting, and which had carved into it the mysterious letters D.O.U.O.S.V.A.V.V.M., whose meaning had yet to be deciphered.

In 1973, an art historian, Professor Christopher Cornford, had discovered that Poussin's painting was designed around a pentagram, and later, authors Henry Lincoln, Simon Miles and David Wood had all demonstrated that the landscape around Rennes-le-Château was also designed around a pentagram, with Wood proposing that its top point was extended.

Shortly after returning to Rennes-le-Château, the priest Saunière had begun spending prodigious sums of money—refurbishing the church, as well as building a tower known as the *Tour Magdala* and additional structures, such as a second tower crowned with a conservatory, the Villa Bethania, an orangerie, and a park with fountains and a menagerie.

On January 17, 1917, he was felled by either a heart attack or a stroke, and suspiciously, there was also some evidence that a coffin had been ordered for him beforehand. Saunière had died five days later, imparting to only his housekeeper, Marie Dénarnaud, the secret of where he had obtained the riches to carry out his many and varied schemes. This, she had promised to reveal on her deathbed. However, curiously, she, too, had fallen victim to a stroke that had left her paralyzed and unable to speak before she had died in 1953.

As a result, speculation about the source of Saunière's wealth had run rife ever since. Had it been buried Visigoth gold? The Visigoths were known to have seized possession of at least some portion of the treasure of the Temple of Jerusalem, which had previously been confiscated by the Romans and removed to Rome. The Cathars, as well, were said to have possessed a treasure, which had disappeared from Montsegur when it had surrendered in March, 1244, to invading forces. Was it this that had been concealed at Rennes-le-Château? Or had it, in fact, been the lost Knights Templar treasure? Or had the priest Saunière simply been employing some awful secret to blackmail the Roman Church? It was this last that many people believed, since it was said that Saunière's confession before his death had proved so shocking that the priest who had heard it had denied him both absolution and the Last Rites.

Subsequently, Noel Corbu, who had purchased the Villa Bethania after Marie Dénarnaud had been rendered destitute by the introduction of the new franc in 1946, had also in 1953 been killed in a terrible car crash that several people alleged had not been an accident at all; and in 1967, a courier, Fakhur el Islam, who had been the bearer of *les dossiers secrets,* a separate collection of secret papers attributed to the Ordre de Sion, had, en route from East Germany to Melun, France, been mysteriously murdered by being thrown from the Paris-Geneva express.

Many people insisted that the cabal behind several of the enigmatic events at Rennes-le-Château was the *Prieure de Notre Dame de Sion*—the 'Priory of Our Lady of Sion'—which, like the Abbey of the Divine, was untraceable.

By this time, Bryony and Hamish had reached the church. Its entrance was a tympanum, a triangular space enclosed between the sloping and horizontal cornices of a pediment, often decorated with a sculpture—in this case, that of Mary Magdalene. Beneath her were the words *Terribiles est locus iste*—"This place is terrible." Also on the typanum were roses and the cross; the coat of arms of Monseigneur Felix Billard, the Bishop of Carcassonne during Saunière's time; and the coat of arms of the yesteryear Pope Leo XIII.

Once inside, Bryony and Hamish were greeted by a statue of Asmodeus, the hideous, goat-horned, Jewish King of Demons, bearing a stoup or holy-water fount upon his hunched back, his ears elongated, his nose aquiline and hooked, and talons on his fingers and toes, where the nails ought to have been. Traditionally, Asmodeus was the custodian of secrets and treasure, and it was he who was said to have been tamed by Solomon and, under the King's direction, to have built the Great Temple of Jerusalem. His proper name, Aesma-daeva, meant "spirit of anger," and he was associated with lust, as well. Surmounting the statue were four angels—perhaps the archangels named in the Bible—and a decorative cornice supported by two chimera, which were wingless monsters with lion heads, goat bodies and serpent tails. A small, circular plaque set into the lower rail of the cornice bore the letters B. S., which were the initials of Bérenger Saunière. However, they were equally as likely to refer to Rennes-le-Château's two nearby rivers, the Blanque and the Sals, which converged at a place known as *Le Bénitier* or "the Stoup."

Other statues placed around the church were of esoteric saints in unusual postures. St. Germaine de Pibrac scattered red roses from her apron. Mary Magdalene held a vase or jar. Like the Grail King of Arthurian literature, St. Roche displayed a wounded thigh, and St. Anthony of the Desert—the saint of David Teniers the Younger's painting—bore a closed book.

Borne by four angels was Saint Antony of Padua, to whom the faithful prayed for help in recovering lost objects. Flanking the altar left and right, respectively, stood Joseph and Mary, each carrying a child, recalling the legend that Jesus Christ had had a twin brother, and on the bas-relief beneath the altar, Mary Magdalene knelt before a cross fashioned of two branches, one of which was alive, the other dead.

On one fresco wall was depicted the Mount of Beatitude, from where Jesus Christ had given his sermon on the eight spiritual blessings. Roses strewed the hillside, and on the left bloomed the flower known as Solomon's seal, while on the right were pomegranate leaves. The penitence bag had a hole in it. Strangest of all were the Fifteen Stations of the Cross, each of which contained bizarre inconsistencies. Among other anomalies, Pontius Pilate wore a veil. A black-veiled woman held the hand of a child dressed in a Scottish tartan. A Roman soldier gambling for the robe of Jesus Christ had thrown a pair of dice, upon one of which showed a three and a four, an impossibility, since they were on opposite sides of an accurate die, while the second die displayed a five—all the numbers thus adding up to twelve.

"It is claimed that Abbé Henri Boudet, once the curé of Rennes-les-Bains, which is not far from Rennes-le-Château, was the real brains behind Saunière," Hamish confided to Bryony as they surveyed the church in detail, making copious notes, just as they had at Rosslyn Chapel. "Boudet was a linguistic scholar who wrote a book entitled *The True Celtic Language and the Cromlech at Rennes-les-Bains*, in which he appeared, however, despite all his expertise, to put forth the utterly mad hypothesis that the Celts spoke Anglo-Saxon…that is, Old English…and that this was also the language spoken by Noah's sons before the Tower of Babel was constructed. Of course, we know none of that is true. But the authors Henry Lincoln and David Wood have argued that what Boudet might actually have been theorizing is that there was, in fact, a universal language prior to the Deluge."

"If aliens or angels or whatever *did* somehow introduce a level of higher intelligence into our prehistoric ancestors, then it would be only natural to assume that they also taught them the rudiments of a language, would it not, from which all language thus originated here on Earth?" Bryony speculated.

"Yes, it would be."

"And you know what, Hamish?"

"What?"

"If all that's true, then it also argues for a commonality of symbological interpretations originally, too. So...why don't we try to take stock here...distill what we've found—as much as we can, anyway?"

"All right. Where do you think we ought to begin?"

"With life and death—because in the end, that's really what *all* of this is all about, isn't it?"

"I believe so, yes."

"Okay, then, let's start with the Green Man and the Black Madonna—Osiris and Isis, as the Egyptians called them—because they seem to be the two predominant figures we've consistently come across, and we've already agreed that the Green Man represents life, rebirth, hope and renewal, while the Black Madonna represents wisdom and death."

"'I, Isis, am all that has been, that is, or shall be. No mortal man hath ever me unveiled,'" Hamish quoted quietly. "The Greek essayist and biographer Plutarch saw those words inscribed on the Temple of Neith at the city of Sais, and recorded them for all posterity. And now, at long last, I think I can make sense of them."

"How?"

"To know and understand 'all that has been, that is, or shall be' is to have acquired complete wisdom and enlightenment, is it not? And 'No mortal man hath ever me unveiled'...of course, that's true, too, because without dying—at least once—one can never truly attain complete wisdom and enlightenment, for the simple reason that one would never have actually experienced death."

"And in the Christian context, death—or at least the knowledge and understanding of it—was brought to Mankind by the Serpent, Lucifer...the Red Snake or Dragon."

"Yes, but why the color red?" the Scotsman mused aloud. "Why not blue or yellow, for instance?"

"Something to do with blood, perhaps? Maybe even a virgin's blood? Historically, both virgins and virgin's blood have always played a large part in myths and ceremonies. Biologically speaking, in ancient times, the only way for a man to be certain his woman's children were actually born of his own seed was if she were, in fact, a virgin when he first mated with her, and if he stuck around afterward to ensure that she didn't mate with anyone else besides him. Thus, offspring produced from such a union would have been 'pure,' so to speak, their 'blood' untainted, their parentage unquestioned. Further, we know from countless archaeological sites that beginning with even the earliest known ritual burials—those of the Neanderthals—the bones of the deceased were often coated with red ocher, and that ancient peoples like the Mayans painted the insides of their royal coffins with cinnabar. King Arthur was said to have been a 'crimson-stained one,' as well. Conversely, all this may have something to do with death, also. Hunters and warriors, for instance, have traditionally been daubed or anointed with the blood of their first kill. In fact, in keeping with *all* these trains of thought, the color red may actually somehow be symbolic of something that is in some way a *first*, or else that is in some way connected with someone who is considered a *first* one, like a virgin or a king."

"Yes." Hamish nodded. "In the Christian context, Adam—whose name is often translated as 'Red Earth'—was the eponymous First Man, and the blood of all Mankind is iron-based, remember, so it turns red when exposed to oxygen, just as iron itself reddens with rust."

"So...perhaps the color red is symbolic of the first humans and of the human life cycle itself...human conception, birth, life, death and possibly even rebirth...reincarnation..." Bryony suggested, considering. "But...why a serpent or dragon? Dragons don't even exist here on earth, and apparently never did—apart from the dinosaurs, of course, which weren't really dragons as we understand them. Yet still, dragons are universally depicted."

"That one is more difficult, I believe," the Scotsman said thoughtfully, "and in some regards, I think the word 'dragon' is something of a misnomer, that it perhaps does not nowadays accurately convey what was originally truly intended, which is a winged or feathered serpent."

"Like the Aztecs' god Quetzalcoatl, for instance, or the Mayans' god Kukulcan?"

"Precisely. Now, let's go back to the idea of a level of higher intelligence and thus sentience somehow having been introduced into our prehistoric ancestors by some kind of more advanced beings. Whether we call them aliens, angels or whatever is irrelevant. The point is that if they existed, they would have come down to earth from the heavens, right?"

"Yes, meaning they were 'winged'—whether they actually were or not—that is to say that like birds, they possessed flight capabilities." Bryony easily followed the Scotsman's line of reasoning. "Either they literally *did* have wings, the way we imagine angels do, or else, probably much more likely, they had 'winged chariots'…that is, spaceships or UFOs."

"Exactly. And the ancient name of Rennes-le-Château, Rhédae, let us not forget, means 'Four-wheeled Chariot.'"

"Like that seen by the prophet Ezekiel in the Bible?"

"Yes."

"And the entire landscape around Rennes-le-Château is unquestionably laid out on an extended pentagram—which, I suppose, could possibly represent some sort of jetlike UFO, rather like the stealth bomber, actually, with the extended point being the nose of the spaceship, the two side points the wings, and the two bottom points some kind of nacelles, so that to those looking up at it from the ground below, it would have had the shape and appearance of an irregular pentagram."

"Yes, that's certainly one possibility," Hamish agreed slowly. "Another is that the pentagram has something to do with the planet Venus, whose orbit around the sun, as seen from the earth, describes a pentagram in the heavens every eight years. Further, the 'chariot' or *merkabah,* as the Hebrews called it, was the 'throne' of God, which sat upon the chariot, just as the Ark of the Covenant is sometimes depicted upon a chariot, as well. Merkabah mystical literature informs us that the ascent of a quester's soul to the divine throne of God upon the chariot was a perilous journey through seven spheres or 'heavens' guarded by hostile angels. Passing each angelic gate-keeper depended upon the successful use of certain magical formulas, known as 'seals'—which, naturally, may also some-how be connected with the Seal of Solomon. Last but not least, the name *Isis* means 'Stone Seat'…that is, a throne, and she is often portrayed as seated upon her throne in a ship…also some sort of an ark, perhaps?'' The Scotsman paused for a moment, reflecting. Then he continued.

"At any rate, all this would account for the wings bit. As for the snake, the Bible informs us that for tempting Eve to eat the forbidden fruit of the Tree of Knowledge of Good and Evil in the Garden of Eden, Lucifer the Serpent was condemned to 'crawl on his belly and eat dust every day of his life'—which, if you think about it, could actually mean that Lucifer was simply deprived of his wings, earthbound, marooned here.''

"True. But still, why a snake? Why not a miserable worm, for example?'' Bryony asked.

"Well, to the best of my own knowledge, aside from the fact that all serpents, whether male or female, shed their skin and thus are 'reborn,' there is one attribute that makes all male snakes unique.''

"And that is…?''

"They have not just one, but *two* penises. Therefore, the Serpent *could* be symbolic of the fact that the so-called Fall, in reality, consisted of Lucifer—whoever or *what*ever he may have been—copulating with the eponymous First Woman, Eve, and Eve then copulating with Adam.''

"Thereby making a cuckold of Lucifer.'' Once more, Bryony contemplated the statue of the hideous, goat-horned demon Asmodeus, associated with anger and lust. "It's true that snakes have always held sexual connotations. And even today, a man whose wife has been unfaithful to him is said to be 'wearing a pair of horns,' and Lucifer, Satan, the Devil, what-ever one wants to call him, is invariably depicted with a pair of goat's horns and often even with a goat's head, as well, just like Pan—the so-called Goat of Mendes—and Eliphas Lévi's Sabbatical Goat.''

"Perhaps because Lucifer was as randy as a goat?" The Scotsman grinned, his eyes suddenly raking her in a way that made her blush.

"Well, how do we know that's *not* the reason?" she inquired archly.

"We don't. Regardless, the point is that in world cosmologies, the winged or feathered serpent, the 'dragon,' as it were, is frequently a messianic or savior figure, while whether a winged or feathered serpent or not, the messianic or savior figure itself is usually depicted as hanging on a tree or a cross, like the Scandinavian Odin or the Christian Jesus Christ, or else as requiring sacrificial victims to be hanged on a tree or a cross, like the Celtic Esus. Further, the caduceus, still even today the symbol of healing and medicine, portrays two snakes—one traditionally malevolent, the other beneficent—coiled or copulating around a wand, and to them, the Greeks added wings. So in other words, we begin with a winged figure who loses his wings and who then, through some significant act of atonement or healing that benefits Mankind, regains them and once more ascends to the heavens, whence he came. In this context, we should also note that Lucifer, Satan or the Devil, whatever, was not originally a demon, but, rather, simply a fallen angel. Lucifer means 'Light-Bringer' or 'Torch-Bearer,' which may possibly have the same connotations as the Greek or Minoan Prometheus being said to have brought fire to Mankind…that is to say, in reality, enlightenment or knowledge to Mankind, whether by means of forbidden fruit or fire or something else altogether. And Satan simply means 'Adversary'…one who opposes another or another's ideas, just as Lucifer opposed keeping Adam and Eve ignorant."

"Well, if all *that's* the secret the priest Saunière was blackmailing the Church with, then it's no wonder his confessor was horrified and refused him both absolution and the Last Rites! This sort of speculation could only be considered heretical and blasphemous by the Church!"

"Yet Rennes-le-Château exists—and one could hardly call

this little church we're standing in 'reverent,'" Hamish pointed out logically. "Its ancient origins perhaps lie with Isis—the Black Madonna—rather than with Mary Magdalene, who has also been called the 'Black Madonna,' by the way. And certainly, nothing about it is as it ought to be. Instead, it's all quite twisted and distorted, even sacrilegious, most would probably insist. Yet here it is, all the same. Surely, the Church must know of its existence and what it contains. But still, they've done nothing about it. Why do you suppose that is?"

"I don't know," Bryony confessed, puzzled by the implications.

"Neither do I. But I'll wager the answer to *that* question would prove very interesting indeed!"

Twenty-Nine

Dipping into Wisdom

For I dipped into the future, far as human eye could see,
Saw the Vision of the World, and all the wonder that
would be;
Saw the heavens fill with commerce, argosies of magic
sails,
Pilots of the purple twilight, dropping down with costly
bales;
Heard the heavens fill with shouting, and there rained a
ghastly dew
From the nations' airy navies grappling in the central blue.

Locksley Hall
—Alfred, Lord Tennyson

En Route from France to Greece, the Present

That night, Bryony and Hamish pitched their dome tent just
outside of Rennes-le-Château, cooking their supper on the
camp stove they had brought with them, and dining before the
open fire. Despite the chill of the late spring evening in the
rugged foothills of the Pyrenees Mountains, Bryony thought
the hot, hearty pot-au-feu that she and Hamish had prepared
tasted so good, consumed in the fresh, invigorating air, along
with thick, warm, crusty slices of French bread spread with

butter, and washed down with a bottle of inexpensive but excellent French wine.

"Hmm...that was wonderful!" She sighed contentedly, as she finished the last of the food upon her tin plate.

"It really was, wasn't it?" Hamish agreed. "I don't know why it is, but for some strange reason, food always seems to taste much better when it's cooked and eaten outdoors. Something to do with getting back to nature and our prehistoric roots, I suspect. Some more wine?"

"Yes, please." She proffered her tin cup, sighing again as the Scotsman refilled it to the brim with the sweet, red wine they had shared over supper.

"Tired?" he asked.

"A little. I've been on a nerve-racking roller-coaster ride ever since Dad was killed, and these last several weeks have had a-a kind of surreal quality—not to mention the fact that they've been just plain frightening, besides."

"I know what you mean. I haven't exactly found them to be a picnic myself, Bryony."

"No, of course you haven't, Hamish." Her face softened with love and concern as she gazed at him. "I didn't mean that you had."

"No, I don't suppose that you did." He smiled at her gently. "However, as I've told you before, the point is that we mustn't allow ourselves to grow dispirited and give up. We've actually made a great deal of progress since we first embarked upon our journey...gathering pertinent information, visiting places like Rosslyn Chapel and Rennes-le-Château, and decoding several of your father's files."

"I know. But still, I'm not at all certain what we're to make of it all. I agree with Dad's hypothesis that all world cosmologies, myths, legends, fables, fairy tales and so on spring from a common source or well of knowledge. I also think it's likely that ancient peoples such as the Egyptians and Greeks, and secret orders like the Knights Templar and the Rosicrucians, had access to at least some of this erudition...the so-called Mysteries, if you will. However, I'm still not sure what these Mysteries actually consisted of, what information they revealed to the Initiate, the Adept, or the Master. Just exactly what is it that this common source or well of knowledge was attempting to tell us?''

''I think that's the million-dollar question, sweetheart,'' Hamish declared. ''If we knew the answer to that, then I believe we'd know everything. Probably, the Mysteries were comprised, in some part, of subjects that every child today studies in school—Pythagoras's Quadrivium of arithmetic, music, geometry and astronomy, for instance. To that list, we could also add chemistry—what the ancients called 'alchemy'—and perhaps one or two other fields. At one time, to the ignorant and uneducated, such arts and sciences must have seemed like magic, rather than the concepts of higher learning. So an architect or builder who understood the principles of design and engineering, and who was capable of constructing something like Stonehenge or the Pyramids, must indeed have appeared to the common people as a sorcerer—or perhaps even as a god.''

''Yes, but again, where did such knowledge originate, Hamish? What *was* the common source or well that Dad called 'Alphêus'? Aliens, angels, whatever...something not of this world, as we—and others—have theorized? Because it does seem hard to believe that Mankind himself simply gradually acquired this kind of knowledge over time—especially when we look at prehistoric peoples like the Neanderthals. They're the first culture of which we're aware to bury their dead. If they had only stuck their deceased into holes in the ground, then we could argue that this practice arose from the fact that the bodies otherwise attracted dangerous, carnivorous wild animals, which posed a hazard to the living. But that wasn't the case. Instead, as we know, the Neanderthals also sometimes coated the bones of the dead with red ocher and interred them with simple grave goods. All this would appear to indicate that the Neanderthals had at least some notion of either an afterlife in some form of Paradise or else a belief in reincarnation. So, since we don't evolve the idea of something from nothing, from where did this concept of the dead somehow rising to live again come? What caused the Neanderthals ever to think of it? Did one of them just make it all up one day? If so, based on what?"

"I don't know. According to Carl Jung, all such beliefs were inherited, and they stemmed from what he termed the 'collective unconscious'—that is, that part of the psyche that can be negatively distinguished from the personal unconscious, because it doesn't owe its existence to experience. The personal unconscious, Jung stated, essentially consisted of contents that had at one time been conscious, born of experience, but that had passed from the conscious to the unconscious through means of forgetfulness or repression. The collective unconscious, on the other hand, Jung declared, is fundamentally composed of archetypes that have never been a part of the conscious, but, rather, seem to have always been present everywhere. Mythologists call these archetypes 'motifs,' while the German ethnologist Adolf Bastian referred to them as 'elemental' or 'primordial thoughts.' Jung's hypothesis was thus that there exists a second psychic system of a collective, universal and impersonal nature, which is hereditary and identical in all individuals.''

"If that were true, then it would mean that all such knowledge was somehow genetically encoded," Bryony mused aloud, "and while I could understand something like the concept of a paradisical afterlife being placed into our so-called collective unconscious, what about things like aliens, dwarves, elves, fairies, giants, monsters, ogres and so on? And should we add gods and goddesses to that list, as well? We know most mythological creatures, like dragons, don't really exist and probably never existed. Does that mean that the gods and goddesses, or even a single Creator, don't exist, either? If that's the case, then who or what coded our genes?''

"That's a good question," Hamish observed. "The entire subject is rather like a Catch Twenty-two, isn't it? If the Creator exists, why did He or She put the idea of multiple gods and goddesses into our collective unconscious? If the Creator doesn't exist, then how were we genetically encoded? No doubt, all this ties in somehow, some way, with your father's own ideas, among other things, about the acquisition of wisdom

and the cauldron of life, especially if we think of the cauldron
as the collective unconscious, and of wisdom as what is gained
by tapping into it. Perhaps that's one of the reasons why your
father appeared to feel so strongly that the ancient Greek city
of Delphi was one of the primary keys to the Mysteries. Its
Oracle was, after all, a wise one who sat upon a tripod-
cauldron, able to examine not only the past and present, but
also to foretell the future, perhaps in some way capable of
accessing the collective unconscious.''

"The so-called Sleeping Prophet, Edgar Cayce, claimed that
the whole of time was recorded upon what he referred to as
the 'Akashic Record,'" Bryony noted, as she sipped her wine,
"and could be consulted by those who knew how. Maybe that
idea, too, is simply a form of Jung's collective unconscious."

"Maybe. What do you say that, tomorrow, we head toward
Greece and Delphi, darling?" the Scotsman suggested, lighting
a cigarette and dragging on it deeply. "Perhaps your father was
right, and there *are* at least some answers to be found there."

Bryony sighed heavily.

"I really don't see how, Hamish. I've seen the ruins at Delphi before, years ago, and while they're beautiful, they're still
only the remains of an ancient city. Nevertheless, I suppose
that it can't hurt to visit them." Pausing, she bit her lower lip.
" Oh, how I wish Dad had been able to provide us with more
information than he has so far—and been less cryptic about
what he *did* know! I can't help but feel that at this point, all
we truly have are a bunch of nebulous notions that could be
interpreted in any number of ways...dozens of puzzle pieces
but, still, no big picture. Sometimes, I feel that the task Dad
set for us is simply monumental and overwhelming! People
have been studying arcana and esoterics for millennia! And all
of them were seemingly no further ahead than we ourselves
are currently. Dad devoted his whole life to his research, and
yet even he had only half-formed notions, with few resolutions.
So how can we possibly hope to figure it all out?"

"Maybe the Knights Templar treasure will help."

"But that's been lost for centuries, Hamish—if it ever even
existed at all—and if it did and the Templars possessed it, then

why didn't they make use of it…whatever *it* may have been? Yes, I'll grant that they were an extremely rich and powerful Order. However, in the end, they don't really seem to have accomplished anything that couldn't have been achieved through intelligence, daring, foresight, shrewd strategies, influential connections and financial acumen.''

"Perhaps that's because they didn't fully understand whatever it was that they had somehow got hold of," the Scotsman speculated thoughtfully, blowing a stream of cigarette smoke into the night air. "Maybe *no one* through whose hands it has passed over the millennia has ever completely comprehended it!''

"If that's the case, then it doesn't bode very well for us, either, if, by some miracle, we should actually discover where it's been hidden," Bryony pointed out glumly.

"True. But then, again, we have access to a lot of data, research and study, and, most important, modern technology that the ancient peoples didn't.''

"Somehow, I think we're going to need it!''

At that pronouncement, she and Hamish fell abruptly silent, each lost in reverie, gazing at the campfire, which blazed brightly and warmly in the darkness, yellow-orange flames crackling, wood snapping and popping, cinders flying—a shower of sparks that resembled a dying Roman candle. Aeons ago, on nights such as this, around fires just like this one, the ancient peoples had sat, Bryony thought, and they had stared up at the black-velvet vault above, in which the Silver Wheel, composed of the constellations of the zodiac, turned. Had the tales the ancient peoples had told about the stars and the myths they had attached to them been only to explain the glittering, stellar objects they had not wholly fathomed? Or were they universal concepts placed into the collective unconscious by means of genetic encoding? Or something else entirely…lost knowledge, long-forgotten memories?

She did not know. It seemed almost as weighty a question as that she had once, as a child, asked of a priest in catechism class: Where did God come from? For Mankind could be explained as having been created by God. Heretics and philosophers wondered if the reverse were also true—and the German existentialist Friedrich Nietzsche had written that God was dead, that all the gods had died laughing when one old grim beard among them had stood up and announced, "Thou shalt have no other gods before me."

It was a long drive from Rennes-le-Château to the city of Ancona, which lay on the eastern coast of Italy, on the western shore of the Adriatic Sea. To reach it, Bryony and Hamish traveled east along the northern coast of the Mediterranean Sea, through Marseille, Monaco and Milan, then swung southeast toward Bologna, Rimini and, finally, Ancona itself. From here, dozens of huge, luxurious ferries cruised the Adriatic Sea on regular, virtually daily, routes between Italy and Greece. The grand ships were known by the nickname of "Ro-Ro" ferries, short for "Roll On, Roll Off," a reference to the fact that, if transporting a vehicle, one simply drove it on to, then off of, the vessel.

After investigation into the various ships currently available, Bryony and Hamish were able to book passage upon the *Kriti II*, one of the nine ferries owned by Anek Lines. The *Kriti II* was an enormous, white vessel, capable of speeds up to twenty-three knots, and of carrying sixteen hundred passengers and twelve hundred vehicles. Among other posh amenities, the ship boasted a restaurant, a bar, a disco, a casino, slot machines, a duty-free shop, a swimming pool, and both elevators and es-calators. The pleasant cabin assigned to Bryony and Hamish was an outside one, on an upper deck, and presently, they were ensconced within it, awaiting departure.

The voyage from Ancona to the city of Patras, which lay on the northern coast of the Peloponnese district of Greece, would take approximately twenty-two hours. Soon, the ferry was un-der way, the whitecapped waves of the Adriatic Sea churning beneath its prow.

Following supper in the restaurant, Bryony and Hamish em-ployed their time to download a freeware HTML program from the Internet to her laptop computer. They then began to develop a Web site devoted to the Abbey of the Divine; its origin, history and current state of affairs. Given the limitations of the program they were using, the Web site couldn't be elaborate, but still, it would serve their purpose of uploading information about the secret order to the World Wide Web. In honor of Bryony's father, they had decided to call their Web site "Alphêus: The Underground Stream," believing that would attract more attention than labeling it with the Abbey's own name, which was as yet unknown to the public.

They planned to send background material about the order to several other Web sites on the Internet, which were dedicated to arcana and esoterics. Because of the very nature of the World Wide Web, which was basically unregulated and therefore rife with copying and theft, they conjectured that it would be only a matter of time until their information was seized and expounded upon by any number of other Web masters, who would perpetuate the data in such a way that it would quickly spread all over the Internet, and thereby the entire world.

"After that, any and all attempts by the Abbey to hack the Web sites or otherwise halt the dissemination of the information about the order will simply be additional proof of its actual existence, thus defeating its goal of continued secrecy," the Scotsman asserted, with a note of satisfaction in his voice. "Thank God for the World Wide Web! Whilst it's an international podium for every ignoramus and crackpot around, it's still a modern marvel, bytes flowing in an endless fount of knowledge for anyone with access to a computer, a modem and an Internet service provider—an educational tool the like of which Mankind has never before seen!"

"Good Lord, Hamish!" Bryony exclaimed softly. "Do you realize what you've just said? In its own way, *it's* an underground stream!"

Thirty

The Flight of Abraham the Jew

Balinas mentions the engraving on the table in the hand of Hermes, which says: "Truth! Certainty! That in which there is no doubt!

That which is above is from that which is below, and that which is below is from that which is above, working the miracles of one.

As all things were from one.

Its father is the Sun and its mother the Moon.

The Earth carried it in her belly, and the Wind nourished it in her belly, as Earth which shall become Fire.

Feed the Earth from that which is subtle, with the greatest power.

It ascends from the earth to the heaven and becomes ruler over that which is above and that which is below."

And I have already explained the meaning of the whole of this in two of these books of mine.

The Emerald Tablet
—as translated by Abu Musa Jabir ibn Hayyan

The Taifa of Córdoba, Al-Andalus, 1236 A.D.

As so many others of his ilk were, Abraham the Jew was desperately fleeing from Córdoba, the capital city of Al-

Andalus—"Land of the Vandals." Since its capture by the Catholic King Ferdinand III of Castile, Córdoba was no longer the safe haven it had been under its series of Muslim emirs and caliphs.

For nearly half a millennium now, Córdoba had hosted a society of cultural and religious tolerance such as the world had scarcely ever before witnessed. Libraries and grand centers of learning for architecture, mathematics, music, philosophy, religion and science had been erected, along with mosques, synagogues and churches; the city's copyists rivaled Christian monks in the production of religious works. Córdoba's ornate brocades, woven silks, fine leather work and splendid jewelry were eagerly sought by traders from both the West and the East, a testament to the city's prosperity and rich commerce, industry and mining. The fertile region abounded with the almonds, apricots, sugarcane and other crops introduced by the Arabs, and an elaborate irrigation system had been built by the Muslims, as well.

The heart of Abraham the Jew was heavy and sore as he crept furtively along the city's labyrinth of narrow, winding, cobbled streets, taking care to avoid the light cast by the flickering streetlamps—the first to be instituted in the whole of Europe—which had been ignited at dusk, despite the current state of upheaval. The Castilian kings were fervent Catholics, whose ultimate goal was to drive not only the Muslims, but also the Jews from the entire Iberian Peninsula. As a result, there was no secure place now in Córdoba for the likes of Abraham and his kind.

Alongside him, the unshod hooves of his donkey, muffled by rags carefully wrapped and tied about them, *clip-clopped* quietly on the cobblestones. Atop the beast's back, concealed in the middle of a bundle of innocuous personal possessions, reposed the intricate, gold, silver and copper puzzle box containing the ancient manuscript that Abraham was smuggling from the city. It must not fall into the hands of the zealous King Ferdinand III, he thought, for there was no telling to what vicious uses that sovereign might put its utterly priceless knowledge!

Even now, information that had escaped in bits and pieces from the book over the millennia was changing the face of the world and drastically altering the course of its events. From mystics dedicated to the study of the Qabbalah, to alchemists devoted to finding the Elixir of Life, the Philosopher's Stone, to the founding of ancient orders such as that of the Architects or Builders, who were also called "Masons," and that of the Rose Cross or Rosicrucians to, more recently, that of the Poor Knights of Christ and the Temple of Solomon, the tome had unwittingly unleashed havoc on the entire globe...havoc wrought by those who did not understand the manuscript's contents.

However incorrect, the book had been given a name—*The Emerald Tablet*—and its authorship had been attributed to an Egyptian god-priest, Hermes Trismesgistos or "Thrice-Great Hermes."

But Abraham believed the name to be a misnomer—derived from the fact that the front piece of the ancient manuscript's goat-leather cover had been dyed a deep green. The book was not about transmuting lead into gold at all, as so many misguided people nowadays wildly imagined. No, Abraham reflected, that was not the key. But what the tome held *was* a means to eternal life—and its immense power would surely bring about the end of the world if turned to the sinister hand of Evil!

He heaved a huge sigh of relief when, leading his donkey, he finally slipped from the capital city, leaving Córdoba behind him, heading north toward the Pyrenees Mountains and the Languedoc-Roussillon region, the crescent sliver of land that had once been the principality of Septimania. Years ago, from Rennes-le-Château, the manuscript had come, passing into the hands of Godfrey of Bouillon, once Duke of Lower Lorraine, who had descended not only from Charlemagne, but also from the Merovingian kings.

Along with his brothers Eustace and Baldwin, Godfrey had been a leader of the First Crusade, and he had been named King of Jerusalem following its capture from the Muslims in July 1099. He had accepted the crown, but had refused the title of "King," calling himself instead the "Defender of the Holy Sepulchre." At Godfrey's death, his brother Baldwin had succeeded him.

It was during Baldwin's reign that the Order of the Poor Knights of Christ and the Temple of Solomon—better known as the "Knights Templar"—had been founded by Hugues de Payen, a vassal to Hugh, Count of Champagne, and a relative by marriage to the St. Clairs of Rosslyn, in collaboration with André de Montbard, the uncle of St. Bernard of Clairvaux. The two knights, along with seven other companions, had presented themselves to King Baldwin I of Jerusalem, declaring their intention to found an order of warrior monks for the purpose of keeping "the roads and highways safe," and "with a special regard for the protection of pilgrims" to the Holy Land. After having taken vows of chastity and personal poverty, swearing to hold all their property in common, they had been granted quarters by Baldwin, which had included the stables of the Temple of Solomon, and the right to wear the red cross *patté* as their insignia.

Contrary to their announcement, however, the Templars had done nothing to patrol and protect the dangerous pilgrim routes of the Holy Land. Instead, they had devoted fully nine years to excavating and mining a series of tunnels under their quarters on the Temple Mount. This demanding task had been carried out with the patronage and full support of Baldwin.

They had certainly not been digging in search of the puzzle box and the ancient manuscript. That much, Abraham felt sure of, for both had already been in the hands of first Godfrey and then Baldwin. But the Ark of the Covenant, which had once held the box and the book, had mysteriously vanished centuries ago. The Ark was sometimes depicted as being transported on a four-wheeled chariot, and Abraham knew that, strangely enough, the old Visigoth name for Rennes-le-Château—Rhédae—meant "Four-Wheeled Chariot."

Following the completion of their excavations in December 1127, the Knights Templar had hurried back to France. Hugues de Payen, who had been named the Grand Master of the Order, and André de Montbard had then traveled to England, from where, having obtained safe passage from King Henry I, they had journeyed directly north across the border into Scotland. There, from de Payen's relatives by marriage, the St. Clairs of Rosslyn, the Knights Templar had gained an immediate grant of land—Ballantrodoch—to serve as the head-quarters of the Order in Scotland.

Meanwhile, during the turmoil of the Crusades, the puzzle box and the book had fallen into the custody of the Jews at Jerusalem, whence both had been carried to Córdoba by Abra-ham.

But now, he thought grimly, they must be returned to Rennes-le-Château, where they would be secure. For the Knights Templar had now spread across the whole of Europe, growing into a supremely powerful and wealthy Order—and more than one-third of their total estates were located in the Languedoc-Roussillon region that had once been the princi-pality of Septimania, to where the deposed boy-king, Sigisbert IV, of the Merovingians had fled for his very life nearly six hundred years ago.

Thirty-One

The Oracle at Delphi

The folly of mistaking a paradox for a discovery,
a metaphor for a proof,
a torrent of verbiage for a spring of capital truths,
and oneself for an oracle, is inborn in us.

> Introduction to the *Method of Leonardo da Vinci*
> —Paul Valéry

The oracles are dumb,
No voice or hideous hum
Runs through the arched roof in words deceiving.
Apollô from his shrine
Can no more divine,
With hollow shriek the steep of Delphos leaving.

> *On the Morning of Christ's Nativity*
> —John Milton

Kastri and the Ruins of Delphi, Greece, the Present

The following afternoon, once they had retrieved the Volvo,
disembarked from the *Kriti II* at Patras, and proceeded through
Customs, Bryony and Hamish decided that it was too late to

set out on the approximately three-and-a-half-hour trip to Delphi. Instead, they found a small, quiet hotel in Patras, where they checked in before taking a short stroll along the beach, which was bathed in the fiery rays of the setting sun. Afterward, they ate supper at one of the local tavernas, then returned to their hotel room.

Getting a relatively early start the next morning, they traveled northeast from Patras to Delphi.

Once, aeons ago, not only the Greeks, but also the peoples of far-flung foreign lands had journeyed to Delphi, the so-called center of the earth, the navel of the world. Some had come afoot along serpentine roads from places like Athens, while others had arrived by ship, landing at the ancient port of Krisa, now known as "Itea," on the northern coast of the Gulf of Corinth. They had come to consult the Oracle, the most famous and most important adviser in all the ancient Mediterranean world.

But now, like the ruins of Delphi itself, only the small village of Kastri soared high above the Gulf of Corinth, clinging precariously to the piney-wooded slopes and rocky crags and crevices of colossal and sacred Mount Parnassus, which, at 8,061 feet, towered second only to Mount Olympus in Greece. Above the ruins and the village loomed the titanic, stark cliffs known as the *Phaedriades*—the "Shining Ones"—so called because they reflected the sun's rays and glowed at sunset. Cutting through the imposing cliffs was a ravine at whose base flowed the Castalian spring where the oracular priestesses had used to bathe and purify themselves. Below was a precipitous drop into the gorge of Pleistos, which itself gave way to a broad plain filled with olive trees that stretched to the edge of the azure waters of the gulf.

The bright, yellow late-spring sun, much warmer here in Greece than in France, had now burned away the morning mist that, earlier, had swathed Mount Parnassus, exposing to Bryony and Hamish a site that had been occupied for perhaps as long as seven millennia, since the arrival of its first settlers in the Neolithic period, several thousand years before the advent of Jesus Christ. In the medieval age, Kastri had occupied the area of Delphi itself. But in later years, the village had been moved to its present location to allow for systematic excavations of the ruins by the French Archaeological School, which had begun in 1893, although various archaeologists had been excavating the site since 1838. Gradually, the removal of massive quantities of accumulated earth—the result of a number of landslides—had revealed the remains of the once-great Delphi.

Now, as the Volvo climbed ever higher, it was not just the thin mountain air that made Bryony's breath catch in her throat, but also the sight of the ruins themselves. It had been years since she had last seen them, and until this very moment, she had forgotten how splendid they truly were, perched like an eagle in an aerie upon the mountainside, aeons-old columns and stones gleaming white in the sunlight, a priceless pearl in a wild, green-gold setting.

"Only imagine what Delphi must have been like at the height of its full glory, Hamish." She spoke quietly. "How it must have awed and dazzled everyone who saw it!"

"Yes. Even in ruins, it's still fabulous!"

After at last reaching their destination, parking their car and getting out to walk the old, twisting streets of both Kastri and Delphi, Bryony and Hamish found themselves amid a strange mélange of ancient classical structures; small, traditional Greek houses clustered close together on the mountainside; and modern restaurants, souvenir shops and hotels. For these days, the renowned ruins served the village as a tourist attraction, drawing thousands of visitors annually.

Hungry after their three-and-a-half-hour drive, Bryony and Hamish decided to eat lunch first before exploring Delphi. At one of the local tavernas, they dined on *horiatiki salata maroulee*—a tasty Greek village salad consisting of lettuce topped with capers, cucumbers, feta, green peppers, olives, oregano and tomatoes, and drenched with olive oil and vinegar; followed by *melitzaness tighanites*, fried eggplant dipped in *tzatziki*—a rich Greek yogurt, cucumber, olive oil, mint and garlic sauce; and then a main course of spicy *souvlaki arni*, spit-roasted lamb served on skewers, on a bed of rice pilaf. They washed it all down not with retsina—the popular, pine-resin-flavored, white wine found in both Greece and Cyprus, but which usually tasted quite bitter to the unaccustomed palate— but, rather, with an *Apéllis* red wine from Kos. Afterward, they ordered cups of strong, black coffee, over which Hamish smoked a cigarette.

"Do you know any of the myths or history of Delphi?" he inquired, taking a long drag from his cigarette, then blowing a stream of smoke through his nostrils.

Bryony shook her head. "No...that is, aside from the archaeological findings, of course, I know only the most basic details," she amended, "such as the fact that it's where the ancient Oracle prophesied, and that it's just one of several such places—Delos, Dodona, Ammon and Rome among them, although I suppose Rome didn't actually have an oracle proper, but, rather, augers...priests who foretold the future through observing omens, like lightning, meeting certain kinds of animals, spilling salt and so forth...many of which are still superstitions even today."

"Yes, that's right," the Scotsman stated. "Delphi, however, is an extremely old oracular site, and there is evidence that it was dedicated to an earth-mother goddess."

According to myth, the Delphic site was where the earth-mother goddess Gaia or Gē used to pronounce her prophecies. It dates from the second millennium before Christ, when the Mycenaeans built a village there. Gaia's oracular cave was said to have been guarded by her child, Pythôn, a huge serpent or dragon coiled around the lofty peak of Mount Parnassus.

"Legend tells that Gaia's cavern was first discovered by a goatherd named Kouretas, who observed his goats behaving quite strangely at its mouth, frisking and gamboling about, and uttering peculiar noises," Hamish explained as he sipped his coffee and smoked his cigarette. "Kouretas investigated the opening, whereupon a fit of madness promptly seized him, and he himself began cavorting and prophesying. Soon, his neighbors and others flocked to the cavity, many growing so frenzied there that, temporarily insane, they flung themselves into the deep fissure in its rocky floor, whence the mysterious fumes that were the cause of all the mental disturbances were emanating. To prevent the suicides, the village officials built a temple over the site, devoting it to the earth-mother goddess.''

In a small room above the vaporous chasm itself had been positioned a tripod-cauldron, upon which the Delphic priestesses had sat to deliver their oracles.

"Although no trace of any such fissure has ever been found—either beneath the lower chamber of the temple or elsewhere," Hamish continued, "it is certainly entirely possible that it actually did exist and has simply been sealed up by earthquakes, which are fairly common in this region. In addition, methane has been found in small quantities in the local rocks, which could account for the hallucinogenic fumes the priestesses allegedly inhaled, although, more recently, it has been discovered that the Castalian spring in which they bathed prior to pronouncing their divinations carries and releases equally small quantities of ethylene, which, when inhaled, acts as an anesthetic, inducing a trancelike state. Also, although the priestesses are thought by most people to have chewed laurel leaves before performing their oracular duties, it is far more likely that they actually burned them in the adytum below the tripod-cauldron, since the smoke from laurel leaves is mildly hallucinogenic, as well. Unquestionably, one or a combination of these things could have been responsible for the oracular fits the priestesses were said to suffer.''

Myth held that, eventually, the infant sun god Apollô had grown jealous of Delphi's fame and, coming down from Mount Olympus, had violently slain Pythôn.

"It is said that upon the site of his battle with the serpent, Apollô built a temple, and that in the earth, at the precise place where he had killed the serpent, he set the fabled *omphalos* or navel stone," the Scotsman elucidated, "allegedly a huge meteorite that, in antiquity, had fallen from the heavens, and Delphi, according to the Greeks, being the center of the world. This last, the great god Zeus had previously determined by loosing two eagles at opposite ends of the earth, proclaiming as the navel of the world the spot—Delphi—where the birds, one flying from the west, the other the east, had at last met. It was supposedly renamed from Pytho to Delphi after Apollô transformed himself into a dolphin—*delphis* in Greek—to fetch sailors from Crete to serve as priests in his new shrine.''

Bryony said thoughtfully, ''Basically, the myth ties in quite well with what we know about Delphi archaeologically...that it was settled by Neolithic peoples sometime between five thousand and three thousand B.C., that the Mycenaeans arrived around fifteen hundred B.C., and that about five hundred years after that, either warlike northern tribes from Thessaly or else Dorians from Crete—perhaps taking advantage of the natural disasters, such as earthquakes and tidal waves, which plague the region—moved into the area, overthrowing what had previously been a peaceful, goddess-worshiping culture and imposing upon it their own god.'' She paused, then went on. ''Shouldn't we go investigate the ruins now, Hamish, before it gets too late in the day? Although it was some years ago, I've seen them before, of course. I expect many archaeologists have. However, I *would* like to refresh my memory, even though I'm still not exactly sure what we're looking for here.''

''That makes two of us. But still, your father seemed to believe strongly that Delphi was somehow important, so I don't think we ought to leave any stone unturned.''

''No, nor do I.''

After paying their bill at the taverna and tipping the pleasant, young Greek who had waited on them, Bryony and Hamish bought tickets to visit the ruins and, hand in hand, started up the Sacred Way, the path that thousands of ancient supplicants, after riding up the shadowy, fearsome gorges that led to Delphi, had trodden afoot aeons ago before them.

Among the important archaeological finds at the ruins were the Altar of the Chians, the Castalian spring, the Gymnasium, the Polygonal Wall, the settlement of Delphi itself and its cemeteries, the Stadium, the Stoa of the Athenians, the Temple of Apollô, the Theater, the Tholos and the Treasury of the Athenians. Of all the monuments uncovered, however, only the Treasury had proved capable of being fully reconstructed from its own original building materials. During the years 1903 through 1906, it had been restored to all its former glory, and it was now the best preserved edifice at Delphi.

It was just one of many treasuries that had been erected over
the centuries to house the *telônias,* the taxes or tolls paid by
those who had wished to consult the Oracle, as well as the
donations of gold and silver and other priceless gifts that had
poured into Delphi from far and wide.

Both the city and its vast wealth had been administered and
protected by a group of sacred scribes representing twelve
Greek tribes. They had met every spring and autumn to vote
on decisions that had then been acted upon by the Senate. Approximately a thousand people had once lived in the city,
hawking sacrificial knives and other religious objects, or working as inscription carvers, servants and at other such profes-
sions.

Eventually, however, several Sacred Wars had broken out
for control of Delphi, and in the end, the Emperor Constantine
the Great had removed the temple's hallowed tripod-cauldron
to Byzantium. Later, the Emperor Julian, the apostate who had
attempted to destroy Christianity, had inquired of the Oracle
whether he should restore the sanctuary. It was said that, keening bitterly, she had replied, "Tell the king this: The glorious
temple has fallen into ruin. Apollô has no roof over his head;
the bay leaves are silent; the prophetic springs and fountains
are dead." At last, around 385 A.D., the sanctuary had been
officially closed down, by decree of the Emperor Theodosius.

As Bryony and Hamish wandered through the ruins, she felt,
as she always did at such places, the immense, awesome power
of the site. Even today, although Delphi was but a mere shadow
of its former self, it still possessed the ability both to daunt and
to inspire. In her mind's eye, she imagined all the monuments
as they must have looked in their glory days, and as always,
she marveled at the aesthetics and architectural knowledge of
their builders.

To the east of the main entrance to the sanctuary rose the
beautiful Temple of Athêna, and to its west flowed the Castalian spring. Just north of the Temple of Apollô curved the Theater, its cavea containing thirty-five rows of stone benches—
approximately seven thousand seats—from which spectators
had once watched the Delphic Festivals. Some yards above the

Theater and slightly to the west lay the Stadium, with its enormous arched entrance, in which the Pythian Games had been held every four years.

Interestingly enough, the Greeks had revered Athêna as the goddess of wisdom, and among the things venerable to her had been the owl, the serpent, and the olive tree. In some myths, she was also credited with having invented the chariot.

"Hamish, here's a thought!" Bryony abruptly exclaimed, with excitement, as they studied the temple. "Idries Shah, in his book *The Sufis,* suggests that the name of the disembodied head or skull—Baphomet—allegedly worshiped by the Knights Templar derives from the Arabic word *Abufihamat,* meaning 'Father of Understanding,' right?"

"That's correct—although many people believe that the word is more accurately translated as 'Source of Understanding,' which source, some say, was the Mother, rather than the Father. Why do you ask?"

"Well, standing here, it just suddenly struck me. According to legend, Athêna was the daughter of Zeus and the Titaness Metis, whom Zeus trapped and swallowed whole when she was pregnant with Athêna, because an *oracle of the earth-mother goddess* had predicted that the child would depose Zeus, just as he had his own father, Kronos! But Zeus's attempt to murder his daughter failed. Instead, he developed a horrendous headache, and the messenger god and psychopomp, Hermês, hearing Zeus's cries of pain, summoned the smith god, Hephaestus, who, with a blow of his mighty ax, split open Zeus's *skull.* Athêna subsequently sprang fully grown and armed *from her father's head!* Last but not least, there are those who claim that the name Baphomet actually derives from the Greek term *baphê-mêtis,* aren't there?"

"Yes!" The Scotsman nodded, also beginning to grow excited. "*Baphê-mêtis* is invariably mistranslated—most often as 'absorption or immersion into knowledge or wisdom,' or, even more erroneously, as 'initiation into measurement.' But what the word *baphê* truly means is 'the dipping of red-hot iron into water...tempering.' The word *mêtis* has several different definitions...'wisdom, skill, craft, counsel, plan, undertaking.'

However, a *mêtietês* is a 'counselor,' and Homer employs that word as an epithet for Zeus, meaning 'all-wise.' Zeus swallowed Metis—'Counsel'—whole, remember? Thereby allegorically digesting wisdom. So what *baphê-mêtis* actually properly translates as is 'tempered by counsel or wisdom.' Further, a silver goblet said to have belonged to the Vienna Preceptory of the Knights Templar is claimed by Joseph von Hammer to bear an incription that reads, 'Let Mete be exalted, who causes all things to bud and blossom; it is our root; it is the one and seven; it is *octinimus,* the eight-fold name.'"

"And wisdom is the province of Isis, Sophia, the Black Madonna—whose number is eight! Perhaps what the Knights Templar worshiped was simply wisdom. The original name of the Knights Templar was the Order of the Poor Knights of Christ and the Temple of Solomon, right? And King Solomon was not only famed for his wisdom, but was also a polytheist who venerated Astarte, the Canaanite Isis, as did King Hiram of Tyre, who contributed to the construction of Solomon's Temple. So maybe that's what the Templar's disembodied head or skull signified...a higher level of intelligence, the human *brain*—because *that's* really the 'source of understanding,' isn't it? I mean, it *is* the human brain that sets us apart from all other animals and that has enabled us to acquire sentience and the knowledge of life and death! One usually achieves wisdom precisely by being 'tempered by counsel'—advice, guidance, instruction, learning, whatever, from those older, wiser and more experienced than oneself." Bryony paused for a moment, ordering her thoughts. Then she continued.

"Additionally, to temper something, such as a sword, is to harden, strengthen and give an edge to it, by immersing it in fire and water...heating the iron to make it malleable, so it can be pounded into the desired shape, then plunging it into water to cool and harden it, so it's better able to take an edge. John the Baptist said that he baptized with *water,* but that Jesus would baptize with the Holy Spirit and *fire*. Fire, however, is traditionally associated with Hell, an inferno, the fiery lair of the Serpent, while baptism by water is a rite performed for the remission of sins and purification of the body and soul...the very first of the sacraments—that of regeneration—and the door to Heaven and eternal life. Yet ceremonial baptism by water is far older than Christianity and was practiced by countless ancient peoples. The Celts, for example, proclaimed themselves to have been baptizers long before the advent of Jesus, and they believed the head to contain the immortal soul, as well. Further, according to the Gospel of Matthew, Jesus said, 'Do not think that I have come to bring peace upon the earth. I have come to bring not peace, but the sword,' while it was John the Baptist, not Jesus, who was beheaded—and it was a disembodied head or skull that the Knights Templar are claimed to have revered, just as the Easter Islanders worshiped giant heads. Last but not least, John the Baptist and his feast day of June Twenty-third are inextricably entwined with both the Templars and modern Freemasony! What do you think all this signifies, Hamish?''

"I'm not sure," he responded slowly, pondering. "But let's try to tie at least some of this together, shall we? Since we're standing at her temple, why don't we start with Athêna Pronaia? As we know, Athêna was the Greek goddess of wisdom, so we may quite legitimately equate her with Isis, Sophia, the Black Madonna and so on. Her name here in her guise at Delphi—Athêna Pronaia—translates as 'Before the Temple of Immortality,' since Athêna derives from the Greek words *athanasia,* meaning 'ambrosia, antidote, elixir of life, immortality,' and *athanês,* meaning 'undying,' whilst Pronaia stems from the Greek word *pronaios,* which means 'before the temple' or 'the front hall of a temple, through which one passes to the *naos*'— *naos* itself referring to 'the innermost part of a temple or shrine, and containing the image of god,' which is the same as the Greek *aduton,* from which we derive the Latin word *adytum,* which we use in English today."

"And Athêna's temple here at Delphi surrounds a *tholos* tomb or rotunda, which is any round building, especially one covered by a dome, and which word itself comes from the Latin root word *rota*—'wheel.' Good Lord, Hamish! That makes me think of the four-wheeled chariot the prophet Ezekiel saw! I mean, it's described as being round, wheeled, and having a dome on it, isn't it?''

''Yes, and the dome contained a throne, upon which God sat, just as Isis is enthroned in a ship or vessel. Who traditionally sits on thrones, Bryony? Only gods, goddesses, kings and queens—and as we noted earlier, the *tholos* tomb was generally used by the Mycenaeans for the burial of kings and other royalty. Was this, then, symbolic of the 'chariot' that carried one to the Creator? I wonder. After all, slain Viking warriors were often burned in ships, and even today, the deceased are transported by hearses to cemeteries.''

''Ancient peoples such as the Urnfield culture cremated their dead, interring them in urns or cauldrons that were frequently placed on small chariots, too. Delphi before Apollô and Athêna became attached to it was originally the center of a chthonic cult—a cult of the Underworld. It dealt with death and rebirth, as did the Essene rituals and those of the Egyptian god Osiris. So it makes perfect sense that both the tomb and the womb—the latter represented by the legendary cave of the earth-mother goddess and the world's navel—would be combined at such a site, even after the Apollô and Athêna myths were grafted on to it,'' she pointed out. ''And so perhaps the serpent Pythôn even has something to do with the umbilical cord, as well.''

''Possibly,'' the Scotsman rejoined. ''Of course, if one believes in reincarnation, then to die and be inhumed in a tomb is actually to return to the womb—which is also, when filled with a child, a domed chamber, after a fashion, is it not? One in which the fetus essentially 'sails' on amniotic fluid or the 'elixir of life,' and which fluid is actually virtually indistinguishable from seawater, in which all life here on earth began...the primordial soup, as it were. So unquestionably, there are several ideas at work here, the principal of which seems to be that wisdom is required to know the Creator, to enter into the Temple of the Creator, and to achieve eternal life, and that such wisdom is acquired by the tempering of the spirit—perhaps through several lifetimes, in fact, if we equate fire with death or the tomb, and water with life or the womb. Thus the fact that Jesus baptized with the Holy Spirit and fire, died, and was entombed becomes increasingly paramount when we consider the fact that we have already agreed that to gain full wisdom or enlightenment, one must actually experience death at least once. So if death *is* the key, then Jesus really *was* the embodiment of the Way, because above all, He demonstrated the significance of death—that even the Son of God must die.''

"While John the Baptist showed the flipside of the coin, so to speak," Bryony observed, "the importance of life, and the symbolism of baptism...the sprinkling of life-giving water upon the head, which contains the immortal soul and the human brain, enabling sentience and the acquisition of knowledge and wisdom throughout the life journey, without which life itself becomes meaningless and we ourselves no different from animals. For the Greeks, the 'brain' was Athêna, sprung from the head of Zeus, the 'All-Wise' One. Sacred to her were the owl, representing wisdom, and the serpent, whose venom is both poison and antidote, as death itself would appear to be both anathema and vital to us, and as the umbilical cord brings death to the infant beyond the womb and life within it. In some tales, Lil, not Eve, was the first wife of Adam, and *Lil* has been variously translated as both 'owl' and 'serpent,' symbols of wisdom and death, while *Eve* means 'life.' But of course, the two women are actually like the planet Venus, with its dual nature, aren't they? Both, in reality, one...Eve, the innocent, naive one who lived and then ate of the forbidden fruit from the Tree of Knowledge of Good and Evil in the Garden of Eden, thereby becoming Lil, the sadder but wiser one who died...Athêna and Aphrodite...Minerva and Venus—the Evening Star and the Morning Star. Do we truly believe that one shines less brightly than the other?''

"No.'' Hamish shook his head. "I don't think so. And of course, all this conforms quite nicely, as well, with Isis's number, eight—which represents the vagina and womb of the earth-mother goddess—and, too, with the fact that Venus's orbit around the sun, as seen from the earth, describes a pentagram in the heavens every eight years.'' He paused, then went on.

"By means of the number eight, we can further correlate all this, as well, with Pythagoras, the Greek mathematician who discovered the octave, which is the foundation of the Western musical scale—and which, on a piano, consists of eight white keys and five black ones. Just as a rainbow has seven colors, the octave is comprised of seven tones, plus an eighth, which is a higher or lower repeat of the first tone, or twelve semitones, plus a thirteeth, which, again, is a higher or lower repeat of the first semitone. Basically, what Pythagoras demonstrated was that if you take two strings of equal length and tension, and divide one of them exactly in half, then when they are plucked, the pitch produced by the shorter string will be precisely one octave higher than that of the string twice its length. He is therefore credited with discovering that the interval of an octave is rooted in the ratio of two to one, that of a fourth in four to three, that of a fifth in three to two, and that of a whole tone in nine to eight.

"This eventually led to the concept known as *Musica Mundâna*—the 'Music of the Worlds.' For some time now, scientists have been aware that the planets in our solar system, including the earth, give off low-frequency sounds, probably as a result of their relative mass, composition and orbital speed, among other things. Further, during the Seventeen Hundreds, the Prussian astronomer Johann Titius discovered that the planets also display a mean orbital distance of a ratio that is roughly two to one from the innermost planet, Mercury. This ratio holds true for the moons from their respective planets, too. After Titius had pointed all this out, it was subsequently formulated as a mathematical expression by the German astronomer Johann Bode, and is now popularly referred to as the 'Titius-Bode Law.' Thus, since the planets' mean orbital distance is the same ratio as that of an octave, it could be argued that they fashion a chain of octaves—"

"As though there were one long umbilical cord stretched along the navels of the worlds!" Bryony interrupted, highly animated.

"Why…yes! I hadn't ever thought of it that way before…but, *yes!* To continue, then, thus when the planets are variously aligned with one another in conjunctions and so forth, they could be legitimately described as 'singing' celestial 'chords.'"

"So astrology truly *could* have some genuine, factual basis in science, with its not being so much the actual *positions* of the planets at the time of one's birth, but, rather, the *sound waves* they produce in those particular positions that affects one's being!" Bryony declared, fascinated. "Maybe the Beach Boys really *were* picking up good vibrations, and maybe we really *do* literally get bad vibes, Hamish!"

"That's certainly a strong possibility," the Scotsman agreed. Then he quoted softly, "'If a man does not keep pace with his companions, perhaps it is because he hears a different drummer. Let him step to the music which he hears, however measured or far away.'" He fell silent for a moment, then went on.

"There's more. Until the late Renaissance period, musical instruments were tuned by means of a single-stringed device known as the 'canon' or 'monochord'—which is also what Pythagoras used for his own experiments—following a phenomenon incorrectly called the 'Circle of Fifths.' This process starts by dividing the monochord's string at two-thirds its original length, the two-thirds, of course, being the Fifth of the undivided string, just as the Fifth—or five diatonic notes—is the Golden Mean of an octave. The Circle of Fifths is then itself produced by continuous division of the string into even-smaller two-thirds segments, with each new division beginning a new scale, in which all the tones of the previous scale will sound again in a higher octave. Theoretically, by applying the proper ratios repeatedly, Pythagoras ought to have been able to cycle through a Circle of Fifths twelve times in ascending sequence, returning to his original tone, eight octaves higher. Only there are no *perfect* circles in nature, so when he got back to his starting point, he was slightly off—by roughly an eighth, some say, although I believe the precise figure is, in reality, somewhat smaller. Regardless, this is referred to as the 'Pythagorean Comma,' and means that the Circle of Fifths is actually a spiral."

"Just as our Milky Way galaxy is a spiral," Bryony noted

shrewdly, "and as a ram's horns spiral, and as a snake coils itself into a spiral, as well—whence perhaps the significance of the ram-horned snake grasped by the Celtic god Cernunnos on the Gundestrup cauldron, for example."

"Exactly! Now, the Italian scholar Leonardo Fibonacci of Pisa—who grew up in the North African city of Bugia, studied under the Muslims, and published *Liber Abaci,* the historic manuscript that was the principal introduction of Arabic numerals to Europe—also stumbled upon a key to the spiral. Only, he did it by proposing an infinite sequence of numbers, beginning with zero and one, and continuing by adding each number to its predecessor to arrive at the next. In other words, zero plus one equals one, one plus one equals two, one plus two equals three, two plus three equals five, and so on. He then found that the formula characterizing the relationship between each of his numbers was one-half of the square root of five minus one, which results in a number that we call 'Phi' or the 'Golden Mean'—and that is also referred to as the 'Golden Ratio,' the 'Golden Section,' and the 'Divine Proportion.' Essentially, in simple terms, it describes any point on a line where the ratio of the line's smaller section to its larger section is equal to the ratio of the larger section to the entire line."

"Which concept the ancient peoples, the Greeks and Egyptians among them, are claimed to have known about and used architecturally in structures like the Parthenon and the Pyramids, long before Fibonacci," Bryony announced, "and which artists like Leonardo da Vinci and musicians like Mozart are said also to have employed in their works. I remember that back in the early twentieth century, a Yale art historian, Jay Hambridge, defined two types of geometric symmetry in classical and modern art, calling them 'static' and 'dynamic.' The former, he based on the straight lines and sharp angles of Roman art, while the latter was based on what he referred to as the 'whirling rectangles' of Grecian art—such as that to be found here at Delphi."

"Yes. In the Sixteen Hundreds, men like Descartes, Toricelli, and Bernoulli discovered that the *spira mirablis* or 'marvelous spiral'—now known as the 'logarithmic spiral' or 'equiangular spiral'—can be fashioned from either a Golden Rectangle or a Golden Triangle, both of which are also based on Phi relationships. Further, if we follow the course of a *spira mirablis,* either inward or outward, we soon find that we will never reach either its origin or termination point, that it has no beginning or end, but, rather, is infinite.''

''Which brings us right back to the number eight, because the symbol for infinity is also the Arabic numeral eight laid on its side—indicating that wisdom is both timeless and without beginning or end, perhaps?''

''Yes—and, surely, that the numbers are somehow the key to attaining it, besides! So, Bryony, let us also not forget the English chemist John Newlands. During the Eighteen-Sixties, in his 'Law of Octaves,' so called in honor of Pythagoras and highly ridiculed as nonsense at the time, Newlands arranged the then sixty-two known elements in ascending order by atomic weight, observing that with every eighth element, similar physical and chemical properties reappeared. Despite the fact that it had initially been poorly received, it was nevertheless upon this Law of Octaves that the Russian chemist Dimitri Mendeleyev later constructed his *Periodic Table of the Elements,* his genius such that he was able to do so despite the fact that several elements, including the entire family of Noble Gases, were completely unknown, not being discovered until later dates—although, with his table, Mendeleyev correctly predicted the existence of some of the missing elements. Among other chemists and physicists, our modern *Periodic Table* owes its current arrangement—which is now based on a model of atomic structure rather than atomic weight—not only to Mendeleyev, but also to Niels Bohr, who, along with Max Planck, developed the foundations of quantum physics.''

''Add to that the fact that the grossly misunderstood and unappreciated Croatian genius and inventor Nikolai Tesla is claimed to have had a succession of revelations, Hamish, in which, among several other things, he envisioned that *everything* in the universe conforms to the Law of Octaves! This led to his inventing the alternating-current generator, thereby instigating the modern technological revolution. Eventually, he had dozens of inventions and hundreds of patents to his name—earning him the jealousy of men like Thomas Edison, who, to protect his own fame and financial profits, did everything possible to defame and undermine Tesla! Fluorescent lights, radio and X rays are all owed originally to Tesla—and *not* to those who later claimed credit for them! In Nineteen Forty-Three, the U.S. Supreme Court, in fact, finally ruled that Marconi—the alleged inventor of radio—had infringed on or flagrantly stolen at least twelve different patents of Tesla's! Last but not least, Tesla was obsessed with the notion of the generation and transmission of wireless power. In his laboratory in Colorado Springs, he somehow managed to harness the forces of nature, creating lightning bolts that were seen and heard miles away, and, on one occasion, accidentally melting one of the municipal power generators! Many of his papers and notes were confiscated by the U.S. government, and, despite the Freedom of Information Act, are still classified even today, due to 'national security issues'!''

"The principles of the positive and negative energy forces of nature—*yang* and *yin*—were also employed by the Taoists of ancient China," Hamish asserted, "to develop a cosmology that resulted in the eight trigrams of the I-Ching, from which sixty-four hexagrams are produced…the exact same number of squares on a chessboard, by the way…eight times eight."

"Sixty-four…my god, Hamish!" Bryony cried. "That's the code for all life itself!"

"What do you mean?"

"I read an article about the fact that today's geneticists have now discovered that DNA, the double helix of life, is a *universal* genetic code shared by *all* living things. Genes provide the directions for the manufacture of proteins—the basic material of all living cells—which are formed from distinct combinations of amino acids, the twenty 'building blocks' of life. Both DNA and RNA work by encoding amino acids with strings of three out of four chemical bases, which are adenine, thymine, cytosine, and guanine. A triplet of these bases is known as a 'codon.' There are *sixty-four* different codons—the very instructions for life! Again, eight times eight…*octinimus,* the eight-fold name of Mete—Wisdom.... Proof that the Creator actually *does* exist...? Because, Hamish, for something to be written in code, it *must* have some kind of an intelligent author behind it! Code doesn't just happen by natural process or random chance. You don't simply turn on a computer with an empty hard drive, for example, and expect it to format itself. You have to install some kind of an operating system on it, which either you or someone else has programmed, so the computer can function and know what to do. Otherwise, it's just a brainless box!''

''All true. But answer me this, then. Once you had successfully mastered the secret of how to write the code yourself, then what further need would you have for the original author?''

''Well...none. You'd be a code author yourself—''

Falling abruptly silent at all the implications of that, Bryony and Hamish stared at each other, awed and reflective. Then, at last, after a long moment, they slowly continued their climb up the Sacred Way of the Delphic sanctuary, which twisted uphill to the Temple of Apollô Pythia above, and which was lined with the remains of the treasuries that had been built over the centuries to house all the riches contributed to the city. Aeons ago, along this very same serpentine path, the supplicants had come, bearing their payments and religious votives, hopeful of wise advice from the Oracle.

Before inquiring of it, however, the questioners had first been required to fast, and to cleanse and purify themselves in the Castalian spring. After that, a goat had been brought forward by the priests or ''Holy Ones,'' who, as though baptizing the creature, had sprinkled it with water. If the beast had shivered, then that had been taken as a sign that the god Apollô could be petitioned that day, and the goat itself had been ritually sacrificed. The inquirer had then paid the necessary fee and, in proper turn, entered the temple. On the lintel above the door had been inscribed the words ''Know Thyself.'' Inside, the supplicant had written down a question upon a tablet, which the priests, as *proxenos* or proxies, had handed to the oracular priestesses, each called the ''Pythia.''

Originally, there had been only one priestess. But eventually as the fame of the Delphic Oracle had spread, it had been necessary to increase the number to three. Initially, the Pythias had all been young virgins. But after an especially beautiful one of them had been kidnapped and raped by a Thessalian scoundrel, only chaste maidens of at least fifty years of age had been chosen to serve.

Before delivering any prophesies, the Pythia, like the petitioner, had first fasted, then cleansed and purified herself in the Castalian spring, which, it was claimed, had burst forth from the earth when a hoof of the winged horse, Pegasus, had struck the ground. After bathing, the priestess had donned her ceremonial garments, then drunk from the sacred Kassotis spring. Entering the small room connecting the upper temple with the adytum—the shrine's lower chamber, where the mysterious vapors had risen from the earth's cleft, and laurel leaves had burned—she had seated herself upon the tripod-cauldron. Inhaling deeply of the pungent fumes—thought to have been the divine breath of Apollô—issuing from the adytum, the Pythia had then fallen into a profound trance and begun to babble prophetically in response to the questions put to her. Her answers had been interpreted by the priests, written down in hexameter verse or otherwise, and given to the inquirer.

Because the priestesses had been consulted on all kinds of matters, from geography, history, money and politics, to mathematics, philosophy, religion and science, and by not only the Greeks, but also by the pilgrims from faraway, foreign lands, they and the Oracle's priests had gained an immense, unusual knowledge of the world and its peoples and state of affairs. For this reason, the divinations uttered by the Pythia, while cryptic, had often been quite shrewd and informed, as well. The most famous of these was her reply to the question posed by King Croesus, who had wanted to know what would happen if he crossed the River Halys and attacked the Persians. The Oracle had responded that he would destroy a great empire. Encouraged by the Pythia's answer, Croesus had consequently invaded Persia, only to endure a definitive defeat. Bitterly condemning the Oracle, he had then demanded to know why the priestess had lied to him, only to receive the rejoinder that she had prophesied truly, for by waging war on the Persians, Croesus *had* destroyed a great empire—his own.

The Temple of Apollô, where the Oracle had once spoken, was the very heart of the sanctuary. But whereas the Temple of Athêna was smaller and round, Apollô's was larger and rectangular, although it, too, had once been surrounded with tall, Doric columns.

"I find it interesting that Apollô needed to be taught the art of divination by the goat god Pan," Bryony remarked, as she and Hamish made their way toward the entrance of the shrine. "What do you suppose might be the relevance, if any, of that?"

"Hmm…well, possibly, for one thing, although he was often mistakenly believed to be the son of the messenger god Hermês, Pan was actually a much older god than his alleged father. In fact, Pan was the principal god of Arcadia—of Poussin's painting *The Shepherds of Arcadia* fame—and by their own reckoning, the Arcadians, who prided themselves on their antiquity, were *proselênoi,* or 'older than the moon.' The Egyptians worshiped Pan as one of the original pantheon of eight— there's that number again!—gods, and there are those who believe him to be the symbol of the whole universe…the 'Great All.'

"Pan instructed on how to cure diseases, bore a shepherd's crook, and played the syrinx—his pipe fashioned of only seven reeds, however, rather than the eight that would have completed the octave, so that ultimately, his music remains as yet unfinished, leaving us listening breathlessly, waiting expectantly for its last, dying note.

"Pan has a dual nature, however, and his other side is not so beneficent, for he is the proverbial randy goat in pursuit of women, a prominent participant in drunken, licentious carousing and promiscuity, as well as being the malicious trickster, the wolf god in sheep's clothing, who savages the flocks, and the source of the sudden, dark, all-consuming, blind fear that can in the blink of an eye overtake us, driving the mind into chaos. Even today, we still call it 'panic.' From the earliest times of the wild festivals, men have donned the hairy skins of goats, sheep, stags and other creatures, assuming the animalistic appearance and behavior of Pan, the man-beast. Over celebrations like Saturnalia, Brumalia, the Feast of Fools, Christmas revelries, and other such carnivals rooted in the winter solstice have presided Mock Kings, Kings of the Bean, and Lords of Misrule—in ancient times ritually slain at the ends of their short reigns, then, later, burned in effigy.

"If the Greek historian Plutarch is to be believed, Pan died during the reign of the Roman Emperor Tiberius and in the time of Jesus Christ, whose birthday has been traditionally celebrated on the last day of the winter-solstice festivities."

"During which, on the longest night of the year, the sun journeys from the sign of Sagittarius the Archer into the sign of Capricorn—the Goat. Strictly speaking, however, Capricorn is only half goat. The other half is either a serpent or else a fish," Bryony mused aloud, "depending on one's point of view. The Babylonians sometimes even called it *kusarikku*—the 'fish-ram.' Come on, Hamish. I want to go down into the adytum."

"Why?"

"Because I want to speak to the Oracle, of course!"

It was, naturally, only a fanciful yearning on her part, for she knew full well that like the Great God Pan himself, the Pythia was aeons dead, her voice silent now for nearly two millennia. Still, carefully picking their way among the large, exposed stones that were all that remained now of the once-magnificent temple, Bryony and Hamish slowly descended into the inner sanctum of the empty, softly reverberating shrine. By this time, the afternoon had grown late, and the warm spring sun had started to sink like butter melting on the western horizon, casting the adytum into long, cool shadows, causing Bryony to shiver a little, as though a goose had just walked over her grave, as she stepped into the temple's innermost recesses—although the chilly tingle she felt was not simply from the lack of sunlight alone.

There was power here…vast, old power—that of Gaia, the Earth-Mother Goddess of Wisdom; of Pythôn, the Serpent, whose venom was both poison and antidote, death and life; of Pan, the All One, the Goat of Two Faces: Man Exalted—the lofty mountain goat nimbly scaling the highest peaks…and Bestial Man—the indiscriminate billy goat heedlessly traipsing through the barnyard mud; and of Apollô Pythia, the Sun One—whose name meant 'Decaying Destroyer'—the Bright, Shining One who would give life to the world endlessly, it seemed, but who was, in reality, decaying, dying, and would one day burn too hotly and brilliantly, going nova, consuming in a titanic, blinding inferno all the planets of the solar system, silencing their music forever. All this was the great, ancient power Bryony felt in the adytum within the earth, the power rushing through her blood and pounding in her very bones, making the fine hairs of her nape stand on end.

Once, in the small room above this very place, the famed priestess had sat upon the tripod-cauldron positioned over the lower chamber and its cryptic, vaporous chasm, whose strange fumes had mingled with the pungent smoke of the burning laurel leaves and risen from the adytum. And entranced, the Pythia had foretold the destinies of the Sons of Heaven and of the Daughters of Men….

Suddenly, compelled by some peculiar, inexplicable but inexorable urge, Bryony closed her eyes and began to breathe slowly, deeply, as though she could smell the strong, fragrant scent of bay permeating her nostrils…taste upon her tongue the clear, sweet water of the sacred Kassotis spring….

The blood sang in her ears, and she felt the vibrations of the place growing ever stronger around her and within her. And then somehow across the aeons, from some wild, primeval vortex of swirling mist and shadows, echoing down the long, dark, labyrinthine corridor of Time, she heard the distant, aged voice of the Oracle speak:

Et in Arcadia Egô. Et in Alphêo Eris.

It was the wind stirring. Surely, it was only the whisper of the soughing wind snaking and slithering its way like the fallen Pythôn around the mountainside….

"But of course," Bryony murmured, unwittingly. "The goat of fools, promiscuity, misrule and chaos…the goat of atonement, who takes away the sins of the world...the goat of sacrifice. Capricorn of the summer solstice in the southern hemisphere, and of the winter solstice in the northern. Half goat, half serpent, its coils evoking the spirals of the ram's horns...the Arien ram of wisdom that grazes on the peaceful, ever-green summer pastures of Arcadia. 'He maketh me lie down in green pastures.' Half goat, half fish...the two Piscean fish of Free Will, the choice to swim either upstream or down in the underground, ever-silver wintry River Alphêus. 'He leadeth me beside still waters. He restoreth my soul.' 'My cup runneth over.' Kusarikku...the fish-ram. 'Thy rod and thy staff, they comfort me.' 'Follow me, and I will make you fishers of men.' 'Shepherds and kings...' Aries and Pisces, the first and last signs of the great Silver Wheel that encircles the world. 'Thus, the last shall be first, and the first, last.' 'Blessed are the meek, for they shall inherit the earth.' 'It is the glory of God to conceal a matter; to search it out is the glory of kings.' *'And in Arcadia I am. And in Alphêus I will be.'''* At long last, trembling with the force of her emotions, Bryony slowly opened her eyes.

"The sepulchre in Poussin's painting, Hamish..." she said softly. "I know who it belongs to now. It's the tomb of the Great God Pan."

Thirty-Two

In the Pindus Mountains

The sounding cataract
Haunted me like a passion: the tall rock
The mountain, and the deep and gloomy wood,
Their colors and their forms, were then to me
An appetite; a feeling and a love,
That had no need of a remoter charm,
By thought supplied, nor any interest
Unborrowed from the eye.

Lines Composed a Few Miles Above Tintern Abbey
—William Wordsworth

En Route from Delphi to Athens, Greece, the Present

"We have managed once more to locate Bryony St. Blaze and Neville, Nautonnier!" Shieldbearer's voice, as he spoke into the telephone receiver, held a note of supreme satisfaction and triumph.

"How? Where?" At the opposite end of the line, the Grand Master of the Abbey's own voice was terse and grim.

"Through a contact on the Italian police force. He has provided us with information that the woman and Neville boarded the Anek Lines ferry *Kriti II*, bound for Patras, two days ago in Ancona. Further, an official with Greek Customs has confirmed that they did, in fact, arrive in Patras late yesterday afternoon. They booked a room in a hotel there, but checked out this morning. We now believe them to be en route to Delphi, Nautonnier, although for what purpose, we are as yet unaware. What are your orders? Do you still wish them placed under observation only?''

"No. They have eluded us far too often, and they killed Hammerbearer, and for that, there must be a reckoning. It was really a most unfortunate and regrettable coincidence that his path should have inadvertently crossed theirs at St. Pancras, was it not? But then, as we know, there is no such thing as chance, and all is part of the Grand Design by the Master Architect, who cloaks his intent in Mystery. Take both Ms. St. Blaze and Neville captive, if you can, Shieldbearer. If not, then although the woman would prove very useful to us now as leverage against Neville, since he is clearly besotted with her, she is nevertheless expendable. We must presume that if she is indeed privy to some information from her father about the lost Knights Templar treasure, then she has now imparted all the details of that to Neville. *He* is the one we want alive, if at all possible, to account for his actions in this entire affair, and to make restitution for Hammerbearer's death. Had you and the others not arrived at the Euro Car Park at St. Pancras when you did, it is highly likely that the body would have been discovered by unwitting citizens, who would have summoned the British police, and then there would have been a lengthy investigation, during which the Abbey would perhaps have been exposed. I cannot countenance that. For centuries now, we have successfully managed to conceal our existence from the world's unwashed masses of ignorant rabble. Not for the likes of us the glorious, bright glare of the kings' spotlight center stage...but only the still, dark shadows of the kingmakers' wings, whence we can wield our great power without consequence to achieve our lofty ambitions, working our will and pulling the strings of the stupid and unenlightened puppets, eh, Shieldbearer?''

"Yes, quite, Nautonnier."

"Then you know you must do whatever is necessary—as

must we all.'' With those parting words of wisdom, the Grand Master, as usual, abruptly severed the telephone connection, leaving the dial tone buzzing sibilantly in Shieldbearer's ear.

That night, Bryony and Hamish camped once more under the stars, not far from the ruins of Delphi. As it had been for weeks now, her mind was in a tumultuous whirl. However, this evening, it was due not to any physical threat to her well-being, but to her attempting to make sense of all she had learned since she and the Scotsman had embarked upon their flight from Drumrose Cottage and the Abbey. Random, fleeting thoughts filled her head, one flowing into another, like the ripples of the River Alphêus, the underground stream.

Upon reflection, it seemed to her that the concept of Dualism—of God and Devil, of infinity and nothingness, of light and darkness, of spiritual and material, of life and death, of knowledge and ignorance, of good and evil, of purity and sin, of savior and beast, and of peace and war—underlay all the world's cosmologies, myths, legends, fables and fairy tales, regardless of whether they purported to be monistic or pluralistic in nature; and that this was the result of Free Will, of the choice faced by Man...whether to swim upstream or down, as symbolized by the astrological sign of Pisces, the two fish, sometimes bound together by a silver cord around their tails, representing the age-old struggle of Man against temptation, to become more than just the sum of his parts.

Et in Alphêo Eris—which translated literally as ''And in Gain, Strife.'' Little girls in sundresses, on green summer lawns, playing Mother, May I? Two steps forward, one step back...forget to ask, ''Mother, may I?'' and return to the very beginning...but touch Mother and win the game. Mother. The Black Madonna. The Virgin Transmuted. Wisdom. Eve and Lil...the eponymous First Woman, and thus the First Virgin, the First Victim, the First Adulteress, the First Mother, the First Widow. The eponymous First Man Adam's wife, tempted by the Serpent—the ithyphallic symbol of Wisdom...Knowledge.

''Hamish,'' Bryony said, ''I've been thinking—among other things—about the earth-mother goddess and the snake, because

based on the various archaeological evidence, these are essentially the earliest known religious cults, and they are frequently
tied together, as well, just as they were here at Delphi, via Gaia
and Pythôn, or as in Christianity, via Eve and the Serpent,
Lucifer. Lucifer, as we know, is often depicted wearing the
horns of a goat, and as having the cloven hooves of a goat,
too. This is also how the Greek god Pan is portrayed. So it
seems to me that three types of snakes can be identified myth-
ologically...the ram-horned snake, the goat-horned snake, and
the winged or feathered snake. Both sheep and goats have cloven hooves, so perhaps it's not so much the hooves themselves
that are of importance as it is the sense of lameness that would
appear to be associated with Lucifer, for example. In other
words, perhaps the original connotation of the cloven hooves
was simply that of being 'crippled'—that is, earthbound—unable to fly any longer, because the wings that Lucifer had once
possessed had been lost when he had fallen from grace. Therefore, he had become like the beasts, rather than the birds.'' She
paused, then continued.

"Further, if we equate the ram's horns with wisdom, represented by the spiral—the *spira mirablis* or 'marvelous spiral'—that is the very nature of the universe, and the goat's
horns with foolishness, represented by the phallus, which
brought about the so-called Fall and Death, then it would appear that the ram-horned snake and the goat-horned snake are
actually symbolic of the choice bestowed upon us by Free
Will—to learn to be wise, or else to remain fools. 'When the
Son of Man comes in His glory, and all the angels with Him,
He will sit upon His glorious throne, and all the nations will
be assembled before Him. And He will separate them one from
another, as a shepherd separates the sheep from the goats,'''
Bryony quoted, from the Gospel of Matthew.

"Significantly, perhaps, in the biblical passage, the sheep are
directed to the right-hand side of God, that which is called the
dexter, while the goats are directed to the left-hand side of
God, that which is even today known as the *sinister*—thereby
'giving the Devil his due'?'' she suggested. "Additionally, we
are told by Jesus Christ, 'Behold, I am sending you like sheep

in the midst of wolves, so be as wise as serpents, and as harmless as doves.' Jesus himself is called the *Agnus Dei* or 'Lamb of God,' while to 'get a man's goat' is to make a fool of him. Last but not least, there is the winged or feathered snake, which, as we've previously discussed, is unquestionably symbolic of the fallen or earthbound one regaining flight, ascending once more into the heavens. These all seem to be universal figures. Therefore, it would appear logical to assume, that, as Dad suggested, there is indeed some common source or well. Jung, we know, called this the 'collective unconscious.' However, what if it isn't? What if all this actually *is* the history of Humankind, misted by aeons and written down by those who did not fully understand what it was they were recording? Or perhaps these things are symbolic guidelines that were set down for us by some unknown being, to teach us wisdom. Mythologists identify so-called motifs like these, which occur over and over, and the primary method of learning *is* by rote. We're also told that history repeats itself. Maybe it does so because Mankind has yet to pass some sort of cosmic examination…we've failed our course of study, so we're caught up now in a never-ending circle.

"The Great God Pan died, Plutarch said, and, with him, paganism as a global religion. At the same time, Jesus Christ was born, and Christianity spread throughout the world. So, in effect, the Goat died, and the Ram or Lamb was born. Now, I'm wondering if this is somehow only a segment of some larger pattern, if we are continuously cycling through a series of Goats and Rams that are but the two faces of some single aspect. The earth's precession of equinoxes through the twelve astrological constellations takes approximately twenty-six thousand years. Maybe, during each of the astrological ages of the precession, either the Goat or the Ram comes."

"The Beast or the Messiah?" Hamish cocked one eyebrow inquisitively. "It's an interesting idea—and if correct, then the biblical number of the Beast, the infamous six-six-six, could be the sum of some mathematical computation based on the precession, to warn us when to expect its next appearance. *Architect* comes from the Greek words *archê* and *tektôn,* meaning

'First Craftsman.' However, they can also be translated as 'Maker of Heavenly Powers and the Powers of Evil.' In this regard, I find it fascinating that Jesus said, 'Do not think that I have come to bring peace upon the earth. I have come to bring not peace but the sword.' Because the Greek word *arês,* which is the name of the Greek war god, means not only 'war,' but also 'sword' and 'sheep.''"

"And the planet Mars—the Roman name for Arês—rules the astrological sign of Aries the Ram. Surely, all that's not just some strange coincidence, Hamish! Maybe it's symbolic of the fact that to wholly appreciate peace, we also need to wholly comprehend war, to understand what it means to be 'slaughtered like sheep'—just as in order to fully esteem life, we also need to fully grasp death. We've done quite a bit of investigation into the goat god Pan, but hardly any into the ram god, whom the Egyptians called Ammon. I'd like to know more about him."

"Well, we could always go to Egypt," the Scotsman declared, "and delve into Isis herself at the same time. Would you like that, sweetheart?"

"Yes, I would."

"Good, it's settled then. Tomorrow, we'll drive into Athens, leave the car in long-term parking, and fly to Cairo."

It was approximately a two-hour trip from Delphi to Athens, along highways that wound through the foothills of the Pindus Mountains, which stretched from the north of Greece to the southern tip of its province of Attica. Partially retracing their path to Kastri, Bryony and Hamish followed gusty Highway 48 southeast toward the capital city of Greece, delighting once more in the splendid mountain views that assailed them on their journey. Overhead, the late-spring sun blazed brightly, as though it now rushed toward summer and the height of its full glory, preening for the earth, which soaked up its heat as a woman does that of a man on a cold night. The morning fog that, earlier, had cloaked the mountains had now burned away, revealing their brilliant sweeps of green and gold, in which, here and there, ancient ruins like Delphi nestled—a reminder that Greece had once been the cradle of Western civilization, whence the great minds of men like Pythagoras, Socrates and Plato had sprung.

Perhaps Eve, too, had been lost in a like contemplation of the beauty of the Garden of Eden when the Serpent, Lucifer, had appeared, offering the temptation of the forbidden fruit, Bryony was to think later. For without warning, into the quiet of the morning, fear came as suddenly as a snake striking, its fangs piercing deeply. It came in the form of a Mercedes as sleek, shiny and black as an Egyptian cobra, barreling up from nowhere behind the Volvo and bashing it in the rear end before Hamish realized what was intended.

"Oh, my God!" Bryony cried, stricken, as the Volvo growled in protest and lurched forward sickeningly, the Scotsman battling furiously to retain control of the steering wheel, speeding up to attempt to avoid the other car.

At first, she did not know what was happening, thought only that the driver of the Mercedes had lost his brakes, so that he couldn't halt his vehicle's impetus. But then, much to her shock and horror, the black automobile abruptly veered from behind them, whipping into the left–hand lane and roaring up beside them. Its windows were all dark-tinted glass, so that she couldn't see inside the car, could put no face to the evil that now assaulted them.

Horn blasting like the Last Trump, the Mercedes deliberately swerved over into the side of the Volvo, smashing it with such force that it jarred every last bone in Bryony's body, before careening away, only to return for yet another horrible blow. Such was her stark, blind terror at the multiple collisions that she wasn't even aware that the screams that now reverberated loudly in the Volvo emanated from her own throat. In some dark corner of her mind, clips from films like *The Hearse* and *Duel* flashed. Because this was the kind of thing that happened in movies—not in real life. She would have thought she had fallen asleep and was dreaming, suffering a nightmare, had the repeated slams of the Mercedes against the Volvo not ruthlessly hammered home to her the fact that this was all too real.

"They want us to pull over, Hamish!" she uttered stupidly, petrified.

"And what do you suppose will happen if we do? It's got to be more of the Round Table members inside that Mercedes! You know that!"

"Oh, Jesus!"

Because the Volvo was a right–hand drive vehicle, Bryony, in the passenger seat, was getting the worst of the continuous impacts, but before he could act accordingly to try to protect her, a paroxysm rocked the Volvo, and her window shattered violently into a spiderweb with an ominous hole at its center, small shards of safety glass flying and spilling like a stream of diamonds into her lap. Just above her left temple, crimson welled to run down her cheek and neck.

"Bloody Christ!" Hamish swore, horrified. "Bryony, are you all right? Are you all right? Get your head down, goddamn it! Get your head down!"

Shaking and sobbing, she hunched forward in her seat, burying her face in her hands, ignoring the seat belt cutting into her skin. She was hardly even cognizant of the fact that she had been wounded and was bleeding. She knew only, dimly, that the left side of her head was warm and sticky, and that her fingers were slowly staining red from the trickle that seeped between them. For one hideous moment, as she slumped downward, the Scotsman believed she was dead. Then the sound of her weeping penetrated his consciousness, and he knew she was still alive, although injured—how badly, he had no clue.

Gritting his teeth, gripping the steering wheel even more tightly, and jamming his foot down hard on the accelerator, Hamish managed to push the automobile to an even greater clip. Burning rubber, the tires screeched on the asphalt as the car fishtailed crazily into the left–hand lane, in front of the Mercedes. The other vehicle responded by smacking them in the rear again before swinging into the right–hand lane, its horn still blaring, insistently signaling them to pull off the road. But the Scotsman knew, as Bryony did, that if they complied, one or both of them would probably be murdered, and he refused to take that risk. At least in the Volvo, they stood some kind of a chance against the onslaught of the Mercedes and the Abbey's henchmen.

Desperately, Hamish began to fight back, jerking the steering wheel hard to the right, so that the Volvo crashed into the black automobile, causing it to slide wildly upon the road. But its driver was experienced, quickly regaining charge and retorting in kind. Like competing chariots in a deadly race, the two cars hurtled down the highway, banging together, twisting and skidding along through the mountains that, only minutes before, had been still and serene.

The horn of the Mercedes shrieked incessantly; engines groaned and whined; metal crunched nauseatingly; and tires squealed. Then, suddenly, at a sharp curve in the road, the two automobiles rammed each other yet again—and in the ferocious wake of the concussion, one of them reeled away convulsively, plunging off the highway, brutally plowing through the low barricade alongside the rocky verge, then savagely plummeting down the steep hillside beyond.

Moments later, the car's gas tank ruptured and ignited; the once-peaceful mountains rang with the resulting, dreadful explosion; and sulfuric smoke from the frenzied flames spewed like the pungent fumes of the Oracle's adytum into the sweet spring air.

Thirty-Three

The Alchemist

> O! he sits high in all the people's hearts:
> And that which would appear offense in us,
> His countenance, like richest alchemy,
> Will change to virtue and to worthiness.

Julius Caesar
—William Shakespeare

Paris, France, 1360 A.D.

Mon Dieu, *what a very strange dream I had last night!* the scrivener Nicolas Flamel thought, for the umpteenth time that day. Anxiously, he glanced over his shoulder, at the small, open bookshop behind him, located in the rue de Marivaux in Paris. He wanted to be certain he had not spoken the words aloud, that the copyists and illuminators who labored therein had not heard him. Much to his vast relief, they were hunched over their desks, busy at their work.

Nicolas sighed. In some respects, life had been much easier when he had been conducting his bookselling trade in the tiny stall that had backed on to the columns of the church of Saint-Jacques la Boucherie, and where he had had no employees. Now, he still stood outside all day long, for French law required all transactions to be made in public and in daylight, so that vendors had fewer opportunities to cheat their customers. But he must constantly watch over his shoulder, too, to be sure that his employees were not idling their time away—and listening to him talk to himself. Not that he did, of course! Nicolas assured himself hastily. Besides running his bookshop and overseeing the copyists and illuminators, he gave writing lessons to nobles who must make the mark of the cross on letters and other documents, being unable to sign their names.

Nicolas's musings returned to his dream. In it, an angel had appeared to him, winged and streaming brightly with light. In its hands, the angel had borne a book, and, holding it out to him, had spoken to him, bidding him to take it. Slowly, Nicolas had stretched out his hands to receive the book, but then both it and the angel had evanesced into the glowing, golden mist of dreams, and disappeared.

Ah, well. He sighed again. However peculiar it might have been, it had still been only a dream, nothing more. Or so Nicolas thought until one day, when he was alone in his bookshop, a poor, unknown beggarman approached him, carrying a worn bundle from which he drew forth the very book that Nicolas had beheld in his dream. Without even haggling over the price, he paid two solid-gold florins for the book.

It was like nothing he had ever before seen, with an old binding of worked copper and brass, on which were engraved enigmatic diagrams and characters, some of them in Greek and others in a language he didn't recognize. Instead of parchment, the gold-patina-edged pages of the book were fashioned of the bark of young trees, and across them flowed writing that had been formed with an iron point. The leaves of the book were divided into groups of seven, and consisted of three parts separated by a page upon which an unfathomable symbol had been drawn. On the first page were written words proclaiming that the author of the book was one Abraham the Jew—prince, priest, Levite, astrologer and philosopher to the nation of the Jews. This was followed by a string of curses and threats against anyone who read the book, unless the reader were himself a priest or a scribe.

Once the bargain had been struck, the beggarman hurriedly

wrapped the resplendent book back up in his bundle. Then,
glancing right and left, as though to be certain he and Nicolas
were not being closely watched, he abruptly shoved the entire
heavy bundle into the other's hands and skittered away down
an alley before the bookseller could protest. By the time Nicolas had gathered his wits enough to start after him, the beggarman had vanished. Shaking his head at the fellow's decidedly peculiar behavior, the bookseller at last went into his
bookshop, where, in the back room, he opened the weighty
bundle. Much to his vast astonishment and horror, not only the
book, but also a decorative, gold, silver and copper puzzle box
spilled from the large square of rough, woolen cloth.

"*Sacré bleu!*" Nicolas swore softly.

"What is it, husband? What's wrong?" his wife, Pernelle,
asked, entering the room.

Swiftly, the bookseller related his incredible tale to her.

"Only two florins I paid him!" Nicolas ended, bewildered.
"And the box itself is clearly utterly priceless! Pernelle, it must
be stolen! Why else would the beggarman not even have shown
it to me—much less given it to me? Naturally, it is my duty
to report all this to the proper authorities at once!"

"No!" his wife cried fearfully. "For only think, husband...what if your story is not believed? What if it is *you* who
is thought to have taken the box? We do not know to whom
it rightfully belongs. But surely, there can be no doubt that it
is the property of some rich and powerful lord, at the very least.
No...no, husband, we must say nothing to no one. Let us open
the box instead and see what is inside. Then perhaps we shall
have a better idea of what to do."

Finally, Nicolas nodded in agreement. Pernelle was not only
attractive, but also intelligent and slightly older than he, as
well. He trusted her good judgment and knew her to be that
rarest of women: one who was capable of keeping a secret all
her life, if necessary.

In the end, it took the Flamels several months to decipher
the key to unlocking the puzzle box. For nineteen years after
that, they studied the ancient manuscript it contained, deter-
mining that the *Book of Abraham the Jew* was but a copy of

some twenty-one pages from the much larger tome. In despair, Nicolas placed the small *Book of Abraham the Jew* on display in his bookshop, in the hope that some customer would be able to help him unravel its mysteries. But his eager, polite inquiries and efforts were all in vain, being greeted with laughter from skeptics and ignorance from would-be scholars.

The bookseller then decided to travel to Spain, believing that, there, he might meet some learned Qabbalist who would be able to translate the *Book of Abraham the Jew* for him. Making a vow to Spain's popular St. James of Compostela, knowing it was safer to travel as a pilgrim, Nicolas accoutred himself with a devotee's garments, shell-covered hat and wooden staff, and set off on his journey. Arriving in Spain, he first diligently fulfilled his vow to St. James. Then he wandered about, trying to find someone who could read the *Book of Abraham the Jew* for him. But there was no one, and at last, disheartened, he began his long trip home. But in León, where he stayed overnight at an inn, his fortunes changed, and he met—through a Boulognese merchant with whom he chanced to sup—one Maestro Canches, an elderly Jewish scholar, who was able to assist him.

After returning home, Nicolas spent three more years on his studies until, on January 17, 1382, at noon, he finally succeeded in his quest. Subsequently, he grew rich, and rumors circulated that he had learned how to transmute mercury first into silver and then gold. However, except to move into a larger establishment at 51 rue de Montmorency—the top two floors of which they turned into a shelter for the homeless—he and his wife, Pernelle, altered little about their own modest lifestyle. Instead, they devoted themselves to succoring the poor, founding hospitals, endowing churches and building or repairing cemeteries. After Pernelle died, Nicolas spent the remainder of his life writing books on alchemy.

Following his own death, greedy fortune hunters desecrated his grave at the Cemetery of the Innocents, and all his former houses, too, hoping to find the great treasure he was alleged to have amassed and hidden. Robbers even lifted the heavy slab off his tomb and broke open his coffin, giving rise to wild tales that the casket had been empty and that Nicolas was still alive, having discovered the Elixir of Life, the Philosopher's Stone.

Cardinal Richelieu was believed to have seized possession of the *Book of Abraham the Jew* and, in a vain attempt to learn its secrets, had constructed a laboratory at the Château de Rueil, where he had conducted countless but wholly unsuccessful experiments. Realistically, it was not to be hoped that he could, in only a scant few years, achieve what it had taken Nicolas nearly a quarter of a century to attain. At the Cardinal's own death, all hints of the book's cryptic text had disappeared, and only seven equally enigmatic pictures had survived. Titled *Mercurius Meets with Saturn, The Workers in the Garden, The Winged Caduceus of Mercurius, Snakes Among the Hills, The Crucified Snake, The Massacre of the Innocents* and *Planetary Dragons on a Hill,* they remained a mystery to the unenlightened.

Of the puzzle box and its own ancient manuscript, there was not a single trace to be found.

Thirty-Four

The Temple of Neith, at Sais

Then out spake brave Horatius,
The Captain of the Gate:
"To every man upon this earth
Death cometh soon or late.
And how can we die better
Than facing fearful odds,
For the ashes of his fathers,
And the temples of his Gods?"

Lays of Ancient Rome: Horatius
—Lord Macaulay

May you, may Cam, and Isis, preach it long,
The Right Divine of Kings to govern wrong.

The Dunciad
—Alexander Pope

My life closed twice before its close—
It yet remains to see
If Immortality unveil
A third event to me

So huge, so hopeless to conceive
As these that twice befell.

Parting is all we know of heaven,
And all we need of hell.

No. 1732
—Emily Dickinson

En Route from Athens, Greece to Sais, Egypt, the Present

Shuddering violently, the Volvo skidded to an abrupt halt that slammed Hamish hard against his seat belt and jerked Bryony like a lifeless puppet. The Scotsman's breath came in harsh rasps, and his heart pounded fiercely. For a moment, he simply sat there, stunned, unnerved and outraged by what had just occurred. Then, in a rush, concern for Bryony overwhelmed him, driving from his mind every thought save those for her. Unfastening his seat belt, he bent over her, taking her gently into his arms.

"Sweetheart, are you okay?" he asked anxiously, his voice rough with emotion.

"I...I don't know...I'm...I'm not sure...." Dazedly, she peeped up at him, one badly trembling hand going to the blood-encrusted wound near her temple. "M-M-My head hurts."

"Let me see what's happened, darling."

Tenderly, Hamish tilted her ashen countenance up to his, grimacing as he spied the blood that matted her hair and smeared her face and neck. Then, tentatively, he probed her injury.

"Thank God, it looks far worse than it actually is!" he announced, vastly relieved. "The bullet only grazed your head. A couple of inches to the left, and it would have put a hole right through it! Jesus Christ! It makes me sick even to *think* about how close I came to losing you!"

"What—What happened to the Mercedes? I thought—I thought I heard an explosion.... I must have—there's smoke coming up from below!"

"Yes, the driver of the Mercedes lost control, and it went

off the road, past the barrier and down the hillside. Its petrol
tank burst and caught on fire in the process."

"Who was in the car? How many of them were there? Are
they dead?"

"I don't know."

"Go and find out, Hamish...please."

"No, I need to get the first-aid kit and attend to your wound,
sweetheart."

"Please. I'll be all right for a minute—and I-I want to be
sure we're truly out of danger now. Besides which, someone
in the Mercedes may have survived the crash and the explosion,
and need help. Please, Hamish," she entreated tremulously.

"If that's what you want, of course I will, darling. You just
sit tight for the time being, then, and I'll be right back. Do you
understand me? Stay in the car, and don't try to move. Just lie
back and rest quietly until I return."

"Yes, I will...I promise...."

In reality, the Scotsman didn't give a damn if whoever had
been in the Mercedes was either dead or else alive and requiring assistance. His fear for Bryony and his anger at how the
Abbey's henchmen had attempted to murder her were such that,
instead, he devoutly hoped the Mercedes' occupants were even
now frying in hell. And if they weren't, he'd help them all
right, he decided, with grisly resolution, as he walked toward
the crash site. He'd help them right into a grave!

When he reached the broken barrier alongside the road,
Hamish saw that the Mercedes was a viciously mangled ruin,
being consumed by flames. It would be difficult for him to
descend the precipitous hillside in order to discover whether
anyone had survived. Returning to the Volvo, he popped the
trunk and removed a pair of high-powered binoculars. Then he
went back to the scene of the accident. Scanning the Mercedes
and the surrounding region, it quickly became clear to him that
at least four bodies were burning in the vehicle, one of which
was sprawled halfway on the ground, apparently having been
partially thrown clear. As he focused in on the corpse, the
Scotsman observed that upon its left, inner wrist was the same
sort of tattoo that he had seen upon both Cauldronbearer and

Hammerbearer—except that on this one, the serpents entwined around a shield.

"Rot in hell, Shieldbearer," Hamish said softly, in his tone a small, grim note of satisfaction as he gazed at the wreckage.

Abandoning his scrutiny of the crash site, he fetched the first-aid kit from the trunk of the Volvo, along with a fresh rag and a container of bottled water. He spent several long minutes gingerly cleaning the blood from Bryony's injury, then applying an antibacterial ointment and a bandage. After that, he administered her a couple of aspirin against the pain, which she washed down with small sips of the water.

"I'm sorry I can't do more for you, sweetheart," he asserted, smiling at her ruefully, his dark, brown eyes filled with concern as he gazed at her pale face. "Although it *is* only a graze I know it must throb like the devil!"

"Yes, it does." Wanly, Bryony returned his smile. "But that's okay. I'll manage. Was there—was there anyone alive in the Mercedes?"

The Scotsman shook his head.

"No, they're all dead...all four of them—and just at the moment, I'm afraid I'm finding it rather difficult to feel very sorry about that. Do you feel up to climbing into the backseat, darling, so you can lie down and perhaps sleep until we get to Athens?"

"Yes...all right."

Unbuckling Bryony's seat belt, Hamish assisted her into the backseat of the Volvo, settling her as comfortably as possibly with one of the pillows and a light, woolen blanket. As he fussed over her, he noticed that the round that had been fired at her had buried itself in the backseat. Withdrawing his Swiss Army knife from his pocket, he dug it out.

"Why'd you do that?" Bryony queried.

"Because I need to get rid of it—and to do something about the passenger window, as well. A car accident's a whole lot easier to explain to the authorities than a chase scene involving an assassination attempt by four members of a secret order whose upper eschelons think they're reincarnates of King Arthur and the Knights of the Round Table."

"I suppose so." She bit her lower lip hard. "They almost killed me, Hamish. They almost killed us both."

"Thankfully, they didn't succeed—and now, as a result of their collective failure, the Abbey's Round Table is short a grand total of six members."

"Six?" A puzzled frown knit Bryony's brow. "But…Hammerbearer and the four in the Mercedes only make five."

"True—but you're forgetting…I'm Mordred, the thirteenth member…officially designated as 'Scythebearer,' or so Cauldronbearer informed me at our lunch together that day in Aberdeen."

She shivered.

"I don't like thinking of you as either Scythebearer or Mordred, the traitor."

"Ah, but he *wasn't* a traitor, according to Scottish tradition. He was a hero."

Employing a small, heavy rock he found on the verge alongside the road, the Scotsman further damaged the passenger window, so that the hole caused by the shot was obliterated. Then he threw the spent round he had prised from the Volvo's backseat down the steep hillside, into the wreckage of the now-smoldering Mercedes. The Greek police could make of it whatever they might. Fortunately, the Greeks weren't nearly as strict about guns as the British were, and Greece had its own share of terrorists, too.

Starting the Volvo, Hamish then proceeded on down Highway 48 toward Routes 3 and 8a, and Athens. In the backseat, her head aching dully, Bryony at last slept.

"I would urge that you fix your eyes on the greatness of Athens as she really is and fall in love with her." So the Greek politician and general Pericles had proclaimed in his oration for the dead of the Peloponnesian War—or so the Greek historian Thucydides had recorded. More than a millennium later, Michael Akominatos, the archbishop of the city, had written to the contrary: "You cannot look upon Athens without tears. She has lost the very form, appearance and character of a city." In truth, while the capital city might indeed be viewed as a metropolis, it was, in reality, a succession of small villages twisting and twining into one another. From the ancient Acropolis, where the ruins of the Parthenon stood, its honey-colored pillars of Pentelic marble soaring from an enormous, limestone foundation, to the nineteenth-century Plaka adored by Lord Byron, to the tall, modern, concrete tenements, Athens was a study in contrasts. Noisy, overcrowded and polluted with a thick cloud of smog, referred to as the *nefos,* it sprawled in the shadow of Mount Hymetus.

Such was the state of traffic and the number of collisions that no one paid any heed to the Volvo as Hamish maneuvered it through the labyrinth of old, narrow, winding streets that mingled with modern, wider, straighter roads. Eventually locating a garage, he explained to the attendant that he and Bryony had suffered an automobile accident outside of Athens, and made arrangements to have the vehicle repaired while they were away in Egypt. Then he telephoned for a taxi to chauffeur them to the Hellinikon Airport, which lay six miles south of the center of Athens. When the taxi arrived at the garage, the Scotsman, as was customary in Greece, haggled with the driver over the fare, finally settling on a sum of two thousand drachma—approximately ten dollars—to transport him, Bryony and all their necessary baggage to the airport's East Terminal, the international hub.

Thirty minutes later, they arrived at the airport, where they bought two tickets on a nonstop Egyptair flight to Cairo. Since it didn't leave until that evening, they had plenty of time to check their luggage and for Bryony to wash up and change her clothes. Hamish had wanted her to see a doctor, but she had demurred, insisting that nothing more would be done for her than he had already taken care of himself, and that she only wanted to rest. Reluctantly, knowing the wound to be relatively minor, he had agreed to humor her.

Once they had passed through Security and found their departure gate, Bryony cuddled up with her head in the Scotsman's lap, eventually drifting again into slumber.

* * *

Thankfully, the two-hour flight from Athens to Cairo passed smoothly and uneventfully. At passport control, they paid fifteen dollars each for a thirty-day tourist visa that permitted them to enter the country. Then they proceeded to the arrivals hall, Bryony feeling quite a bit better at the sight of the Tourist Police who patrolled the Cairo International Airport, identified by their white armbands. Surely, if the Abbey had somehow divined that she and Hamish had fled to Cairo, its Round Table members would refrain from any incident at the airport.

Out front, both taxis and limousines were lined up at the curb, awaiting fares. From previous experience, Bryony knew it was best to hire a limousine to drive them into Cairo. But now, seeing the queue of old, black Mercedes cars, she shuddered visibly.

"Don't worry. We'll get a taxi." Hamish spoke comfortingly, sensitive to her distress.

"No." She shook her head. "It's all right. It's late, and a limo will be far less trouble."

"Are you sure, my love?"

"Yes."

Stepping up to the dispatcher, the Scotsman made all the necessary arrangements, and was assigned one of the limousines. Before leaving the airport, they were required to stop at a Tourist Police booth, where, for security reasons, their names were taken down, along with the license number of their limousine, and they were asked to sign the log book. Forty-five minutes after that, they reached Cairo.

Like its Greek counterpart, the capital city of Egypt was a mélange of the ancient and the modern, winding like a serpent along the east bank of the Nile. It was only in the past forty years or so that it had grown to spread across the river to the west bank, its population having swollen to more than ten or even fifteen million—no one knew for sure. Labyrinthine streets and narrow alleys wound through the various districts that were like a living historical guide to Cairo, for each of its successive rulers, rather than destroying the old city, had chosen simply to add to it. From Old Cairo in the south, the city snaked north through Fustat and east to Islamic Cairo, then

west to the colonial downtown district and *Maydan Tahrir*—
"Liberation Square." New office and apartment buildings mingled with old marketplaces and small cafés, where a cup of
mint tea could be had and a cigarette smoked at hardly any
cost.

Across the River Nile, at Giza, the Pyramids and the Sphinx
rose in crumbling, but still-majestic splendor, tangible remind-
ers of the fact that Egypt had once been the greatest civilization
on earth, privy to architectural knowledge that, even now, had
yet to be truly fathomed.

Employing their aliases of Jessamine Winthorpe and Ian
MacCallum, Bryony and Hamish checked into the Hotel
Golden Tulip Flamenco, situated in the heart of the residential
and diplomatic district of Cairo, on Zamalek Island. Since room
service was available twenty-four hours a day, the Scotsman
ordered up a very late supper for them, while Bryony took a
long, hot shower to wash away the remaining vestiges of blood
that matted her hair from the graze near her temple. As she
thought of her harrowing brush with death, she shivered. Finally, after eating, the two of them tumbled into bed, Hamish
cradling her gently against his chest in the darkness.

The following morning, they hired another limousine to take
them to Sais, called by the Egyptians *Sa-el-Hagar,* which lay
some miles northwest of Cairo, on the Canopic or Rosetta
Branch of the River Nile. From prehistoric times, the city had
been the site of the chief shrine of Neith, the Egyptian goddess
of war and of the loom, who had become cognate with Isis.
During the reign of the Pharaoh Psamtik I, Sais had also served
as the capital of Egypt. Now, it was only a small village of
about 12,500 people, who relied mostly on the production of
cotton to sustain them.

Egypt's road system was poor, and travel was often dangerous, especially at night, beyond the major cities. Vehicles frequently operated with no headlights in the darkness, and at high
speeds, and traffic regulations were routinely ignored. To journey off road was even more hazardous, as land mines that were
remnants from the numerous conflicts over the years were still
buried in many regions. Known minefields, while unmarked by

signs, were normally enclosed with barbed wire. But after heavy rains and flooding in desert areas, the land mines could shift, lurking in dunes of blown sand on the roadways. So the limousine driver was careful to avoid the piles of golden grit.

The considerable, commanding mound of Sais had been little excavated, and since it had first been detailed by Jean-François Champollion, who had translated the renowned Rosetta Stone, it had been extensively stripped, besides, by pilferers and thieves. So, as Bryony and Hamish stepped from the limousine upon its arrival at Sais, there was actually very little for them to see, although still visible were the ancient ruins of the Temple of Neith, the Egyptian earth-mother goddess cognate with Isis. However, as only fragments insufficient for archaeologists to reconstruct the shrine remained, it was the Greek historians Plutarch and Herodotus who were the main sources for how it had looked in its glory days.

"Early mythology of Lower Egypt claimed that Neith was the first entity to emerge from Nun, the primordial chaos, and that she then, by means of song, created her firstborn child, Ra, the sun god, who initially appeared as a light on the eastern horizon," Hamish explained, as they walked toward the ruins of the temple. "Afterward, it is said, Neith assumed the form of a bee and flew to Sais. Thus, her shrine here, Sapi-meht, was also referred to as the 'House of the Bee.'"

"One of the emblems of the Merovingian kings was the bee," Bryony noted, remembering all the golden bees that had been discovered in the sovereigns' tombs in France. "And since Rhédae or Rennes-le-Château was thought to have originally been dedicated to the earth-mother goddess Isis, there may be some connection."

"Undoubtedly."

"Archaeologically speaking, we don't really know much about the Temple of Neith," Bryony elucidated, as they began to explore what few ruins still remained. "But Herodotus reports that it was raised by the Egyptian King Amasis, and that its gate—the opening to the ways, as it were—was constructed first, being fashioned of 'stones of rare size and excellency.'"

A friend to the Greeks, who had equated Neith with their

own goddess Athêna, King Amasis had also contributed funds to the building of Delphi, although, plainly, the shrine at Sais to his own goddess of wisdom had proved his first priority. Herodotus had further averred that the temple enclosure had, at its rear, contained a mausoleum that had covered the whole rear wall, and that there had been huge, stone obelisks, and a circular lake, besides. The Saites, he had reported, had buried all the kings who belonged to their canton inside the Temple of Neith, which he had described as having a court, as well as a cloister of stone adorned with pillars carved to resemble palm trees.

The vegetation god Osiris had been entombed at Sais, too, although other myths asserted that he had instead been dismembered and cast into the River Nile, but that his widow, Isis, gathering his body parts from its banks, had interred them in cities throughout Egypt, to promote fertility and rebirth. Only his missing phallus had never been recovered—becoming the "Talisman of Set" and a potent source of occult power.

"The Greeks equated Osiris with their own Diônysus, by the way," Hamish revealed, "and like the goat god Pan, Osiris is depicted as bearing a flagellum and a shepherd's crook."

"And just like Pan, Osiris died!"

"Yes…and *that* is quite an interesting tale, indeed. Depending on the various legends, Set was either the brother or the son of Osiris, and, growing jealous of him, sought to do away with him by trickery. Using measurements he had secretly obtained of Osiris's body, Set ordered an opulent, ornate chest to be constructed, into which only Osiris would fit. Then Set held an elaborate feast in Osiris's honor and at the end of the meal, with great ceremony, brought forth the chest, promising that it would be a gift to whoever could fit inside it. Naturally, Set offered Osiris first crack at it, and when Osiris had climbed into the chest, Set quickly slammed down the lid, nailed it shut, and sealed all the cracks with molten lead, so Osiris couldn't escape. Then Set commanded that the chest be borne to the mouth of the River Nile and, there, pitched into the sea.

"Eventually, news of her husband's fate reached the ears of Isis, and she embarked on a quest to find him. The chest, it seemed, had washed ashore on the Phoenician coast at Byblos, coming to rest among the branches of a tamarisk bush. Such was the power of Osiris that the bush rapidly grew into a stout and mighty tree—''

"Like Yggdrasil, the Great Ash Tree of the Scandinavians!" Bryony exclaimed.

"Yes. And as it burgeoned, it formed a solid trunk around the chest containing Osiris." The Scotsman withdrew a pack of Marlboros from his pocket, shook out a cigarette, and lit up, dragging on it deeply, then blowing a cloud of smoke from his nostrils.

"So Osiris, too, then, was essentially 'hanged' on a tree— just as the Scandinavian god Odin was, in order to obtain wisdom!"

"Yes. Impressed by the tree, King Melcarthus of Byblos chopped it down and, from its trunk, had a pillar fashioned to support the roof of the Royal Palace, and such was the sweet fragrance that the pillar exuded that it's fame spread far and wide. Presently, Isis, hearing about it, traveled to Byblos and begged King Melcarthus to give her the pillar, which he did, being informed by her that it harbored the corpse of her husband. Cutting the chest from the heart of the pillar, Isis carried it back to Egypt and hid it from Set. But despite all her precautions, he chanced upon the chest, anyway, and recognizing it, he opened it, hacked Osiris's body up into fourteen pieces, and threw them into the River Nile, hoping they would be devoured by crocodiles. But because of their love for Osiris and their fear of Isis, the crocodiles didn't eat the corpse, and instead, its parts were cast up on the banks of the River Nile, there to be discovered by Isis and buried—all except for Osiris's phallus, which had been consumed by a fish," Hamish said, ending the story.

"Okay, let's think about this now," Bryony insisted. "Say that I'm right about Pan being entombed in the sepulchre with the Arcadia epitaph in Poussin's painting."

"All right." The Scotsman's eyes twinkled with both interest and delight at the workings of her mind, as he gazed at her lovingly.

"Now, here's Osiris, interred in a chest."

"Yes."

"Well...the chest was essentially both a coffin and an ark of a sort, since—probably because it was so well sealed—it floated on the River Nile and out to sea, right? And the Latin word for both 'chest' and 'coffin' was *arca*, which also means 'Noah's Ark' and the 'Ark of the Covenant'! So what we really have here, I think, is a concept of Death as a ship that bears one to knowledge, Hamish...either because for whatever reason, the ancient peoples really *did* believe the deceased were ferried across underground rivers like the Styx, by boatmen or navigators—*nautonniers!*—like Charon, or else perhaps because they had some distant recollection that Death had 'arrived' here on earth in a ship! You said the Arcadians called themselves *proselênoi*—'older than the moon'—and now, I'd be willing to bet it wasn't just because their patron god was Arkas or the 'Bear,' but also because they considered themselves the People of the Ark—"

"The Greek *arkê,* which is the equivalent of the Latin *arca.*" Contemplating this, the Scotsman slowly nodded his agreement. "Not Noah's Ark or the Ark of the Covenant, as most persons would suppose, but something even older...an ark or ship or spaceship, which carried an ark or chest, which brought an ark or coffin—Death or the knowledge of Death, and thus Wisdom—to Mankind."

"Just as the two stone tablets inscribed with the Ten Commandments—the Wisdom of God—were placed into the Ark of the Covenant! So maybe that's what the Knights Templar treasure was, Hamish...some kind of an ark or chest containing wisdom of some sort."

"Strangely enough, legend relates that the *Book of Thoth,* which was said to be the key to immortality, was stored in a golden box, in the inner sanctuary of the temple. Further, Plato's *Timaeus* and *Critias* state that at the Temple of Neith, secret halls held historical records that had been maintained for more than nine thousand years. If an ancient book or manuscript, or something like it, *is,* in fact, what we're searching or, then it probably won't be very large, but something easily carried by one or perhaps two men at the most.''

"Or else borne by a chariot," Bryony suggested, "just as he Ark of the Covenant is sometimes depicted. Also in this egard, we should take note of the Arcadians' association with he constellation Ursa Major or the 'Great Bear,' which you Brits call the 'Plow' or, jocularly, the 'Saucepan,' and we Americans call the 'Big Dipper.' Diverse cultures throughout he ancient world not only all portrayed this constellation as a bear, but also, often, as a chariot or wagon, and as a bier or coffin. As we know, the chariot was said to have been invented by Athêna, the goddess of wisdom, and sacred to her was the owl. One of the deep-sky objects in Ursa Major is the Owl Nebula, Hamish, so called for its two dark, core areas that resemble the eyes of an owl, but which can be seen from earth by only the largest of our telescopes! Yet perhaps the ancient peoples somehow knew about this nebula, even so. Spurred on by *Boötes* or the 'Bear Driver,' both Ursa Major and Ursa Minor wheel around Polaris or the Pole Star, which deceptively appears fixed in the night sky, like an axis or a fulcrum. Rather than bears, however, some cultures, such as the Romans and he Persians, saw the seven stars of the Big Dipper as oxen or bulls, pulling a plow. Now, the most-interesting thing about all his, Hamish, is that in 1996, after eight years of surveillance at the Lick Observatory, in San Jose, California, it was announced that a planet had been discovered orbiting Forty-Seven Ursae Majoris, which is a star in the region of Ursa Major. This planet, it is believed, has an atmosphere that would permit liquid water!''

"The elixir of life. So it's possible that life has, in fact, originated there, just as it has here on earth!''

"It is truly a pity that there isn't more to see here. If Mankind had only guarded the temples and monuments and libraries of the past more carefully, we would be a great deal further ahead. It's a shame that such great treasures are allowed to crumble into ruins, or else are wantonly destroyed by the barbaric, bigoted, fanatic, ignorant or terroristic peoples of this world. As both an archaeologist and the daughter of a historian, it sickens me. It strikes me that on the whole, Hamish, Mankind has proved a very poor caretaker of this planet!"

"I couldn't agree more."

As there was little more to investigate at Sais than the few remnants of the Temple of Neith, Bryony and Hamish strolled back to the waiting limousine, deciding to return to Cairo. There, the Scotsman intended to devote the rest of the afternoon to putting together what would initially be a simple, straightforward Web site about the Abbey of the Divine.

"I'm also going to e-mail Cauldronbearer," he told her, "attaching a copy of what we propose to upload to the Internet."

"Do you really believe that's wise, Hamish?"

"Just the threat alone may be enough to buy us some more time, sweetheart. By taking out five of its Round Table members, we've already managed to deal the Abbey a punishing blow. The idea of their existence being exposed to the world, coming so hard on the heels of the deaths of Hammerbearer and the others, may cause the order to back off—at least for a while—to regroup, recognizing that we're more formidable opponents than they at first thought."

"Yes, but then...won't they be even more determined to best us?"

"Perhaps. We'll just have to wait and see. Why don't you lie down and rest, darling, while I concentrate on the Web site and my letter to Cauldronbearer? Even though the injury you received was only a graze, thank God, I'm concerned that you don't overdo things, that you take it easy until you're feeling better."

"I'm all right, Hamish. Really, I am. In fact, it's somehow ironic to think that aside from a slight wound and a mild headache, I don't feel too bad physically. It's the mental stress of the entire ordeal that has truly affected me. When I dwell on how close to death I actually came—"

"Don't," the Scotsman ordered bluntly. "You're alive, and that's all that matters!"

"Yes, I know you're right." She bit her lower lip. "Would you mind very much if I left you alone here to work, Hamish, and went over to Giza? I'd like to spend some time at the pyramids.''

''No, my love, but, please, be careful! While I genuinely don't believe the Abbey is much of a threat currently—I wouldn't let you go, otherwise—I don't think we ought to take any chances, but should remain on guard at all times.''

''Don't worry. I don't intend to make an easy target of myself!''

Of all the Seven Wonders of the Ancient World, only the oldest, the Pyramids of Egypt at Giza, still survived. The rest— the Colossus of Rhodes, the Hanging Gardens of Babylon, the Mausoleum of Halicarnassus, the Pharos or Lighthouse of Alexandria, the Statue of Zeus at Olympia, and the Temple of Artemis at Ephesus—had all fallen prey to earthquakes, fires and other disasters. Even the Pyramids had not escaped unscathed but had been savaged over the millennia, stripped of their outer limestone casings, their inner chambers and tombs robbed.

Still, they stood upon the sweeping, red-gold desert plateau...silent sentinels and witnesses to the passing of the millennia. The Great Pyramid, built for the Pharaoh Khufu, whom the Greeks had called ''Kheops,'' had at one time stood nearly five hundred feet tall, and covered thirteen acres. It was believed to have taken one hundred thousand laborers approximately twenty years to construct Khufu's pyramid, and to have utilized an estimated two-and-a-half million stones. The other two of the primary three pyramids at Giza were smaller, but only slightly less impressive.

Although various theories abounded, it was not really known how the ancient Egyptians had made the nearly precise astronomical, geometrical and mathematical calculations required to build the Pyramids, or how they had then maneuvered the huge blocks of stone into place, either.

But Bryony was aware that in 1994, in his book *The Orion Mystery,* author Robert G. Bauval had proposed the theory that the three Pyramids had been laid out to correspond with the stars of the constellation Orion's belt. The Egyptians had viewed Orion—the "Hunter"—as Osiris. Further, in the Great Pyramid of Khufu had been fashioned shafts from both the King's and Queen's chambers, which had, respectively, been aligned with the belt stars of Orion and with Sirius, the Dog Star associated with Isis.

Because of her interest in both astrology and astronomy, Bryony knew the heavens had appeared differently from the earth in ancient times than they did now, and that because the earth wobbled slightly on its axis, the Pole Star that marked the approximate Celestial Pole changed over the millennia. To-day, the Pole Star was Polaris, which lay in the constellation Ursa Minor. During the time of the Pyramids, however, it had been Thuban, located in the constellation Draconis. In the year 12,000 A.D., it would be Vega, found in the constellation Lyra.

As she gazed at the Pyramids in the distance, reflecting on all this, she wondered if the ever-changing Pole Star had any-thing to do with the dragon having become such a universal symbol, just as the ark-bear-chariot had, and if, ten thousand years from now, the lyre would spring into prominence, as well. This last made her think of Pythagoras and his strings, of the Circle of Fifths that was really a spiral, and of the *Musica Mundâna*—the "Music of the Worlds." This was all a signif-icant piece of the puzzle, she felt. But how did it fit in?

The zodiac was a circle, too, but of twelve astrological signs, rather than musical fifths, and each of these was consequential in some fashion. The first was Aries the Ram, worshiped in Egypt as ram-horned or ram-headed and sacred to the god Am-mon, whose name meant "Hidden," just as the Mysteries were concealed or veiled. In predynasitc times, he had been the god of the wind, and rites celebrating him had included enshrouding his shrine. Later, he had been the king of the gods, the lord of time, the keeper of the years, and, as Ammon-Ra, a personifi-cation of the sun. At his temple in Thebes, a ritual boat known as *Woserhat* had been kept, elaborately constructed and adorned with golden ram's heads, and the god's image had been placed on the ship's deck. Across from the Temple of Ammon at Thebes, on the opposite bank of the River Nile, had stood the Temple of Khem—the goat god Pan—the two shrines like twin pillars guarding the river of life...or the doors to the Temple of Solomon, and Wisdom. Ammon...like Isis, a boatman or navigator...his ship an ark or chariot, whereupon he was enthroned...the chariot invented by Athêna, who was Wisdom...the chariot of the biblical Ezekial, with its four wheel of four faces: the ox, the lion, the eagle, the man....

Taurus, Leo, Scorpio, Aquarius...earth, fire, water, air...the four elements, the four corners of the earth and of the zodiac...spirals...wheels within wheels...

Reaching into her handbag and withdrawing her notepad, Bryony sat down on the desert ground and began to sketch furiously, informing the limousine driver that she had changed her mind and no longer wished to tour the Pyramids, after all. Some confusion ensued when he mistakenly thought she had decided to go for a camel ride instead, or else to wander around the bazaar of souvenir shops and other tourist traps at Giza.

"No...no..." She shook her head firmly. "I want only to sit here for a little while and draw."

At last, the pleasant, young Egyptian driver understood. The beautiful American woman was an artist, he observed shrewdly. She wished to paint the Pyramids! Bryony did not bother to correct his mistaken impression, for in truth, she did not know *what* she was doing...only that she felt she was on the verge of some pivotal, monumental discovery, having to do with the stars...with the twelve astrological constellations. No, not the constellations, she amended, but, rather, the *signs*. There *was* a difference, which, except for astrologers, most people did not realize or understand.

In her notebook, she drew the circle or wheel that was used to calculate horoscopes or birth charts, dividing it into thirty-six segments of ten degrees each, then dividing the ten-degree segments into groups of three to come up with the twelve signs. There was nothing revelatory about this, since what she had sketched was a standard astrological wheel, relying on what was termed the "Equal House System," from which all astrologers initially worked.

After Bryony got the astrological wheel down, she began to play around with it in various fashions, having only one concrete goal in mind: somehow to connect Taurus, Leo, Scorpio and Aquarius, which she had determined must be what the four faces—the ox, lion, eagle and man—on the wheels of the chariot seen by the Prophet Ezekial in the Bible referred to.

To start, Bryony tried to join the four signs by means of a pentagram, but as she lacked either a compass or protractor, that proved difficult, since the degrees were skewed, and she couldn't get the angles even, thus ending up with a pentagram that was badly distorted. Scrapping that, she then employed equilateral triangles to connect the four signs, which initially resulted in the hexagram that was part of the Seal of Solomon, and then, as she continued, burgeoned into a rosette...the Rose of the Rose and the Cross, she realized. Even more interesting was the fact that at the center of the rosette was an octagon— an eight-sided figure.

Next, she joined the four signs by means of a square, symbolic of the Hiram key and the four corners, which produced triangles whose top points intersected the octagon. As she contemplated the ever-growing and changing design, it then occurred to her that, using those intersections as reference points, she could now place an extended pentagram into the heart of the octagon, and that had she so desired, she could also have put a second inverted, extended pentagram there, to complete the whole. But she didn't. Instead, for several long minutes after she had finished, Bryony studied with fascination the design she had ultimately created, pondering what, if any, significance it might hold.

Strangely enough, even though, at the moment, it didn't look like much more to her than a bunch of esoteric symbols placed into an astrological wheel, she still felt as though, somehow, some way, she were on the right track. The question was: the right track for what? Actually, the more she stared at the design, the more it also, to her, resembled a multifaceted jewel, with a star at its center. Even as they were today, gemstones had been highly prized by the ancient peoples, she considered, and stones with stars, like opals and sapphires, had been surrounded with more superstition than most.

What should she do next? she wondered, her brow knitted

in a thoughtful, bemused frown. The pentagram, probably, was the key, she reasoned, since it was at the heart of the design and such a universal symbol, besides. Because it was extended—just like the pentagram described by the landscape at Rennes-le-Château—it occurred to her that perhaps the angle formed by its two long sides might be important. With that idea in mind, Bryony decided to use a series of those to join the signs Taurus, Leo, Scorpio and Aquarius yet again, employing a new astrological wheel, and having some vague notion about triangles and spirals.

When she was done, she had a twelve-pointed star in the center of the wheel. As she grasped that fact, old, long-forgotten memories stirred nebulously in the back of her mind. The design reminded her of something...something having to do with some kind of atomic, crystalline or molecular structure, perhaps...? Moments later, however, the only half-formulated idea slipped elusively away. She should have paid more attention in her science classes! Bryony chided herself, biting her lower lip hard with annoyance. But then, maybe she was remembering all wrong, anyway.

Yet even as that thought arose, another entered her mind, and she suddenly realized that the series of angles she had constructed had generated the exact same type of triangles with inverted bases that comprised the eight-pointed Maltese Cross of the Order of the Knights Hospitaler of St. John of Jerusalem, later known as the "Knights of Malta" and closely associated and allied with the Knights Templar.

Presently, she drew two straight lines to connect the four solitary points that had resulted from the series of pentagram angles, thus arriving at what astrologers termed a "Grand Cross"...the Cross of the Rose and the Cross, which cross, in her second design, lay at the center of an octagon, just as the extended pentagram had in her first design.

"X marks the spot," Bryony murmured whimsically to herself, a small half-smile curving her mouth. Then at that, of a sudden, an icy grue chased up her spine, making the fine hairs on her nape stand chillingly on end. "Oh, my God," she exclaimed softly, utterly stunned and incredulous. "It's a *treasure map!*"

Thirty-Five

Loch Awe and Ben Cruachan

Poets are the hierophants of an unapprehended
inspiration; the mirrors of the gigantic shadows
Which futurity casts upon the present.

A Defense of Poetry
—Percy Bysshe Shelley

O Caledonia! stern and wild,
Meet nurse for a poetic child!
Land of brown heath and shaggy wood;
Land of the mountain and the flood!

The Lay of the Last Minstrel
—Sir Walter Scott

But if you name me among the lyric bards,
I shall strike the stars with my exalted head.

Odes, Book I
—Horace (Quintus Horatius Flaccus)

*En Route from Cairo, Egypt, to Loch Awe and Ben Cruachan,
Scotland, the Present*

Returning hurriedly to their room at the Hotel Golden Tulip Flamenco in Cairo, Bryony could scarcely contain her excitement.

"Hamish... *Hamish!*" she cried, as she stumbled into the room, bubbling over, laughing, dancing and whirling around, before she hugged him tightly. "I've found it! *I've found it!*"

"Found what, my love?" From where he sat at the desk, working at her laptop, he glanced up, his eyes sparkling and his mouth grinning broadly with amusement. "Some fabulously mysterious, energizing potion you discovered in the Pharaoh Khufu's great tomb? I've never before seen you so animated! Sit down, sweetheart... *slow* down—please—and tell me what has happened to excite you so."

"I told you! Weren't you listening? *I've found it*... the Knights Templar treasure! Well, not the treasure, exactly—but what I believe is the map to its location!"

The Scotsman eyed her askance, shaking his head disbelievingly, starting now to chuckle.

"I get it. Instead of visiting the Pyramids at Giza, you went to one of the local cafés, where you imbibed far more than your fair share of potent Egyptian spirits, right? Or else you are teasing me—as punishment for your having to spend all afternoon alone, whilst I've slaved over our Web site devoted to the Abbey and my e-mail to the enigmatic Cauldronbearer."

"No! I mean it, Hamish! I'm serious! Look!" Withdrawing her notepad from her purse, Bryony flipped it open to show him the fruits of her labors, explaining how she had come to sketch the two designs on the astrological wheels. "While it's true that I don't yet really understand precisely *how* they're supposed to work, I'm still somehow certain they *are* the map to the Knights Templar treasure, Hamish!" she insisted.

"Darling, I'm truly delighted to see you so happy—especially in light of all that's befallen us—and further, you must know I would be absolutely the very last person on this earth to rain on your parade. However, if I understand your hypothesis correctly—that the two designs you've shown me will somehow identify some as-yet-to-be-determined location in the heavens, which will then pinpoint someplace here on earth as the burial site of the Knights Templar treasure—then I'm very much afraid

I must inform you that there are entirely legitimate astronomical, geographical and mathematical reasons why what you've proposed simply won't work."

"Oh." Her elated expression abruptly grew crestfallen. Then she demanded suspiciously, "Why not?"

"Well, my love, because you are attempting to impose what is essentially a two-dimensional, flat map—your astrological wheel—onto three-dimensional objects that are either curved or spherical in nature, and for which one would also thus require a different kind of cartography. In other words, when we see a flat map of our planet, it is to a certain extent distorted, in a way that a globe is not; and if we were to attempt to fold the flat map around the globe, for example, we would find that we simply could never make everything line up properly."

"Well...*damn!*" Bryony sighed heavily. "And yet, I was *so* sure I'd somehow discovered the key—"

"Hmm...yes, well, *that* is a horse of a different color altogether! I'm not saying your idea is totally useless, sweetheart—not at all...only that it's simply impossible for it ever to be successful in the way in which you are trying to implement it."

"What would you suggest, then?"

"Well, of course, it's entirely feasible that your astrological wheel containing the Grand Cross could be laid down upon any *flat* map—as opposed to trying to make it correspond to the heavens or a globe—to pinpoint a specific geographical location. Because, essentially, your astrological wheel itself isn't really a map. Rather, it's a sort of compass—one in which if the axes that comprise the Grand Cross were properly aligned with some as-yet-unknown directional coordinates, the hub *would,* in fact, fall upon a precise point."

"Yes, I understand now," she said slowly, the wheels in her mind turning. "But, then...how would I ever determine the correct degree of tilt of the axes, assuming that a zero inclination would indicate due north?"

"You'd require some kind of geographical clues or instructions for calculating at least one set of directional coordinates for each axis of the Grand Cross, or else for figuring the degree of tilt for one of the axes, presuming, of course, that they are intended to maintain their right angles."

"A geographical clue...like *Le Bénetier*—'The Stoop'!" Bryony exclaimed.

"What do you mean?" Hamish inquired, puzzled. "I hardly see how a holy-water fount—"

"No—not the fount in the little church at Rennes-le-Château. Rather, the confluence of the Rivers Blanque and Sals! It's called *Le Bénetier*, remember? We even discussed at the time that perhaps the church's statue of the Demon Asmodeus *was* a clue to that! So...say that one of the axes of the Grand Cross should be aligned with *Le Bénetier*, and the other with the Temple Mount at Jerusalem or something...."

"Yes...*yes!* I see what you're driving at now—and possibly, you truly *are* on to something, you clever lady! Get my collection of highway maps out, darling, while I do something about redrawing these crude sketches of yours into more accurate designs. We'll need to put them on tracing paper, besides, so we can see what turns up when we lay the Grand Cross on the maps. I'll run downstairs and find out whether the hotel's front office or any of the nearby shops have anything like that."

"Do that!" Bryony was already digging excitedly through the Scotsman's overnight bag, in which he had several Ordnance Survey maps, which he habitually carried with him whenever he traveled and which he had thought would stand them in good stead when they had fled from Drumrose Cottage. "Oh, and, Hamish—"

"Yes?" He raised one eyebrow inquisitively.

"I love you...."

Momentarily, as he gazed at her, his dark, hawkish visage softened.

"I love you, too, sweetheart."

"Well?" The voice of the Abbey's Grand Master was cool, distant. "I'm waiting, Cauldronbearer. You said you had something of vital importance to report. So either tell me what it is, or I shall have to assume that you had no good reason for disturbing me."

"My deepest apologies, Nautonnier, but I'm afraid the news I have to impart to you is so profoundly distressing that I-I hardly even know where to begin."

"It is always wise to begin at the beginning, Cauldronbearer," the Grand Master reminded him.

"Yes, you are right, as usual, Nautonnier." Cauldronbearer cleared his throat nervously. "I-I have been contacted by Neville, via e-mail."

"Indeed?" Despite how he attempted to repress it, a note of genuine interest and excitement crept into the normally taciturn Grand Master's voice. "And this, I take it, is at the root of your upset?"

"Quite. Nautonnier, Neville has…he has constructed a *Web site,* to which he intends to upload *every single thing* he knows about the Abbey! I'm sure I don't need to point out to you that if he should carry out such a dire and drastic plan, it will be the ruin of us! For only look what has happened to the Prieure de Sion since they were foolish enough to speak to Henry Lincoln, et al., and publicized in that book *Holy Blood, Holy Grail.* They've had not a moment's peace or privacy ever since! Everyone from amateur sleuths to complete crackpots has investigated their order! Centuries of secrecy and relative obscurity have now disappeared where the Priory is concerned—and while they may continue to involve themselves in worldly matters, certainly, they can no longer expect to do so without observation and with total impunity! Nautonnier, what are your instructions? Surely, you must now concur that Neville has betrayed us, that he poses a significant threat to us! He has destroyed five of our number already! Nor have we yet any evidence whatsoever that he has somehow managed to locate the hiding place of the lost Knights Templar treasure!"

For a long moment, there was no answer, so that Cauldronbearer wondered if the Abbey's Grand Master were so incensed that he had hung up on him. But still, no dial tone buzzed furiously in Cauldronbearer's ear.

"Nautonnier?" he at last queried tentatively.

"Yes, I'm here—not out giving interviews!" the Grand Master asserted dryly. "So you needn't worry, Cauldronbearer. I merely wished to reflect on these revelations of yours. Despite everything, I confess I still cherished some small—and, now, clearly vain—hope that Neville would, in the end, prove to be one of our own. After all, he killed Hammerbearer in self-defense and to protect the woman...Bryony St. Blaze...and what happened on the road to Athens was in all likelihood a terrible accident born of Shieldbearer's knowledge and fear that yet another failure on his part would not be tolerated. But that Neville would deliberately threaten us in this way, even consider exposing the Abbey to the world and its unwashed masses of ignorant rabble...no, that I cannot and will not countenance, Cauldronbearer. He must be destroyed—and the woman with him, of course."

"Unfortunately, I fear that is no longer quite the viable option it was previously, Nautionner. He who hesitates is lost—and in my opinion, we have left decisive action against Neville far too late. Thank God, he was never actually formally initiated into our innermost ranks! In his e-mail to me, he claims to have written some computer-programming script that, if he does not enter into it some password at regular intervals, will automatically upload all the information about the Abbey to the World Wide Web, as well as dispatch it to dozens of other Web masters who maintain esoterical sites on the Internet!"

"But...how is that possible? The man's a history lecturer, for Christ's sake!"

"True. Nevertheless, information about such things is available everywhere these days, Nautonnier. The World Wide Web is a fount of knowledge—for those who are intelligent enough to make proper use of it. Even television would never have proved capable of disseminating so much material on a global basis! It's the Age of Aquarius—and of the Digital Generation. Only think, Nautonnier, how from the time of our prehistoric ancestors, Mankind has plodded along for millennia, scarcely making any discernible progress at all as a species, aside from a few rare flashes of brilliance, as evidenced by such monuments as Stonehenge, the Pyramids, Machu Picchu, the Hanging Gardens of Babylon and the Forbidden City. But now, suddenly, in only the last one hundred years or so—hardly the blink of an eye, as far as history and its timeline is concerned—he has put men on the moon and regularly sends astronauts in space shuttles to orbit the planet! Among other things, the astrological sign of Aquarius rules inventions and technology. Some say its age has not yet dawned, but I...I tell you, Nautonnier, that it is already upon us!''

"Such was the shape of the things to come, Cauldronbearer. All the great cultures and prophets foretold it, did they not? Once, knowledge was the province of the Great Minds of the world, of the Enlightened Ones. Now, it is the playground of every idiot with a modem! Truly, I shudder to think about it, Cauldronbearer—for a little knowledge is, indeed, a very dangerous thing, and misinformation is even worse than ignorance!'' The Grand Master sighed heavily.

"Continue the search for Neville and Ms. St. Blaze. When they are again found, maintain a prudent watch upon them. However, no further attempts to capture or get rid of either of them are to be made at this time. Contact Crownbearer and Scepterbearer to assist you. In the meanwhile, I will be in touch with Hornbearer and Stonebearer, in order to discover whether there exists some means of outwitting Neville's alleged computer-programming script. That is all.''

At that, Cauldronbearer did not even need to hear the dial tone buzzing in his ear to know the Grand Master had ruthlessly severed the connection.

As well as exploring ancient Egypt, Bryony and Hamish had also worked on the "compass and the treasure map,'' as they had come to call the astrological wheel and the as-yet-unfathomed map leading to the lost Knights Templar treasure— or so they now fervently believed. Yet despite the fact that they had now opened and decrypted all of Simon St. Blaze's files contained on the two CDs he had sent to Bryony before his death, as well as collected and collated reams of information of their own, they felt as though they were no closer now to solving the puzzle than they had been at their first meeting.

Now, this evening, growing discouraged once more at the enormity of the task they had set for themselves, Bryony, sitting cross-legged on the bed, buried her face in her hands, then combed her fingers through her hair, sighing deeply.

"I'm starting to think sorting all this out is absolutely hopeless," she announced, smiling wanly at Hamish, who sprawled beside her on the bed. "We could read and cross reference for aeons—and still miss half of what's been written about arcana and esoterics over the ages! I swear to God...whoever burned down the Library at Alexandria ought to have been marched out and shot! The ancient Egyptians were great because they possessed thousands of years' worth of knowledge, Hamish! Once all their papyrus texts went up in smoke, they declined something pitiful!"

"It was Julius Caesar and the Romans who initially burnt the Library, and Arab invaders who later finished off whatever little of it still remained, using the books and scrolls as fuel to heat bathhouses. Literally hundreds of thousands of manuscripts were destroyed. I don't believe Egypt declined *quite* as rapidly afterward as you imagine. However, I suspect there *is*, nevertheless, a great deal of truth in your observation. Fools burn books. Wise men learn from them—no matter who wrote them, or why."

"Well, I've never understood why anybody would want to burn books—or even to ban them. Without books or other records of some kind, we'd all be virtual ignoramuses! Only look at the Neanderthals. They existed for thousands of years, yet never made any real progress whatsoever. No books, of course— way too early in the timeline for that—but still, no written or pictoral records to speak of, since very little art has been found, and of music only a flute or two. And probably, the Neanderthals possessed only limited linguistic abilities, if any, besides. Contrast all this with the Cro-Magnons, who displaced them—maybe even exterminated them—and who were exceedingly more developed and sophisticated, leaving behind extensive cave art as pictoral records. Books are how we remember the accumulated knowledge and history of Mankind, Hamish, so we don't slide back into nescience and barbarism...so we don't keep on repeating the past...caught up in a vicious cycle!"

"You're preaching to the converted, my love," the Scotsman

reminded her, grinning, then, at her feigned scowl, leaned forward on the bed to kiss her lightly upon the mouth.

At first, it seemed that he would only tease her. But then, after a moment, his dancing eyes darkened, and the pressure of his lips grew harder and more demanding, as though the taste and feel of her had wakened some hitherto sleeping beast inside him. Bryony felt the sudden surge of force and desire that emanated from him as hard as a physical blow, and then the powerful quiver and leap of her own involuntary response as she wrapped her arms around him, clinging to him with a hunger and need that was as age-old as time. Her mouth yielded to his...kissed him back with a fervency that caused him to inhale sharply and tighten his grip on her. His fingers cupped her face, tunneled through the strands of her hair, pulling her down beside him on the mattress.

They tumbled together on the rumpled bedclothes, unfastening and discarding their garments with a haste born of mutual passion and yearning, each longing to feel bare skin against bare skin, with nothing between them, separating them, however little. Outside, from below the towering Hotel Golden Tulip Flamenco drifted the sounds and scents of Cairo...of the residential and diplomatic district of Zamalek Island, and of the River Nile...the traffic of the capital city, the voices speaking foreign tongues, the ripple of water against the shore...the heady bouquet of exotic flowers, the pungent aroma of strong tobacco, the earthy perfume of rich, fertile, black Delta soil.

Time was old and ceaseless here, but in this moment, there was only now for Bryony and Hamish, no thought of tomorrow, of their uncertain future. There was only each other, heated flesh pressed against heated flesh, lips and tongues and hands unstill, moving surely and sweetly, tasting and touching...tantalizing....

She melted like ice in the desert sun against him, melding herself to the lean, hard length of his body as he crushed her to him, burying his dark, hawkish visage in her long, blond hair, inhaling deeply of the vanilla fragrance of her. His hands roamed where they willed, upon her breasts and between her thighs, arousing within her the first of the exquisite sensations that would presently overtake her, making her breath catch in her throat and scattering her senses to the four winds.

Like summer wine, he intoxicated her. She reveled in the feel of him, in the strong, supple muscles that bunched and rippled in his broad back and chest, his arms and thighs, beneath her palms that caressed and kneaded him, enfolded his maleness, potent and throbbing with his burgeoning want and need for her. She felt herself a goddess, all powerful, all wise, knowing that at this instant, in the throes of unbridled desire, he would deny her nothing. So Cleopatra—Isis incarnate—must have felt with Caesar and Antony...as though, with merely a deft flick of her wrist, a damp lick of her tongue, she had brought the entire Roman Empire to its knees. Slowly lowering her head, Bryony took Hamish in her mouth, her tongue delicately swirling and teasing, eliciting a low groan of rough emotion and deep pleasure from his lips. Her hands stroked him tauntingly.

Somewhere, time passed. But not here, not now. Here in this ancient city, it somehow hung suspended like the moon over the Delta and the desert, while she wove her magic as surely as, with her loom, the goddess Neith had woven the world into existence. And perhaps she really had, Bryony thought, in some dim corner of her mind. For was it not women who tended the hearths and birthed the children, so that Man might live? Was this not the primal secret known to Lil and Isis, to Sophia and Athêna? To the earth-mother goddesses, all? Dusky, innocent Eve of the dark, coarsely curling hair...unwittingly tempting the Serpent, Lucifer, into tempting her, in turn, to taste of the succulent, forbidden fruit...as Bryony tasted—and gained the ancient knowledge of the power of Woman. It lay not in her own strength—but in the weakness of Man for soft, swollen breasts, generously curved hips and trembling thighs wide spread to reveal the sweet, mellifluous Mysteries of Life....

His fingers covetous cords that bound her hair, Hamish at last lifted her head and savagely drew her to him, his mouth seizing hers possessively, his tongue plunging full and deep, his strong, sure, slender hands forcefully rolling her over and sliding her beneath him. His urgent weight pressed her down, and Bryony welcomed it eagerly, lost in a place as dark and timeless and atavistic as the primeval void…a place where only flesh and the senses reigned, and lips and tongues and hands worked their sweet, savage sorcery, casting the honeyed spells that would blind and bind, honing passion to the keen-edged blade that would claim the nectarous offering. With a single, sharp thrust, it pierced her to the very core.

The blood sang in her ears, and the tide rushed through her, bearing her away like a ship upon the waters of an underground stream. And then, without warning, the earth tilted on its axis, and the sun and the moon fell into the primal, madding sea and were swallowed by its storm. Emerging from the blackness into the light, Bryony soared ever higher, no longer earthbound, but unfettered. Winged. Eternal…

And Hamish flew at her side.

"We can't stay here, sweetheart," he told her gently, the following morning. "You know that. But we can't continue to run away and hide from the Abbey forever, either. I desperately want a life together with you, Bryony—and this isn't it!"

"I know…I know…." She spoke softly

Catching another Egyptair flight, they returned to Athens, retrieved the now-repaired Volvo from the garage where they had left it, and started to retrace their labyrinthine route back to Scotland and Drumrose Cottage. As the miles passed, Bryony and Hamish went on trying to make some logical rhyme and reason of their compass and the treasure map, although without success.

"Far from having too few clues, we have too many!" Refolding their map of Greece, she flung it with frustration onto the floor of the automobile. "We'll never figure it out, damn it! For pity's sake, Hamish! *You're* the historian and expert author on the medieval ages. If you had been a Knight Templar back then, where would *you* have concealed the treasure?"

"Well, I…I would have taken it to Argyll," he replied slowly, thoughtfully.

"Why?"

"Because for one thing, if I'd fled from France during the time of Philip the Fair, carrying the treasure away with me, then I would undoubtedly have sought refuge in Scotland—which is where most of the Knights Templar who escaped from King Philip's persecution actually *did* go. Further, Argyll is wild and isolated, yet not nearly as far away and difficult to access from Europe as the New World would have been at the time—which is why I have always thought 'Prince' Henry St. Clair wouldn't, sensibly, ever have hidden the treasure there, no matter *what* outlandish rumor may claim to the contrary!"

"So…Argyll's your pleasure, is it? Well, I'm really loath to burst your bubble, Hamish, but to the very best of my own knowledge, there's not one single damned thing about Argyll that stands out as even a mere hint…much less a real, concrete clue—esoterical or otherwise—to the whereabouts of the missing treasure, or about anything else of relevance, either, for that matter! No Rosslyn Chapel, no Rennes-le-Château, no Oracle at Delphi, no Temple of Neith…nothing, nada, zilch—"

"Hmm…well, that's not exactly true, you know…."

"What do you mean…*'that's not exactly true'?*" Bryony questioned, frowning. "We've nothing at all about Argyll in any of our own notes, and all Dad had to say about it in the files he sent to me before his death was that there was tangible evidence of a Knights Templar presence there during the Middle Ages— which, as you've already demonstrated, was probably true for most, if not all, of Scotland!"

"Yes…however, there *is* one highly interesting little detail not about Argyll, but, rather, its neighbor Perthshire that, more often than not, is simply discounted, ignored or overlooked by those delving into the whereabouts of the Templar treasure."

"And what 'little detail,' as you termed it, might that be?"

"Viscount 'Bonnie' Dundee was killed there, in Sixteen Eighty-nine, at a little place called 'Killiecrankie.'"

"So?"

"So…he was the Grand Master of the Scottish Templars at the time, and he was wearing the Grand Cross of the Order and other Templar regalia when he died—which means that he may have known where the treasure was and had access to it. It may, in fact, have been after his death, during the Glorious Revolution against King James the Second and the influx into Britain and Ireland of the Protestant Orangemen under King William the

Third of Orange, a principality in southern France, that the Templar treasure was actually lost. It may have disappeared when, following Bonnie Dundee's untimely demise, it was removed from his holdings on the Firth of Tay, or from elsewhere, and conveyed west into Argyll, toward Oban, the so-called Gateway to the Isles. Under the circumstances, secreting the treasure would have been a sensible precaution at the time—and although the clan doesn't appear to be related to the Sinclairs of the North, there *is* a branch of Sinclairs in Argyll and the west of Scotland.''

"All right…let's find out where—if anyplace—all that leads us.''

As Hamish drove, Bryony dragged out their *Ordnance Survey* map of Scotland from their cartography collection, along with the astrological wheel that served as their compass. Laying it over the map, she then carefully lined up one of the axes of its Grand Cross with Killiecrankie, which lay in the Grampian Mountains, some miles to the northwest of the city of Dundee. Then she slowly swung the compass around to see if the other axis lined up with anywhere else that might prove to hold some significance to them, however small.

"Found anything yet?'' Briefly, the Scotsman glanced over interestedly before returning his gaze to the road ahead.

"I…I don't know…maybe… With the first axis on Killicrankie, the second can line up with Dumbarton.''

"And?''

"And so I'm thinking about Dumbarton Rock…that huge, dark, red mass of basalt that rises like some primal giantess's breasts from the Firth of Clyde. It's a very well-known Scottish landmark, Hamish. Moreover, it could tie in fabulously with the statue of St. Roch at Rennes-le-Château—and with King Arthur and the Holy Grail, too! Because the French word *roche* means 'rock,' and Dumbarton was often called *Castrum Arthuri*—'Arthur's Castle.' Additionally, St. Roche is depicted at Rennes-le-Château as being wounded in the thigh—just like the Grail or Fisher King of Arthurian legend! Last but not least, if I turn the compass so the sign of Pisces, the Fish, lies toward Dumbarton, then one of the axes of the Grand Cross runs straight

through it!—while the other runs straight through Killiecrankie!''

"Where do the axes intersect?"

"Let's see…hmm…at a mountain called 'Ben Cruachan'—
but in all honesty, I have to admit that there doesn't seem to be
any importance attached to *that,* esoterical or otherwise," Bryony observed, her earlier excitement now fading, leaving her
once more downcast. "So I guess it's just another wild-goose
chase, like every other location we've tried thus far—damn it!"

At that, softly, devilishly, Hamish began to laugh.

"What's so funny?" she demanded crossly, glowering at him.

"*Ben Cruachan*…it's Gaelic, my love. It means 'Head Hill'
or 'Hill of the *Head*'!"

The Head. Baphomet. Wisdom. Bingo.

From Dumbarton, Bryony and Hamish took the A82 highway
north to Tyndrum, then followed the A85 west, deep into Argyll,
which was some of the wildest and most beautiful countryside
in all of Scotland, dappled with clear lochs and murky bogs,
sweeping moors and dark forests, hidden valleys and rugged
mountains.

To the southwest of the village of Dalmally, Loch Awe uncoiled like a serpent in the midst of striking, its northern fork a
gaping maw poised as though to swallow Ben Cruachan, the
great, soaring munro that, rising to 3,695 feet, was the highest
of the Cruachan range and loomed like a ponderous colossus
over the breathtaking land. Islands dotted the loch, home to ancient crannogs; and the cloaking mist that drifted across the still
water, snaking its way through the deep glens and clinging to
the summits of the towering peaks, lent the savage terrain an
eerie air, making it seem as though Bryony and Hamish had
somehow traveled back to a time as old as the very lake dwell-
ings themselves. In spite of the modern roads that twisted
through far-flung villages with names like Cladich, Kilchrenan,
Taynuilt and Oban—this part of Argyll was so desolate that it
appeared frozen in the past, hardly touched by contemporary
civilization, as though at any moment, barbaric Picts or Highland
warriors would charge from the hills and woods, shouting their

fierce battle cries and brandishing their iron spears and claymores, their faces ritually tattooed or otherwise painted with blue woad.

Thirty-four miles in length, Loch Awe met its furious, foaming, namesake river at the daunting Pass of Brander, which crouched ferociously at the foot of Ben Cruachan and was bounded by frightening, precipitous crags that ascended in rapid steps and terraces from the water to wall in the declivity and to fashion the base of the mountain, falling away to only a narrow, rocky beach that crept along the rough shore. Upon the jagged steeps grew dense forests of oaks and firs and other trees, home to wild cats, deer, foxes, martens, badgers, squirrels and eagles alike; and the river itself roiled over a broken jumble of upthrusting chunks of granite and whinstone. At the northern end of the pass rose a cliff called "Craiganuni," where the giant Rocks of Brander formed a natural strait of sorts, supports upon which ancient peoples had aeons ago positioned huge tree trunks to serve as a bridge, however unstable and dangerous. Some distance below the Rocks had once lain an equally perilous ford employed as a cattle crossing by those daring enough to brave the churning current.

As her eyes drank in the awe-inspiring region, Bryony felt her breath catch in her throat and her heart pound with a strange, primitive, erratic rhythm. There was something not only dazzling and exquisite, but also fearsome and atavistic about the entire scene that, coupled with her own uneasy realization that almost-certain death awaited should the Volvo somehow plunge off the highway, disturbed her. The fine hairs on her nape prickled, and every now and then, she looked anxiously over her shoulder, through the rear window, to be sure that she and Hamish were not being followed, as they had been on the road to Athens.

"I know," the Scotsman said quietly, observing her action and glancing himself into the rearview mirror again, to check the road behind them. "The idea of another car chase in this kind of an area has me on edge, as well. However, I've seen no one tailing us—yet."

"Nor have I—much to my vast relief! I keep trying to reassure myself. But I have to confess that even the landscape here, despite how gorgeous it is, has me a trifle unnerved.''

"Yes, it's quite primeval, isn't it? There's an old folktale attached to this part of Argyll, which recounts how Loch Awe came into being. Legend says that the Cailleach Bheur, a supernatural guardian of fountains, springs, streams and wells, was in charge of a spring that fed a magic well of youth at the top of Ben Cruachan. Every single evening at sunset, to staunch the water's flow, it was her responsibility to cover the fount with a large, stone slab, which she also removed again every sunrise. But one dusk, after driving her goats across Connel and then bathing, the Cailleach Bheur was so exhausted that she fell asleep beside the spring, neglecting to put its slab back into place beforehand. As a result, the fount overflowed, gushing down the mountainside and bursting through the Pass of Brander. The roaring of the torrent awoke the Cailleach Bheur, but it was too late. All her efforts to stem the rushing tide were in vain, and the water flooded the plain below, drowning man and beast alike, and forming Loch Awe. The Cailleach Bheur was so horrified by all the destruction she had inadvertently caused that she turned herself into the great, stone mountain of the same name, which lies near Ben Cruachan—although some say that it was the gods who punished her.''

"I've often thought that no matter how fantastic it might seem to us, some grain of truth lurks at the heart of every folktale,'' Bryony mused aloud. "Perhaps once, long ago, the Cailleach Bheur really *did* exist—not as some supernatural creature, of course, but as a wise, old woman steeped in ancient knowledge…a fount of information and experience, as it were. Maybe she lived all alone in these hills, and people mistakenly believed that she controlled the flow of the river.''

"Perhaps,'' Hamish agreed. "It's as good an explanation as any other, I suppose.''

Under Hamish's competent guidance, the Volvo wound through the Pass of Brander, where both the highway and railroad track competed for space along the narrow, curving strip of terrain at the water's edge. Ahead, Ben Cruachan rose, its four ridges culminating in a sharp summit, its principal ridge, which ran east to west, strewn with boulders.

Eventually, after circumnavigating the southern skirt of the mountain, Bryony and Hamish arrived at the local campgrounds located at the southwest corner of the huge munro. There, they found an out-of-the-way place to park and set up camp. After that, the Scotsman suggested that they enjoy an early supper at the historic pub in Kilchrenan.

"There's little point in trying to climb Ben Cruachan today," he insisted. "'Munro bagging,' it's called here in Scotland. It'll be dark soon, so we wouldn't be able to see anything, anyway, even if we could make the ascent, which we couldn't—and I'd rather not have to spend the night on the mountain, besides…cold and miserable…when we can be warm and snug in the tent. Better for us to rest tonight and get an early start in the morning."

"Yes, but even so, Hamish, I still don't see how we can possibly hope to find the Knights Templar treasure." Bryony sighed. "Ben Cruachan is so massive that the treasure could be hidden anyplace on it, and even with our compass, there's nothing to indicate where—and we don't even know that we've got the map right, besides! In reality, we're only speculating, after all."

"True. But if we *are* right about the map, then my own guess is that there ought to be something physical—some kind of a marker, if you will—on or visible from Ben Cruachan itself that will give us a tangible clue as to the location of the treasure."

"And if there isn't?"

"Then we'll just have to cross that bridge when we come to it. In the meanwhile, you know what they say about all work and no play. So…let's be off to Kilchrenan for a bite to eat, then, shall we?"

"Sounds good to me. I'm famished!" Bryony smiled, brightening. "It must be all this fresh mountain air and hard labor! You'd think I'd be used to setting up a camp by now. But, somehow, it just never seems to get any easier."

"Well, at least it's a good, tidy, serviceable camp," Hamish noted as he scrutinized their campsite, "and hopefully, with any luck, we won't have to use for it very long."

The short drive to the West Highland village of Kilchrenan passed quickly and pleasantly, and in no time at all, the Scotsman was steering the car into the small, paved parking lot that surrounded the green lawn in front of the Kilchrenan Inn. The pub itself was an old, long, pebbled-ash building, painted white, with five gabled windows set into its dark, pitched roof, from which chimneys rose at either end. Cheerful, leafy plants framed the front door and lower windows. Attached to one end of the pub was Dunloamin, a holiday house with its own separate front and rear access. At the other, a hedge ran halfway across the front of the building. Inside, the Kilchrenan Inn boasted a cozy, traditional bar, as well as a dining room that served both lunch and supper during the tourist and holiday seasons.

After making their way to the dining room, Bryony and Hamish ordered a simple but tasty meal of Scottish fare, which they shared over pints of ale, while they discussed their plans for the following day.

"We'll need to climb to the *top* of Ben Cruachan," the Scotsman ventured, as he sipped from his glass.

"Why?"

"Well, if our deductions about the compass and map *are* actually correct, and there *is* indeed some kind of a marker pointing the way to where the Knights Templar treasure is cached, then the indicator must be either on or visible from the munro...probably from its peak. That's really the only thing that makes any sense. Otherwise, anyone searching for the treasure would be compelled to scour the *whole* mountain."

"That seems reasonable enough," Bryony concurred. "But still, you're assuming that whoever concealed the treasure wanted it to be found. Maybe they didn't."

"That is a possibility. Nevertheless, I think it's extremely unlikely. In my opinion, it's not apt to be anything of monetary value, although the treasure—whatever it may be—was clearly priceless to the Knights Templar. The Templar Grand Master, Jacques de Molay, during the time of Philip the Fair, endured torture and was burned at the stake rather than revealing Templar secrets. So the Templars wouldn't have wanted their treasure to be lost...only hidden from those who either would not understand and appreciate its import, or else who would misuse it in some fashion—which is no doubt what they feared, where Philip the Fair was concerned. Since they wouldn't have known how long the treasure would remain secreted, any marker indicating its whereabouts would need to be able to withstand the elements, perhaps for centuries, which argues for something permanent...and something that would mean nothing to the casual observer, but everything to the enlightened eye.''

''Like what?''

''I don't know.'' Hamish shrugged. ''Maybe a carving on a rock face, for example—although even that would be difficult to find up on Ben Cruachan, since its main ridge is littered with boulders. No...I'm guessing that it's going to be something concealed somehow in the landscape itself.''

''Something like the Nazca lines in Peru, for instance?'' Bryony suggested, beginning to grow faintly excited at the possibility.

''Precisely! Yes, that's exactly what I'm talking about! On the ground, it's difficult to make out the Nazca lines at all, much less to see the figures they actually depict. But overhead, from the air—''

''Or from the *summit* of a mountain— Yes...yes, Hamish, now, I see what you're driving at! A map that doesn't exist—but must be *deduced* from esoterical clues to an astrological wheel that fashions a compass—and a marker that must also be deduced in a similarly discerning way! It's all exceedingly clever, actually.''

''Designed to outwit both the ignorant and uninitiated...hard even for the intelligent and enlightened. It was never meant to be easy.''

''You can say that again. Nothing about any of this has been easy!'' Bryony declared. ''I only hope we're right about all of this—that we aren't off on some wild-goose chase.''

''Well, I guess we'll soon know, one way or another.''

They ordered dessert, which they ate over strong, black coffee. Then they returned to the campgrounds, making love beneath the shelter of their dome tent under the stars before falling asleep in each other's arms.

It took Bryony and Hamish four days of combing Ben Cruachan before they finally discovered what they had been searching for all along: a series of large stones laid out in such a way that from above, the design they created resembled a Knights Templar sword. But it was on such a grand scale and so skillfully blended into the terrain that it only became visible when viewed from a particular high spot on one side of the munro. Identification of the blade was further complicated by the fact that over the intervening centuries, vegetation had grown up to screen several of the stones that fashioned it, while others had been shifted from their proper alignments by the elements. Had Bryony and Hamish not been deliberately looking for such a marker, they would doubtless have missed it. It was only keen observation through Hamish's high-powered binoculars, and a little luck—or destiny—that enabled them to discern the weapon in the landscape.

"As nearly as I can make out, the Templar sword is pointing toward some small, stone ruin in the distance, where the rough terrain slopes down toward Loch Etive." Hamish slowly lowered his binoculars. "Possibly, it's the remains of an ancient shrine, or else an old dwelling of some kind from later centuries." He paused for a moment, then continued. "It's growing late. Let's go back to camp and investigate the ruins tomorrow morning, when we've plenty of time."

"Agreed," Bryony said.

Centuries ago, the small, stone cottage, secluded on the mountainside, had doubtless served as a shepherd's summer shelter. But now, having been long abandoned, it was nothing more than a ruin...roofless, its walls crumbling, its single, solitary room open to the elements and filled with the accumulated earth and debris of nearly half a millennium. Still, tenaciously, it clung to its rocky acclivity overlooking a tributary that wended its way southwestward to flow into the River Awe below.

"It's truly difficult to believe there could be anything of value here, darling—much less the missing Knights Templar treasure," Hamish remarked as they quietly surveyed their humble surroundings. "But still, this *is* definitely the place to which the Templar sword points—I'm sure of it—and a shepherd's hut certainly fits in with the esoterical shepherd theme, also…with Pan, the god of shepherds, and with Jesus Christ, the shepherd of the Christian flocks…with Poussin's painting *The Shepherds of Arcadia*…and so forth. So despite the fact that this cottage ruin would appear less than promising, now that we're actually here, we might as well have a look around."

"I think so, too," Bryony concurred thoughtfully. "Besides which, most archaeological sites don't—at least initially—ever seem very promising on the surface, either. Yet they often yield priceless objects."

From long, professional habit, she knelt, withdrew a gardening trowel from her backpack, and began experimentally to dig up a small section of the hut's soft, damp, loam floor. Little by little, as she carefully worked at scooping away the centuries of amassed soil and decay, a series of stone slabs started to emerge.

"Well, now, *that's* very interesting!" the Scotsman observed, a sudden note of excitement creeping into his voice as he hunkered down beside her, watching intently as she continued to labor.

"Why?"

"Because centuries ago, a *real* shepherd's cottage wouldn't have had a properly slabbed, stone floor—especially one so meticulously laid that the centuries have scarcely disturbed it. For that, in ages past, one would have required a skilled mason, such as those of the Templar artisan class. As your father reported in his files, in this part of Argyll, there *are* stories—as well as many genuine clues—that several mysterious but highly skilled masons *did* operate around Loch Awe in the fourteenth century, and perhaps even afterward. They could have been fugitive Templars. Even a Templar from a later century could have sought refuge in this region, particularly after the Battle of Killiecrankie in Sixteen Eighty-nine. We know 'Bonnie' Dundee—as John Graham of Claverhouse, Viscount Dundee—was affectionately called, was slain whilst leading the charge of the Highlanders at Killiecrankie, against General Hugh MacKay and his troops…the Orangemen of King William the Third, Prince of Orange, who, at the behest of the Protestants, had invaded England and deposed the Catholic King James the Second. As I told you before, Dundee is reputed to have been wearing the Grand Cross of the Order, as well as other Templar regalia, at the time of his death. Historically, Scotland has always been a Templar haven—and even though they don't appear to be connected with the Sinclairs of the north, the Sinclairs of Argyll and the west of Scotland *are* known as the *Clann na Cearda* or 'Clan of the Craftsmen,' so perhaps there *is* some link between the two families, after all.''

"Under the circumstances, that *would* seem likely.'' Biting her lower lip thoughtfully, Bryony fell silent for a moment, concentrating on her examination of the cottage. Then she went on. "It will take time to uncover this entire floor, remove each stone slab and properly excavate the ground underneath.''

"Maybe that won't be necessary,'' the Scotsman suggested. "Because if I'm right, there will probably be another marker somewhere…perhaps on one of the quoins.''

Reflecting on this possibility, she slowly nodded.

"Yes, the cornerstones usually *are* the last part of a foundation to collapse or otherwise fall to rack and ruin over the ages. Shall we check the perimeter?''

Hamish nodded.

Outside, the two of them spent considerable time methodically scraping centuries of moss and blown earth from each of the four quoins, growing increasingly disheartened when they found nothing beneath. But then, finally, on the last cornerstone, all their determined, hard efforts revealed a single date—1689—and the distinctive, square-handled Hiram key of the Freemasons, chiseled into the granite.

"Look! The key's pointing straight down, Hamish,'' Bryony exclaimed, excitement now rising in her own voice. "Maybe the Templar treasure's buried in a cache underneath the quoin! The Egyptians often concealed objects in just such a manner.''

"Yes, however my own thinking is that in this particular instance, whatever's hidden here is more likely beneath the flagstones in this corner inside. Otherwise, there wouldn't ever have been any need to lay the floor to begin with, would there?'' the Scotsman pointed out, glancing up from his scrutiny of the cornerstone. ''So which do you want to try first...removing the stone slabs inside or else excavating under the quoin?''

''Well, it will certainly be much easier to cope with the flagstones—besides which, I can't fault your logic about the floor!''

Together, inside the shepherd's hut, they painstakingly loosened each of the stone slabs in the corner marked by the keystone, then lifted them away to reveal the ground beneath. After that, with their foldable camping shovel, Hamish started slowly and cautiously to dig up the earth, while Bryony assisted with her gardening trowel and a soft paintbrush she employed to whisk away fine soil. Because of their prudence, the entire process took a little more than two hours, at the end of which they struck rock. Cleaning away the remainder of the dirt exposed the stone as the flat, top slab of a small crypt, as though the tomb of an infant had been set into the ground. Upon the slab was chiseled a pentacle.

As she stared at it silently, Bryony scarcely even breathed, so great was her anticipation and excitement. Hamish, too, was caught in the same strange, suspenseful grip. Finally, wordlessly, they slid away the slab to reveal the treasure inside: a breathtakingly beautiful, highly ornate, gold, silver and copper puzzle box—at the very heart of its lid, a huge, highly polished, green, cabochon gemstone shaped to resemble an eye.

''My God, Hamish...it's an *ark!*'' Bryony whispered, stunned and disbelieving. ''Set with an alexandrite! How can that be? That jewel wasn't even discovered until Eighteen Thirty, in the Ural Mountains of Russia! Look at the size of it, and the clarity and fire of its green color in the sunlight! Too bad we had no need to bring a flashlight with us!''

''Why?''

''Because alexandrite has an exceedingly peculiar and singular quality called 'pleochroism,' meaning that it changes color in different lights. True alexandrite shines green in daylight and red at night, under incandescent light. This particular stone is chatoyant, as well, meaning that it's not only cut into a cabochon, but that it also, at its center, reflects a single streak of pure light—called a 'cat's eye,' because it opens and closes like one, depending on the amount of illumination to which it is exposed. It's believed that a cat's-eye stone, if pressed between your eyes at the point of the so-called Third Eye, will endow you with the gift of prophesy! You simply cannot imagine how incredibly infrequently cat's eye occurs in alexandrite, Hamish, and if it *does* exhibit that invaluable quality, then it becomes one of *the* rarest and costliest of gems on the whole planet! That jewel alone must be priceless!''

''How do you know so much about gemstones?'' he queried curiously.

''All of the astrological signs rule different jewels, which vary, depending on the astrologers' interpretations of them. But alexandrite belongs properly to Capricorn—the Goat. Help me lift the ark out, Hamish, so we can examine it more closely.''

Slowly, carefully, they raised the elaborate puzzle box from the crypt wherein it had lain for more than three hundred years. They were startled by the strange power, an inexplicable energy force, that appeared to emanate from the ark when they touched it. They attempted to open the lid but quickly discovered that they would be unable to do so without first learning the secret of the puzzle. Momentarily setting the ark to one side then, they conscientiously positioned the stone slab back into place on the crypt, then refilled the cavity with the earth they had earlier removed, and replaced the flagstones. After that, Hamish carrying the box, they stepped from the ruins of the shepherd's cottage.

''Well, well. How very clever the two of you have proved, indeed! Countless people have searched for the Knights Templar treasure since it disappeared more than three hundred years ago. Just how *did* the two of you ever manage to find it? By some means quite ingenious, I should imagine. Congratulations! You've played the game brilliantly! After all your dedication and hard work, it seems almost a shame somehow to deprive you of the winner's laurels. Still, we all must do what we all must do. So I'll take that box, if you please—or even if you don't, I'm afraid!''

The stranger who had spoken to them, who blocked their path confrontationally, was tall, lean and young. Standing there with the warm, buttery sunlight spilling down on his golden hair, he looked like a reincarnation of the Greek sun god Apollô. His gaze glowed the blue shade of the sky that stretched behind him, and his teeth flashed in his tanned face as he smiled at Bryony and Hamish—a charmingly deceptive smile that did not quite reach the corners of his bright eyes. He was dressed in a cream-colored, linen shirt and a pair of khaki chinos, and in his hands, he bore a stout, wooden hiking stick. On the inside of his left wrist was a tattoo that identified him as a member of the Abbey's Round Table...Staffbearer.

Neither Bryony nor Hamish made the mistake of thinking this was because the stranger was cut from the same cloth as the yesteryear Celtic monks who had traveled across Europe, staffs in hand, as a symbol of their office. No, the stranger's stave was a cudgel, and they had no doubt that he knew full well how to use it—and would.

"Well, now, the truth is that I *don't* please," Hamish declared softly, also smiling—but it, too, was a smile that sent a chill up Bryony's spine. "So it seems we are at an impasse."

"Only if you wish it. I've been sent to offer you a bargain, Neville," Staffbearer announced. "Give me the box. Give *up* the idea of a Web site devoted to the Abbey. And we shall give you our most solemn and sacred word of honor never to trouble you *or* the lady again, so long as you both shall live."

"Indeed? Well, to be honest, despite your oath, I don't much fancy the terms of your bargain, Staffbearer—or Galahad, if you prefer. So here's one of my own for you and the rest of the Abbey's Round Table to consider. Ms. St. Blaze and I keep the box...and if anything untoward happens to either one of us—if one of us even accidentally slips on a bar of soap in the bath-tub—the Web site devoted to the Abbey will be immediately uploaded to the Internet, and the box goes straight to Sotheby's auction block in London, for sale to the highest bidder!"

Although he continued to smile with feigned pleasantness, Staffbearer's blue eyes narrowed and hardened ever so slightly. Imperceptibly, his grip on the stick he held tightened.

"As you observed, Neville, it seems we are at an impasse. However, despite that being the case, I nevertheless feel certain we can settle our differences in a gentlemanly fashion. I'm quite sure you don't want the lady to get hurt...."

At that unveiled threat, Hamish's smile abruptly disappeared, and his molasses-brown eyes glittered like shards of smoky quartz in his dark, hawkish visage.

"And I'm equally quite sure you don't want me to pitch this box down the mountainside, into the tributary below, where it will certainly be damaged or lost—perhaps even swept into Loch Etive, the Firth of Lorne, and out to sea—and possibly destroyed forever."

Despite himself, Staffbearer could not contain his shock and horror at that caveat.

"For God's sake, Neville! You can't be serious! The box alone is worth a king's ransom, while the treasure it contains is priceless and utterly irreplaceable! You simply *can't* be serious!" he reiterated, incredulous.

"I assure you that I have never been more serious in my entire life!" Hamish rejoined grimly. "Now, back off, Galahad—or I warn you, I'll throw this box down the mountainside and into the tributary below so hard and fast that you won't stand a prayer's chance in hell of stopping me! Back off, I said!" he growled furiously, raising the box as though he would, in fact, hurl it into the distance at even the slightest provocation.

For one tense, frightening moment that seemed to last an eternity, Staffbearer did not move. Finally, his blue eyes as cold as Arctic ice, his mouth tight with anger at his impotence in the face of Hamish's threat, he wordlessly pivoted on his heel to disappear down the old mountain track that wended its way up to the ruined shepherd's cottage. Once he had vanished, Bryony heaved a huge sigh of relief, her knees suddenly giving way beneath her, so that she sank to the grassy ground.

"My God, Hamish," she breathed, shaken, "would you *truly* have done it? Cast the Knights Templar treasure down the mountainside and into the tributary...perhaps destroying it forever?"

"That, my love, is something to which I don't believe either one of us will ever know the answer."

Thirty-Six

Rosslyn Chapel

> Wherever God erects a house of prayer,
> The Devil always builds a chapel there;
> And 'twill be found, upon examination
> The latter has the largest congregation.
>
> *The True-Born Englishman*
> —Daniel Defoe

Rosslyn Castle, Scotland, 1446 A.D.

More than a hundred years had come and gone since the famous Battle of Bannockburn. Nevertheless, its details were well known to Sir William St. Clair, Baron of Rosslyn and Grand Admiral of Scotland.

On that grim June day in 1314, Scotland's King Robert the Bruce and his army had been outnumbered by at least two to one and fighting desperately against the troops of England's King Edward II. On the first day of the battle, the Scots had entrenched themselves above a rocky ridge on Coxet Hill, inflicting serious casualties upon the English cavalry, so that King Edward and his soldiers had been forced on to the Carse Plain. The following morning, King Robert and his own warriors had advanced to attack—the Scottish schiltrons standing firm against the English horsemen, and the Scots' own cavalry determinedly driving back the English archers. As a result, an exhausted stalemate between the two sides had ensued. But then, from nowhere, there had appeared on the horizon behind the flank of Coxet Hill a highly professional and well-trained band of knights, accoutred in full, shining, silver armor, well equipped with gleaming weapons, and mounted on splendid destriers.

Some claimed that, strangely enough, the knights had borne no battle standards flying their colors, and that all their shields had been bare of identifying markings, while others insisted that the warriors had flown and worn the regalia of the Knights Templar. Either way, charging at a furious gallop into the midst of the fray, they had joined King Robert and his infantrymen. Clearly being well experienced in military war tactics, the band of knights had rapidly turned the tide of the battle in favor of the Scots, for it was seen that the warriors' goal was to cut straight through King Edward's lines and kill the English monarch himself. At this point, the Bruce's own reserve, the Highlanders and Islemen, had been sent in to take advantage of the resulting confusion in the English's ranks, and King Edward's bodyguards, the Earl of Pembroke and Sir Giles d'Argentine, had insisted that he ride for the safety of Stirling Castle.

With the decamping of the royal standard, the remainder of the English forces had hastily and ignominiously fled in fear from the battlefield, abandoning all their supplies and baggage; without revealing their names or whence they had come, the mysterious knights who had brought about this decisive rout had vanished over the horizon as quickly as they had appeared upon it.

Later, legend declared that the warriors *had* been Knights Templar, whom King Robert had permitted to take refuge in Scotland when the Order had been persecuted and dismantled by King Philip the Fair of France.

As he gazed out over the land upon which he now stood, William St. Clair smiled faintly to himself. His ancestors Sirs Henri and another William St. Clair had fought at the Battle of Bannockburn. The latter had been the nephew of the Bishop of Dunkeld and, along with Sir James Douglas, had undertaken, at the Bruce's death, to carry his heart to the Holy Land. So William knew the legend to be true. Since the days of the Knights Templar founder, Hugues de Payen, who had married Catherine St. Clair, the St. Clairs had been inextricably bound up with the Order and its secrets.

In 1391, William's grandfather, "Prince" Henry St. Clair, Earl of Orkney, had traveled to Fer Island, located between the Orkneys and the Shetlands, to meet with the renowned Venetian explorers and cartographers Nicolos and Antonio Zeno, who were famous for their maps of Iceland and the Arctic. He had contracted with them to dispatch an exploratory fleet to the New World, and with the aid of monies from the Knights Templar coffers, he had eventually secured a flotilla of twelve ships for the voyage.

They had set sail for the New World in 1398, led by Prince Henry himself, under the guidance of Antonio Zeno. Their purpose had been to establish a safe haven for the Knights Templar and the Order's treasure. They had landed and wintered in Nova Scotia, building a castle, it was rumored, and exploring the eastern seaboard, before returning to the Orkneys. Shortly afterward, however, Prince Henry had been assassinated, so that nothing had ever actually materialized of the proposed, new Knights Templar base.

Now, William felt that as his illustrious St. Clair ancestors before him had done, he, too, must contribute to the Knights Templar cause. Because of that, he had decided to design and construct a church at Rosslyn, his barony—a great sanctuary in the Knights Templar tradition. It was to be erected in the form of a large cross, with a high tower at its center, and with a Lady Chapel, as well. The edifice would be known as the "Collegiate Church of St. Matthew," and like others of its ilk, it would be a secular foundation for intellectual and spiritual knowledge, a Guardian of the Mysteries.

To that end, William had hired from all across foreign lands far and wide the best stonemasons, carpenters, smiths, barrowmen, quarriers and other guild tradesmen possible, and he had built a small village, Roslin, to support and house them while they worked on the church. The master mason received the sum of forty pounds annually; the rest of the laborers were paid ten pounds per year. The whole of the church was to be laid out in accordance with sacred geometry, with the floor plan based on the distinctive Knights Templar cross. On every surface would be carved esoteric symbols and other elaborate, fantastic figures; and on imported Baltic timber, William had drawn up patterns for the carpenters to cut, so that the masons could recreate them in stone.

Today, the foundation stone for the grand church was to be laid, and William could hardly contain his excitement at the prospect. He did not know it would take more than forty years just to finish the Lady Chapel alone, or that the entire, huge church would never be completed. William knew only that the building he intended to raise would stand for centuries—and be a fitting place indeed to shelter the priceless treasures it would hold.

Truth. Knowledge. Wisdom.

Epilogue

The Angel's Face

Abou Ben Adhem (may his tribe increase!)
Awoke one night from a deep dream of peace,
And saw, within the moonlight in his room,
Making it rich, and like a lily in bloom,
An Angel writing in a book of gold:—
Exceeding peace had made Ben Adhem bold,
And to the presence in the room he said,
"What writest thou?"—The Vision raised its head,
And with a look made of all sweet accord
Answered, "The names of those who love the Lord."
"And is mine one?" said Abou. "Nay, not so,"
Replied the Angel. Abou spoke more low,
But cheerily still, and said, "I pray thee, then,
Write me as one that loves his fellow men."

The Angel wrote and vanished. The next night
It came again with a great wakening light,
And showed the names whom love of God had blessed,
And, lo! Ben Adhem's name led all the rest.

Abou Ben Adhem
—Leigh Hunt

The Shepherd's Book *or* Isis Unveiled

I took one Draught of Life—
I'll tell you what I paid—
Precisely an existence—
The market price, they said.

> *No. 1725*
> —Emily Dickinson

Come live with me, and be my love;
And we will all the pleasures prove
That valleys, groves, hills, and fields,
Woods or steepy mountain yields.

> *The Passionate Shepherd to His Love*
> —Christopher Marlowe

If all the world and love were young,
And truth in every shepherd's tongue,
These pretty pleasures might me move
To live with thee, and be thy love.

> *The Nymph's Reply to the Passionate Shepherd*
> —Sir Walter Raleigh

Drumrose Cottage, Scotland, The Present

It had taken Bryony and Hamish six months to unlock the secret of the puzzle box, and afterward—even with the assistance of all their own notes, her father's files, the world's archives, and the modern technology of a new, high-speed computer—another two years for them to decrypt the ancient book inside.

And in the end, what they had learned was that it had never truly been about the manuscript at all....

Once they had gained possession of the Knights Templar treasure, they had uploaded everything they knew about the

Abbey of the Divine to the World Wide Web. They had been certain the order would be deeply hesitant to make any untoward move against them, for fear that they would either auction off the ark and, on the Internet, publish the contents of its tome, or else would destroy the box and book both. So, by e-mail, Hamish had warned the Round Table—informing them that he and Bryony had taken any number of precautions to safeguard both themselves and the treasure, although not revealing details, deliberately leaving the Abbey in the dark, thereby keeping the Round Table speculating and uneasy, reluctant to act.

Deciphering the ancient manuscript had proved relatively easy in some respects and exceedingly difficult in others. They discovered that portions of it had actually already been decoded over the millennia and had made their way into the world, in one fashion or another. However, other parts of the tome were deliberately obscure. Eventually, Bryony and Hamish were able to determine that the crux of the book was the opening of some great cosmic gate—a Gate of God. But even in the manuscript, the precise means of accomplishing this remained cloaked in mystery.

"Gate of God," Bryony mused aloud one evening. "What do we know about such a thing? King Nebuchadnezzar the Second of Babylonia tried to build one—the Tower of Babel—and failed miserably. Why? Because God came down and 'confused the speech of all the world.' So the people no longer spoke a common tongue and therefore could no longer communicate with one another, which meant they couldn't work together on the tower anymore, since no one could understand anyone else."

"Right. Thus, point number one is language," the Scotsman observed. "So let's assume that in order to open the Gate, one needs first to be able physically to speak—that an animal couldn't do it, for example—and, second, not just to speak in any old tongue, either, but, rather, one specifically. The question is, which one?"

"No, I disagree that a *specific* language is required, Hamish. The whole point of the story is that God '*confused* the speech of all the world.' To me, that indicates simply that a *common* tongue is somehow necessary to open the Gate. In other words, everyone involved in opening the Gate has to speak the *same* language."

"Okay. I'll buy that. So…we have a group of people who are thirteen in number, let's say, and they all speak English, so they can communicate with and understand one another. What next? It can't be as easy as merely waving a magic wand and saying, *'Abracadabra!'*"

"Hmm…well, maybe it is," she answered slowly, thoughtfully. "I mean, I think it's really strange that the tale of *Ali Baba and the Forty Thieves* is one of the texts in the book—and he *did* open the cave by saying, 'Open, Sesame.' Further, both the ark and the manuscript have 'Remember the Word' emblazoned upon them, and Jesus Christ said He was the Word, while the Gospel of John starts out, 'In the beginning was the Word, and the Word was with God.'"

"All right. So point number two is the Word. But…*what* Word? Just what *is* the Word we're supposed to remember?"

Bryony shook her head.

"I don't know—except that I'm pretty sure I *do* know what it means."

"What?"

"'I am.' That's what both God and Isis said, remember? 'I am.' Or in the words of René Descartes, 'I think, therefore I am.'"

"Then, for the moment, for lack of any other, let's call the Word *Yahweh.* So…two or more people get together and say, *Yahweh,* and the Gate opens…? *That,* I *don't* buy. Otherwise, the Gate would surely have opened by now after all these millennia, even if only quite by accident. So there's got to be more to it than simply the Word alone."

"Well, even though you joked about waving a magic wand, maybe you *do* need something like that, some source of power to make the Word work," she speculated.

"Like the earth's magnetic field, perhaps, which is generated from within our planet? All the ancient peoples have tales about fishermen's nets and spiderwebs and so on. The Curry Net and the Hartmann Grid, proposed by two German professors, Dr.

Manfred Curry and Dr. Ernst Hartmann, are described as lines of energy encircling our world, while other people point to the old tracks from one ancient, sacred place to another, insisting that the paths follow so-called ley lines. Dowsers claim to find water by utilizing these kinds of earth energies, as well, of which underground streams are also believed to be a part of," Hamish asserted.

"So perhaps places like the Pyramids, the Oracle at Delphi, Stonehenge, Machu Picchu and so forth were built by the ancient peoples to try to harness some type of geomagnetic power. Such sites often boast dolmens or pillars, too, that form 'doorways' or 'gates' that generally face east and thus toward the rising, rather than the setting, sun. The Greek word *hôros-kopeô*, from which we derive our own 'horoscope,' means 'to be in the ascendant,' while *hôros* and *skopeô*, taken separately, mean 'Behold time.' So maybe direction and timing are aspects, also, with the latter involving the Silver Wheel, the ecliptic—the great circle formed by the intersection of the plane of the earth's orbit with the celestial sphere—wherein all the astrological constellations lie."

"Yes, but the ancient peoples all had concepts like this, too—and still, the Gate has never opened. The Silver Wheel has kept on turning. The unending cycle of the Goat and the Ram, of the Fool and the Sage, of the Red Demon and the Green Man, of the Beast and the Messiah has never been broken. The Elixir of Life has yet to be drunk, the Philosopher's Stone found, the Holy Grail achieved. The Serpent has yet to regain his Angel Wings. So…what are we doing wrong? What more is needed, I wonder?"

"I don't know." Bryony sighed heavily, rubbing one side of her aching head. "And I'm too tired, and my mind's too badly drained at the moment, to concentrate on all this any more tonight. Open the ark again, please, so we can put the book away."

Obligingly, as exhausted and overtaxed as she, the Scotsman unlocked the puzzle box and slowly lifted its lid. As it always did whenever it was opened, the ark softly, almost indiscernibly, played a fleeting, solitary diatonic scale of seven notes, then broke off into silence.

"That always drives me crazy," Bryony declared. "It's like what you said about Pan's pipes leaving one waiting breathlessly, expectantly, for the final note to finish out the octave.... Oh, my God! Octaves! *Angels!* Hamish, that's it! Angels...*harps!* Why have we always envisioned and depicted angels as carrying harps? No one really knows. But I'll tell you why. It's because harps have *strings*...the same kind of strings that Pythagoras used to formulate his theory of the *Mundâna Musica*—the 'Music of the Worlds.' Pan's pipes have only seven reeds because he's the Goat and the Fool! And the Ram's horn...it's what warriors and hunters, priests and shepherds blow to sound warning—a *Word* to the *Wise* to take *note*...the herald of kings...the Last Trump!

"The earth-goddess mother Neith, who was Isis, created her firstborn, Ra, by means of *song,* and every wise mother from Time's beginning has quieted her fretful child by *singing* it a lullaby...the *lull* of the storm...music soothes the savage breast... Make love, not war. The Bible's *Shiyr HaShiyrm*— 'Song of Songs,' penned by Solomon. *Coda*...Italian for 'tail' and meaning the last section of a piece of music. *That's* why Ursa Major and Ursa Minor have tails in the night sky—and bears here on earth don't! Oh, Hamish, don't you see? It's *we—all* of Humankind—who have to *sing* the Word, the coda, the final note of the octave! The Creator is listening—and he has never heard us sing it in *unison. That's* why the Gate to Him has never opened! We're a dissonant chord, not in harmony with the universe!"

I looked over Jordan, and what did I see?
Comin' for to carry me home?
A band of angels comin' after me,
Coming for to carry me home.

Swing low, Sweet Chariot,
Comin' for to carry me home,

Swing low, Sweet Chariot,
Comin' for to carry me home....

Traditional Spiritual
—preserved and arranged by Henry Thacker Burleigh

Place Unknown, the Present

"Are you quite certain you want to do this, my dearest love?" Hamish asked gently.

"Yes...yes...." Bryony nodded regretfully. "It's the right thing to do. I'm certain of it. Tragically, Humankind has not yet grown wise enough to appreciate the value of this beautiful, incomparable gift of destiny that was bestowed upon us aeons ago. We can only hope and pray that maybe, someday, we will be...."

Together, a fortnight past, the two of them had crafted a small, stone crypt—not unsimilar to the one in which they had discovered the puzzle box in the ruins of the shepherd's cottage at Ben Cruachan—and, earlier this day, set it deep into the cool, dark cavity they had dug into the ground. Now, carefully, reverently, they slowly lowered the exquisite ark that held the ancient book into the crypt, then slid the heavy top slab securely into place, burying it beneath the rich, fertile soil of the melodiously unquiet earth. When, finally, they had finished, Bryony—lightly brushing the remaining vestiges of damp loam from her hands and gazing off into the distance at the westering sun on the horizon—once more spoke.

"More than twenty years ago now, the author Gary Zukav called the dancing *Wu Li* masters enlightened beings who dance with the universe. But it isn't about dancing, ultimately, Hamish. Pythagoras was right. It *is* about the *Mundâna Musica*— the 'Music of the Worlds.' The *song*. Because only think what would happen if all of us everywhere on our entire planet—if even for just a few incredibly precious, absolutely priceless minutes—laid down our weapons, set aside our religious, racial, cultural and political differences, and, wherever we were, stopped whatever we were doing to join together in a common, worldwide song. It would, in essence, be that one, brief, shining moment that was King Arthur's Camelot....

"Because for that single, glorious, unparalleled interlude, Hamish, the whole earth would be united in heart, mind and spirit...utterly at peace...voices making the proverbial joyful noise...raised in transcendental harmony with one another, the universe and the Creator—in one song...." She fell silent for a moment, reflecting...hoping...dreaming things that had never been—but that *could* be, if only Humankind would learn to sing the Music of the Worlds. Then, as Hamish drew her to him and they embraced sweetly and passionately, their hearts like a fount welling and overflowing with love for each other, she continued softly.

"That's what the word *universe* means, you know. It's Latin...from *ûnio*—'to join together, unite; one'—and *versus*—'a dance; a poetic verse; a song, a note.'"

One song...

One last, clear and perfect—

Author Note

Dear Reader:

I hope you enjoyed reading my novel *Destiny's Daughter*. But more than that, I hope it has given you food for thought—and music for the soul.

It is said that when Pandora—who may indeed, as some scholars believe, actually have been Minoan rather than Greek, and thus to be found in the shadow of Mount Ida instead of Mount Olympus—opened her fabled jar or box, all the wickedness inside escaped into the world, and that only hope was not lost. Hope has always proved the bright beacon that guides us—and our world—through our darkest times, just as the pillar of smoke and fire guided Moses and the Hebrews on their Exodus. The proposed Pharaoh, sequence of historical events, and Exodus route you read about in these pages are matters of debate, although not without several merits worthy of consideration. However, the truth is that we don't really know who Moses's Pharaoh was, whether the explosion of Thera was to blame for the plagues and cataclysms, or what route the Hebrews traveled on their Exodus.

But with rare exceptions, most all the historical personages to be found in *Destiny's Daughter* actually did exist, although their interludes spent with the puzzle box and its ancient book are my own inventions.

On a personal note, I want very much to thank my dear friend and Welshman, Den Robinson, who told me the strange story that first inspired this novel and who drew my Map of the Exodus Route for me. His advice, critiques, insights and assistance with both historical and esoterical research throughout my writing of *Destiny's Daughter* proved invaluable to me.

There is a wise Chinese proverb that says, "A book is like a garden carried in the pocket." I believe that to be true. There are few things on this earth more beautiful than a garden—especially a secret garden with high stone walls; a wrought-iron gate covered with English and grape ivy; riotous flower beds in which a profusion of lush, multicolored blooms grow, permeating the air with their rich and fragrant scents; and a lone, soaring, old yew tree beneath whose spreading, gnarled branches one may recline upon cool, shaded grasses—book in hand.

For books do indeed go hand in hand with gardens. Like flowers, books, too, spring from seeds and bulbs...the seeds of dreams and the bulbs of imagination that grow in the fertile minds of writers the world over. The first words on every page are like new green shoots in spring, holding the promise of something magical and wondrous; if they are carefully and lovingly nurtured, they may indeed blossom into something that will remain with you, the reader, for the rest of your life—a memory cherished long after the book itself, just like a flower pressed between its yellowing pages, has faded and crumbled with age and is no more.

We, as human beings, once had a vast store of knowledge painstakingly recorded for all posterity, on ancient clay and stone tablets, papyrus and parchment, and which manuscripts were the first books of our ancestors, the roots and first green shoots, as it were, of Humankind and our history. But tragically, we did not tend our treasure troves of books, just as today we do not tend the gardens—the atmosphere, the rain forests, and the rivers and oceans—of our earth. Instead, the huge Egyptian library at Alexandria was burned to the ground by first the Romans, then, later, the Arabs, many of its ancient books and scrolls used, in fact, to heat bathhouses. The immense Celtic library at the far-from-legendary Grail Castle of King Arthur was sacked and destroyed by ignorant, barbaric Vikings. Spanish missionaries, in their religious zeal, consigned countless MesoAmerican works to bonfires. And sadly, the list goes on.

We will never know what was lost, what priceless knowledge may have been contained on those tablets and scrolls now gone forever. The Celts and the Greeks both performed successful brain surgery. Where might our own neurosurgery be today if we knew how they had done it? The Babylonians and the Egyptians charted the courses of our stars (it took twentieth-century technology to prove their theories, by the way), and the Mayans created the most accurate calendar our world has ever known.

The knowledge and history, the philosophy and theology, the stories and dreams of Humankind can live on in books. That is the "big secret" that every single writer who has ever lived has always known. Today, we know the words of individuals like Aesop, Aristotle, Chuang-tzu, Dante Alighieri, Leonardo da Vinci, Hippocrates, Homer, Lao-tzu, Machiavelli, Milton, Sir Isaac Newton, Nostradamus, Plato, Pythagoras, Socrates, Virgil and so many other because the works of their lifetimes somehow survived. Their manuscripts and the texts of their followers who cited them were not forever banned and burned by those who, in their prejudice or ignorance or fervor, would tell us what we can and cannot read—which is a very dangerous thing indeed. For if we are told what to read, it will soon be only a matter of time before we are told also what to think and dream. *And no one must ever tell us that.*

Alone, we are born into this world, and alone, we die. But between the beginning and the end is an extraordinary gift—a precious journey that is ours to make of whatever we can and will. Writers will tell you all kinds of reasons why they write: for love, for fame, for fortune, for the thrill of it, for lack of anything better to do, or because they are compelled by some intangible muse to put derrière to chair and pen to paper. But the real truth hidden deep in all writers' hearts and minds and souls is that they write because they want and hope to be heard across the aeons, to leave something lasting behind. For it *is* in the poet's word and the bard's song that the archives of Humankind can be preserved for all posterity, so that we may learn from our mistakes of the past, rather than being doomed to repeat them endlessly in the future.

If you ended *Destiny's Daughter* on the right *note,* then you heard the music I hoped you would hear when I wrote this book.

Please visit me at Ravenscroft Castle, my virtual home: *http://www.brandewyne.com.* Send e-mail to me at: *rebecca@brandewyne.com.* Although I regret that I cannot answer all your letters personally, I do always read each and every one of them myself, and I enjoy and appreciate them all!

Pax vobiscum.

Rebecca Brandewyne

New York Times Bestselling Author

JAYNE ANN KRENTZ

The Wedding Night

Owen Sutherland's whirlwind courtship has left Angie Townsend breathless and in love—and hopeful that the fierce rivalry that had divided their powerful families would finally end. But now, nestled in their honeymoon suite, Angie suspects she may also be a fool. A sudden, hushed phone call warns her of the terrible truth: her marriage is a sham, nothing more than a clever corporate raid orchestrated by her powerful new husband. The very husband reaching out to lead her to their wedding bed… Is Owen Sutherland a calculating stranger…or the man she's married for better or for worse? Until Angie knows for certain, her wedding night is on hold…indefinitely.

"A master of the genre—nobody does it better!"
—*Romantic Times*

*Available the first week
of December 2001
wherever paperbacks are sold!*

If you enjoyed what you just read,
then we've got an offer you can't resist!

Take 2
bestselling novels FREE!
Plus get a FREE surprise gift!

Clip this page and mail it to The Best of the Best™

IN U.S.A.
3010 Walden Ave.
P.O. Box 1867
Buffalo, N.Y. 14240-1867

IN CANADA
P.O. Box 609
Fort Erie, Ontario
L2A 5X3

YES! Please send me 2 free Best of the Best™ novels and my free surprise gift. After receiving them, if I don't wish to receive anymore, I can return the shipping statement marked cancel. If I don't cancel, I will receive 4 brand-new novels every month, before they're available in stores! In the U.S.A., bill me at the bargain price of $4.24 plus 25¢ shipping and handling per book and applicable sales tax, if any*. In Canada, bill me at the bargain price of $4.74 plus 25¢ shipping and handling per book and applicable taxes**. That's the complete price and a savings of over 15% off the cover prices—what a great deal! I understand that accepting the 2 free books and gift places me under no obligation ever to buy any books. I can always return a shipment and cancel at any time. Even if I never buy another book from The Best of the Best™, the 2 free books and gift are mine to keep forever.

185 MEN DFNG
385 MEN DFNH

Name	(PLEASE PRINT)	
Address	Apt.#	
City	State/Prov.	Zip/Postal Code

* Terms and prices subject to change without notice. Sales tax applicable in N.Y.
** Canadian residents will be charged applicable provincial taxes and GST.
  All orders subject to approval. Offer limited to one per household and not valid to current Best of the Best™ subscribers.
® are registered trademarks of Harlequin Enterprises Limited.

BOB01   ©1998 Harlequin Enterprises Limited

REBECCA BRANDEWYNE

66430	HIGH STAKES	___ $5.99 U.S.	___ $6.99 CAN.
66276	GLORY SEEKERS	___ $5.99 U.S.	___ $6.99 CAN.
66063	DUST DEVIL	___ $5.99 U.S.	___ $6.50 CAN.

(limited quantities available)

TOTAL AMOUNT	$_____
POSTAGE & HANDLING	$_____
($1.00 for one book; 50¢ for each additional)	
APPLICABLE TAXES*	$_____
TOTAL PAYABLE	$_____
(check or money order—please do not send cash)	

To order, complete this form and send it, along with a check
or money order for the total above, payable to MIRA Books®,
to: **In the U.S.:** 3010 Walden Avenue, P.O. Box 9077, Buffalo,
NY 14269-9077; **In Canada:** P.O. Box 636, Fort Erie, Ontario,
L2A 5X3.

Name:_____
Address:_____ City:_____
State/Prov.:_____ Zip/Postal Code:_____
Account Number (if applicable):_____
075 CSAS

   *New York residents remit applicable sales taxes.
    Canadian residents remit applicable GST and provincial taxes.

MIRA®